Works of Ivo Andrić

Ex Ponto—POEMS, 1918
Unrest—POEMS, 1919
The Voyage of Ali Djerzelez—NOVELLA, 1920
Tales I—1924
Tales II—1931
Conversations with Goya—ESSAY, 1934
Tales III—1936
The Bridge on the Drina—NOVEL, 1945
Bosnian Chronicle—NOVEL, 1945
Miss—NOVEL, 1945
New Tales—1948
The Vizier's Elephant—NOVELLA, 1948
Devil's Yard—NOVELLA, 1954
Under the Hornbeam—NOVELLA, 1952
Faces—STORIES, 1960
Notes on Goya—ESSAY, 1962

BOSNIAN CHRONICLE

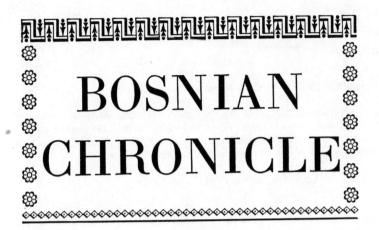

BOSNIAN CHRONICLE

BY

IVO ANDRIĆ

Translated from the Serbo-Croatian by

JOSEPH HITREC

ARCADE PUBLISHING • NEW YORK

First Arcade Paperback Edition 1993

The characters and events in this book are fictitious. Any similarity to real persons, living or dead, is coincidental and not intended by the author.

Library of Congress Cataloging-in-Publication Data

Andrić, Ivo, 1892–1975.
    [Travnička hronika. English]
    Bosnian chronicle / by Ivo Andrić ; translated from the Serbo-Croatian by Joseph Hitrec—First Arcade paperback ed.
      p.   cm.
    ISBN 1-55970-236-2
    1. Travnik (Travnik, Bosnia and Hercegovina)—History—Fiction.
I. Title
PG1418.A6T713   1993
891.8′235—dc20   93-8695

Published in the United States by Arcade Publishing, Inc., New York

Distributed by Little, Brown and Company

10 9 8 7 6 5 4 3 2

BP

Printed in the United States of America

Translator's Note

In October 1961, the Swedish Academy awarded Ivo Andrić the Nobel Prize for literature, citing him for "the epic force with which he has depicted themes and human destinies from the history of his country." The Academy paid special tribute to the three works that comprise his Bosnian trilogy—of which *Bosnian Chronicle* is the longest and most monumental. The other two are *The Bridge on the Drina* and *Miss*.

While the subject of all three are the people of Bosnia, *Bosnian Chronicle* delves deepest into those elements of the turbulent Bosnian heritage which give it its unique ethnic and spiritual flavor. This is the territory—roughly the size of West Virginia—which has been the contending ground of Eastern and Western cultures for almost two thousand years. Roman legions and the phalanxes of Philip of Macedon have roamed over it in search of plunder and new frontiers. Byzantium and the Church of St. Peter have wrangled for its soul. The Ottoman tide, cresting into Europe in the sixteenth century, made of Bosnia a buffer province and a base for its incursions against Vienna and Budapest. Later, it became a precarious East-West trade route in Napoleon's Continental System. And after the Austrian occupation in the nineteenth century, it was the fatal shot fired at Sarajevo in 1914 that plunged the world into the first global war.

This, then, is the tortured, flamboyant tapestry of Andrić's stories—stories in which Bosnian men and women live their perilous and extraordinary lives amid oppression and cruelty, ever haunted by visions of freedom and human dignity which history has dangled before them but has been painfully slow to deliver.

Born in Travnik in 1892, Andrić was part of the struggle of

which he writes. At the age of nineteen, while studying in Sarajevo, he joined the Bosnian Revolutionary Youth Organization, which fought for the liberation of Bosnia from Austrian rule and for the unification of the South Slavs. Thrown in jail by the Austrians, Andrić read Kierkegaard and wrote two volumes of brooding poetry, *Ex Ponto* (1918) and *Unrest* (1919). After World War I, when the South Slavs finally realized their historic dream of independence, he entered his country's new diplomatic corps and served with distinction in Italy, Rumania, Spain, and Switzerland. He also wrote a great number of stories and novellas which quickly established him as one of the foremost Yugoslav writers of the day. Among his critical writings of that period, *Conversations with Goya* occupies a special place in that it states his credo as a writer and humanist.

On the eve of World War II he was appointed Minister to Germany. When the Nazis attacked Yugoslavia he returned to Belgrade and lived as a recluse in his apartment. "The long night of the occupation seemed to have no end," he told a friend later on. "Hope was an act of desperate defiance against monstrous odds." Hope and the oblivion of work. He translated Giardini's *Riccordi*, wrote a score of tales, and read everything in sight. He began work on his Bosnian trilogy—first *Bosnian Chronicle*, followed by *The Bridge on the Drina* and *Miss*. Four and a half years later the trilogy was ready for publication.

The three books, published one after another during 1945, made him, overnight as it were, a dominant figure in Yugoslav letters. He was hailed as a prose-poet of the past, a storyteller of genuine power with a philosophic viewpoint, whose style of expression perfectly fitted his material. Moreover, the epic sweep of his canvas and the deeply compassionate spirit playing over it gave his writings a universal quality that raised them from the purely regional and placed them in the European mainstream. Here was a small-nation writer who was "big" in a fashion that transcended his "local" subject matter. It was largely through Andrić that Yugoslav literature—talented and interesting but flourishing on the European periphery—gained international recognition and a world audience for the first time. By the late fifties, Andrić's stories, novellas, and novels were read and admired in some twenty-eight languages.

In the years following World War II Andrić served in his country's National Assembly and was elected president of the Yugoslav Federation of Writers. He received the highest literary award of Yugoslavia. He wrote more stories, essays, and several important novellas, notably *Devil's Yard*, a phantasmagoric study of an oriental prison that has drawn critical comparisons with Gogol, Dostoevski, Kafka, and Orwell. Since the Nobel Prize, he has been living and writing in Belgrade and is now completing another chronicle of his native Bosnia.

The main themes of Ivo Andrić's writing—causative interplay of guilt and human suffering, the individual versus tyranny, the warping of men's destinies through historic circumstance—which are explored singly in some of his stories, are woven in *Bosnian Chronicle* into a harmonious whole. The elegiac mood of his early poetry, the preoccupation with personal sin as an agent of general evil, which marks his longer stories written between the wars, are transmuted here into a relentless, many-leveled scrutiny of the character, psychology, and moral sap of a whole people. What is the truth behind the harshness of Bosnian life and its tormented heritage, how real is that audible and visible melancholy which the Austrian Colonel von Mitterer, in *Bosnian Chronicle*, speciously calls *Urjammer*—ancient misery? Why, as a discerning Yugoslav critic has asked, is "everything weighed down by some heavy and sinister burden, as if paying back who knows what kind of ancient and eternal debt"?

For his answer Andrić turns to the past, and his quest is absorbing and illuminating. The act is neither escapism nor a deliberate turning back on the modern world, but a clear-eyed, unsentimental pursuit of durable values and pertinent atavistic wisdom. It is the method of a compassionate researcher who knows that much of the truth of an individual and his group lies locked in his antecedents and must be dredged up for the sake of the total truth. So his answers are neither pat nor necessarily flattering to his subject.

The past, like the present, is ridden with guilt and evil, individual as well as communal, but it also yields a residue of good. Long centuries of oppression have forced the Bosnian character to grow like a stubborn plant in one of the country's mountain passes, close to the ground and bending with the wind. But there is also a hard core of patrimony that shows through, a hardy perennial undergrowth which no wars, tyranny, or brutalities could trample out of existence. In that patrimony, heroism, nobility, and greatness of heart exist side by side with moral turpitude and coarseness. Enduring values are handed down through generations and become a distinctive heritage. And all of it together, in Andrić's special amalgam of storytelling and large-scale canvas, makes for powerful, often shocking, but always fascinating and engrossing reading.

The Bosnian usage of the name "Turk" to denote a Moslem of local origin and domicile has been retained in this translation. Thus "Turk" may mean either a member of the ruling Osmanli race or a Bosnian Moslem, usually of Slavic origin, whose ancestors became converts to Islam.

The Serbo-Croatian original contains a good many Turkisms and Bosnian adaptations of Turkish titles of respect, rank, and social status. Most of these have been changed into rough-and-ready English equivalents, but a few, resisting this method, are used here in their original forms. To avoid italicizing them in the text, their meanings are given here:

Aga: Military title, used loosely of any higher rank.
Beg: A title of honor, usually connected with Moslem landed gentry.
Divan: Council or council chamber; also audience or reception.
Effendi: Master, or sir.
Hodja: Muezzin.
Kavass: Groom, attendant, or bearer.
Illyria: Name of Roman province, revived under Napoleon.
Pashalik: Territory under the jurisdiction of a pasha.
Rayah: Subject Bosnian Christians, collectively.
Schwabe: A Swabian, popular generic term for Germans.

J.H.

BOSNIAN CHRONICLE

Prologue

On the outskirts of the bazaar at Travnik, under the cool and clamoring springs of Shumech, there stands, older than the town's living memory, a little coffeehouse known as Lutva's Café. Not even the oldest inhabitants remember Lutva, the original owner of the café—he has been lying in one of the scattered cemeteries of Travnik for at least a hundred years—but they all go to Lutva's for coffee and his name is remembered and spoken where the names of sultans, viziers, and begs have long been forgotten. In the garden of this coffeehouse, under a cliff at the foot of the hill, there is a secluded spot, cool and slightly elevated, where an old lime tree grows. Around this lime tree, between the bushes and the rocks, low benches of irregular shape have been set up, on which it is a pleasure to sit and from which it is difficult to rise. Warped and worn smooth with the years and long use, the benches have completely blended into and become a part of the tree, the earth, and the stone around them.

During the summer months—that is to say, from the beginning of May to the end of October—it is a place where, according to a long-standing tradition, the begs of Travnik and the more distinguished citizens who are admitted into their company foregather in the afternoon about the time of prayer. At that hour of the day, no one else in town would dream of going up to the elevation and sitting down to drink a coffee.

The place is called "the Sofa." In the popular usage of Travnik the word has acquired, through generations, a particular social and political connotation of its own, and anything said, discussed, and settled at the Sofa may be taken with almost the same authority as if it had been settled among the town elders in the Vizier's divan, or council.

On this particular day, there are some ten begs sitting at the Sofa, even though the sky has clouded over and a wind is rising, which at that season of the year means there is rain in the offing. It is the last Friday in the month of October 1806. The begs are chatting quietly, sitting in their accustomed places; most of them are thoughtfully watching the hide-and-seek of the sun and clouds and coughing in a moody fashion.

They are discussing an important piece of news.

One of them, a certain Suleiman Beg Ayvaz, who in the last few days had gone to Livno on business, had talked there with a man from Split—a serious person, from all appearances—and had learned from him the piece of news which he is now communicating to the begs. The latter, however, can't quite make head or tail of it, and they are pressing him for details and asking him to repeat what he has already told them. And Suleiman Beg obliges them: "Well, here's how it was. The man asked me a perfectly civil question: 'Are you people over in Travnik getting ready for visitors?' 'Not we,' I said to him, 'we've no use for visitors.' 'Well, maybe you do and maybe you don't,' he says, 'but you'd better get ready all the same, because you have a French consul coming. Bonaparte has asked the Porte at Istanbul to be allowed to send his consul to open a consulate at Travnik and stay on there. It has already been approved, so you can expect a consul some time this winter.' I laughed it off as a joke. 'For hundreds of years we've got along quite well without any consuls,' I told him, 'and we can live without them from here on too. Besides, what would a consul do in Travnik?' But he stuck to his story. 'How you've lived so far is neither here nor there,' he said. 'From now on you'd better get used to living with consuls. That's how it is these days. And he'd find something to do, don't you worry. He'll sit beside the Vizier, ordering this and arranging that, he'll watch and see how you begs and agas are behaving and how the Christian rayah is treated, and he'll report everything to Bonaparte.' 'That's never happened before and never will,' I protested. 'No one's ever poked his nose into our affairs and this fellow's not likely to either.' 'Well, then, I don't know about that,' he says to me, 'but you'd better get used to the idea, because when Bonaparte asks for something there's nobody can refuse him, not even the government in Istanbul. And not only that, but as soon as Austria sees you've accepted a French consul, she'll demand that you take one of hers as well, and after Austria there'll be Russia . . .' 'Oh come now, stop it, neighbor,' I said to him, but he kept on grinning, the Latin pest, and stroking his mustache. 'You can cut it off if it doesn't turn out just as I'm telling you,' he said. So there you are, my good friends, that's what I have heard and I simply can't get it out of my head," Ayvaz finished his tale.

Conditions being what they are—the French army occupied Dalmatia over a year ago and Serbia is in continuous revolt— a vague rumor of this kind is sufficient to baffle and disturb the begs, who have enough worries of their own. They are stirred and anxious, though no one would guess it from the expressions on their faces and the calm way they puff at their pipes. They speak slowly, in fits and starts, one at a time, conjecturing what this might mean, how much truth and untruth there is in the news, what steps they should take to verify it and perhaps stop the whole thing before it develops.

Some are of the opinion that the rumor is a lurid exaggeration, invented by someone who wanted to disturb and frighten them. Others again say, with bitterness in their voices, that the rumor is not surprising, seeing how such things are happening in Istanbul and Bosnia and all over the world, and that one ought to be ready for anything. Then, there are those who comfort themselves with the thought that this is Travnik—Travnik! —not just any little market town, and that whatever happens to other people need not and cannot happen to them.

Each one of them makes a remark or two—enough to show that he is participating—but none will commit himself definitely, for they are all waiting to hear what the oldest of them will say. And the oldest is Hamdi Beg Teskeredjich, a big-boned old man, slow of movement but still boasting a powerful body of giant proportions. He has been through many wars and suffered wounds and captivity; he has had eleven sons, eight daughters, and a numerous progeny between them. His beard and mustache are sparse, the skin of his keen regular face is tanned and full of scars and livid blotches from a blast of gunpowder long ago. The heavy eyelids are leaden in color and perpetually half-lowered. His speech is slow but clear.

At length, Hamdi Beg cuts short their guessing, speculation, and fears in his strangely youthful voice: "Come, come, let's not wail over the judge before he's really dead, as the saying goes. Let's not get stirred up prematurely. One should listen to everything and remember everything, but not take everything to heart right away. As for these consuls, who knows what's what?

Maybe they'll come, maybe they won't. And even if they come, the Lashva won't turn around and flow backwards—it will run the same as now. We're here on our own ground, anyone else who may come will be on strange ground and he won't tarry long. Armies have gone through here before and they never could hold out for long. Many have come here to stay, but so far we've always managed to see the back of them, just as we will see the back of these consuls too, even supposing they come. For the moment, they're not even in sight. And as for Bonaparte's request to Istanbul, that needn't be final, for all we know. For years a good many people have asked for a good many things, but what a man asks and what he gets is not always the same thing. . . ."

Hamdi Beg has spoken the last words testily. Now, in complete silence, he blows a cloudlet of smoke and continues. "Well, let them come! Let us see what happens and how many there are. No man's candle burns forever, nor will this . . . this fellow's . . ."

Here Hamdi Beg gulps a little and gives a cough of suppressed annoyance, thus managing not to pronounce Bonaparte's name, which is in everyone's thoughts and on everyone's tongue.

As no one has anything further to add, the discussion of the latest piece of news is over.

Soon the clouds veil the sun completely and a strong gust of cold wind blows through the valley. The leaves of the poplars along the riverbank rustle with a metallic sound. The cold shudder sweeping down the Travnik valley means that for this year an end has come to the sessions and chatting on the Sofa. One by one the begs commence to get up; they gesture silent greetings to one another and then scatter to their homes.

1

At the beginning of the year 1807 strange things began to happen at Travnik, things that had never happened before.

No one in Travnik had ever supposed that the town was made for an ordinary life and for the workaday grind—no one, not even the last Moslem bumpkin from the mountain hinterland. This deep-seated feeling that they were somehow different from the rest of the world, that they were created and called for better and higher things, was as much a part of their life as the cutting winds from Vlashich, the cool waters of Shumech, and the sweet-tasting maize of the sunny fields around Travnik, and the people never lost this feeling, not even in sleep or the times of great difficulties or in the moment of death.

This was especially true of the Moslems who lived in the town itself. But even the humble and the poor of the three faiths—the so-called rayah—scattered along the hilly outskirts or crowded together in separate suburbs, shared this feeling in their own way and each according to their station. And this was also true of their town itself, about whose situation and layout there was something special, typical, and proud.

In reality, this town of theirs was a narrow and deep gorge which successive generations had in the course of time built up and brought under cultivation, a fortified passageway where men had paused and then settled down permanently, adapting themselves to it and it to themselves down the centuries. On both sides, mountains tumble down steeply and meet in the valley at a sharp angle, leaving barely enough room for a thin river and a road running beside it. It all reminds one of an oversize half-opened book, the pages of which, standing up stiffly on each side, are generously illustrated with gardens, streets, houses, fields, cemeteries, and mosques.

No one has ever reckoned the number of hours of sunlight which nature has withheld from this town, but it is certain that here the sun rises later and sets earlier than in any other of the numerous Bosnian cities and small towns. The people of the town—Travnichani—do not deny it either, but they claim that, while it shines, it does so with a light that no other town can boast of.

In this narrow valley, where the river Lashva flows along the bottom and the steep hillsides are full of the whisper of springs, rivulets, and water-mill channels, a valley full of damp and drafts, there is hardly a straight path or piece of level ground where a man may step freely and without paying attention. All is steep and uneven, crisscrossed and angled, linked and chopped up by private right-of-ways, fences, blind alleys, gardens, wicket gates, graveyards, and shrines.

Here by the water, that fickle, mysterious, and powerful element, generations of Travnichani are born and die. Here they grow up, sallow-faced and delicate of body, but hardened and equal to anything; here they live, with the Vizier's Residency ever before their eyes, proud, sensitive, haughty, fastidious, and cunning; here they work and thrive, or loaf around in genteel poverty; cautious and persevering, they don't know how to laugh aloud but are masters of the sly leer; scant talkers, they are fond of the whispered innuendo; and here they are buried when their time comes, each according to his faith and custom, in marshy graveyards, making room for a new generation like themselves.

So the waves of posterity go on, bequeathing one to another not only a peculiar common heritage of body and spirit, but also a land and a faith, not only an inherited sense of what is right and fitting and an instinct for recognizing and distinguishing all the byways, gateways, and alleys of their intricate town but also an inborn flair for judging the world and men in general. Thus equipped come the children of Travnik into the world;

of all their attributes pride is the most conspicuous. Pride is their second nature, a living force that stays with them all through life, that animates them and marks them visibly apart from the rest of mankind.

This pride has nothing in common with the naïve ostentation of prosperous peasants and small-town provincials who, smug in their pleasure with themselves, swell visibly and are loud in self-congratulation. On the contrary, their pride is of an inner and private kind; it is more like a burdensome legacy and an exacting obligation toward themselves, their families, and their town, set and conditioned by nothing less than the lofty, exalted, and quite abstract image which they have formed of themselves and their city.

Still, every human feeling has its measure and limit, and the sense of one's own grandeur is no exception. While it is true that Travnik is the seat of the Vizier and its people are well bred and neat, moderate and wise enough to deal with emperors, there are times in the lives of Travnichani when their pride becomes a nuisance and they yearn secretly for a relaxed and carefree existence, when they would settle for a humble life in one of these obscure small market towns that do not figure in the reckoning of emperors or in the clashes of states, that are bypassed and unaffected by world events and do not lie in the path of great and celebrated men.

Indeed, times had become such that one couldn't look forward to anything pleasant or expect anything good. For that reason the proud and discerning people of Travnik hoped that in fact nothing would happen and they would be allowed, as far as possible, to lead their lives without changes or surprises. Anyway, what good could possibly result from rulers being locked in combat, from nations giving each other bloody noses, from scorched and burning lands? A new vizier? He would not be worse or better than his predecessor, while his swarming entourage would be an unknown quantity, hungering and lusting for Lord knew what new things. ("The best vizier we ever had," they said, "was the one who got as far as the frontier, then went straight back to Istanbul and never even set foot in Bosnia.") Some foreigner? A distinguished bird of passage, perhaps? But one knew exactly what that meant. They spent a little money and distributed a few gifts, and the moment they were gone, next day as it were, questions were asked and police inquiries instituted. Who were they and what were they, with whom did they spend the night, who was seen talking to them? And by the time you disentangled and cleared yourself, you regretted it ten times over and lost more money than you may have made on the stranger. Or perhaps a spy . . . ? Or a secret agent of an unknown power, with dubious intentions? When all was said and done, it was hard to tell what a man might bring or whose scout he might be.

In short, things were not too promising nowadays. It was better by far to eat one's bread and live one's days in peace— as much as one had left of either—in this the noblest of all cities on earth, and may the good Lord save us from glory, from important visitors, and from great events.

Such, in the opening years of the nineteenth century, were the thoughts and private hopes of the leading men of Travnik, although, naturally, they kept them to themselves; for it was characteristic of the Travnichani that between their wishes and thoughts and a visible or audible expression of them there was a long and devious road not easily traversed.

In the last few years especially—at the end of the eighteenth and the beginning of the nineteenth century—events and changes had come rather fast and thick. Indeed, there was a regular assault of events from every quarter, a clashing and a tumble that ranged all over Europe and the great Turkish Empire and reached even into this tight little valley, settling here like flood water or a sand drift. Ever since the Turks had withdrawn from Hungary, the relations between the Ottoman Empire and the Christian world had grown steadily worse and more complex, as had conditions in general. The warriors of the great Empire, the agas and the spahis, who had been forced to relinquish their rich estates on the fertile Hungarian plain and to return to their cramped and poor country, were bitter and resentful of every- thing Christian; and while they multiplied the number of mouths that had to be fed, the number of hands available for work remained as before.

On the other hand, these same wars of the eighteenth cen- tury that were easing the Turks out of the neighboring Christian lands and bringing them back to Bosnia, filled the local rayah —or subject Christians—with bold new hopes and opened up daring new horizons; and this too was bound to influence the attitude of the rayah to their imperial overlord, the Turk. Both sides—if one may speak of two sides at this stage of the struggle —fought each in its own way, and with the means that were suited to the times and circumstances. The Turks elected repression and force, the Christians fought back with passive resistance, cunning, and conspiracy, or readiness to conspire. The Turks defended their right to live and their way of life, the Christians fought to gain those rights. The rayah was getting "uppish" and was no longer what it used to be. This conflict of interests, beliefs, yearnings, and hopes produced a convulsive atmosphere which the long Turkish wars with Venice, Austria, and Russia made only tenser and more constricting. In Bosnia the mood grew somber and brooding, clashes became more frequent, life more difficult; order and sense of security waned by the day.

The beginning of the nineteenth century brought an uprising in Serbia that was symbolic of the new times and new methods of struggle. The Bosnian knot tightened more ominously still.

As time went on, the rebellion of the Serbs caused more and more worries, trouble, damage, expense, and loss throughout Turkish Bosnia, and thus to Travnik as well, though more to the Vizier, the authorities, and the other Bosnian towns than to the Turks of Travnik itself; to the latter no war was big or important enough to warrant a contribution of their wealth, let alone their persons. The Moslems of Travnik spoke of "Karageorge's rebellion" with rather forced contempt, just as they always found some sneering epithet for the army which the Vizier sent against Serbia and which the fumbling and bickering local chieftains assembled, in their slow and chaotic way, in the environs of Travnik.

A more deserving topic of conversation in Travnik was the European campaigns of Napoleon. At first, these were discussed as if they were distant events that needed retelling and interpretation but which had not, and could not possibly have, any connection with the daily life of Travnik. The arrival of the French army in Dalmatia unexpectedly brought this fabled "Bonaparte" much nearer to Bosnia and Travnik.

Simultaneously there came to Travnik a new vizier, Husref Mehmed Pasha, bringing with him a new respect for Napoleon and an interest in everything French—an interest far greater, the Travnichani felt, than was becoming to an Osmanli and a high representative of the Turkish Empire.

Perturbed and irritated by it all, the local Moslems began to express their feelings about Napoleon and his exploits in terse and cryptic sentences or else with a disdainful pursuing of lips.

Still, none of it could quite remove and protect them from Bonaparte or from the events which, like ripples of water radiating
from their center, spread from him with mysterious speed to
every corner of Europe, or which, like a blaze or the plague,
caught up with all men whether they tried to run from it or
hoped to escape it by staying put. The unseen and, to them, unfamiliar conqueror seemed to inject their city, as he did so many
other cities of the world, with unrest, excitement, and commotion. For years to come the hard ringing name of Bonaparte was
to echo through the valley of Travnik and, whether they liked
it or not, the townspeople were often to mouth its gnarled, angular syllables; the name would long buzz in their ears and
hover before their eyes. For the "Times of the Consuls" were at
hand.

All Travnichani, without exception, like to appear unruffled and
to affect an air of impassivity. Yet the rumored arrival of a
consul —now a Frenchman, then an Austrian or a Russian,
then again all three of them together—caused them to worry
and entertain hopes; it touched off desires and anticipations that
were difficult to hide altogether, that in fact set their minds
working more briskly and gave a lively new note to their conversation.

Very few of them understood the real import of these rumors,
which had been bandied about since the fall, and no one could
say specifically which consuls were expected or what their business in Travnik was supposed to be. In the prevailing mood, a
single scrap of news, a chance hint of something unusual, was
enough to stir their imagination, to call forth much talk and
guessing; and, beyond that, many doubts and fears, many secret
thoughts and longings of the kind which a man does not admit
or broadcast but keeps to himself.

The local Moslems, as we have seen, were apprehensive and
inclined to sound churlish when discussing the possible arrival
of a consul. Mistrustful of everything that came from abroad
and hostile in advance toward anything new, the Turks hoped
privately that these rumors were no more than spiteful gossip
typical of unsettled times, that the consuls might never come,
or that, if they came after all, they would shortly pack up and
vanish again, together with the bad times that had brought
them.

The Christians, on the other hand, Catholics and Orthodox

alike, received the news with joy and passed it along by word of mouth, stealthily and in whispers, extracting from it vague new hope and a promise of change to come. Any change could only be for the better. And of course each of them thought of the prospect in his own fashion and from his own point of view, which was often diametrically opposed to the viewpoints of others.

The Catholics, who were in the majority, dreamed of an influential Austrian consul who might bring with him the help and protection of the mightly Catholic Emperor at Vienna. The Orthodox, who were fewer in number and had been steadily persecuted during the last few years on account of the Serbian rebellion, expected little—either from a French or an Austrian consul—but they saw in it a good omen and a proof that the Turkish authority was weakening and that better times were on the way—times of unrest and therefore of deliverance. But they were quick to add that naturally "nothing would be accomplished without a Russian consul."

Even the small but lively community of Sephardic Jews found it hard, in the face of such news, to maintain the businesslike reserve which the centuries had taught them; they were stirred by the hope that Bosnia might get a consul of the great French Emperor, Napoleon, "who is good to the Jews like a good father."

The rumor of the imminent arrival of foreign consuls, like most rumors in our land, cropped up suddenly, grew to fantastic proportions, and then ceased just as suddenly, only to reappear in a new form and with new intensity several weeks later.

In the middle of winter, which happened to be short and mild that year, these intimations took on an appearance of reality for the first time. There arrived from Split a Jew by the name of Pardo who, together with a Travnik merchant called Juso Atias, began to look around for a suitable house for the French consulate. They went everywhere, consulted with the town mayor and inspected the properties of the Moslem trust foundation with the administrator. Finally they chose a large, rather neglected house belonging to the foundation where, as far back as anyone could remember, the itinerant merchants from Dubrovnik used to put up and which, for that reason, was called Dubrovnik Lodge. The house stood on one side of the town, above a Moslem school, in the middle of a large, steeply sloping garden traversed by a brook. As soon as terms were agreed upon, they engaged artisans, carpenters, and masons to repair the house and put it in order; and this dwelling which up till then had languished apart and gaped at the world with empty windows, came to life all of a sudden and began to attract the attention of the townspeople and the curiosity of children and loiterers. There was talk that a coat of arms and a flag were to be displayed, permanently and conspicuously, on the building of the foreign consulate. These were things which, in fact, no one had ever seen before; the Moslems pronounced the two weighty and important words seldom and with a frown, while the Christians whispered them often and with a certain malice.

The Moslems of Travnik were, of course, too shrewd and too proud to show their true feelings, but in conversation among themselves they made no attempt to conceal them.

For some time now they had been fretting and troubled in the knowledge that the fences of the empire were tumbling along the frontiers and that Bosnia was fast becoming an open territory, trampled not only by the Osmanlis but by unbelievers of the whole wide world, where even the rayah dared to raise its head more boldly than ever before. And now they were about to be overrun by some infidel consuls and spies, who were sure to use every opportunity to boast of the power and sway of their emperors. And so, little by little, the death knell would be sounded to the good order and "beautiful quiet" of Turkish Bosnia, which in any case had been progressively more difficult to keep and defend for many years past. It was plainly Allah's will and design that the Turks should rule up to the river Sava, and the "Schwabes" beyond. Yet now all Christendom was challenging this patent ordinance of the Almighty, tugging at the frontier fences and digging under them day and night, both openly and in secret. Lately too the divine will itself showed unmistakable signs of blurring and softening. "What else is likely to happen, who else is likely to come?" the older Turks asked themselves with heartfelt bitterness.

And in fact what the baptized folk were saying about the rumored opening of foreign consulates only went to prove that the chagrin of the Moslems was not unjustified.

"There will be a flag!" the Christians whispered to one another; and their eyes were bright with defiance, almost as if the flag would be their own. In reality no one had any idea of what kind of flag it was supposed to be, or what was likely to happen once it appeared, but the very thought that beside the green Turkish flag other colors would be unfurled and allowed to flutter with impunity brought a joyous new luster to people's eyes and aroused such hope as only the oppressed can know and entertain.

Those five bare words—"There will be a flag"—brightened many a poor devil's home for a few moments, made his empty stomach easier to bear, his threadbare suit of clothes warmer; the sound of those five plain unassuming words caused many a peasant's heart to skip a beat, bemused his vision with flaming colors and gilded crosses, filled his ears, like a gust of irresistible wind, with the victorious flapping of all the standards of all the emperors and kings of Christendom. For man can live on a single word, as long as he has the will to fight and by fighting to keep himself alive.

Apart from all this, there was yet another reason why many a shopkeeper in the bazaar thought hopefully of the change. The advent of these unknown but almost certainly well-to-do newcomers held out prospects of new income, for they were bound to shop and spend money. In the last few years, trade had declined and the bazaar had gone into a slump, particularly since the Serb rebellion. Mounting taxes, forced labor, and frequent requisitions had driven the peasant away from the city, and now he had little to sell and bought only the barest necessities. Government purchases were spotty and payments irregular. Slavonia was shut off, while the landing of French troops in Dalmatia made that market insecure and problematical. In these circumstances the business community at Travnik clutched at every straw and looked in every direction for some sign of change for the better.

At last, the thing of which everybody had been talking for months became a reality. The first of the consuls to arrive was the French Consul-General. It was the end of February, the last day of the Moslem fast of Ramadan. An hour before the evening prayer, as the chilly February sun was setting, the people in the lower bazaar were able to observe the arrival of the Consul. The storekeepers had already begun to move their merchandise indoors and to lower the shutters when a scramble of inquisitive gypsy urchins announced his coming.

The procession was a short one. At the head of it rode the Vizier's envoys, two courtiers of the highest rank, escorted by half a dozen horse soldiers. They had gone down to Lashva to meet him. They were smartly got out and their mounts were

good. On either side and in the rear rode the guards of the
mayor of Livno, who had accompanied the Consul all the way;
frozen and tired out, they cut a rather poor figure on their
shaggy, small ponies. In the middle of the procession, riding
a sturdy and elderly gray, was the French Consul-General—
M. Jean Daville, a tall, pink-cheeked man with blue eyes and
a light-colored mustache. He had a co-traveler beside him, a M.
Pouqueville, who was on his way to Janina, where his brother
was also a consul. Bringing up the rear, several paces behind
them, was Pardo, the Jew from Split, and two strapping big
Dalmatians from Sinj, who were in the French service. All three
were bundled up to their eyes in black tunics and scarlet peasant
shawls, and there were traces of straw on their riding boots.

The procession, it will be evident, was not especially large or
brilliant, and the winter weather conspired to rob it of the little
glamour and pageantry it might otherwise have had, as cold
makes bulky clothing unavoidable and cramps one's posture and
lends the whole thing an air of unseemly haste.

And so, except for a handful of shivering gypsy children, the
little cavalcade passed through the town arousing little or no
interest among the Travnichani. The Moslems pretended not to
see it, while the Christians dared not show undue attention. And
even those who saw everything, whether out of the corner of
their eye or from some hidden place, were disappointed that
Bonaparte's Consul should make so colorless and prosaic an
entry, for most of them had visions of the consuls as exalted
dignitaries who wore splendid uniforms decked with gold braid
and decorations, riding spirited thoroughbreds or else reclining
in glittering carriages.

2

The Consul's retinue lodged at the state inn, the Consul and M.
Pouqueville at the home of Joseph Baruch, the wealthiest and
most respected Jew in Travnik, as the large house that was being fitted out for the French consulate would not be ready for
another few weeks. Thus, on the first day of the festival of
Bairam—which marked the end of the fast of Ramadan—the

unusual guest woke up in the small but cozy house of Joseph Baruch. The entire ground floor was placed at his and M. Pouqueville's disposal. Daville was given a large corner room, with two windows overlooking the river and another two with wooden grilles, facing the garden, which was frozen and desolate under a coating of white frost that did not thaw the whole day long.

On the floor above one could hear the patter, scuffling, and cries of Joseph Baruch's many children and the shrill voice of their mother, vainly trying to keep them quiet with threats and shouts. From the town there came the boom of firing cannon, the crackle of children's popguns, and the ear-rending wail of gypsy music. A couple of drums beat out a dull rhythm and over their somber resonance a reed pipe gamboled and pranced, improvising strange melodies full of unexpected trills and pauses. It was one of those rare days in the year when Travnik emerged from its silence.

As it would not be fitting for the Consul to show himself in the streets before he had paid an official call on the Vizier, Daville remained in his big room during the three days of the feast of Bairam, with the same little river and frozen garden constantly in front of his eyes; but if the view was bleak, the unusual sounds of the house and the town gave him an earful. The rich, abundant Jewish food, a mixture of oriental and Spanish cooking, spread a heady aroma of oil, burnt sugar, onions, and powerful spices through the house.

Daville passed the time in conversation with his compatriot, Pouqueville, in issuing orders, and in being briefed on the ceremonial aspects of his first visit to the Vizier, which was to take place on Friday, immediately after the conclusion of the three-day feast of Bairam. From the Residency, meanwhile, he received a gift of two large tallow candles and a basket of almonds and raisins.

Liaison between the Residency and the new Consul was performed by the Vizier's physician and interpreter, César D'Avenat, whom both the Turks and the local people called "Davna." He had called himself by this name the better part of his life. Actually his family came from Piedmont, though he was born in Savoy and was French by adoption. As a young man he had studied medicine at Montpellier and had called himself Cesare Avenato at the time; it was there that he had chosen his present name and opted for French nationality. From there, in circumstances that had never been satisfactorily explained, he had somehow made his way to Istanbul and there entered the service of the redoubtable Kutchuk Hussein, Chief Admiral of the Navy, as surgeon and medical adviser. The Admiral had passed him on to Mehmed Pasha, who was then Vizier of Egypt, and who later brought him to Travnik as his personal doctor, interpreter, and a general factotum of many talents, useful in any kind of exigency.

He was a tall, sinewy, and thickset man of swarthy complexion and dark hair that was always carefully powdered and braided in an impeccable queue. There were a few deep pockmarks on his broad, clean-shaven face; he had a large, sensual mouth and burning eyes. He was neatly groomed and wore French clothes of a prerevolutionary cut.

D'Avenat brought genuine good will to his task and tried to be as helpful as possible to his distinguished compatriot.

To Daville, everything was new and strange and took up all of his time; but it couldn't shut out the thoughts which, especially in the slow hours of the night, flashed through his mind uninvited, leaping swiftly from the present to the past and then again to the future, as if straining to divine its shape and visage.

The nights were oppressive and seemed endless.

He couldn't get used to lying on the low mattress on the floor, which made his head feel heavy, or to the smell of wool in the hard-packed and newly refilled pillows. He woke up often from the stuffy warmth of too many eiderdowns and blankets, feeling soured and bilious from the overspiced oriental food which makes heavy eating and which the body takes and assimilates with the utmost reluctance. He rose several times and drank ice-cold water that shocked his gullet and painfully cooled his stomach.

During the day, as he talked with Pouqueville or D'Avenat, he gave the impression of a calm and decisive man, one who had a well-ordered profession, rank, and name, a man of clear purpose, carrying out palpable tasks that happened to bring him to this God-forsaken Turkish province, just as they might have to any other part of the world. But at night he was not only his present self but also his past selves and the self he hoped to be in the future. And this man lying in the darkness of the long February nights appeared a stranger to himself, a person of many sides who at times was not to be recognized.

And even as the dawn startled him awake with its drums and

pipes of Bairam, or with a scuttling of children's feet on the floor above, Daville had trouble rousing himself and realizing where he was. For a while he would nod between sleeping and waking, since his dreams were bound up with the reality of his life thus far, whereas the reality of the moment was more like the sort of dream in which a man suddenly finds himself cast into a far and weird landscape and facing a most fantastic situation. So his waking was like a dream that failed to end, from which one passed slowly and with an effort to the unwanted reality of being a consul in the distant Turkish town of Travnik.

And in this welter of exotic new impressions, memories of the past came to haunt him irresistibly, mingling with the tasks and cares of the present. Incidents from his past life swam to the surface of his mind, often abruptly and disconnectedly, only to take on a new light and strange new dimension. For the life he had left behind had been a full and restless one.

Jean-Baptiste-Etienne Daville was in his late thirties, tall, of light hair, with an erect carriage and a firm walk. He had been seventeen when he left his native town on the north coast of France and went to Paris, like so many before him, to seek a life for himself and make a reputation. After his early quests and experiences, he was soon drawn to the Revolution, together with millions of other people; and the Revolution became his private, all-exclusive destiny. A volume of his verse and two or three ambitious flings at historical and social plays remained tucked in a drawer; he gave up his modest job of apprentice clerk in the government. Jean Daville became a journalist. He still published verses and literary articles, but now his main interest was the Constituent Assembly; he poured his youth and all the enthusiasm of which he was capable into exhaustive reports of its proceedings. But under the grindstone of the Revolution all things crumbled, changed their substance, and vanished, swiftly and without leaving a trace. It was like a dream. Men passed rapidly and directly from position to position, from honor to honor, from infamy to death, from poverty to fame, some moving in one direction, others in the opposite.

In those extraordinary times and circumstances Daville had been in turn a journalist, then a volunteer in the war against Spain, then an official in the hastily improvised Ministry of Foreign Affairs, which sent him on various missions to Germany, Italy, the Cisalpine Republic, and the Knights of Malta.

Then, back in Paris once more, he resumed journalism and became literary critic at *Le Moniteur*. And now finally he was Consul-General at Travnik, with orders to establish a consulate and initiate and develop trade relations with this Turkish province, while assisting the French occupation forces in Dalmatia and watching the pulse and temper of the Christian rayah in Bosnia and Serbia.

Such, in a few words, was the biography of this guest in the house of Joseph Baruch. Yet now, looking at it from the strange perspective of his unexpected three days' confinement, Daville often had to make an effort to remember exactly who he was and where he came from, what his earlier life had been, why he had come to this place, and how it happened that he was now pacing this red Bosnian rug all day long.

So long as a man leads a normal, ordered life among his own kind, such details of his career represent important phases and significant turning points in his life; but as soon as chance, illness, or an assignment separate and isolate him, these highlights begin suddenly to fade and gutter, to wither and shrivel like so many papier-mâché masks that one has no use for any more. And from underneath there begins to emerge our other life, known to only ourselves, the "true" story of our spirit and body, one that has not been set down anywhere and which no other person can begin to guess at, a story that has no visible connection with our successes in society but which, in the final tally of good and evil in our existence, is the only concrete and decisive one.

Lost in these wilds, in the long nights when every last sound petered away in darkness, Daville looked back on his life as a long succession of bold endeavors and fainthearted backsliding, known only to himself; an erratic patchwork of quest, bravery, lucky turns, triumphs, sudden wrenches, setbacks, contradictions, useless sacrifices, and vain compromises.

In the darkness and silence of this town, which he had scarcely seen as yet but where trouble and worries surely awaited him, the truism that the world would never know peace and order acquired a stark new meaning for Daville. At times it seemed to him that life demanded unconscionable efforts and each effort a disproportionate amount of courage. In the darkness that surrounded him, he could not see the end of these efforts. Terrified of faltering and remaining still, a man deceived himself by burying his unfinished business under new tasks, which he

would never finish either, and in these fresh enterprises and
endeavors sought new strength and a new lease of courage. And
so he cheated himself and as time went on piled up an ever
greater and more hopeless debt to himself and to everyone
around him.

Still, as the day of his first official reception drew near, these
memories and reflections gave way increasingly to new impressions and to the practical cares and work of the moment.
Daville pulled himself together. Remembrance and brooding
thoughts receded to the back of his mind, from where, in days
to come, they would often reappear to give an odd and surprising dimension to daily events or to the strange experiences
of his new life in Travnik.

At last the three long days, with their three nights of soul
searching, came to an end. With a premonition that is usually
not far wrong in people who have received many hard knocks
in their lives, Daville thought that morning: "It is quite possible
that these three days were the best and quietest I'm ever going
to spend in this cramped little valley."

In the early morning of that day there was the sound of
neighing and stamping horses under his windows. Strapped in
his gala official uniform, the Consul awaited the captain of the
Vizier's Mameluke Guard, who came accompanied by D'Avenat.
Everything went off as arranged and discussed beforehand.
There were twelve Mamelukes, from the detachment which the
Vizier Melmed Pasha had brought from Egypt as his personal
bodyguard and of whom he was particularly proud. Their smartly
rolled turbans of finely woven silk and gold, their curving sci-
mitars dangling picturesquely from their horses' flanks, their
ample cherry-colored greatcoats attracted everyone's attention.
The mounts of Daville and his escort were caparisoned from
head to tail with choicest cloth; the men were smart and showed
good discipline. Daville tried to mount his horse as naturally as
possible; the animal was a quiet old black, rather broad-crouped.
The Consul's dark blue cloak was generously parted at the chest
to show the gilded buttons, the silver sash, the medals and service decorations. Sitting straight as a ramrod, his handsome
virile head held up high, the Consul cut a fine figure.

Up to the point where they turned into the main street, everything went well and the Consul had reason to be satisfied. But
as soon as they reached the first Turkish houses, suspicious calls
began to be heard and there was a sudden banging of courtyard

gates and a closing of window shutters. Already at the first gate a little girl opened one wing of the door and, muttering something unintelligible, began to spit thinly into the street, as if casting a spell. A moment later other doors flew open and shutters were raised, one after another, revealing faces that were full of hate and fanatical zeal. Veiled women spat and cursed, and small boys shouted abuse, accompanied by obscene gestures and unmistakable threats, as they smacked their bottoms or drew their fingers across the throats in a vicious slitting movement.

As the street was narrow and shut in by jutting balconies on both sides, the procession ran a double gamut of abuse and threats. At first, taken aback, the Consul tightened his reins and slowed down, but D'Avenat spurred his horse nearer and, without turning in the saddle or moving a single facial muscle, began to urge in an agitated whisper: "I beg Your Excellency to ride on quietly and pay no attention. They are wild ignorant people. They hate everything foreign and greet everyone in this way. It is best to ignore them. That's what the Vizier does, ignore them. It's their barbarian way. Please ride on, Your Excellency."

Baffled and outraged, although trying his best to hide it, the Consul rode on, realizing that none of the Vizier's guards did in fact pay any attention to what was happening; but he felt a rush of blood to his head. Confused, rash, and contradictory thoughts raced through his mind. His first thought was whether, as a representative of the great Napoleon, he ought to tolerate this or whether he should return to his house right away and create a scandal. It was a hard decision to make, for as much as he wanted to stand up for the honor of France, he was equally anxious to avoid any impetuous action that would lead to a clash and so ruin his relations with the Vizier and the Turks right on his very first day. Failing to summon up enough resolution to act quickly, he felt humiliated and bitter toward himself; and he was disgusted with the Levantine D'Avenat who kept repeating behind him: "I beg Your Excellency to ride on and pay no attention. These are just loutish Bosnian customs and ways. Let us proceed quietly."

In this irresolute and unhappy frame of mind, Daville was conscious of his burning cheeks and his clammy armpits, which were full of sweat in spite of the cold. He hated D'Avenat's persistent whispering, which struck him as boorish and revolting.

It was an intimation, it seemed to him, of the kind of life a Westerner might expect if he moved to the Orient and hitched his destiny to it permanently.

Throughout this time, from behind their window grilles, invisible women spat down on the horses and the riders. Once more the Consul halted for a second; one more he went on, yielding to D'Avenat's urgings and carried along by the stolid progress of his escorts. Soon they left the residential quarter behind them and gained the market street, with its single-storied shops, where Turkish storekeepers and their customers sat on little wooden platforms, smoking and bargaining. It was like passing from an overheated room into a cold one. All of a sudden there were no more blazing looks, no gestures indicating how the throats of unbelievers are slashed, no more sputtering by superstitious womenfolk. Instead, on both sides of the street, there were blank inscrutable faces. Daville saw them dimly, as if through a veil that shivered in front of his eyes. Not one of them paused in his work or stopped smoking or lifted his eyes and deigned to acknowledge with a glance the uncommon sight of a solemn procession. Here and there a shopkeeper did turn his head, as if looking for merchandise on the shelves. Only Orientals knew how to hate and feel contempt so intensely, and to show it in this way.

D'Avenat had fallen silent and backed away as required by protocol, but Daville found this incredible mute contempt of the bazaar just as hard to take, just as insufferable as the loud-voiced hatred and abuse of a little while before. At last they veered to the right and saw the high, long walls and the white building of the Vizier's Residency, a large well-proportioned dwelling with a row of glazed windows. He felt a little easier.

The agonizing journey that now lay behind him would long remain etched in Daville's memory; like an unhappy but portentous dream, it would never be entirely erased. In years to come he was to retrace his steps along the same road a hundred times, in similar circumstances; for as often as he would have an audience with the Vizier—and they would be frequent, especially in times of unrest—he would have to ride through the same residential quarter and the same market street. He would sit upright and rigid on his horse, looking neither to the left nor to the right, neither too high nor between the horse's ears, appearing neither distracted nor worried, neither smiling nor dour, but quietly and soberly alert, displaying the kind of studied air with which generals in their portraits contemplate a battle in the distance, gazing at a point somewhere between the road and the horizon where promised and well-timed reinforcements are supposed to appear. For a long time yet Turkish children would spit at his horse's legs, in frantic but childish imitation of spell-casting, which they had learned from their elders. Moslem shopkeepers would turn their backs to him, pretending to look for something on the shelves.

Only a rare Jew here and there would greet him, coming face to face with him unexpectedly, unable to dodge him. Time and again he was to ride by like this, outwardly calm and dignified but inwardly trembling at the hate and the studied indifference closing in on him from all sides, shuddering at the thought of some sudden, unexpected incident, loathing his work and his present life, yet trying to hide by a convulsive effort both the alarm and the revulsion he felt.

And even much later, when in the course of many years and changes the populace had finally accepted the presence of foreigners, and when Daville had met a number of people and got to know them much better, this first ceremonial procession would linger in his consciousness like a black and burning line which continues to hurt and is only gradually salved and healed by oblivion.

With a hollow clatter, the procession crossed a wooden bridge and came up to a large gate. All at once, with a loud scraping of locks and a bustle of attendants, both wings swung wide open.

Jean Daville was about to enter the stage on which, for nearly eight years, he would play the varied scenes of a singularly exacting and thankless role.

Time and again he would stand before this yawning, disproportionately wide gate; and always, at the moment when it gaped open, it would seem to him like the hideous mouth of a jinnee, spewing and belching the smell of everything that lived, grew, steamed, was used up or ailing in the huge Residency. He knew that the town and the district, which had to feed the Vizier and his staff, daily stocked the Residency with almost a ton of assorted provisions and that all of it was distributed, stolen, or consumed. He knew that besides the Vizier and his close family there were eleven other dignitaries, thirty-two guards, and as many, and maybe more, parasites, hangers-on, Christian day workers, and petty clerks; over and above that, an indeterminate number of horses, cattle, dogs, cats, birds, and monkeys. The air was heavy with the stomach-turning reek of rancid butter and tallow, which overpowered those who were not inured to it. After every audience this sickly sweet odor would haunt the Consul for the rest of the day and the very thought of it produced in him a feeling of nausea. He had the impression that the entire Residency was permeated with the smell, as a church with incense, and that it clung not only to people and to their clothes but also to the walls and all other inanimate objects.

Now as the unfamiliar gate swung open to receive him for the first time, the Mameluke column detached itself and dismounted, while Daville rode into the courtyard with his own escort. This first, outer courtyard was narrow and shadowy, closed over by the upper story of the house from one end to the other; but beyond was a regular open courtyard, with a water well, with grass, and flowerbeds along the walls. At the far end, a tall and impenetrable fence shut off the Vizier's private garden.

Still shaken by his experiences during his passage through the town, Daville was now startled by the polite fuss and ceremonious attention extended to him by the entire population of courtiers and officials of the Residency. They all milled and scurried around him with an avid, overwhelming concern that was unknown in the ceremonials of the West.

The first to greet the Consul was the Vizier's Secretary; the Vizier's Deputy, Suleiman Pasha Skoplyak, was not in Travnik. Behind him came the Keeper of Arms, the Quartermaster, the Treasurer, the Protocol Officer, and behind them shoved and elbowed a whole crowd of people of unknown and indeterminate rank and occupation. Some murmured a few indistinct words of welcome, bowing their heads, others spread their arms ceremoniously, and the whole throng moved toward the great hall where the divan—or reception—was to be held. Through it all, the towering and swarthy D'Avenat made his way deftly and with practiced indifference, loftily brushing aside those who stood in the way, and issuing orders and instructions rather more loudly and conspicuously than the occasion warranted. Inwardly confused but calm and self-possessed on the outside, Daville couldn't help seeing himself as one of those saints in the Catholic holy pictures, borne to the heavens by a swarm of angels; the throng simply carried him up the few broad steps that led from the courtyard to the divan.

The divan was a dim but spacious hall on the ground level. There were a few rugs scattered on the floor; all around were couches draped with cherry-red cloth. In an alcove by the window were cushions for the Vizier and his guest. The walls contained a single picture, the imperial coat of arms: the Sultan's initials in gold letters on a green parchment. Underneath, a sword, two pistols, and a scarlet mantle of honor, gifts from Sultan Selim III to his favorite, Husref Mehmed Pasha.

Above this hall, on the upper story, there was another like it, much brighter though more sparsely furnished, in which the Vizier held his divan during the summer months. Two entire walls of this great room were taken up with windows, one half of which overlooked the garden and the other the river Lashva and the bazaar beyond the bridge. These were the "panels of glass" about which songs were sung and tales told, the likes of which were not to be found in all Bosnia; it was from Austria that Mehmed Pasha had imported them at his own expense, hiring a famous master glazier, a German, to cut and install them. Seated on his cushion a guest could look out through the windows and see the open veranda where under the eaves a nest of swallows perched high on a juniper beam, and he could listen to their twitter and watch the shy mother swallow dart in and out amid the trembling stalks of straw.

Sitting beside these windows was always delightful. It was bright there and full of flowers and greenery, and one sat in a soft breeze, lapped by the purling sound of water and chirruping birds, and there was always peace enough to rest in and quiet for reflection or talk. Many a hard and thorny decision was reached or sanctioned there; but all problems, when discussed in this place, seemed somehow easier, clearer, and more human than in the reception hall on the ground floor.

These two rooms of the Residency were the only ones Daville would ever get to know during his stay in Travnik, and they would be the scene of his trials and satisfactions, failures and successes. Here, in the years to come, he would learn to understand not only the Turks and their peculiar strengths and terrible weaknesses, but also himself, his own capacity and limitations, and mankind in general, and the world and human relationships within it.

This first audience, as was customary in the winter, was held in the divan on the ground floor. Judging by the stale and moldy air, the hall had been opened and heated for the first time that winter, especially for the occasion.

As soon as the Consul crossed the threshold, a door opened on the opposite side of the hall and the Vizier appeared in a colorful gala robe, accompanied by courtiers who walked with their heads slightly bowed and arms humbly folded on their chests.

This was the great ceremonial audience which Daville had sought and negotiated for three days through D'Avenat, and which he hoped would lend special color and spice to his initial report to the Minister. The Turks had suggested that the Vizier await the Consul reclining on his couch, as he did all his other visitors, but the Consul demanded that he greet him standing on his feet. The Consul had invoked the might of France and the battle glory of his sovereign, the Turks their ancient traditions and the greatness of their Empire. At length it was agreed that both the Vizier and the Consul should make their entrance at the same moment and meet in the center of the hall, whence the Vizier would lead the Frenchman to the platform by the window where two identical cushions would be set, on which they would lower themselves at the same instant.

This was in fact what happened. The Vizier, who had a limp in his right foot for which the people had nicknamed him the Lame Pasha, walked up briskly and energetically, as lame people often do, and cordially invited the Consul to be seated.

Between them, but a step lower, squatted the interpreter D'Avenat. He sat doubled up, with hands folded in his lap and his eyes downcast, as if anxious to make himself smaller and less conspicuous than he was, obtruding with his presence and his breath only as much as was necessary to enable these two dignitaries to communicate their thoughts and declarations to each other. The rest of the throng melted away quietly. There remained only servants, standing at a respectful distance, awaiting their master's bidding. During the whole conversation, which took up more than an hour's time, everything that ceremonial hospitality required was passed discreetly from one shadowy boy to another and offered to the Vizier and his guest.

First, lighted chibouks were brought in, then coffee, then sherbet. Then one of the boys, approaching on his knees, held out a shallow bowl of strong aromatic essence and passed it under the Vizier's beard and around the Consul's mustache, as if censing them. Then again more coffee and fresh pipes. All of it was served while they were talking, with the utmost efficiency, inconspicuously, swiftly, and yet with a practiced sense of timing. For an Oriental, the Vizier was unusually lively, cordial, and outspoken. Daville had already been told about these traits of the Vizier and although he knew they were not to be taken at face value, he still found the man's cordiality and friendliness most agreeable, especially after the humiliating experience in the bazaar. The throbbing of blood in his head subsided. The Vizier's talk, the aroma of coffee, and the smell of pipes were pleasant and soothing, even if they could not altogether erase the earlier sickening impressions. The Vizier tactfully alluded to the backwardness of the land and to the coarse and boorish manners of the people. It was a difficult country and the natives were a problem. What could one expect of women and children, creatures on whom God had not lavished much reason, in a country where even the men were irresponsible louts? Nothing these people did or said could have any significance or importance or any effect on the affairs of serious and enlightened persons. The dog barks but the caravan moves on, said the Vizier in conclusion; for he had obviously been informed of everything that had happened during the Consul's ride through the city and was now trying to minimize and smooth over the incident. Then, without further ado, he passed from these unpleasant trivia to a fresh subject, the signal greatness of Napoleon's victories and the enormous importance of close and realistic collaboration between the two empires, the Ottoman and the French.

These words, spoken quietly and sincerely, were like a balm to Daville, intended as they were to be an indirect apology for the insults of a little while before; in his own eyes, at any rate, they lessened the humiliation he had endured. Feeling reassured and better disposed, he now gave the Vizier more of his attention and remembered all that D'Avenat had told him about the man.

Husref Mehmed Pasha, nicknamed "the Lame," was a Georgian. Brought to Istanbul as a slave in his youth, he had entered the service of the great Kutchuk Hussein Pasha. There he was noticed by Selim III, even before the latter ascended the throne. Brave, shrewd, bright, eloquent, genuinely devoted to his superiors, this Georgian became, at the age of thirty-one, Vizier of Egypt. His tenure was cut short, however, as the great

Mameluke rebellion drove him out of the country; even so, he
was not disgraced altogether. After a short stay at Salonica he
was appointed Vizier of Bosnia. As punishment this was com-
paratively mild, and he made it appear lighter still by keeping
up a shrewd pretense before the world that he did not regard
it as a punishment at all. He brought with him from Egypt a
detachment of thirty loyal Mamelukes whom he liked to exercise on the drilling field of Travnik. Well fed and lavishly uniformed, the Mamelukes attracted general curiosity and served
to bolster his prestige with the people. The Bosnian Moslems
eyed them with hatred but also with fear and secret admiration.
   Even more than the Mamelukes, the people admired the Vizier's stud, which far surpassed any other yet seen in Bosnia for
both the number and quality of its horses.
   The Vizier was young and looked still younger than his years.
Of less than medium build, he somehow managed, with his
whole bearing, and particularly with his habit of smiling, to
give an impression of being an inch or two taller than he was.
Although he limped with his right foot, the skillful cut of his
clothes and his crisp, energetic movements somehow disguised
this defect. Whenever obliged to stand on his feet, he invariably
struck a pose that concealed his disability; and when he was
obliged to move, he did so swiftly, nimbly, and in short spurts.
This gave him a characteristic air of freshness and youth. He
had none of that monolithic Ottoman dignity of which Daville
had read and heard so much. The color and style of his clothes
were simple, though it was evident that they were chosen with
the utmost care. There are people who can impart a special glitter and elegance to their dress and adornment by the mere act
of wearing it. His face was unusually ruddy, like a seafaring
man's, with a short dark beard and slanted black, shiny eyes;
it was an open and smiling face. He seemed to be one of those
men who hide their true mood in a steady smile and their
thoughts, or lack of them, in animated talk. In everything he
touched upon he seemed to imply a greater knowledge of the
subject than the words themselves might have indicated. His
every cordiality, attention, and kindness appeared to be only a
preamble, a first installment of what one might still expect of
him. Regardless of how much one might have been briefed and
forewarned, it was impossible to escape the impression that here
was an honorable and sensible man who would not only promise but also carry out a good deed, where and whenever he

could; at the same time no person, however astute, could really judge or discern the subtle limits of those promises or the actual scope of the good deed.

The Vizier and the Consul turned to those subjects for which each knew the other had a secret weakness, or which happened to be a favorite topic. The Vizier kept referring to the exceptional personality of Napoleon and to his victories, while the Consul, who had learned from D'Avenat about the Vizier's love of the sea and seafaring, spoke of matters connected with navigation and naval warfare. The Vizier did, in fact, have a passionate love of the sea and of a sailor's life. Besides his secret shame over his failure in Egypt, he suffered most of all from the fact that he had been torn away from the sea and imprisoned in these cold, wild mountain regions. Deep down inside him the Vizier still nurtured the hope that one day he might succeed his great chief Kutchuk Hussein Pasha and, as Chief Lord of the Admiralty, pursue his plans and designs for the revival of the Turkish battle fleet.

After an hour and a half of conversation the Consul and the Vizier parted as old acquaintances, each believing that much might be achieved with the help of the other, each pleased with the other and with himself.

The Consul's leave-taking occasioned an even greater bustle and hubbub than before. Fur cloaks of really considerable value were brought out; sable for the Consul, coats of fox fur and cloth for his retinue. Someone voiced a prayer and invoked blessings on the imperial guest, and the others chorused after him. The high-ranking courtiers led Daville back to the mounting block in the middle of the inner courtyard; they all walked with open arms, as if bearing him along. Daville mounted his horse. The Vizier's sable cloak was slung over his greatcoat. Outside the Mamelukes were waiting, mounted and ready. The procession turned back the way it had come.

In spite of the heavy robe weighing him down, Daville shuddered a little at the thought of having to ride once more between those worn shutters and jutting window grilles amid the cursing and contempt of the crowd; but, it seemed, his first public appearances in Travnik were to be full of surprises, even, sometimes, agreeable ones. True, the Turks in the shops along the way were sullen and impassive, their eyes conspicuously averted, but this time neither insults nor threats were heard from the houses. Arching against his will, Daville had a feeling

that behind the wooden grilles many a curious and hostile pair
of eyes watched him, although he heard no sound and saw no
movement. It seemed almost as if the Vizier's cloak were shield-
ing him from the people, and he drew it instinctively tighter
around him and sat up straight in the saddle and thus, with
his head held high, he reached the walled courtyard of Joseph
Baruch.

When at last he was alone in his warm room, he sat down on
a hard couch, unbuttoned his uniform, and took a deep breath.
He was worn out with excitement and tired in every part of his
body. He felt empty, blunted, and confused, as if he'd been
hurled down from a great height onto this hard settee and
couldn't yet come to himself and grasp clearly where he was
and what had happened. He was free at last, but had no idea
what to do with his free time. He thought of resting and going
to sleep, but his glance fell on the hanging fur cloak he had got
from the Vizier a little while before, and all at once the thought
came back to him, unwelcome and a little jolting, that he must
write a report on all this to the Minister in Paris and the Ambassador at Istanbul. That meant he must live through the whole
thing again and, moreover, paint a picture that would not be too
damaging to his prestige but not too far from the truth either.
This task now loomed before him like an impassable mountain
that he must somehow negotiate. The Consul laid the balls of
his palms on his eyes and pressed them. He sighed heavily a
few more times and said under his breath: "Dear God. Dear
God!" He remained sprawled like this on the settee, and there
he slept and rested.

3

As happens to the heroes in Eastern fables, Daville encountered
his greatest obstacles at the outset of his consulship. Everything
seemed to pounce on him at once, as if to scare him and head
him off the road he'd chosen. Everything he met with in Bosnia
and all that reached him from the embassy in Istanbul, and from
the military governor in Dalmatia, was contrary to what he'd
been told when he left Paris.

After several weeks Daville moved out of Baruch's house into the building that was to be his Consulate. He furnished and fitted out two or three rooms as well as he could and lived alone with his servants in the large, empty house.

On his way to Travnik, he had been obliged to leave his wife with a French family in Split. Madame Daville was expecting the birth of her third child and he did not dare to take her with him, in that condition, to an unfamiliar Turkish town. After her delivery, she had been slow to recuperate and her departure from Dalmatia had to be put off again and again.

Daville, who was used to living with his family and up to now had never been separated from his wife, found the isolation particularly hard to bear in his present circumstances. Loneliness, disorder in the house, worries about his wife and children tormented him more and more as the days went by. Monsieur Pouqueville had left Travnik some days before on his way further east.

Other things combined to give Daville a sense of being forgotten and left to fend for himself. Funds and equipment for his work and administration, which had been promised to him before he set out for Bosnia, or which he had demanded since then, turned out to be inadequate or else failed altogether to materialize.

Lacking assistants and clerical help, he was forced to do all the writing, copying, and office work himself. Not knowing the language and being unfamiliar with the land and local conditions, he had no choice but to employ D'Avenat as full-time interpreter to the Consulate. The Vizier generously released his medical adviser and D'Avenat was delighted at the opportunity to enter the French service. Daville hired him with some misgivings and a certain private aversion, and decided to let him handle only those affairs which the Vizier could be allowed to know about. But he soon came to see how indispensable this man was to him and how great was his usefulness in practical matters. D'Avenat managed to get two reliable kavasses right away, an Albanian and a man from Herzegovina, and he took over the management of the staff and relieved the Consul of a good deal of petty and distasteful detail. Working with him day by day, the Consul was able to observe him and got to know him better and better.

Having lived in the East from his early youth, D'Avenat had acquired many of the traits and habits of the Levantine. The Levantine is a man with no illusions and no scruples and with-

out a face of his own—that is to say, a man of several faces,
forced to put on an act of humility one moment and one of
boldness the next, a man melancholy and bubbling by turns, for
these faces are his indispensable weapons in the fight for survival, which in the Levant is tougher and more complex than
in any other part of the world. A foreigner who is pitched into
this bitter and unequal struggle founders in it and loses his true
personality. He spends a lifetime in the East but never gets to
know it completely, or else gets to know it one-sidedly—that is
to say, only from the viewpoint of his success or failure in the
struggle to which he is condemned. Those foreigners who, like
D'Avenat, stay on and live in the East, acquire from the Turks,
in most cases, only their bad and cruder characteristics, and are
unable to see and assimilate any of their better and nobler qualities and habits.

D'Avenat was a man like that in many ways. In his youth he
had led a life of pleasure, and contact with the Osmanlis had
not taught him anything good in this respect. People of this
type, when their sensual life begins to blunt and burn out, become moody and bitter, a burden to themselves and to others.
Exceedingly humble and servile in the presence of power, authority, and wealth, he was rude, brazen, and merciless to all
that was weak, poor, and unfortunate. And yet there was something that redeemed this man and raised him above these faults.
He had a son, a bright handsome lad over whose upbringing
and well-being he worried constantly, and for whom he did, and
was ready to do, anything. These intense feelings of fatherly
love gradually cured him of his bad habits and made him better
and more human. And as the boy grew, so D'Avenat's life grew
purer and clearer. Every time he did someone a good turn or
refrained from doing something disreputable, he did so in the
superstitious belief that "it will be repaid to the little one." As
often happens in life, this peccant and many-faced parent
nursed the secret ambition to see his son grow up to be a man
who lived honorably and respectably. And there was nothing he
would not have done or sacrificed to realize this desire.

Though motherless, the child received all the care and attention that it was possible to give a boy, and he grew beside his
father like a young sapling tied to a drying but sturdy stake.
The boy was good-looking, he had his father's softer and gentler
features, he was physically and mentally sound and showed no
bad traits or distressing legacies.

Deep in his heart D'Avenat cherished one secret wish, one ultimate aim: that the child should be spared his fate of being a Levantine lackey to all and sundry, that he might instead be sent to some school in France and afterwards be accepted into French service. This was the main reason that D'Avenat worked for the Consulate with such exemplary zeal and devotion, and one could believe that his loyalty was genuine and lasting.

The new Consul also had financial problems and difficulties. Remittances were slow and irregular; considerable unforeseen expenses kept showing up on the ledger. The credits that had been granted him arrived late, and those he requested for fresh contingencies were turned down. Instead there came a spate of perfunctory and bewildering orders from the Department of Accounts and lengthy circular letters that made no sense whatever, and which struck Daville, forlorn and isolated as he was, as purest nonsense. In one of them, for example, he was directed to confine his social contacts to foreign diplomats only and to attend the receptions of foreign ambassadors and envoys only when called upon to do so by his own ambassador or envoy. Another brought detailed instructions for the celebration of Napoleon's birthday on August 15. "The orchestra and decorations for the ball which the Consul-General will arrange on this occasion will be at his expense." Daville read it with a wry smile. The words called up an irresistible vision before his mind's eye: Travnik musicians, consisting of three ragged gypsies of whom two were drummers and one puffed away on a small flute, who all through Ramadan and Bairam had split the ears of any European condemned to live there.

He would always remember the first celebration of the Emperor's birthday, or, more accurately, his misbegotten effort to organize festivities. Several days previously he had tried, via D'Avenat, to secure the attendance of at least some of the more respected local Turks; but even the few at the Residency who had accepted the invitation failed to put in an appearance. The Brothers and their fellow Catholics declined, politely but firmly. The Orthodox abbot Pakhomi neither accepted nor declined the invitation, but he did not come either. Only the Jews came. There were fourteen in all; and some, contrary to Travnik custom, even brought their wives.

Madame Daville had not yet arrived in Travnik; and Daville, wearing his gala uniform and assisted by D'Avenat and the kavasses, acted the gracious host and served refreshments and a sparkling wine which he had obtained from Split. He even made a little speech in honor of his Sovereign, in which he flattered the Turks and praised Travnik as an important city, for he assumed that at least two of those Jews were in the Vizier's service and would report to him forthwith, and that all of them together would carry his words up and down Travnik. The Jewesses, who were seated on the couch, their hands folded in their laps, fluttered their eyelashes and moved their heads now to the left shoulder, now to the right. Their menfolk looked straight in front of them, as if to say: "That's how things are and they'll never be otherwise, but we haven't said a word."

They were all a little flushed from the sparkling wine. D'Avenat, who didn't greatly care for the Jews of Travnik and translated their good wishes a little condescendingly, could barely attend to all of them, as everyone now had something he wished to say to the Consul. Then they began to speak Spanish, which suddenly loosened the tongues of the women, and Daville racked his brain to recall the hundred or so Spanish words he had once picked up soldiering in Spain. Before long the younger among them started to sing. Awkwardly enough, not one of them knew any French songs and they refused to sing Turkish ones. In the end Mazalta, Benzion's daughter-in-law, sang a Spanish romance, puffing a little from excitement and premature stoutness. Her mother-in-law, a lively and earthy woman, caught the mood so well that she took to clapping her hands, swinging the upper half of her body, and pushing back her lacy headdress which kept slipping off on account of the sparkling wine.

The unpretentious merrymaking of these simple and good-natured folk was all that could be improvised in Travnik to celebrate the mightiest ruler on earth. This both touched and saddened the Consul.

Daville thought it best not to remember it, and in reporting officially to the Ministry on how the birthday of the Emperor was first celebrated at Travnik, he wrote coyly and with deliberate vagueness that the great day had been marked "in a style suitable to the circumstances and customs of the country." Yet now, as he read the belated and pompous circular letter about balls, orchestras, and decorations, he felt a fresh pang of shame and discomfort and couldn't make up his mind whether to laugh or cry.

.   .   .

One of his constant worries was having to take care of the officers and soldiers who passed through Bosnia on their way from Dalmatia to Istanbul.

The Turkish government and the French Ambassador at Istanbul had signed a treaty under which the French army was to place at the disposal of the Turks a certain number of officers, as instructors and engineers, gunners and sappers. A short time before, the English fleet had forced the Dardanelles and threatened Istanbul itself, and Sultan Selim had set about bolstering the defenses of his capital with the aid of the French envoy Sebastiani and a small group of French officers. The French were then urgently requested to send a certain number of officers and men, and Paris ordered General Marmont in Dalmatia to dispatch them right away in small detachments via Bosnia. Daville was instructed to provide their passage and secure horses and escort. He then had an opportunity of seeing how a treaty made with the government at Istanbul worked out in practice. Passage permits did not arrive in time and the officers had to sit it out in Travnik. The Consul did his best to expedite matters with the Vizier, and the Vizier in turn with the capital. And even if the permit had come in time, this would still not have been the end of the business, for fresh complications kept cropping up with annoying suddenness and the officers had to break their journey elsewhere and waste their time in obscure little Bosnian towns.

The Bosnian Moslems looked with suspicion and hatred on the French occupation army in Dalmatia. Austrian agents had spread the rumor among them that General Marmont was building a wide highway down the entire length of the Dalmatian coast, with the object of annexing Bosnia as well. The advent of French officers to Bosnia confirmed the town in this mistaken belief; and these French officers, who had come as allies at the request of the Turkish government, were greeted already at Livno, just across the frontier, by jeering and abusive mobs, and their reception went from bad to worse as they continued into the interior.

There were times when thirty or forty of these officers and other ranks were stranded in Daville's house at Travnik, unable to go forward and not daring to turn back. In vain did the Vizier call together the leaders and notables of the town and enjoin them to treat these people as friends who had come at the invitation of, and with the full knowledge of, the High Porte.

The thing was patched up and settled with words, as usual. The town elders made promises to the Vizier, the Vizier made promises to the Consul, the Consul to the officers, that there would be no more hostility from the populace; but when the officers set out again the next day, they usually walked into such a hornet's nest in the next small town that they turned around and marched back to Travnik more indignant than ever.

In vain Daville wrote to his government about the real sentiments of the local Turks and about the helpless attempts of the Vizier to restrain them and impose his will. Istanbul continued to demand new contingents, Paris kept up its instructions, and Split kept obeying them faithfully. Again fresh groups of officers would arrive in Travnik, one after another, only to loaf around embittered, waiting for further orders. Everything went appallingly wrong and made the Consul feel as though his head were buffeted from all sides.

In vain did the French authorities in Dalmatia print friendly proclamations to the Turkish population. The posters, written in a high-flown, literary Turkish, were hardly read; and if anyone took the trouble to read them, he could not understand them. No appeal made any headway against the ingrained mistrust of the entire Moslem population, which had no desire to read or hear or look at anything and acted solely from its deep instinct of self-preservation and of hatred toward these foreigners and unbelievers who had advanced to their frontiers and were beginning to enter their country.

Only after the May palace revolution in the capital and the deposition of the Sultan were the orders suspended for sending French officers to Turkey. But although new orders ceased, the old ones continued to be carried out blindly and mechanically. So it came to pass that, for a long time after, groups of two or three French officers would suddenly pop up in Travnik, even though their trip was now purposeless and nonsensical.

But although the events in Istanbul freed the Consul of one kind of nuisance, they soon threatened him with another and much bigger one.

Daville had come to depend on the help and support of the Vizier, Husref Mehmed Pasha. He had already, it was true, had many opportunities of observing the man's limited power and his lack of influence among the Bosnian begs; many of his promises had gone blithely unfulfilled and many of his commands had died a quiet death, although the Vizier himself pretended not to notice it. At the same time, the Vizier's good will was clear and beyond doubt. Both from natural inclination and from policy, he wished to be considered a friend of France and to prove it by his acts. And besides this, Mehmed Pasha's happy disposition, his unshakable optimism, and the smiling ease with which he approached a problem and weathered every kind of mishap, acted as a pure balm on Daville and gave him courage to deal with the many niggling as well as real difficulties of his new life. And now he was faced with the possibility of losing this great and only help and comfort.

In May of that year there was the *coup d'état* in Istanbul. The fanatical opponents of Selim III deposed that enlightened and reform-minded Sultan and shut him up in the Serai, installing Sultan Mustapha in his place. French influence in the capital declined and, what was still worse for Daville personally, the fate of Husref Mehmed Pasha became uncertain, since the fall of Selim had deprived him of support in the capital while in Bosnia he remained unpopular because of his friendship for France and his partiality to reform.

The Vizier, it was true, never for a moment lost his broad seaman's smile before the world, nor his oriental optimism that seemed to have no other foundation than his invincible inner self; but these things deceived no one. The Travnik Moslems, all of whom to a man were implacable foes of Selim's reforms and hostile to Mehmed Pasha, said that "the Vizier's feet were dangling." A sort of vexed silence fell over the Residency. All hands quietly made preparations for a move that might take place at any moment; everyone was wrapped in his own cares and spoke little and looked straight in front of him. The Vizier himself was apt to be distracted and listless in his talks with Daville, though he tried with kindness and brave words to cover up his utter inability to help anyone or anything.

Special couriers came and went, and the Vizier sent his own confidential agents to Istanbul with mysterious messages and gifts to those friends he still had left. D'Avenat, who had managed to learn a few details, asserted that the Vizier was fighting as much to save his head as to save his position under the new Sultan.

Knowing what the removal of the present Vizier would mean for himself and his work, Daville at once dispatched some urgent messages to General Marmont in Dalmatia and to the Ambassador in Istanbul, urging them to use their best offices with the High Porte to ensure that Mehmed Pasha remained in Bosnia, irrespective of the political changes in the capital, for that was how the Russians and Austrians interceded for their own friends and the Turks would judge the influence and strength of a Christian power by its success in this direction.

The Bosnian Moslems were jubilant.

"Gone is the infidel Sultan," said the hodjas in the bazaar. "The time has come to scrape off the mud that has collected around the true faith and the Moslem way of life these last few years. The Lame Vizier will go and take his friend the Consul with him, just as he brought him here." The ragtag of the streets spread the words and grew steadily more aggressive. They taunted and molested the Consul's servants; they jeered and abused D'Avenat in the streets, asking whether the Consul was packing to leave, and if not, what he was waiting for. The interpreter, dark and hulking on his dappled mare, gave them a withering look of disdain and replied caustically that they didn't know what they were talking about; that obviously they'd picked up this nonsense from a nitwit whose brain was soaked in plum brandy; that, on the contrary, the new Sultan and the French Emperor were the best of friends and Istanbul had already sent word that the French Consul in Travnik was an official guest of the state, and if anything happened to him Bosnia would be scorched from one end to the other and not even the babes in their cribs would be spared. D'Avenat kept telling the Consul that at a time like this it was essential to put on a bold and resolute front since this was the only thing that would carry weight with these savages, who were apt to pounce on anyone betraying the slightest sign of quailing or retreat.

The Vizier, in his own fashion, acted on the same principle. The Mameluke Guard went every day to drill and exercise on the field near the Tombs and the townspeople looked with a mixture of hate and respect at these athletic horsemen in their shining heavy armor, dressed up and spangled like a wedding party. The Vizier rode out with them to inspect the exercise, he raced with them, and did target practice, much like a man who had not a care in the world and no thought either of departure or death, but, on the contrary, was getting in shape for combat.

Both sides, the Vizier and the Moslems of Travnik, awaited the decision of the new Sultan and the news from the capital about the outcome of the struggle going on there.

Toward the middle of summer a special envoy, one of the

confidential assistants to the Sultan, arrived with his retinue. Mehmed Pasha arranged a particularly glittering reception for him. He was met outside the town by the entire Mameluke Guard and all the courtiers and dignitaries. The guns boomed a salute from the fortress and Mehmed Pasha himself waited at the gates of the Residency. Word spread through the town with lightning speed that this meant the Vizier had won the grace of the new Sultan and that he would remain in Travnik. The Moslems refused to believe it and maintained that the Sultan's emissary would go back to Istanbul with the Vizier's head in his saddlebag. However, the facts seemed to bear out the rumor. The emissary had brought a royal decree confirming Mehmed Pasha in his post at Travnik; and at the same time he solemnly gave the Vizier a jeweled sword as a gift from the new Sultan, together with orders that he mobilize a powerful striking force and move against Serbia the next spring.

The day after the arrival of the emissary—it happened to be a Friday—Daville was scheduled to see the Vizier by previous appointment. Far from canceling the audience, Mehmed Pasha received the Consul in the presence of the emissary, whom he introduced as an old friend and an auspicious bearer of the Sultan's grace. At the same time he showed him the sword which he had received as a gift from the Sultan.

The emissary, who took pains to assure the Consul that he too, like Mehmed Pasha, was an admirer of Napoleon's, was a tall man, obviously of mixed blood, with rather pronounced Negroid features. There was an undertone of gray in his sallow complexion, his lips and nails were almost purple, the whites of his eyes unclear, all but muddy. He spoke emphatically and at great length about his sympathies for France and his hatred of the Russians. As he talked, the deep notches on both sides of his fleshy mulatto mouth filled with white specks of froth. Looking at him, Daville wished that the man would take a breath and wipe himself, but he went on talking in his fevered manner. D'Avenat, who translated, could barely keep up with him. With a fresh surge of hatred, as it were, the emissary went on to tell them of his old campaigns against the Russians and of a skirmish somewhere near Otchakov in which he had been wounded; and all at once, with startling alacrity, he pulled up the tight sleeve of his tunic and displayed a thick scar on his forearm. The slender but muscular dark-skinned arm shook visibly.

Mehmed Pasha seemed to enjoy the conversation of his

friends and chuckled more than usual, like one who cannot conceal his satisfaction and happiness at being allowed to bask in imperial grace. That day the audience went on much longer than usual. As they were going home, Daville asked D'Avenat: "What do you think of the emissary?"

He expected, as always, that the interpreter's answer would be couched in a wealth of details—all the details he had collected about the man up to that moment; but this time D'Avenat was surprisingly short: "He is a very sick man, Your Excellency."

"Yes indeed. A very strange guest."

"Very, very sick," muttered D'Avenat, looking straight in front of him and refusing to elaborate.

And two days later, before the usual time, D'Avenat made an urgent request to see the Consul. Daville received him in the dining room, where he was finishing breakfast.

It was Sunday, one of those mornings in midsummer whose freshness and limpid beauty were like a reward for the dark, bone-chilling, and unpleasant autumn and winter days. The air was cool and alive with the purl and blue shimmer of countless invisible streams. Daville had spent a restful night, pleased with the news that Mehmed Pasha would be staying on at Travnik. Before him were the remains of breakfast and he was wiping his mouth with the air of a man who has just appeased his hunger, when D'Avenat came in, dark and tense as usual, his lips drawn and his jaw set. In a low voice D'Avenat informed the Consul that the Sultan's emissary had died that night.

Daville got up abruptly and pushed away the breakfast tray. D'Avenat, not budging from where he stood or changing his voice, met his agitated questioning with terse, barely intelligible replies.

On the previous afternoon, the emissary, who lately had not been in the best of health, had suddenly felt unwell. He had taken a warm bath and gone to bed and had died suddenly during the night, before anyone knew what was going on or could help him. They were planning to bury him this morning. Anything further that he, D'Avenat, might learn about it, concerning either the death itself or the effect which this news might have in the bazaar, he would report later. That was all he would say. To Daville's query as to whether there was anything he could do, such as offer condolences or the like, D'Avenat answered that it was better not to do anything that might be taken as a

breach of custom. Death in these parts was not anything to be
talked about, and everything connected with it was disposed
of swiftly, without many words or much ceremony.

Left alone, Daville felt as though his day that had started so
buoyantly had suddenly gone dark. He could not help thinking
of the tall, rather unpleasant man with whom he had been talking only two days before, who was now dead. He wondered
about the Vizier too, and about the unsavory repercussions that
were bound to follow from having an important personage die
in his house. And D'Avenat's ashen and sepulchral face was
constantly before his eyes, and also his silence and impassivity,
the way he bowed and went out, as cold and somber as when
he entered. But he followed D'Avenat's advice and made no
move of any kind, though he never for a moment stopped thinking about the death at the Residency.

Next morning D'Avenat came again and, in an alcove by the
window, told the shocked Consul the true purpose of the emissary's mission and the cause of his death.

The emissary had in fact been the bearer of the Vizier's death
sentence. The imperial firman confirming the Vizier in his present office and the sword of honor were intended only to camou-
flage the sentence, to put the Vizier at ease and to bemuse the
people at large. On the eve of his departure from Travnik, after
he had lulled the Vizier into a sense of security, the emissary
was supposed to produce a second imperial decree, the so-called
katil-firman, which condemned the Vizier to death, together
with all those who had worked directly or indirectly with the
ex-Sultan; he was then to command one of his escort to cut the
Vizier down before any of his people could spring to his defense.
But the cunning Vizier, anticipating something of the order, had
overwhelmed the emissary with attentions and honors, pretending to believe his words and to be delighted with the Sultan's
graciousness, while promptly bribing the man's retinue. Meanwhile he showed him the town and introduced him to the French
Consul in a formal audience.

On the following day he treated him to a splendid picnic in
a meadow by the road that leads to the Tombs. On their return
to the Residency, after much entertainment and an abundance
of highly spiced food, the emissary developed a sudden high
fever—"from the sharp Bosnian water." The Vizier offered his
guest the use of his sumptuously appointed steambath. While
the emissary was steaming on the hot stone slabs, working up

a sweat and waiting for the masseur whom Mehmed Pasha had particularly recommended to him, the Vizier's men skillfully opened the lining of his long cloak where, according to a bribed attendant of the emissary, the death decree was hidden. The death firman was thus discovered and taken to the Vizier. And when the emissary, parboiled and tired out, came out of the bath, he suddenly felt a painful, burning thirst that no drink could assuage. The more he drank, the faster the poison worked. At dusk, panting like a man whose mouth and guts were on fire, he collapsed and then stiffened and fell silent. When they saw that he had lost the power of speech and was completely paralyzed, that he could not communicate either by voice or sign, they rushed out of the Residency looking for doctors and summoning the hodjas. For a doctor it was too late, but for a hodja there was always time.

Stiff as a dead fish, his face the color of indigo, the emissary lay on a thin mattress in the middle of the room. Only his eyelids trembled a little and he rolled them up from time to time with the utmost effort as, goggling and with a terrible look, he scanned the room, perhaps trying to locate his cloak or one of his men. The big glassy eyes of the dying, hoodwinked man, who himself had come on a mission of treachery and murder, were the only part of him that was still alive and they expressed all he could no longer say or do. Awed and fearful, the Vizier's servants moved around him on tiptoe, showing him every possible attention and communicating with one another only by signs and terse whispers. No one was able to say exactly when he gave up his ghost.

His host, the Vizier, appeared inconsolable. It was as if the sudden death of his old friend had soured all his pleasure in the recent good news and the great honor he had received. His flashing white teeth now remained hidden under his thick black mustache. Unsmiling, not to be recognized, the Vizier spoke to everyone, but only briefly, in a voice that was unsteady and full of barely controlled pain. He summoned the Mayor of the town, Ressim Beg, a man of aristocratic lineage but weak and aged before his time, and requested his help during these difficult days, although he well knew that the Mayor was a useless fumbler who couldn't even look after his own affairs. He spoke bitterly of his grief in front of the Mayor: "It was written that he should come all this way only to die before my eyes. That is Fate, but I would sooner have lost my own born brother." The

Vizier sounded like a man who, with all his self-control, cannot keep his anguish bottled inside him.

"There's nothing you can do, Pasha," the Mayor consoled him. "Remember the old saying, 'All of us die, we're only buried at different times.' "

The *katil*-firman, that was to have cost Mehmed Pasha his head and was to have buried him, was carefully sewn back into the same place in the lining of the emissary's cloak. He was to be laid to rest that morning in one of the finest of Travnik's cemeteries. His entire retinue, bribed and richly rewarded, was leaving that day for Istanbul.

So D'Avenat concluded his account of the latest events at the Residency.

Daville was shocked and dumb with amazement. It all sounded to him like a lurid, improbable tale and he was on the point of interrupting the interpreter several times. The Vizier's action seemed to him not only revolting and criminal, but dangerous and illogical as well. Covered with gooseflesh, he paced up and down the room and peered into D'Avenat's face, as if to see whether he had spoken seriously or had gone out of his mind.

"How is it possible? How?" the Consul kept saying. "How can anyone do such a thing? How dare he? They're bound to find out! And in the end what good will it do him?"

"Oh, but it will. It seems as if it might do him a lot of good," D'Avenat said calmly.

The Vizier's scheme, bold and reckless though it was, was not as far-fetched as may appear at first sight, D'Avenat explained to the Consul, who had stopped pacing.

First and foremost, the Vizier had escaped the immediate danger, and rather skillfully at that, by outwitting his opponents and forestalling the emissary. The people were bound to gossip and cast suspicion, of course, but no one could point to anything, much less prove it. Secondly, the emissary had publicly brought good news and extraordinary honors to the Vizier. It stood to reason that the Vizier would be the last man to wish to see him dead; and those who had sent the emissary on his double-faced errand would not dare, at least for the time being, to initiate fresh plots against the Vizier, for in so doing they would show their hand and give away the conspiracy and confess their failure. Thirdly, the emissary had been an unpopular man, with a bad reputation, a mulatto without any real friends, who lied and betrayed as easily as he breathed and talked, and was not particularly esteemed even by those who used him. So his death would not be a great surprise to anyone, much less the cause of bitterness or vengeance on anybody's part. His bribed retinue would do their best to see to that. Fourthly, and most important of all, Istanbul was in a state of utter anarchy at the moment; and Mehmed Pasha's friends, to whom only a few days before the unexpected arrival of the emissary he had sent "everything necessary," would be able to complete their "countermove" to reinstate the Vizier in the Sultan's favor and, if possible, have him confirmed in his present post.

Cold with excitement, Daville listened to the calm exposé of his interpreter. Unable to refute him, he could only stammer: "But still . . . still . . ." And D'Avenat, who did not think the Consul needed further convincing, merely added that the bazaar was quiet and that the untoward death of the emissary had not stirred up any special agitation, although there was much comment.

It was only after he was left alone that the full horror of what he had just heard overcame the Consul. As the day went on, his restiveness grew also. He ate little and couldn't stay put in any one place. Several times he was on the point of calling D'Avenat and questioning him some more, if only to prove to himself that the tale he'd heard that morning was really true. He began to wonder what kind of report he should write about it, whether it might not be better to keep silent altogether. He sat down at his desk and began to write. "At the Vizier's Residency last night there was enacted . . ." No, that was fatuous and in poor taste. "The events of the last few days seem to indicate that, by the use of methods and stratagems which are customary here, Mehmed Pasha will succeed in keeping his post, even in the face of altered circumstances, and that, accordingly, it is safe to assume that this Vizier who is sympathetic to us . . ." No, no. That was dry and nebulous. At length it came to him that the best way to describe it was to report the thing exactly the way it had happened and the way it appeared to an outsider: that a special emissary had arrived from Istanbul with an imperial decree confirming the Vizier in his present post and had brought him a sword of honor as a sign of the Sultan's favor and a symbol of the imminent campaign against Serbia. He might point out at the end that this augured well for the continued success of French aspirations in these parts, and then add, parenthetically as it were, that the emissary had died unexpectedly while carrying out his mission in Travnik.

Phrasing and drafting the official report in his head, Daville calmed down somewhat. The crime which had occurred only yesterday, here, under his very eyes, began at once to seem less heinous and appalling the moment it became the subject of his report. In vain the Consul looked in himself for the excitement and moral confusion of the morning.

He sat down and wrote out the document, interpreting the event as it appeared to the people at large. And later, as he made a fair copy, he felt more at ease with himself, even a little smug in the thought that the report wisely left untold the great and sinister secrets that were at the core of it.

So he waited for the summer twilight, full of silence and oblique shafts of light between the dark shadows on the steep hillsides. Quieter now, the Consul stood by the open window. Someone came into the room behind him with a lighted taper and began to light the candles on the desk. At that moment the thought assailed him: Who could have prepared the poison for the Vizier, set the dose and measured its action so expertly that the whole thing would go off fairly quickly (each stage at the appointed time), yet not too suddenly or suspiciously? Who, if not D'Avenat? Drugs were part of his profession. He had been in the service of the Vizier until quite recently, and perhaps he still was.

All at once, his apparent calm left Daville. Once more there surged through him that morning's feeling of dread, the sense that here, in his close proximity, impinging on his work as it were, and therefore involving him too, a crime had been committed in which his interpreter might well be a bribed and sordid accomplice. The horror of it swept him like a flame. Was anyone living here safe and protected from crime? And so he stood rooted, between the candles that were flickering on in the room one by one and the dimming light on the steep slopes beyond the window.

The evening came, heralding the onset of one of those insomniac nights with which he had lately become so familiar at Travnik, in which a man could neither sleep nor think properly. And even when he managed, for a moment, to doze off fitfully, there passed before him, unbidden and spectral, a restless suc-

cession of images that changed, blended, and overlapped without pause: Mehmed Pasha's broad pleased grin of two days before, the slender wiry arm of the emissary with its broad scar;
the dark and incoherent D'Avenat, quietly mouthing the words:
"A very, very sick man indeed." There was no order or logic to
any of it. Each picture seemed to have a life of its own that had
no connection whatever with the others, as if all certainty and
decisions were suspended, as if the crime were entirely possible
and then again might even now be prevented. In this tormented
half-sleep, Daville hoped with all his heart that the murder
would somehow go uncommitted, and yet couldn't help feeling,
somewhere in the depths of his consciousness, that it had been
carried out already.

Often an oppressive, fevered night of this kind sums up an
entire experience and shuts it off forever like a soundproof iron
door.

In the days that followed, D'Avenat came to the Consulate as
usual. He was quite unchanged. Nor did the sudden death of
the Sultan's emissary cause much disaffection among the Moslems of Travnik; the voices of suspicion, the finger-pointing
lasted but a short time; the fate of the Osmanli did not seem
to interest them a great deal. They saw only one thing, that their
detested Vizier was going to stay on in Travnik, and had even
been rewarded. They gathered from this that the May revolution
in the capital had left things pretty much as they had been.
Accordingly, they relapsed into disillusioned silence, gritted their
teeth and lowered their eyes. It was plain to them that even the
new Sultan was under the influence of unbelievers and had
surrounded himself with bad and corrupt advisers, and that
victory of the good and just cause had once again been put off.
All the same, they continued in their unshakable belief that the
true and pure faith was bound to triumph in the end and that
this was only a matter of waiting. And no one could wait like
the Bosnian Moslems, for they were people of stolid faith and
a granitelike pride, who could be as impetuous as a spring torrent and as patient as the earth.

Once more Daville felt a recrudescence of his dread—a pang
of sick, cold fear in his innards. This was during the first audience following the emissary's death. Twelve days had gone by.
The Vizier was unchanged and cheerful. He spoke of his prepa-

rations for the campaign against Serbia and agreed readily to all Daville's plans for Turco-French collaboration on the frontier between Bosnia and Dalmatia.

With studied calm and straining to appear as natural as possible, Daville had, toward the end of his talk, incidentally, as it were, expressed his sincere regrets over the death of the imperial envoy and Vizier's friend. Even before D'Avenat had finished translating the words, the Vizier's smile vanished and his black mustache covered the flashing white teeth. His face with the slanting almond eyes grew somehow wider and more compact and remained like that until the interpreter finished conveying Daville's expressions of sympathy. The rest of the interview was again conducted with the old smile.

The general indifference and short public memory of the event helped to calm Daville. Seeing that life went on unchanged, he said to himself: Evidently this is how things are. He stopped talking to D'Avenat about the crime at the Residency. His time was pre-empted by duties. Day by day he shook off a little more of that unexplainable turmoil of conscience and his first sense of bitter dismay, and let himself be carried along by the stream of workaday life, submitting to the laws that govern all living things. True, he would never again, it seemed to him, be able to face Mehmed Pasha without remembering that he was the man who, in D'Avenat's words, "was the quicker and craftier and had outsmarted his opponents"; yet he would work with him again and talk with him on every subject, save this one.

It was about this time that the Vizier's Deputy, Suleiman Pasha Skoplyak, came back from the river Drina, after having thoroughly routed the insurgent Serbs—or so it was said at the Residency. Suleiman Pasha himself used more restrained and less definite language on the subject.

The Deputy Vizier was a Bosnian and came from a leading family of begs—Moslem landed gentry. He owned large estates in Skoplye on the river Kupres and some ten houses and shops in Bugoyno. Broad-shouldered, tough, slender-waisted despite his mature years, with piercing blue eyes, he was a man who had seen many wars and piled up a fortune and become a pasha without having to flatter or bribe his way. He kept peace with a firm hand and was cunning in war, he was greedy for land and not particularly subtle in his method of getting it, but he was also incorruptible, forthright, and free of the usual Turkish vices.

It would be too much to say that this half-peasant pasha of fierce visage, with the keen eye of "the best sharpshooter in the whole of Bosnia," was a pleasant or attractive person. In his dealings with foreigners he was, like most Osmanlis, mistrustful and procrastinating, wily and stubborn, as well as brusque and coarse in his speech. For the rest, he spent the greater part of the year either in punitive expeditions against Serbia or on his estates, and lived at Travnik only during the winter months. Now his presence in the town signified the end of the campaign, at least for this year.

Life became more settled and orderly as the months passed. Autumn came: first, the early autumn, with its harvests, weddings, bustling trade, and swelling profits; and then the late autumn of rains, coughing, and worries. The mountains turned impassable, the people less enterprising and more inclined to stay put. Everyone prepared to spend the winter where he happened to be, figuring how best to get through it. It seemed to Daville that even the vast machinery of the French Empire was ticking ever more slowly, more softly. The Congress of Erfurt had come to an end. Napoleon was turning his attention toward Spain, which meant that for the time being the whirlpool was sweeping westward. Couriers were few, instructions from Split less frequent.

The Vizier, on whom Daville counted most of all, would remain, it seemed, at his post; once again he put forth his brightest smile. (The counterstrategy of his friends at Istanbul seemed to have been eminently successful.) The Austrian Consul, whose coming had long been talked about, had still not arrived. Paris informed Daville that, before the year was out, they would send him a career officer who spoke Turkish. In those difficult days D'Avenat showed himself resourceful, dependable, and devoted.

The onset of autumn brought Daville his greatest joy of all. Quietly and almost unnoticed Mme Daville arrived with their three children, the sons Pierre, Jules-François, and Jean-Paul. The first was four years of age, the second two, while the third had been born a few months before in Split.

Madame Daville was blond, petite, and slender. Under her thin hair, which was gathered up in a style of no particular fashion, there was a small lively face with a healthy complexion, delicate features, and blue eyes of a high metallic sparkle. Behind an exterior which at first sight was plain and unremarkable was a clever, sober, and versatile woman of strong will and a robust constitution; one of those women of whom one says, "She's nobody's fool." Her life was one long fanatical but sensible and patient service to her family and home. To this service were dedicated all her thoughts and feelings; her slender, always red, and seemingly fragile hands were never still for a moment and grappled with work as if they were made of steel. Of a good bourgeois family that had lost everything in the Revolution, she had grown up in the house of her uncle, the Bishop of Avranches, and was imbued with that special French piety that was both staunch and thoroughly human, that never wavered and was yet free of bigotry.

As soon as Mme Daville arrived, a new era began in the huge and forlorn house of the French Consulate. Saying little, uncomplaining, asking no help or advice from anybody, she worked from early morning until all hours of the night. The house grew clean and orderly; a good many changes were carried out, to make it as suitable as possible for the new inmates and their needs. Rooms were partitioned off, doors and windows were walled in, new ones opened up. For lack of cabinets and furnishings, Turkish chests, rugs, and local fabrics were used. Curtained and rearranged, the house looked quite different. Footsteps no longer sent up a hollow echo as before. The kitchen was done over from scratch. Little by little everything took on the stamp of French daily life, frugal and sensible but rich in true satisfactions. The following spring would find the house and its inmates and surroundings utterly transformed.

On the flat ground in front of the dwelling there would be two cultivated plots whose design and flowerbeds would be a modest imitation of a French garden. In the rear there would be a barn, a storehouse, and a woodshed. All this work, planned by Mme Daville herself, was now started under her supervision.

The Consul's wife had to contend with all kinds of difficulties and especially with the servant problem. It was not the usual servant problem about which all the housewives the world over have always complained, but a real dilemma. At first no one wanted to serve in the Consul's household. Turkish servants were out of the question. The few Serb-Orthodox families wouldn't let one of their members enter the house; while the Catholic girls, who were sometimes found working in Turkish homes, did not at first dare to come near the Consulate, because the friars had threatened them with damnation and dire penances. Presently the wives of some of the Jewish merchants managed to talk a few gypsy women into working at the new Consulate for good wages. It was only when Mme Daville, after frequent visits and donations to the church at Dolats, had demonstrated that she was a good Catholic in spite of being married to the "Jacobin Consul," that the Brothers relented a little and grudgingly approved of women working for the French Consul's wife.

In other ways too Mme Daville did her best to cultivate and improve her relations with the parish priest at Dolats, with the Brothers of Gucha Gora, and their congregations. And despite all his troubles, the ignorance and the mistrust with which he was surrounded, Daville hoped that before the Austrian Consul came to Travnik he might at least succeed, with the help of his devout and clever wife, in securing for himself some influence with the Brothers and the Catholic community at large.

In short, the first days of autumn brought with them a pleasant sense of calm and purpose, reflected alike in the Consul's home and in his work. A feeling persisted in Daville, clear and reassuring, that everything was falling into place and taking a turn for the better, or at least was beginning to seem easier and more tolerable.

A pale autumn sun shone over the streets of Travnik, and in its light the rain-washed cobblestones stood out clean and spanking. Bushes and woods changed color and grew thinner, more transparent. The river Lashva ran swift and clean in the sun, straight and narrow in its bed, humming like a plucked string. Paths were dry and hard, with here and there a trace of squashed fruit that had dropped out of somebody's market basket, and with wisps of hay hanging from the shrubbery and the fences along the roadside.

Daville went out for a long ride every day. He rode up over Kupilo along a straight footpath under towering elms and looked down over the dark-roofed houses enveloped in blue smoke, over the mosques and scattered white graveyards; and it seemed to him as if all of it, the houses, the alleys, and the gardens, were blending into a single hue that was slowly becoming more familiar and recognizable. An air of ease and respite spread out on every side. The Consul breathed it in with the autumn air and felt like turning in the saddle and confiding it, if only by a smile, to the groom who rode behind him.

In reality, it was only a pause for breath.

4

In his official reports during the first few months Daville complained about all the things a consul in his circumstances could possibly complain about. He deplored the malice and the spite of the local Moslems, the feebleness and dilatory tactics of the authorities, his meager pay and insufficient credits, the leaking house roof and the climate that made his children sickly, the intrigues of the Austrian agents, the lack of understanding he encountered from his superiors at Istanbul and Split. In a word, everything was difficult, half-done, topsy-turvy, and everything gave fresh cause for plaints and indignation. Most of all, Daville regretted the Ministry's failure to send him a reliable assistant, a career official with a thorough command of the Turkish language.

He could use the interpreter D'Avenat in an emergency, but he was unable to trust him completely. The unquestionable zeal of the man still had not dispelled the Consul's doubts. Besides, although D'Avenat spoke French, he could not do official correspondence in French.

For information work among the general public Daville had hired Rafo Atias, a young Travnik Jew who preferred the job of interpreting the "Illyrian" language to the rolling and stacking of tanned hides in his uncle's store. He could be trusted even less than D'Avenat. In every report, therefore, Daville begged for an assistant.

At length, just as he was beginning to lose all hope and was getting used to D'Avenat and gaining confidence in him, a new secretary and interpreter arrived, young Desfosses.

Amédée Chaumette Desfosses was of the new generation of Parisian diplomats, the first crop of those who, after the turbulent revolutionary years, had received proper schooling in a climate of comparative calm and were specially trained for service in the East. He came of a banking family that had managed to keep some of its old established wealth both during the Revolution and under the Directory. At school he had been a precocious youngster and had amazed his teachers and schoolmates with his memory, bright judgment, and the ease with which he accumulated all types of knowledge. He was tall, of an athletic build, with a rosy face and large brown eyes that glowed with curiosity and restlessness. Daville saw at once that he had before him a true child of the new epoch, a new kind of Parisian youth, bold and poised in his speech and movements, carefree, close to reality, with boundless faith in his own strength and knowledge, and inclined to overrate both.

The young man handed over the mail pouch and made a brief and concise report, not hiding the fact that he was cold and tired. He ate heartily and generously and let the Consul know, without too many excuses, that he would like to lie down and rest. He slept all night and through the forenoon of the following day, then got up fresh and invigorated, radiating a sense of well-being that was as natural and spontaneous as the exhaustion and drowsiness of the day before.

By his directness, his assurance, and his relaxed tone of voice, the young man caused a stir in the little household. He seemed to know right away where to go and what he wanted, and he asked for it without hesitation or too many words.

Several days and conversations later, it became clear that between the Consul and his new officer there were not, nor could there be, many points of contact, much less close rapport. However, each of them understood and accepted this in his own way.

To Daville, who was at the stage of life when most things easily turned into a problem of conscience and a burden to the spirit, the coming of young Desfosses brought new complications instead of relief; it opened up in his mind a string of fresh difficulties that could neither be solved nor brushed aside, and which tended to deepen his isolation and loneliness. To the young Chancellor, on the other hand, nothing seemed to be any trouble or presented any obstacle too big for him to overcome— in any case, not his superior, Daville.

Daville was getting on to forty, while Desfosses was barely twenty-four. In other times and circumstances this gap in their ages would not have mattered too much; but a period of great and stormy changes and social dislocation creates and deepens an unbridgeable chasm between generations and, in fact, makes of them two different worlds.

Daville could remember the ancient regime, although he was only a boy at the time; he had experienced the Revolution in all its aspects, as part of his own destiny; he had met the First

Consul and had become a supporter of his government with a zeal in which there was both suppressed doubt and boundless faith.

He had been twelve years old when, lined up with the other children of bourgeois families, he had watched Louis XVI visit their town. It was an unforgettable event for the imaginative and spirited boy who was always hearing at home that the whole family lived in fact on the King's bounty. Now this King passed before him in person, an embodiment of everything grand and beautiful that life could possibly offer. Through it all, unseen bands were playing, cannon were thundering, and the town's bells were pealing all at once. Dressed in their finery, the people almost broke the police cordon in their enthusiasm. Through his own tears, the boy saw the tears in the eyes of others, and in his throat a knot tightened that he would always associate with moments of great emotion. The King, himself moved, ordered the carriage to go slowly, took off his wide-brimmed hat in a gallant gesture, and, in answer to a loud chorus of "Long live the King!" cried in a clear voice, "Long live my people!" All this the boy saw and heard as if it were an impossible dream of paradise, until the ecstatic crowd behind him pushed his brand-new and somewhat foppish hat over his eyes so that everything was suddenly plunged in a blind mist of his own tears, streaked over with golden flashes in a dappled swarm of blue spots. By the time he managed to pull the hat up, the procession had gone by like a mirage and only the shoving throng remained and a sea of flushed faces and shining eyes.

Ten years later, as a cub reporter on a Parisian newspaper, with the same choking lump in his throat and brimming eyes, Daville heard Mirabeau harangue fiercely against the old order and its abuses. His enthusiasm flowed from the same wellspring, but this time it was inspired by a vastly different object. Changed, Daville found himself in a world that too was utterly changed, cast upon it by the Revolution which now swept along hundreds of thousands of young men like himself, with great and irresistible force. He felt as if the whole world were growing young again alongside his own youth, as if the old humdrum of existence were suddenly shot up in a fireworks of dazzling vistas and unimagined opportunities. All at once everything became easy, rational and simple, all striving took on a loftier purpose, every thought and step grew somehow larger than life in

a blaze of superhuman grandeur and dignity. It was no longer
a case of the King's bounty seeping down to a limited number
of people and families, but a titanic eruption of divine justice
over the whole of mankind. Like the others, Daville was light-
headed with irrational happiness, as weak and befuddled people
often are when they stumble on a catchall and generally accepted formula that holds out a promise of meeting their needs
and catering to their instincts at the cost of other people's harm
and ruin, while at the same time freeing them of responsibility
and a nagging conscience.

Although he was only one of a large group of journalists covering the meetings of the Constituent Assembly, it seemed to
young Daville that his own reports, in which he detailed the
speeches of the leading participants or described the rousing
scenes of patriotic and revolutionary fervor among the listeners,
had a global, permanent significance, and his own initials at
the foot of the column struck him at first as two pinnacles that
nothing could surpass or scale. At times he thought he was not
just chronicling the daily doings of the Assembly but was knead-
ing, with his own hands and with giant force, the soul of mankind as though it were made of some obedient putty.

But those years went by and, sooner than he could have
thought possible, he saw the dark side of this Revolution which
had claimed his whole being. He still remembered how it all
began.

One morning, awakened by a shouting street crowd, he had
got up and flung open the window. Suddenly he had found him-
helf face to face with a severed human head, swinging pale and
blood-spattered, on the pike of a sans-culotte. At that moment,
rising from his Bohemian stomach that hadn't seen food since
the day before, something terrible and sickening, like a cold
fluid gone bitter, flooded first his chest and then his whole body.
From that day on, for many years, life never ceased plying him
with that same sour potion, to which no man can ever become
accustomed. He went on living as before, spawning his articles
and howling with the mob, but tormented now by the deepening
split inside him, which for a long time he would not admit even
to himself and which he would continue to hide from others to
the very end. And when the time came to decide about the
King's life and the fate of the Kingdom, when he had to choose
between the bitter brew of the Revolution, which had once in-

toxicated him so powerfully, and the "royal bounty" on which
he had been nurtured, the young man suddenly found himself
once more on the other side.

In the month of June 1792, after the first revolutionary wave
had broken over the Court, a strong reaction set in among the
more moderate elements and a collection of signatures was
started for an address expressing the people's sympathy for its
King and Royal House. Borne along on this wave of protest
against violence and chaos, young Daville swallowed his fear,
shut his mind to any other thought, and wrote his signature
beside those of twenty thousand other citizens of Paris. So great
was the inner struggle that preceded his signature that it seemed
to Daville as if his name were not lost among those thousands
of names, most of them more prominent and better known than
his own, but were branded in fiery letters across the evening
skies of Paris. He learned then how a man could bend and break
and go against himself, how he could fall and rise in his own
eyes; he learned, in short, how ephemeral passions are, how
tangled and contradictory while they last, what price they exact,
and how bitterly they are repented when they pass away.

A month later began the great persecution and mass arrests
of suspicious persons and "bad citizens," especially among the
twenty thousand who had signed the petition. To escape arrest
and gain time to resolve his private conflicts, the young journalist Daville volunteered for military service and was sent to
the Army of the Pyrenees on the Spanish frontier. There he saw
the harshness and terror of war at first hand and learned too
that war could be a healing and positive thing. He discovered
the value and limits of bodily strength, he proved himself in
danger, learned to obey and to command, he grew familiar with
suffering in all its forms, and also with the beauty of friendship
and the meaning of discipline.

Some three years after his first great inner crisis, Daville once
again found his feet, appeased and toughened by military life.
Chance took him to the Ministry of Foreign Affairs, where at
that time muddle and confusion were the order of the day. No
one, from the Minister on down, was a professional diplomat;
they were all learning, from scratch, those skills which until
then had been the privilege of men of the old regime. When
Talleyrand came to the Ministry, things began to liven up and
take a turn for the better. It was pure chance again that Talley-

rand should notice young Daville's articles in *Le Moniteur* and decide to take him under his wing.

Like so many weak, easily shaken, and vacillating spirits, Daville, in his inner wavering and indecision, looked hopefully to a bright and constant light: the young General Bonaparte, the victor of Italy and the hope of all those who, like Daville, yearned for a middle way between the old regime and the Emigration on the one hand and the Revolution and the Terror on the other. And when Talleyrand gave him the post of Secretary in the new Cisalpine Republic, Daville, before his departure for Milan, was received in audience by the General, who wished to give him a personal message for his envoy, Citizen Trouvé.

Daville knew well Napoleon's brother Lucien, who had recommended him; he was therefore received with every sign of attention, in the General's private quarters, after supper.

When he found himself before this haggard man, with the strained white face, smoldering eyes, and cold glance, when he listened to his words, warm and rational at the same time, great, daring, clear, seductive words that opened up unimagined vistas well worth living and dying for, it seemed to Daville that all his doubts and uncertainties vanished without a trace, that everything grew calm and harmonious, all goals attainable, that all efforts were worth making and were blessed in advance. Talking with this unique person was like receiving the healing touch of a miracle worker. All the silt of past years was washed clean out of his soul, all the lamed ecstasies, all the agonizing doubts found their meaning and their justification. This extraordinary man had the gift of picking the safe course between extremes and contradictions which Daville, like so many others, had for years been seeking passionately and in vain. And when, toward midnight, the new Secretary to the Cisalpine Republic left the General's quarters in rue Chantrennes, tears mounted to his eyes and he felt the same hard knot tightening in his throat as he had when he had waited for Louis XVI or sung revolutionary songs and listened to Mirabeau's speeches. He felt intoxicated and soaring, almost as if the blood in his temples and in his chest pounded in time with the great pulse of the universe, throbbing up there somewhere beneath the stars of the night.

Once more the years passed. The haggard General made the world his stage and rode the horizon like a sublime sun that knew no setting. Daville held a succession of posts in a succession of places, hatched literary and political plans, turning toward this sun like the rest of the world. But fervor, like all passionate feelings of weak men in great and unstable times, betrayed him and failed to keep its promises; and Daville felt that he too, on his side, was secretly betraying his vision and slowly turning his back on it. How long had this been going on? When did the estrangement begin and how far had it gone? He could not find an answer, but each passing day made it clearer that it was so. Only this time everything was harder and more complicated. The Revolution had swept away the old regime like a whirlwind, and Napoleon had come as a salvation from both, an intercession of Providence—the "middle way" of reason and dignity that so many had longed for. Now it began to look as if this way too were a kind of blind alley—one of the many false starts—that indeed there was no such thing as a true road and that men frittered away a lifetime in their dogged quest of it, while constantly shifting from one blind alley to another. Even so, one must keep looking for the right way.

After so many ups and downs, this was no longer as simple and easy as it once had been. Daville was not a young man any more; time and his earlier crises, which had been many and enervating, had worn him out; like so many of his coevals, he yearned for stability and quiet work. But instead of that, the rhythm of French life spun faster all the time, flying off on unexpected tangents. More and more peoples and countries outside France caught the germ of this ferment; one after another joined this ring of footloose, entranced dervishes. Six years had gone by since the Peace of Amiens, and Daville was still tossed between hope and doubt, as in a game of chiaroscuro. After each new victory of the First Consul, and later of Emperor Napoleon, the middle way of salvation seemed to appear firm and dependable, but a few months later one groped around in a wilderness once more. People began to live in fear. They all moved forward, but some began to look over their shoulders. During the few months he spent in Paris just before he was appointed Consul at Travnik, Daville could see mirrored in the eyes of innumerable friends the same fear which, unacknowledged and repressed, kept bobbing up obstinately in himself.

Two years before, immediately after Napoleon's great victory in Prussia, Daville had written a poem, "Battle of Jena," perhaps because he hoped that an unabashed encomium of the victorious Emperor might still his doubts and ease his fears. As he was about to give the poem to the printer, a fellow countryman and old friend of his, a retired officer now working in the Ministry of the Navy, told him over a glass of Calvados: "Do you know what you're praising and whom you're celebrating? Do you know that the Emperor is mad—yes, mad!—and is kept up only by the blood of his victories, victories that lead nowhere and mean nothing? Do you realize that we're all rushing toward some kind of calamity that is surely waiting for us at the end of all these victories, even if we can't name it as yet? You don't, eh? Well, maybe that's why you can write those poems."

His friend had had a few too many that evening, but Daville could not forget his dilated pupils, staring fixedly into the distance, nor his low-pitched voice with its warm breath of alcohol and conviction. And sober people voiced the same thought in other words or hid it behind a worried look. All the same, Daville resolved to have the poem printed but lost his taste for it and also his belief in the value of poetry and the permanence of victories in general. This blighted faith, which was only just beginning to be felt in the world at large, grew like an insidious dry rot in Daville's soul. Harboring these gloomy and involuted thoughts, he had gone to Travnik as Consul, and all his experiences there had done nothing to quiet or encourage him; on the contrary, it had only shaken and confused him more.

These emotions were further stirred and exacerbated by his first contacts with the young man with whom he was now to live and work. Watching his ease of manner, listening to him as he held forth with aplomb and with perfect naturalness on all sorts of subjects, Daville thought: "The terrible thing is not that we grow old and weak and die, but that a new, younger, different breed comes pushing behind us. This is the essence of death. No one drags us toward the grave, we're pushed in from behind." The Consul was startled by these thoughts, for they were not typical of his way of thinking; he promptly shrugged them off and put them down to the "oriental poison" which sooner or later was bound to attack every man, and which even now, as it were, was seeping subtly into his brain.

The young man, who was the only Frenchman and his one real colleague in this wilderness, was so different from him in every respect, or so it seemed, that Daville at times had the impression he was living with a stranger and enemy. What vexed and grated on him most of all was the young man's attitude (lack of it might be a better word) to those "burning questions" that were the content of Daville's life: the Monarchy, the Revolution, and Napoleon. To the Consul and his generation those three concepts represented an appalling, raveled web of conflicts, passions, sallies, and prodigious achievements, as well as indecision, inner betrayals, and invisible stumblings of conscience, never clearly resolved and holding out less and less hope of a respite; they were like a load of guilt one carries from childhood and takes to the grave. But at the same time, and because of it, this load was as close and dear to them as their very life itself.

But to young Desfosses and his contemporaries these things were neither a torment nor an enigma, they were neither food for reflection nor ground for regrets—or so, at any rate, it seemed to Daville. To them all these were simple and natural matters over which there was no point in wasting words or bothering one's head. Monarchy was a fairy tale, the Revolution a vague memory from the nursery; but the Empire was life itself, life and a career, a natural and familiar arena of boundless opportunities, of action, achievement, and glory. To Desfosses, in fact, the system in which he lived—the Empire—represented the one and only reality; whether he saw it in spiritual or material terms, it filled his vision from one end to the other and gathered in it all that life contained. To Daville, on the other hand, it was only a brittle and accidental phase of a process whose tortured beginnings he had lived through and witnessed with his own eyes, whose fleeting nature was never far from his mind. In contrast to the young man, he well remembered what had gone before and often wondered what was yet to come.

The world of "ideas," which to Daville's contemporaries was their spiritual home and their true life, seemed not to exist for the new generation, who chose to believe in the "living life," the world of actuality, of tangible facts and visible, measurable successes and failures, a desolate new world that spread before Daville like a chilly wilderness, more terrifying than the agonies, the soul-racking, and the gore of the Revolution. Spawned in blood, it was a generation stripped of everything, inured to everything, burnished and tempered as if it had passed through fire.

Influenced by his strange environment and difficult conditions of life, the Consul doubtless generalized and exaggerated these things, like everything else. Often he would tell himself as much, since it was not in his temperament to suffer contradictions gladly or to admit that they were eternal and unsolvable. Still, he was constantly reminded of it by this young man of unflinching eyes, who seemed to him both cold and sensual, relaxed and yet self-conscious, who was burdened neither by doubts nor circumspection, who saw all things around him nakedly, as they were, and called a spade a spade without batting an eye. His talents and basic goodness notwithstanding, he was still one of the new generation—"animalized" generation, as Daville's coevals called it. So this was the fruit of the Revolution, the free citizen, the new man, thought Daville whenever he remained alone after a chat with the young man. "Could it be that the revolutions breed monsters?" he would then ask himself anxiously. And more often than not the answer would be: "Yes, they begin in greatness and moral purity and end up by producing freaks."

Later in the night, dark preying thoughts would return and threaten to overwhelm him, and he would be helpless to turn them back.

While Daville brooded like this and searched his heart following the arrival of the young Chancellor, the latter jotted down the following terse sentence about Daville in his modest diary, which he intended to send to his friends in Paris: "The Consul is just as I had imagined him." And what he had imagined was based on Daville's own early dispatches from Travnik, and even more on the accounts of an older colleague in the Ministry, a man called Querrenne, who had the reputation of knowing every official in the Ministry of Foreign Affairs and who was able, in a few words, to give a more or less accurate "moral and physical" description of each. Querrenne was a bright and witty but otherwise sterile fellow, with whom the drawing of such oral portraits had become a habit and a passion. He gave a great deal of effort to this jejune business, which sometimes sounded like a consummate skill but more often like plain slander; and he could do a sketch like this over and over again, word for word, as if he carried a printed text in his head. What Querrenne had told him about his future chief, Daville, was this: "Jean Daville was born healthy, upright, and mediocre. His whole nature, origin, and upbringing incline him to a simple and quiet life, without any great ups or flopping downs; in short, without any sudden changes. A plant for a temperate climate. Has a native capacity for quick enthusiasm and is easily carried away by ideas and personalities, with a particular weakness for poetry and poeticized spiritual poses. All this within the confines of a happy mediocrity. Peaceful times and settled circumstances make mediocre men even more mediocre, whereas upheavals and great changes make them into complex characters. That is the case with our poor Daville, who kept finding himself in the thick of great events, none of which made the slightest dent on his fundamental nature but merely added some new and contrary qualities to what he already had. Since he cannot, and doesn't know how to, be ruthless, cunning, unscrupulous, and underhanded, he has protected and maintained himself by becoming timid, discreet, and cautious to the point of superstition. By nature he is healthy, honest, enterprising, and cheerful, but time has made him touchy, slow, undecided, chary, and inclined to melancholy; and as none of this corresponds with his true character, it has made his personality oddly ambiguous. In other words, he is one of those men who are predestined victims of great historic changes, because they neither know how to withstand these changes, as forceful and exceptional individuals do, nor how to come to terms with them, as the great mass of people manage to do. He is the type who complains and will go on complaining just about everything under the sun, even about the sun itself—a not uncommon case in these days of Our Lord," this colleague concluded.

With these fundamental differences between them, the two men began their life together. Although the autumn was cold and wet, Desfosses explored the town and the surrounding country and met a number of people. Daville presented him to the Vizier and to the top men at the Residency, but the young man did the rest himself. He met the parish priest at Dolats, Fra Ivo Yankovich, a man weighing about three hundred pounds but with an alert mind and a sharp tongue; and Pakhomi, the pale and self-effacing monk who was then looking after the Orthodox Church of St. Michael the Archangel. He visited the houses of the Travnik Jews and the monastery of Gucha Gora, where he made the acquaintance of several Brothers who filled him in on the country and its people. He intended to look over the ancient settlements and tombs in the vicinity as soon as the spring thaw set in. As early as the third week he confided to Daville that he would probably write a book about Bosnia.

The Consul, who had been brought up and schooled in the prerevolutionary classical humanities, functioned strictly within the limits of thought and expression set by that education, not-

withstanding his revolutionary activities. So he looked askance,
even with suspicion, on this undoubtedly talented young man,
on his enormous intellectual curiosity and amazing memory,
his bold and impulsive way of talking, and his enviable bubbling
imagination. He was intimidated by this energy, which nothing
could check or sidetrack. He found it hard to keep up with and
yet felt that there was no way of curbing or stopping it. The
young man had studied Turkish in Paris for three years and
had no qualms about accosting and talking to anyone. ("His
Turkish is the kind they teach at the College of Louis Le Grand
in Paris, not the sort that is spoken by the Turks of Bosnia,"
wrote Daville.) If sometimes he failed to make himself clear,
he nevertheless won the people with his broad and frank eyes.
Even the Brothers, who avoided Daville, and the scowling reserved Pakhomi, talked to him. The only ones who kept their
distance were the Travnik begs. But even the bazaar could not
remain indifferent to the "young Consul" for long.

Defosses never missed a market day, when he would stroll
up and down the bazaar inquiring about the prices, examining
the merchandise, and jotting down phrases and names of things.
Very soon a crowd would collect and watch this foreigner,
dressed à la français, as he tried out a sieve or bent down to
examine a display of chisels and drills. The "young Consul"
would, in turn, be fascinated by some peasant buying a scythe,
by his intense air of concentration as he drew a calloused thumb
over the blade and then knocked and knocked the scythe on the
stone threshold, listening in rapt attention to its sound and
pitch; as, at last, he screwed up one eye and peered down the
long curve of the blade, like a man taking aim, in order to judge
its keenness and temper. Desfosses would go up to the old but
still hardy countrywomen and ask the price of wool that lay on
sacks of goat's hair in front of them, still smelling of the sheep-
fold. Seeing a foreigner before her, the woman would be dumbfounded at first and think that the gentleman was joking. Finally, after a good deal of prodding from Desfosses's groom,
she would come out with the price and swear that the wool was
"soft as a soul" once it had been washed. He inquired about the
names of different cereals and seed stocks, tested the grains
for size and quality. And he showed interest in the workmanship and the types of wood used in making the various
handles and hafts for axes, hatchets, hoes, and other imple-
ments.

The "young Consul" got to know all the colorful personalities in the bazaar, such as Ibrahim Aga, the overseer of weights and and scales, the town crier Hamza, and the bazaar idiot, "the Mad Schwabe."

Ibrahim Aga was a lean, tall stooping old man with a white beard and a dignified, almost forbidding manner. He had once been well off and used to collect the scales tax himself; his sons and assistants did the measuring and checking of everything that was sold in the bazaar, under his supervision. But with time he became poor and was left without sons or helpers. Now the Travnik Jews ran the public scales and collected the weight tax, and Ibrahim Aga worked for them—a fact that was quietly ignored by the bazaar. To the peasants and to all those who either bought or sold in the bazaar, the one and true overseer was still Ibrahim Aga, and he would remain that until he died. Every market day he could be seen standing by the public scale from morning till dusk. When he began to weigh, a solemn silence fell all around him. As he set about adjusting the scale, he held his breath; then, with an air of intense concentration, he grew and shrank as the scale tip rose and dipped. With one eye firmly shut, he scrupulously adjusted the weights and carefully nudged the counterweights in the opposite direction from the goods on the scale, a little more, and then another tiny notch again, until the scale steadied and stopped swinging and the true measure was there for everyone to see. Then he took his hand away, lifted his face, and, with his eyes riveted on the figure, called out the correct weight in a loud firm voice that brooked no question or appeal: "One and sixty, less twenty drams."

There was no disputing the measure. The rest of the bazaar might well be a mad hustle, but where he stood there was an island of order, silence, and the sort of respect which all men show for a true measure and a task well done. Ibrahim Aga's whole personality was such that no other reaction was possible. And when sometimes a suspicious peasant whose stuff was being weighed edged closer to the scale, the better to see and verify the weight behind the scale keeper's back, Ibrahim Aga at once clapped his hand over the counterweight, held up the measuring, and chased the pest away.

"Get back! Stop pushing and coughing into the scale! True measure's the same as faith, a breath can spoil it. And it'll be my soul that'll burn for it, not yours. Step back!"

So Ibrahim Aga spent his whole life suspended over the public scale, living for it and from it, a walking example of what a man can make of his calling, whatever that may be.

This same Ibrahim Aga, who kept his soul pure by blameless measuring, Desfosses once saw thrashing a Christian peasant in the middle of the market place in full view of everybody. The peasant had brought for sale a dozen axe handles and had leaned them against a crumbling wall that enclosed an abandoned tomb and the ruins of an old mosque. Ibrahim Aga, who watched over the market, flew at the peasant in a rage and kicked over all the axe handles, fuming and threatening the bewildered peasant, who scrambled after his scattered merchandise.

"Do you think the mosque wall is there for you to lean your filthy handles on, you pig of pigs! There's no infidel bell-ringing here yet, and no church organ, you son of a she-pig!"

The crowd went on with their bargaining, haggling, measuring, and counting, and paid scant attention to the fracas. The peasant quickly collected his stuff and disappeared in the throng. When Desfosses got home, he made this entry in his diary: "Turkish authority has two faces. Their methods appear mysterious and illogical to us. They never stop puzzling and amazing us."

Hamza the crier was something else again—a different sort of destiny as it were.

Famed at one time for his voice and his good looks, he had been a wastrel and a loafer from his early youth, one of the most notorious drunkards in the whole of Travnik. In his younger days he had been known for his pluck and his wit. Some of his brash but clever sayings were still remembered and recounted. When asked why he had chosen the job of town crier, he answered: "Because I don't know of any easier one." On one occasion, a few years back, when Suleiman Pasha Skoplyak led an army against Montenegro and burned the town of Drobnyak to ashes, Hamza was ordered to broadcast the great Turkish victory and to announce that one hundred and eighty Montenegrin heads had been cut off. One of those who always gather around a town crier asked out loud: "And how many of ours lost their heads?" "Well, that's the business of the crier in Montenegro," replied Hamza flatly and went on shouting what had been ordered.

His dissipation, singing, and the strain of a crier's profession had long since ruined Hamza's voice. He no longer roused the bazaar with his old ringing baritone, but announced the official and market news in a hoarse pipsqueak, heard only by those near him. Still, it would never have occurred to anyone that Hamza should be replaced by someone younger and more sonorous, and he himself appeared to be hardly aware that he no longer had any voice. Striking the same poses and using the same gestures with which he had once sent his famous voice echoing down the lanes, he now delivered his messages to the world as best he could. Now the small fry would gather and skip around him, giggling at these histrionics which had long been too extravagant for his croaking and piping, and they stared open-mouthed and in awe at his bull neck which swelled with the strain like a bagpipe. Nevertheless, he needed these children, for they were the only ones who heard the croaking and promptly spread the news all over town.

Desfosses and Hamza soon became friends, as the "young Consul" occasionally bought some rug or bauble which Hamza was crying for the merchants and on which he made a handsome profit.

The Mad Schwabe was an old "character" in the Travnik bazaar. He was a halfwit of uncertain parentage, from somewhere across the border. The Turks left morons severely alone, and so he was allowed to live here and fend for himself, sleeping under shop counters and feeding on charity. He was a man of giant strength and, when he had a little inside him, he was willing to play the fool to the crude pranksters of the bazaar. On a market day someone would buy him a drink or two and thrust a wooden club in his hand, and the poor idiot would then stop the passing Christian peasants and begin to drill them, always with the same words: *"Halbrechts! Links! Marsch!"* (Half-right! Left! March!)

The peasants would dodge him or clumsily try to run away, well aware that the Mad Schwabe was put up to it by the Moslems, and he would chase them up and down the street, to the amusement of the younger shopkeepers and the idle agas.

One market day Desfosses was returning to the Consulate after a visit to the bazaar. His kavass walked behind him. As they reached the spot where the square narrows down and becomes the market street, the Mad Schwabe suddenly popped up in front of Desfosses. The young man saw before him a square-headed colossus with wicked green eyes. The drunken halfwit blinked at the stranger, then lunged toward the nearest shop,

snatched up a wooden bar, and made straight at him. *"Halbrechts! Marsch!"*

The merchants squatting on their platforms began to crane
their necks in malicious anticipation, eager to see how the
"young Consul" would dance to the nitwit's bidding. But the
thing turned out quite differently. Before the groom could come
to his aid, Desfosses managed to duck under the swinging bar
and, in one nimble and lightning movement, grabbed the idiot's
wrist; he then reeled around with his whole body, twisting the
giant after him like a stuffed doll. As the idiot tottered backwards around the youth, the bar flew out of his clutching hand
in a wide arc and fell to the ground. Meanwhile the groom had
run up with his small rifle at the ready; but the idiot's wind had
already been knocked out of him by the painful backward wrench
of his arm, about which he could do nothing. Desfosses handed
him over to the groom, then picked up the bar from the ground
and quietly put it back in its place by the store. With a contorted face, the nitwit looked now at his hurting hand, now at
the young stranger, who shook his finger at him, as at a child,
and admonished him in his clipped high-flown Turkish accent:
"You're a rowdy. You're not to be a rowdy, understand!" Then
he called the groom and calmly went on his way, past the flabbergasted shopkeepers on their little platforms.

Daville took the young man sternly to task over the incident,
which only proved, he said, that he was right when he warned
him not to go through the bazaar on foot, as one never knew
what those spiteful, uncouth, idle people might do or think of
next. But D'Avenat, who otherwise had little love for Defosses
and thoroughly disapproved of his free-and-easy ways, was
obliged to admit to Daville that the bazaar was buzzing with
admiration for the "young Consul."

The "young Consul" continued to explore the neighborhood,
rain and mud notwithstanding, and to accost the people freely
and talk to them, and so managed to see and learn things which
Daville, grave and stiff and unbending as he was, would never
see or learn. Daville, whose bitterness caused him to look on
everything Turkish and Bosnian with distaste and mistrust,
could see no purpose or official advantage in these excursions
and reports of Desfosses. The easy optimism of the young man
irritated him, as did his eagerness to delve deeper into the his-

tory, customs, and beliefs of the natives; his habit of explaining away their faults; and, lastly, his passion for discovering their good traits, which he believed were corrupted and smothered by the strange circumstances in which they were forced to live. This business impressed Daville as a fool's errand, a harmful straying from official propriety. So his talks with the young Secretary always ended in an argument or petered out in offended silence.

One cold autumn evening Desfosses came back from one of his excursions, soaked, pink-cheeked, frozen, full of impressions and aching to talk about them. Daville, who had been pacing for hours up and down the warm lighted dining room, his mind churning with melancholy thoughts, was at first astonished to see him. The young man, still a little out of breath, ate with gusto and gave a lively account of his visit to Dolats, a crowded Catholic settlement, and of the enormous trouble he had had in making the short trip there and back.

"I sometimes think there's no country in Europe as roadless as Bosnia," said Daville, who picked at his food without any real appetite, for he was not feeling hungry. "These people, more than any other people in the world, have a peculiar and perverse hatred of roads, which in fact represent progress and prosperity. In this God-forsaken country the roads are not kept up and they don't last, they almost fall apart by themselves. You see, the fact that General Marmont is building a great highway through Dalmatia is doing us more harm with the Turks here, even with the Vizier, than our boastful and eager friends in Split could possibly imagine. These people don't like to see roads anywhere near them. How can you explain that to our friends in Split? They're busy bragging to all and sundry how these new roads of theirs will improve communication between Bosnia and Dalmatia, and they have no idea how suspicious the Turks are about it."

"Well, it's no wonder," Desfosses told him. "I can see it all rather clearly. As long as Turkey has the kind of government it has, as long as conditions in Bosnia remain what they are, there'll be no roads or communication. On the contrary, both the Turks and the Christians, though for different reasons, oppose the opening and maintenance of all traffic links. As a matter of fact, I had a good example of it today when I was talking with my friend Fra Ivo, the fat priest of Dolats. I was complaining how steep and eroded the road was from Travnik to Dolats, and wondering why the people of Dolats, who had to use it every day, did nothing to keep it in at least some kind of order. The Brother first looked at me with a grin, as if I didn't know what I was saying, then winked shrewdly and told me in an undertone, 'The worse the road, sir, the fewer are the Turkish visitors. What we would like to see is a great big mountain between us and them. As for ourselves, well, we can manage any road with a little trouble when we have to. We are used to bad roads and every kind of difficulty. Indeed, we live on difficulties. Don't repeat what I'm telling you, but, you know, as long as there are Turks in Travnik, we don't need a better road. Between you and me, as soon as the Turks repair it, our folk break it up and spoil it at the first rain or snow. It all helps to keep the unwelcome guests away.' As he said this, the Brother opened his closed eyes and, pleased with his cunning, begged me once more not to repeat his words to anyone. Well, there you have one reason why the roads are unspeakable. And the other is the Turks themselves. Every new link with the Christian world outside is like opening a door to enemy influences. It gives the enemy a chance to work on the rayah and to threaten Turkish authority. And when everything is said and done, M. Daville, we French have swallowed half of Europe and shouldn't really wonder if the countries we have not yet occupied look with a jaundiced eye on these highways, which our armies are building right on their frontiers."

"Yes, I know, I know," Daville interrupted him. "But Europe needs roads and we can't stop to consider backward peoples like the Turks and the Bosnians."

"Those who maintain that roads have to be built, build them. Which means they consider them necessary. But the point I'm trying to make is that these folk here don't want any roads, that there are reasons why they don't want them, and that the roads do them more harm than good."

As always, Daville was annoyed by the young man's urge to explain and justify everything he saw.

"Really, it's not anything one can defend," the Consul said. "And you can't explain it with rational arguments. The backwardness of these people is in the first place the result of their bad nature—their congenital worthlessness, as the Vizier puts it. *That* certainly can explain all of it."

"Very well then. How do you explain the bad nature itself? Where does it come from?"

"Where from? They're born with it, that's where. You'll have plenty of opportunity to see for yourself."

"Good, but until that happens allow me to stand by my own view that the goodness and badness of a people are the product of conditions in which they live and develop. It's not goodness that motivates our road-building, but need and our desire to expand useful links and our influence, which many people regard as our own brand of wickedness. So our bad nature drives us to build roads, and theirs to hate them and destroy them whenever possible."

"You're exaggerating just a little bit, my young friend."

"No, life is the one that exaggerates—so much, in fact, that we can never quite keep up with it. I am just trying to clarify single facts, even if the total picture escapes me."

"You can't know and explain everything," Daville said wearily, in a somewhat offhand voice.

"No, of course not, but one ought to keep trying."

Desfosses, whom the food and wine had warmed up after his ride in the cold air and whose youth now impelled him to think out loud, went on with his recital. "Anyway, how do you explain this?" he said. "The same clever and sensible priest from Dolats, who is certainly in possession of his faculties, gave a sermon from the Dolats pulpit last Sunday. If I'm to believe my groom, who's a Catholic, the priest claimed in all seriousness that a certain very pious Brother who died the other day in the monastery at Foynitsa was, if not a saint, at least in close touch with the saints, and that it was known beyond doubt that a special angel brought him messages every night from various saints and from Our Lady herself."

"You don't know yet how bigoted these people are."

"All right, let's call it bigotry. But that's a word that explains nothing."

Daville, who considered himself a "wise and moderate liberal," was apt to chafe at any discussion of faith, however innocent. "It explains everything," he said rather tartly. "You don't hear our preachers spreading such tales."

"That's because our conditions of life are not the same, M. Daville. I wonder what we would be preaching if we had led the life of these Christians here for the last three centuries? There wouldn't be miracles enough in all heaven and earth for our arsenal of faith in the struggle against the Turkish overlord. Believe me, the more I see and listen to these folk the more I realize our mistake, as we subdue one European country after another, of trying to foist on them our concepts and our ways of life and rule, strictly and exclusively rational as they are. I realize more and more that it's an unsurmountable and witless task, because it's no earthly use trying to remove abuses and prejudices when you haven't the power or the inclination to eradicate the causes that are at the bottom of them."

"That would take us rather too far afield," Daville broke in on his Chancellor. "And doubtless there must be someone who's thinking about it, never you fear."

The Consul got up and rang sharply and impatiently for the table to be cleared.

Whenever the young man, in the sincere and forthright manner that was part of his nature, of which he seemed not to be conscious and which Daville secretly envied him, began to sound as though he were critical of the Imperial regime, Daville would squirm and lose his control and patience. Because he himself was of two minds and harbored secret doubts that he couldn't admit even to himself, he found it hard to put up with someone else's disparagement. He felt as if this carefree, unguarded young man bared and put his finger on his rawest spot, which he was doing his utmost not only to hide from the world but, if possible, to forget about himself.

Nor could Daville talk to Desfosses about literature, and still less about his own writing.

This was a subject on which Daville was particularly sensitive. For as long as he could remember, he had been planning literary works of various kinds, churning out verses and devising plots. Some ten years before, he had edited, for a while, the literary column of *Le Moniteur* and had attended the meetings of literary societies. He had to give it all up when he rejoined the Ministry of Foreign Affairs and was sent to Malta as Chargé d'Affaires, and later to Naples, but he continued writing.

The verses which he published in various reviews from time to time, and the neatly copied poems which he sent to his friends, superiors, and important personages, were neither much better nor much worse than thousands of other verse products of the day. He called himself a "faithful disciple of the great Boileau," and in articles that no one ever dreamed of challenging, he vigorously espoused the stern classical rule, pleading for a poetry free from the excesses of imagination, from undue experimentation, and from spiritual confusion. Inspiration was a *sine qua non,* Daville asserted in his articles, but it must be guided by rational measure and sound content, without which there could be no work of art. Daville put so much emphasis on these principles that readers had the impression he was more concerned with order and discipline in poetry than with poetry itself, almost as if these things were constantly threatened by poets and poetry and must be protected and upheld by any and all means. His model among the poets of the time was Jacques Delille, author of *The Gardens* and translator of Virgil. Daville printed a series of articles in *Le Moniteur* in defense of Delille, and again no one paid any attention, either by way of praise or rebuttal.

For some years now Daville had been occupied with plans for a momentous epic on Alexander the Great. Conceived in twenty-four cantos, the poem had gradually become a kind of disguised diary of Daville's soul. All his experience of the world, his brooding about Napoleon, war, and politics, his secret wishes and displeasures, were shunted to those far-off times and woven into the hazy circumstances in which his hero had lived, and there he let them roam unchecked save for the modest discipline of metered verse and a more or less mandatory rhyme. Daville was so steeped in the life of his epic that, in addition to the names Jules-François, he gave his second child the name of the Macedonian King Amyntas, Alexander's grandfather. In this "Alexandriad" of his, Bosnia too came to life as a barren country with a harsh climate and peopled by an odious race, but under the name of Tauris. In it could be found Mehmed Pasha and the Bosnian begs and Catholic friars; and all the others with whom Daville had to work or struggle were depicted and disguised as one or another of Alexander's retinue or his opponents. All of Daville's loathing of the East and of the Asiatic spirit in general was here, expressed in terms of his hero's struggle against distant Asia.

As he rode above Travnik and gazed down on the roofs and minarets of the town, Daville was often absorbed in mental descriptions of the fabulous Eastern city that Alexander happened to be investing at the time. And when he sat in audience at the Residency and watched the silent, hurrying servants and courtiers, he kept putting the final touches to his description of a senate session in the besieged city of Tyre, in the third canto. Like all writers who lack the gift and the true vocation, Daville was the victim of an obstinate, deep-seated illusion: namely, that a man can arrive at poetry by a certain deliberate exercise of the mind and that creating poetry rewards and consoles man for the evils with which life burdens and surrounds him.

In his youth Daville had often asked himself whether he was a poet or not. Did his work in this discipline have any significance and promise, or not?

Now, after all those years of hard work that failed to bring success, even if they had brought no outright failure, it was fairly clear that Daville was no poet. Meanwhile, as often happens, Daville "worked at poetry" more and more doggedly as the years went on, methodically and somewhat mechanically, no longer asking himself that question which youth, in its frank and fearless appraisal of itself, can ask with impunity.

In his younger days, when he was still acknowledged and encouraged, he wrote less; now, in his years, when no one any longer took him for a poet, he worked steadily and diligently. The spontaneous need for expression and the deceptive energy of youth had given place to a sluggish habit and application. For application, the virtue that so often appears where it is out of place or when it is no longer needed, is the comfort of ungifted writers and the undoing of art. Unusual circumstances, the loneliness and tedium to which he had been condemned for many years, had driven Daville to this futile sidetrack, this artless sin he called poetry. In reality, Daville had gone astray the day he penned his first verse, for his bond with poetry was not a genuine one. He had no feeling for it, even at its most felicitous, and still less could he evoke or create it.

The spectacle of evil in the world aroused in Daville either rancor or depression; the spectacle of good, enthusiasm and satisfaction, a kind of moral thrill as it were. And out of those thrills, which plucked at him in a way that was sharp and perfectly real, wayward and fitful though they were, he constructed verses that were everything but poetry; and it was true that the fashion of the time abetted and confirmed him in his mistaken notions.

And so, pushing harder and harder as the years went by, Daville continued to use his considerable good qualities toward middling ends, and to expect of poetry what it plainly did not have to give: easy moral euphorias and harmless intellectual games and diversions.

It was understandable that young Desfosses, being what he was, was not a suitable listener or critic, or even a desirable

partner in a literary conversation. All of which led to a further
widening of the already marked distance between them, to which
the Consul was particularly sensitive.

The young man's mind revealed itself chiefly by its endless capacity to store facts, by its efficient reasoning and boldness in
drawing conclusions. Experience and intuition seemed to work
hand in hand in him and complemented each other in a most
striking fashion. With all their differences and temperamental
incompatibility, Daville couldn't fail to see that. He often had
the impression that this youth of twenty-four had read whole
libraries, without, at the same time, attaching any special importance to the fact. Indeed, time and again the young man
irritated the Consul with his far-ranging knowledge and the audacity of his judgments. He would talk about Egyptian history
or the relation of South American colonies to their motherland
like someone playing a game; and then, just as fluently, he
would discuss oriental languages, the clashes between races and
religions in God knew what part of the world, the aims and
prospects of Napoleon's Continental System, or the problems of
communications and tariffs. He would unexpectedly quote from
the classics, usually from lesser known texts, and the sentiment
would always be crisply appropriate, revealing the subject in
a new light. And although quite often the Consul felt that his
youthful pose and runaway imagination had got the better of
order and actual value, he could not help listening to the young
man with a kind of pained and helpless admiration, and also
with an enervating sense of his own weakness and inadequacy
which he tried in vain to overcome and crush.

Ah well, the young fellow was deaf and blind to what Daville
held dearest and what seemed to him the only thing worth re-
specting, besides his duties to the state. Desfosses frankly admitted that he did not care for poetry and that the French verse
of the day impressed him as foggy, thoroughly insincere, bloodless, and unnecessary. He did not, however, for a moment deny
himself the right or the satisfaction to argue and chatter freely
and impetuously—without spite, it was true, but also without
respect or very much thought—about the very thing which, in
his own words, he could neither feel nor had much liking for.

About Delille, for instance, the adored Delille, he said without
hesitation that he was a clever literary-salon type who earned
up to six francs per verse, and that, understandably enough,

Mme Delille locked him up every day and did not let him out until he had completed his daily quota. This cynicism of the new generation both angered and saddened the Consul. At all events, it only helped to make his isolation profounder.

It happened sometimes that Daville, driven by his need to talk and communicate, would brush these things aside and start a warm and intimate conversation about his literary views and plans—a forgivable lapse in his circumstances. And so one evening he drew a complete outline of his epic on Alexander the Great and explained the moral framework of his epic work. Without pausing for a moment to consider the validity of these thoughts and conceptions which made up the brighter half of the Consul's life, the young man, all brisk and smiling, suddenly began to quote from Boileau:

"Que crois-tu qu'Alexandre, en ravageant la terre,
Cherche parmi l'horreur, le tumulte et la guerre?
Possédé d'un ennui qu'il ne saurait dompter
Il craint d'être à lui-meme et songe à s'éviter."

(What do you imagine Alexander, as he lays waste the earth,
Is seeking amid horror, tumult and war?
Possessed by a tedium he cannot master
He fears to be left to his resources and longs to escape from himself.)

And he added quickly by way of apology that he had once read the lines in one of the Satires and happened to remember them.

All at once Daville felt offended and immeasurably lonelier than he had been a few minutes before. It was as though he were confronted with the embodied image of the "new generation" and could feel it with his fingers. So this was the wave of the future, this generation of diabolical restlessness and destructive ideas, quick and vapid in its mental associations! A generation that professed "no interest in poetry" but had no qualms about resorting to it—and with a vengeance—whenever it might serve their warped ambitions, to bring the world down flat on its face, to belittle and humble it, their one wish being to reduce everything to what is lowest and worst in man.

Swallowing his indignation (which was considerable), Daville at once broke off conversation and withdrew to his apartment. He could not sleep for a long time, and even in his dreams he felt the bitterness which an innocent remark can leave behind. For some days afterward he couldn't bring himself to touch or open the manuscript that lay in its cardboard folder, tied with a green ribbon, so profaned and disparaged did his beloved work appear to him.

And on his part Desfosses was not in the least aware that he had offended the Consul. On the contrary, since quoting verses by ear was not a strong point of his otherwise remarkable memory, he was pleased that he had remembered them so well and gave no thought to the possibility that they might reflect in some way on Daville's work and perhaps even displease him, and so affect their relationship. Always, it seems, two consecutive and overlapping generations find it hardest to tolerate each other, and in fact know each other least. Yet so many of their differences and so much of their wrangling rests, as always, on misunderstanding.

What particularly poisoned the Consul's sleepless nights and gnawed away at his dreams was the idea that the young man who had so upset him that evening, of whom he thought with bitter displeasure, was now sleeping fast and sound, a sleep as natural and callous as everything he did and said by day. However, the Consul might have spared himself this one indignity at least, for he was wrong. Those who laugh by day and move lightly among men do not necessarily sleep in blissful peace. Young Desfosses was not entirely the carefree, self-contained example of the "new type," as Daville often supposed—matured too soon and loaded with knowledge, a contented child of a contented Empire, and little else. That night, each of the two Frenchmen nursed his own private malaise, each in his own way, with no possibility of completely understanding the other. Desfosses too was paying, in his own coin, the price of living in new surroundings and unfamiliar circumstances. His means of resistance might be more effective and numerous than Daville's, yet he too was bogged in the languor of "Bosnian silence" and felt as if the country, and his own vegetation in it, were straining to bend and break him, to sap, whittle, and flatten him down to the level of all things around him. It was no easy or simple matter to be hurled, at the age of twenty-four, from Paris to Moslem Travnik, to be full of plans and ambitions that reached far beyond and above one's immediate surroundings, and to be forced to wait patiently while all the leashed powers and unappeased hungers of youth chafed and rebelled at waiting.

The process had begun already at Split. It was like the contraction of an invisible iron hoop. Everything required an extra effort, and the effort itself took more and more doing. Each new step was a little more arduous, each decision less decisive and its implementation less certain, while behind it all, like a constant threat, there lurked mistrust, inadequacy, and possible disaster. It was the East making its appearance.

The commanding officer at Split who had provided a wretched-looking carriage (to take him only as far as Sinj, on the frontier), with ponies for the luggage and a four-man escort, was harassed, in a bad mood, almost spiteful. Young though he was, Desfosses recognized in it the legacy of long wars. For years men had gone about staggering under a load, as it were, each hefting his own misery, all of them displaced, watching for the moment when they could foist some of their burden on the others and so make it easier for themselves, by coarse abuse and unkind words if in no other way. So the common plight rolled on and shifted from place to place, from person to person, and in moving became, if not lighter, at least easier to bear.

Desfosses felt this when, in an unguarded moment, he made the mistake of asking whether the carriage springs were solid enough and the seats comfortable. The commandant stared at him and there was a light in his eyes that was almost like a drunken man's.

"It's the best we can do in this bloody country. Anyone going to work in Turkey ought to have an arse of steel, anyway."

Not batting an eyelash, the young man looked him in the eye and replied with a grin: "My instructions in Paris said nothing about that."

The officer nibbled his lower lip, realizing that here was someone who didn't run away from an argument but seized the opportunity to talk and get a few things off his chest.

"Well, you see, monsieur, there wasn't too much of that in our instructions either. It was all put in later, right here on the spot," and he did a wicked imitation of a scribe wielding a pen.

With this cynical blessing young Desfosses then set out on a dusty road that presently turned to bare rock as it heaved up steeply beyond the town of Split, taking him farther and farther away from the sea, from the last civilized buildings and green cultivation, only to ease him down once more, on the other side of the craggy ridge, into that other vast sea, Bosnia, where his young credentials would be tested for the first time.

As he went deeper and deeper into the barren mountain country, he noticed the huts and shepherd girls by the roadside, lost among rocks and clumps of thornbush, clutching wooden distaffs in their hands but no flock beside them that he could see. Observing it all, he asked himself if that was the worst he could expect, just as a man going through an operation asks himself over and over whether his pain has reached the highest point they had warned him about, or whether he is to brace himself for more and greater pain yet to come. But these were no more the usual fears and trepidations of youth. In reality, he was ready for anything and *knew* that he could go through with it.

Some miles farther on, as he paused on the stony heights above Klis and looked at the bare wilderness yawning ahead and at the blanched stony hillsides spattered here and there with thin flecks of olive-hued vegetation, there wafted up toward him, from the Bosnian side, the silence of a new world such as he had never known. The young man shivered and shook himself, more from the silence and desolation of the view than from the cool breeze that ruffled the pass. He drew his cloak around his shoulders, tightened his legs around the horse's flanks, and plunged down into that new world of silence and uncertainty. Bosnia, that muffled land, was in the air, and the air itself was already impregnated with a chilly anguish that was wordless and not to be explained.

They passed Sinj and Livno in good order. On the Kupres Plain a blizzard blew up unexpectedly. The Turkish guide, who had waited for them on the frontier, managed with an effort to get them to the first khan, a resthouse. There, exhausted and cold, they slumped around the fire, where several people were already warming themselves.

Although tired, chilled to the bone, and hungry, the young man sat upright and put on a cheerful air, bearing in mind the impression he might leave on these strangers. He refreshed his face with toilet water and did a few of his customary exercises, while the others watched him out of the corner of their eye, as if he were doing a ritual prescribed by his law. Only after he had sat down did one of the men by the fire speak a few words in Italian, explaining that he was a Brother from the monastery at Gucha Gora, that his name was Fra Julian Pashalich, and that he was traveling on business for his monastery. The others were team drivers and muleteers.

Making the best of his poor Italian, Desfosses told him who

and what he was. The friar had beetling eyebrows and thick bushy whiskers, behind which, as under a mask, a smiling young face was hidden; when he heard the words "Paris" and "Imperial French Consulate-General at Travnik," his face darkened at once and he fell silent without any further ado.

For some minutes the young man and the cleric observed each other mutely and with suspicion.

The Brother was very young but a giant. He wore a thick black cloak, under which one could dimly see a dark blue cassock and a leather belt with some kind of weapon in it. Desfosses gazed at him incredulously, asking himself, as in a dream, if this could possibly be a churchman and a member of a monastic order. And the friar, in his turn, watched the foreigner, the slender, fresh-faced young man of fine, proud, and carefree bearing, and he did so wordlessly and rather sternly. He did not hide his disapproval when he heard what country he came from and what government had sent him.

To break the silence Desfosses asked the friar whether his vocation was a hard one.

"It's like this, monsieur," the other replied. "While we here, in the face of truly great difficulties, try to keep up the prestige of our holy Church, you over there in France, living in complete freedom, persecute and destroy it. It's a shame and a sin, monsieur."

Desfosses already knew from his talks in Split that the friars and the entire Catholic community in these parts were opposed to the French occupation authorities, believing them to be godless "Jacobins"; still, he was astonished at this opinion and asked himself how a consular official of the Empire was supposed to proceed in a delicate situation like this. He met the friar's frank and questioning gaze and bowed lightly. "It is just conceivable that Your Reverence is not too well informed about the affairs of my country."

"May the Lord grant it," the friar said. "But from what one hears and reads there was much harm done, and it is still being done, to the Church and her leaders and followers. That sort of thing never did anyone any good."

The friar was hard put to find appropriate words in Italian, and his mild and carefully chosen phrases were in sharp contrast to the upset, almost bellicose expression on his face.

Their dialogue broke off when the servants brought plum brandy and the supper began to sizzle on the fire in front of them. In offering each other food and drink, the friar and the stranger were forced to meet each other's eyes from time to time and slowly warmed up, as two frozen and hungry men will under the influence of fire and food.

Young Desfosses was beginning to feel rather hot and drowsy. The wind howled in the high, blackened smoke vent; on the roof hail beat a tattoo that was like pebbles falling. The young man's head went around and around. "Well, my job has started," he thought. "So these are the woes and hardships one reads about in the memoirs of old consuls in the East!" He tried to view his predicament objectively: he was somewhere in Bosnia, under several feet of snow, and forced into an extraordinary argument in a strange language with a strange kind of friar indeed. His eyes were drooping, his brain exacted a disproportionate effort in return for sluggish service, it was all like a complicated dream in which the dreamer is put to difficult and unsporting tests. He only knew that he must hold up his head, which was getting heavier all the time, and keep looking at the other man, so as not to let him have the last word. He was a little bewildered and also rather proud that in this unexpected place and weird company he was called upon to do his share of duty, to test his skills of persuasion on an opponent and his not very considerable knowledge of the Italian language, acquired at college. At the same time, at his very first step as it were, he felt an almost physical sense of man's enormous and implacable responsibility, parceled out though it was among separate individuals and scattered like traps the world over.

His frozen hands were now burning. The smoke stung his eyes and made him cough. His struggle to keep awake was as much a nuisance as his drowsiness, as if he were on sentry duty somewhere, but he kept his eye on the friar as on a target. The sleepiness was like a warm milky liquid that filled his ears with a soft hum and glazed his eyes, through which he saw the quaint friar, as if from a distance, and heard his broken sentences and Latin quotations. His native gift of observation made him think: "The monk is filled to the brim with energy and crammed with quotations and it is evident that he has no one on whom to unload them." The friar kept saying how no man opposing the Church could ever enjoy lasting success, not even a whole country like France, and how it had been said long ago: *Quod custodit Christus, non tollit Gothus* (what Christ guards, no Goth can take away). Mixing French and Italian words, the young man once more tried to explain how Napoleon's France had proved that it desired peace in the world and had given the Church its due place, thus making amends for the violence and mistakes of the Revolution.

Things began to blur and soften under the influence of food, drink, and warmth. The eyes of the friar grew less hard, even though they remained stern, and at times there was a hint of a smile in them. As he watched him, it seemed to Desfosses that this was a signal for truce between them and also proof that big and momentous questions could wait, since in any event they could not be solved in a Turkish khan in the chance meeting between a French consular official and an "Illyrian" friar, and that, therefore, this might be the moment to relent and show consideration, without prejudice to the honor and good name of the service. At peace with himself and lulled by these thoughts, he yielded to exhaustion and sank into a deep sleep.

When they woke him, he needed some moments to come to himself and realize where he was.

The fire had burnt down to embers. Most of the travelers were already outside. Their shouting, as they saddled their horses and strapped their loads, was clearly audible inside. The young man rose and began to get ready, feeling stiff and sore. He checked his belt and wallet and then called his escort, rather more loudly and sharply than was necessary. He was oppressed by the thought that he had forgotten or failed to do something, but as soon as he found that everything was in its place and his men ready and waiting by the harnessed carriage, he calmed down. His acquaintance of the night before, the friar, was coming out of the stable with a fine black horse. In dress and bearing he resembled one of the Croat frontiersman and bandits in the book illustrations. They smiled at each other like old friends whose differences have been ironed out. With an easy, unforced air, Desfosses asked him if they could travel together. The friar explained that he must take another road—he wanted to say "short cut" but couldn't find the right word and waved his hand toward a wooded hill. Desfosses didn't quite understand him, but took his hat off all the same and bade him adieu. *"Vale, reverendissime domine!"* (Farewell, most reverend sir!)

The blizzard was over, like a bad joke. A few thin white suds lingered on the slopes. The ground was soft as in the springtime, the view rinsed clear and far, the mountains blue, and up in the pure gentian sky there were a couple of fiery bands of in-

candescent clouds tilted at the horizon, from behind which the
sun cast a strange diffused light over the whole countryside.
Everything reminded one of a far northern country, and the
young man cast back in his mind to the Consul at Travnik, who
had often dotted his reports of the Bosnians and Moslems with
words like "wild Scythians" and "Hyperboreans," which had
caused some amusement at the Ministry.

And that was how young M. Desfosses had entered Bosnia,
which promptly made good all her promises and threats at the
first contact, and now enveloped him more and more in the cold
cutting air of her barrenness, and especially in her silence and
loneliness, with which the young man wrestled every night when
sleep wouldn't come and there was no help from anywhere.

Months passed and the end of the year drew near, but the Austrian Consul, who everyone believed would come hard on the
heels of the French one, did not appear. The people began to
put him out of their minds. Toward the end of summer a rumor
spread that the Austrian Consul was coming. The word went
through the bazaar, occasioning new smiles, new frowns, and
whisperings. Weeks went by again, and there was no trace of
him. Then, during the last days of autumn, he arrived.

Long before he ever set foot in Bosnia, Daville had heard,
while passing through Split, that the Austrian government was
getting ready to open a Consulate-General at Travnik. Later, at
Travnik itself, this prospect had hung over his head like a threat
for a whole year. Yet now, when after all these months of waiting the threat was about to materialize, he was less disturbed
than one might have expected. He had, in fact, become reconciled to it. What was more, in the wondrous logic of human
weakness, he was flattered by the fact that another great power
should attach importance to this outlying spot. His stature increased in his own eyes and his strength and fighting spirit revived.

Already since the middle of summer D'Avenat had been gathering information, spreading intelligence about the dark intentions of Austria, and generally spinning a web around the arrival of the new Consul. He had, to begin with, sounded various people on what they thought of the news. The Catholics were jubilant and the Franciscans made ready to place themselves at the new Consul's disposal as cordially and devotedly as they had been cool and aloof to the French Consul on his arrival. The Serb-Orthodox, who were persecuted on account of the uprising in Serbia, avoided any public discussion of it but would, when asked in confidence, repeat their stubborn assertion that "there's no consul without a Russian consul." The Turks at the Residency, occupied for the most part with their own troubles and mutual intrigues, kept a lazy, dignified silence that was heavy with contempt. The local Moslems were even more perturbed than they had been over the news of the French Consul's arrival.

If Bonaparte was a distant, shifty, and slightly fantastic force which had to be reckoned with for the time being, Austria, on the contrary, was a real and familiar danger quite close at hand. With the infallible instinct of a race that has held and dominated the country for so many centuries exclusively on the basis of status quo, they had a feeling for any danger, even the smallest, which might threaten that system and their habit of domination. They knew well that every foreigner coming to Bosnia pushed the gate open another crack—the gate that stood between them and the hostile world outside—and that a consul, with his special privileges and resources, could open it wide and let in all manner of things that bode no good, and possibly bode evil, for them, their interests, and their holy faith.

They were especially bitter about the Turks in Istanbul for permitting a thing like this. Their fear was greater than they were willing to let D'Avenat see. They parried his insistent questions with vague and general answers and kept their hate of the invading foreigners well hidden, though not their contempt for his pestering. And when he tried to find out from a merchant in the bazaar which consul he preferred, the French or the Austrian, the man told him flatly that there wasn't much to choose between them. "One is black, the other is pie. The one is a dog, the other his brother," the man said.

D'Avenat gulped his reply. At least now it was clear how the people felt and thought, although he would have trouble translating and explaining it to his Consul without offending him.

In spite of this, the French did everything in their power to foil the work of their antagonist and make his stay uncomfortable.

Daville had long, though vainly, argued with the Vizier that the new Consul constituted a danger for Turkey and that it would be best to withhold the imperial exequatur and not allow him to take up residence. The Vizier had looked blank and refused to commit himself. He knew that the imperial permit had already been issued, but he let the Frenchman talk on, while he speculated what harm or advantage he might derive from the tug of war that was obviously beginning between the two consuls.

All the same, D'Avenat had used his old connections and done some fresh bribing to delay the dispatch of the exequatur. When the Austrian Consul-General, Colonel von Mitterer, arrived in the town of Brod at the frontier, he was unpleasantly surprised to find that neither the imperial firman nor his consular exequatur had been sent to the local Austrian commander, as promised. Von Mitterer moped around in Brod for a whole month, vainly dispatching couriers to Vienna and Travnik. At length he was informed that the exequatur had been sent to the Turkish commander at Derventa, Nail Beg, who was to hand it over and so enable the Consul to have the permit with him when he arrived in Travnik. At that von Mitterer left Brod, with his interpreter Nicholas Rotta and a couple of escorts. At Derventa another surprise awaited him. The local commander declared he had nothing for the Consul, neither an exequatur nor any other instructions. He made him break his journey and stay at the fort of Derventa with his party—in a damp barrack room, in fact, as the local resthouse had burned down only a short time before. Although he was a man of experience, grown old working and battling with the Turkish authorities, the Consul was quite beside himself with indignation. The commander, a dour and tough Bosnian, sounded offhand as he told him over a cup of Turkish coffee: "You'd better wait, sir. If it's true they have sent the firman and the exequatur, as you say, then they are bound to arrive. They can't get lost. Anything the High Porte sends, must arrive. So you'd better wait here. You are no trouble to me."

Even as he was talking, under the cushion on which he sat there lay hidden the firman and the exequatur, neatly folded and wrapped in heavy brocade, issued in the name of Herr Joseph von Mitterer, the Imperial and Royal Consul-General at Travnik.

In baffled despair, the Consul once again sent urgent letters to Vienna, imploring them to demand the exequatur from Istanbul and to rescue him from this invidious situation, which could only tarnish the prestige of the country that had sent him and was certain to jeopardize his future work at Travnik. He ended his letters with: "Written at the fort of Derventa, in a dark cell, on the floor." At the same time he hired special messengers and dispatched them to the Vizier at Travnik, with the request that they either send him the permit or allow him to proceed to Travnik without it. Nail Beg intercepted the messengers, confiscated the letters on the grounds of suspicion, and tucked them calmly under his cushion, next to the firman and the exequatur.

So the Colonel spent another two weeks at Derventa. During that time he was visited by a Jew from Travnik who offered his services and claimed that he was in a good position to spy on the French Consul. The wary Colonel, who was used to dealing with spies and informers, turned down the dubious offer but made use of him as a messenger and gave him a letter for the Vizier. The man accepted the reward, took the message to Travnik and handed it to D'Avenat, who had originally bribed him to go to Derventa and pretend to offer his service to the Austrian Consul. Daville saw from this letter in what an unsavory and grotesque situation his opponent now found himself, and read with gloating his requests and futile entreaties to the Vizier. The letter was sealed again and returned to the Residency. The surprised Vizier ordered an inquiry and set his men to trace the firman and the exequatur, which had been forwarded over a fortnight before to the commander at Derventa, with orders to hand them over to the new Consul on his arrival. The Vizier's Chief Records Keeper rummaged two or three times through his dusty files in a vain attempt to determine where the dispatch might have got stuck. The Tartar dispatch rider, who had taken it to Derventa and had since returned, swore that he had delivered the Vizier's mail to the commander in good order. Everything seemed to have gone according to plan, and yet the Austrian Consul was still sitting at Derventa, waiting impatiently for his exequatur.

In reality, the thing was perfectly simple and clear. With the help of D'Avenat and the Jew, Daville had bribed the commander at Derventa to hold up the permit as long as possible. The commander had no objection to sitting on his cushion for two weeks, with the firman and the exequatur under him, and he assured the Colonel day after day, coolly and with a straight face, that there had been no dispatch for him—for which service he received a gold thaler per day. Moreover, the commander was not in the least concerned about the consequences as he had long before stopped answering any correspondence or complaints which were not to his liking and was keeping away from Travnik altogether.

At last everything was straightened out. The Colonel had a letter from the Vizier telling him that the documents were being traced and inviting him to move to Travnik forthwith, without the exequatur. That same day the Colonel joyfully left Derventa and started on the road to Travnik; the day after, the commander returned the consular papers to the Vizier, with apologies for having mislaid them.

And so the Austrian Consul-General went through the same disheartening merry-go-round that is the invariable lot of foreigners who go to Turkey or do business with the Turks. Before the stranger can properly turn around, the Turks manage to harass, humiliate, and tire him, often deliberately and consciously, but sometimes quite unwittingly, through the accident of circumstances, so that when the stranger finally gets down to the business which was the object of his visit his energy is already spent and his confidence in himself quite shaken.

Nevertheless, it was also true that, while waiting for his exequatur at Brod, von Mitterer had secretly began to open the French Consul's mail from Ljubljana.

The entry of the Austrian Consul into Travnik passed off in much the same way as Daville's own. The only difference was that von Mitterer didn't have to put up in a Jewish home, as the Catholic community was humming like a beehive and the leading merchant families vied with each other to have him. His reception by the Vizier, according to D'Avenat's intelligence, was a trifle shorter and cooler than Daville's had been; and the reaction of the local Moslems was neither better nor worse. ("One is a dog, the other his brother!") In the streets he was showered with the same abuse and curses from women and brats, he was spat on from windows, and the older men in the shops ignored him with an air of stony dignity.

The new Consul first called on two leading Moslem worthies

and then visited the Apostolic Delegate, who happened to be staying at the monastery of Gucha Gora; only then did he drop in on his French colleague. During these visits he was shadowed at every step by D'Avenat's spies, who reported all they could find out and invented and embellished what they couldn't. All of it, nevertheless, helped to crystallize the impression that the Austrian Consul desired to bring together all those who were against the French Consul, and that he did so carefully and unobtrusively, without uttering a single word against his colleague and his work, while listening to everything others had to say. Even so, he managed to hint that he was sorry for his colleague for having to represent a government which had sprouted from revolution and was, at bottom, godless; that was his line with the Catholics. With the Moslems, he regretted Daville's bad luck in having to pave the way—what an ungrateful task!—for a gradual infiltration of French Dalmatian troops into Turkish territory, thus visiting on this quiet and lovely land all the troubles and suffering which wars and armies bring with them.

It was on a Tuesday, exactly at noon, that von Mitterer at last called on Daville.

Outside the sun shone with all the brilliance of late autumn, but in the large room on the ground floor of Daville's residence the air was brisk, almost chilly. The two consuls studied each other carefully, trying not to sound forced in their conversation; each told the other in his most natural tone of voice how long he had looked forward to this occasion. Daville spoke about his stay in Rome and added, as if parenthetically, that his Sovereign had happily put an end to the Revolution and had restored not only the social order but respect for religion in France. Accidentally—or so it seemed—he discovered on his desk the order for the creation of a new imperial nobility in France, which he explained in some detail to his visitor. Von Mitterer, on the other hand, following the established custom, dwelt on the wise policies of the Vienna Court, whose objectives were peace and peaceful collaboration, although it was obliged to maintain a strong army in view of the delicate frontier situation at the eastern reaches of Europe.

Both consuls fairly bristled with the dignity of their profession and with a zeal reminiscent of neophytes. This made it impossible for them to see the absurd side of the high tone and solemn formality of their meeting, though it did not prevent them from observing and sizing each other up.

Daville found von Mitterer looking much older than hearsay had led him to believe. Everything about him—the pine-green military uniform, the old-fashioned style of coiffure, the stiff pomaded mustache on a sallow face—seemed to him lifeless and antiquated.

To von Mitterer, on the other hand, Daville seemed a lightweight and much too young. In his whole manner of speech, in his casual red mustache and the pile of blond hair above the high forehead, innocent of powder or queue, in fact in everything about him, the Colonel detected revolutionary coarseness and an unpleasant surfeit of fantasy and freedom.

Who knows how much longer the consuls might have dilated on their courts' lofty intentions, if they had not been interrupted by shouts, screaming, and a wild commotion in the yard?

In spite of the strictest warnings, a flock of Christian and Jewish children had gathered on the street and clambered onto the fence to see the Consul in his splendid uniform. As they could not keep still during the long wait, someone gave the youngest one a push from behind, and he slipped and tumbled into the yard where Daville's servants and von Mitterer's escort were standing around. The other children scattered like sparrows. After the first shock, the youngster—a Jewish child—began to bawl as if he were being flayed alive, while his two brothers hopped around by the locked gate outside and called him, weeping in unison. The shouting and commotion caused by all this turned the conversation of the two consuls to children and family matters. Thereupon they began to resemble a couple of soldiers who had been ordered "at ease," after an excruciating drill.

From time to time, one or the other, remembering his professional duty, vainly endeavored to put on a hard-bitten official air. Their common trouble and the similarity of their lot proved stronger than airs. Behind their poses, uniforms, decorations, and memorized phrases there lapped the tide of their common discontent at the coarse and grubby life they were condemned to. In vain Daville cited the extraordinary cordiality with which he had been received at the Residency from the beginning; in vain did von Mitterer emphasize the great, secret, and powerful sympathy he enjoyed among the Catholics. The tone of their voice and the look in their eyes showed only sadness and the profound human understanding of two fellow sufferers. And only the lingering sense of duty and propriety kept them from patting each other on the shoulder, as any two sensible private people might have done in their common plight.

And so their first meeting ended on a note of children's illnesses and problems of feeding and in a general discussion of their dreary life in Travnik.

But that same day, and at about the same time, the two consuls sat long over sheets of coarse draft paper, penning long columns of their official reports on the subject of their first confrontation. Here the visit came off quite differently. Here, on paper, it was a bloodless duel of wits, subtlety, and zeal between a couple of giants. Each imputed a strength and quality to his opponent that fully corresponded to his high opinion of himself and of his task; save that in the Frenchman's report it was the Austrian who in the end, morally speaking, lay floored and pinned by both shoulders, while in the Austrian's report it was the Frenchman who was rattled and dumbfounded by the sublime reasoning of the Imperial and Royal Consul-General.

However, each heavily scored the fact that his rival was unhappy over the extraordinarily harsh circumstances in which a civilized European and his family were forced to live in this wild and mountainous backwater. And of course neither mentioned his own unhappiness.

Thus the consuls enjoyed double solace and satisfaction that day: they had talked and sympathized with each other as human beings, insofar as that was possible at a first meeting, and each had portrayed the other in undiluted acid, which served to flatter his own image by contrast. With it, each of them assuaged two inner needs, both vain and contradictory, and at the same time equally human and equally understandable. And that was some gain at least, in this strange life of theirs, in which any kind of satisfaction, real or imagined, was rare and likely to become rarer still.

From then on, the two consuls lived on the two opposite sides of Travnik with their families and helpers—one house against the other. Predestined to be rivals, the two men had been sent here to deceive and foil each other, to advance the interests of their Court and country among the authorities and the people at large, while, in the same breath, combating and damaging those of their rivals. This they did to the best of their capacity, each according to his own temperament, upbringing, and opportunities. Often they fought bitterly, with no quarter given or asked, forgetting everything else, swept along entirely by their instincts of struggle and survival, like two bloodied fighting cocks loosed by unseen hands into a narrow, shadowy arena. Every success was a failure of the other, every defeat of the other a small triumph. When they were outmaneuvered, they hid the fact carefully, or minimized it in their own eyes; when they outmaneuvered their rival, they magnified and stressed it in their dispatches to Vienna and Paris. As a rule, the rival Consul and his activities were painted in these reports only in the darkest of colors; and so these careworn patresfamilias, meek citizens well on in years, appeared at times bloodthirsty and terrifying, like raging lions or sinister Machiavellians. This at any rate was the picture they conveyed of each other, each goaded by his own troubles and confused by the strange environment into which they had both been plunged, in which, only too quickly, both lost their sense of proportion and all feeling for reality.

It would be time-consuming and superfluous to relate all these consular storms in a teacup, all their dogfights and tricks, many of which were laughable, some depressing, all pointless and quite unnecessary. The consuls strove to enlarge their influence with the Vizier and his senior assistants, they bribed the officers in the frontier posts and egged them on to plunder and pillage in their enemy's territory. The Frenchman sent his hirelings northward across the Austrian border; the Austrian directed his south to Dalmatia, occupied by the French. Through their agents each spread false rumors among the people, refuting those of his rival. Before long, they were abusing and slandering each other like two embattled women. They intercepted each other's couriers, opened each other's mail, stole and bribed each other's servants. If one might believe all they said about each other, they were, it seemed, actually poisoning each other, or attempting to.

Yet at the same time there was a great deal, after all, which brought the rival consuls closer together and even linked them. Here, in effect, were two grown men, "burdened with families," each with his own scheme of life, his own plans, cares, and frustrations, forced to struggle and carry on in an alien and unfriendly country, each grimly holding on, each simulating, in his own small way, the larger movements of his distant, unseen, and often incomprehensible masters. Bad luck and a hard life brought them close together, and if there were two people in the world who should have understood and even helped each other, it was these two consuls who in fact spent their energy, their days and nights, putting obstacles in each other's path and embittering their lives wherever possible.

In reality, it was only the aims of their official work that differed—everything else was identical or nearly so. They struggled under the same conditions, with similar weapons and varying success. Besides fighting with each other, they had to wage a daily battle with the slow and unreliable Turkish authorities and with the town Moslems, whose spite and obstinacy had to be seen to be believed. Both had their own family cares and the same disputes with their own governments which were tardy in forwarding instructions, with their respective ministries which were reluctant to issue grants, and with the frontier officials who made mistakes or failed to get things done. Above all, both had to live in the same oriental town, without company and diversions, without any comfort, sometimes even without the barest necessities, among wild mountains and backward peoples, in a running battle with mistrust, vagueness, squalor, sickness, and mishaps of all kinds. In short, they lived in a place that first unnerves a Westerner, then makes him sickly and irritable, a burden to himself and others, and at last, after some years, utterly changes and crushes him and buries him in a dull apathy long before his death.

As conditions changed and the relations between their two countries improved, the consuls readily sought each other's company. In those moments of truce and respite they looked at each other bewildered and a little ashamed, like men roused from a dream, and each tried to summon up different, more personal feelings toward his rival, at the same time wondering how safe it was to indulge them. They associated freely at such times, cheered each other up, gave presents and wrote notes to each other, in the warm friendly fashion of two people who have harmed each other and are at the same time linked by a common misfortune and dependent on each other.

But as soon as the brief lull showed signs of ending and the tug of war between Napoleon and the Court of Vienna was resumed, the consuls began to space out their visits and ration their amity, until a rupture of relations or war separated them and once more left them at loggerheads. Then both the weary men would take up their struggle afresh, echoing, like two obedient puppets on long strings, the twitchings of the distant momentous struggle, whose ultimate design was hidden but whose vast scope and fierceness filled them both to the depths of their souls with the same feelings of terror and insecurity. But even then the subtle link failed to snap between the two consuls— the two "exiles," as they called themselves in their letters. They stopped meeting and visiting each other and their families; they were up to their ears now in prodigious intrigue against each other. At night, long after the town had sunk in deep darkness, a light would remain burning in one or two windows of each Consulate, where the two men kept watch over sheets of paper, reading the reports of their agents, drafting dispatches. And it happened sometimes that M. Daville, or von Mitterer, pausing for a breather, would go to the window and gaze at the lonely light on the hill, by which his neighbor-adversary was dreaming up unknown tricks and fresh traps in which to snare his colleague on the other bank of the Lashva River.

At those moments it was as if the town huddling between them no longer existed, as if they were separated only by darkness and an empty silence. Their lighted windows stared at each other, like the pupils of men in a duel. But hidden behind the curtains, one of the consuls, or both at once, would peer through the dark toward the feeble ray of light on the opposite slope, and they would think of each other with deep and heartfelt understanding and with genuine compassion. Then, once more, they would wrench themselves away and go back to their work by the guttering candlelight, to continue writing their reports in which there was not a vestige of the sympathy they had felt a moment before; in which they blackened and libeled each other in that spuriously lofty tone which officials adopt toward the whole world when writing to their superiors in all confidence, and which they know will never be seen by those who are the subject of it.

6

If the hand of luckless chance lay heavily on this encounter of the two men in a Bosnian valley, in those anxious years of universal war, it was no more than an aspect of the bad luck that ran like a thread through the life of Joseph von Mitterer, the Austrian Consul-General.

He was a dark-haired man, with a sallow face and a black pomaded mustache, slow-spoken, cold and reserved in his manner; everything about him was stiff, angular, clean, and neat, but unobtrusive and strictly "regulation," as if the whole figure, man and uniform, had just been issued by the Imperial and Royal Quartermaster for the immediate outfitting of a stock colonel. Only his round brown eyes, with their perpetually red and inflamed eyelids, gave an impression of some mute goodness of heart and a sensibility carefully kept out of sight. They were the opaque eyes of a man who suffers from bad liver, eyes tired from years of service on the frontier and the grind of office routine, eyes that had spent themselves in long vigils over the constantly threatened frontiers of the Empire; sad and uncomplaining eyes that had seen much evil in the course of this work and witnessed the limitations of man's capacity, man's freedom, and man's humanity to his fellow men.

Born some fifty years before at Osiyek, where his father had been an officer in a Slavonian hussar regiment, he had been sent to cadet school and graduated as an ensign in the infantry. After his commission as lieutenant, he was sent to Zemun as an information officer. There, except for short intervals, he spent some twenty years—hard years crowded with campaigns against the Turks and the mutinous Serbs. During that time he not only organized agents, gathered intelligence, set up communications, and submitted reports, but also crossed into Serbia several times disguised as a peasant or monk, and reconnoitered the Turkish strength, under the most difficult conditions, sketching their fortifications and important positions and sounding the mood of the people. In this work, which wears a man out before his time, von Mitterer was eminently successful. As often happens in life, it was the sort of success that breaks a man's neck. After several years of this work, the Ministry was so pleased with his reports that he was summoned to Vienna in person and there received the rank of captain and a purse of one hundred ducats. The success filled the young officer with the daring hope that he might finally rise above the dreary, monotonous rut in which all his forebears had plodded before him.

With a hundred gold ducats and a high commendation in his pocket, the frontier officer, who had just passed his thirtieth year, indulged in all kinds of visions, but especially in the vision of a more peaceful, more attractive, and socially more reward-ing way of life. He believed he had found the embodiment of such a life in a young Viennese girl. She was the daughter of a military judge, a Germanized Pole, and a landless Hungarian baroness. This pretty, romantic, and somewhat too lively young lady, Anna Maria, was promptly, and indeed rather hurriedly, given in marriage to the unassuming but worthy frontier officer from the Empire's periphery. It was as if destiny had only waited to hang this woman around his neck to lash him completely and for good to the dead round of subordinate duties from which he yearned to escape at all costs. The marriage, which was to have opened the door to a finer and more congenial life, in fact closed it and tied him fast forever, robbing him even of his peace and equanimity, which are the only saving grace and dignity of humble and anonymous lives.

The information officer "who'd done it" soon discovered that there were things which no one could "reconnoiter" and foresee, namely the moods and caprices of a vain and restless woman. The "unhappy Polish-Hungarian-Viennese mixture," as the com-manding officer of the Zemun garrison described Frau von Mit-terer, suffered from an excess of imagination and from a mor-bid, irresistible, and insatiable need for excitement.

Frau von Mitterer became excited over music, nature, mis-guided philanthropy, old pictures, new ideas, Napoleon, or any-thing else outside herself and her own circle, anything in fact that was inimical to her family life, her own good name, and the reputation of her husband. This unquenchable need for en-thusiasm in the life of Frau von Mitterer often found an outlet in fleeting and impulsive love affairs. Driven by a mysterious and irresistible craving, this frigid woman of seething imagi-nation occasionally developed a passionate attachment for a young man, usually younger than herself, imagining each time that in the particular young man of the moment, whom she felt to be endowed with a strong personality and an uncorrupted heart full of pristine emotions, she had found the model of her dreams and a kindred soul. By the unwritten law of such cases, they invariably turned out to be gifted but uninhibited young men with but a single thought in their mind, to sleep with her, just as they would with any other woman who came their way and offered no resistance. But after the first bloom of enthu-siasm, when the first caresses inevitably revealed the vast chasm between her soaring esoteric passion and the man's real intentions, Anna Maria would shrink back disenchanted. "Love" would quickly change to hate and disgust of the fallen idol, of herself, of love and life in general. After a slow convalescence, she would recover and cast about for a fresh object of enthusiasm and disappointment, thus gratifying her inner need for crises and renunciations. And so it went on until the next time, when everything would begin all over again.

Von Mitterer had tried many times to disabuse his wife of her illusions, to bring her to reason and protect her, but it had all been in vain. His "ailing child," who was now getting on in years, succumbed every now and then, in the cyclic pattern of an epileptic, to new crises in her quest for pure love. The Colonel had learned to recognize both the advance symptoms and the probable course of each new "groping," and could tell beforehand the exact moment when she would fling herself around his neck in tears of despair, sobbing that they were all after her but no one really loved her.

How could such a marriage exist and continue? No one would ever know how this sober and conscientious man managed to endure it and why he forgave it all in advance; it was one of those ineffable mysteries that so often cruelly divide two people and yet throw them together inseparably.

Already in the first year of their marriage, Anna Maria had gone back to her parents in Vienna, confessing that she had a mortal loathing of physical love and was quite unable to give her husband his connubial due. Agreeing to everything, the Captain managed to bring her around and take her back. Later, a daughter was born to them; but the truce was short-lived. Two years later it all started again. The Captain bowed his head and sought refuge in the hard work of the Zemun quarantine station and in his intelligence activities, reconciled to the fact that he had to live with a demon to which endless sacrifice must be offered, and which could only pay him back with fresh unhappiness and new alarms.

Like all unstable flighty women, the handsome, wayward, and extravagant Frau von Mitterer did what she pleased without ever quite knowing what it was she wanted. Rushing headlong into her enthusiasm of the moment, she would then flinch away in disenchantment. It was impossible to say which was harder for the Captain to bear or more painful for him to watch, her exaltations or her disappointments. He bore the one and then the other with a martyr's patience. The fact was that he loved this woman, inflicted on him like an undeserved punishment, and he loved her staunchly and selflessly, as one loves a sick child. Everything about her, within her, and around her, down to the small inanimate objects that belonged to her, appeared to him as something rare and exquisite, deserving adoration and justifying every sacrifice. He suffered from her whims and lapses, he felt embarrassed before the world and ashamed before himself, but at the same time he trembled at the thought that this bewitching woman might leave him or do violence to herself and disappear from his home or from the world altogether. He rose in the service, his daughter grew up, a frail, earnest, and sensitive child, but Frau von Mitterer continued her erratic wanderings with undiminished energy, seeking from life all the things it couldn't give, transforming everything into an object of enthusiasm or regret, and distilling from either fresh torment for herself and for those around her. The baffling and untamable fury that raged in this woman took new forms and directions as the years went by, but it showed no signs of weakening or abating.

When von Mitterer was somewhat unexpectedly appointed Consul-General at Travnik, Anna Maria, who just then was passing through one of her big depressions, began to rage and weep, saying that she would not leave the semioriental market town where she had languished up till then in order to go and live in a "real Turkish graveyard," nor would she let her child go "to Asia." The Colonel tried to calm his wife, explaining that the new appointment was a significant change and an important step forward in his career; it was a hard assignment, true, but the pay was much better and would enable him to assure the child's future. Finally he proposed that if she absolutely refused to go, she should remain with the child in Vienna. Anna Maria first agreed to the compromise, then quickly changed her mind and decided to make the sacrifice. The Colonel, it seemed, was not to be granted a few quiet months of that paradise which was another name for the absence of his wife.

As soon as von Mitterer had found a house and fitted it out as best he could, Frau von Mitterer and the child also arrived. It was obvious at first glance that she was a woman who expected the world to give her a lot of elbow room. She was still handsome and looked as youthful as ever, though perhaps running to fat just a little. Her whole appearance, the glow of her flawlessly white skin, the strange brilliance of her eyes that graded from emerald to dusty gold, like the shimmery waters of Lashva, the color and style of her coiffure, her gait, movements, and imperious way of talking, all brought to Travnik for the first time something of the glamor and style which the local people ascribed to foreign consuls in their imagination.

At Frau von Mitterer's side was her daughter Agatha, a thirteen-year-old girl who was quite unlike her mother. Wistful and silent, mature and sensitive beyond her years, with thin drawn lips and the fixed gaze of her father, she walked at her mother's side like a constant mute reproof, never showing her feelings, almost as if she were unaware of the world around her. In reality, the child was bewildered and overwhelmed by her temperamental mother and by the things she guessed were going on between her parents; she loved her father, although that love was passive and undemonstrative. She was one of those delicate, fine-boned girls who develop early and become grown women in miniature, so that they constantly surprise and mislead, with their intermittent visages of utter childishness and unexpectedly mature airs. The living opposite of her mother in everything, the girl had no ear for music and liked to be alone with her books.

Immediately after her arrival, Frau von Mitterer threw herself with all her energy into the arrangement of the house and garden. Furniture was sent from Vienna, workmen were brought in from Slavonski Brod. Everything was changed, moved around, turned upside down. (Over at the French Consulate, in the course of gossip about "those people on the other side of the river," it was said that Frau von Mitterer was building "a new Schoenbrunn." In her turn, Frau von Mitterer, who was fond of the French language and relished what she considered to be French wit, gave back as good as she got. Speaking ironically of Mme Daville's furnishings, which included, as we have seen, a number of cleverly draped and disguised old Bosnian chests, she said that Mme Daville had decorated her house in the style of "Louis Caisse"—Louis the Coffin.) The garden was closed off with a high picket fence from the noisy, muddy courtyard of the town's caravansary and its stables. In fact, the old family house of the Hafizadich was remodeled completely to Frau Consul's specifications, of which no one could see the end or sense, except that they were in keeping, or were meant to be, with certain lofty ideas of perfection, grandeur, and gentility which were not clear even to herself.

As sometimes happens with women of this type, the passing years produced new eccentricities. Anna Maria now became a monomaniac for cleanliness. But although her mania was a burden to her, it was a greater burden to those around her. For her nothing was ever fresh enough or well enough washed, no one was ever clean enough. She waged war on filth and disorder with all the intensity of which she was capable. She changed servants, terrorized the inmates, dashed about, crackled like a rifle, and spent herself in her war against mud, dust, vermin, and the strange habits of the new milieu. This would be followed by days when Anna Maria, suddenly discouraged, lost faith in the outcome of her struggle; wringing her hands in despair, she shrank back from the dirt and confusion of the oriental jack warren that seemed to come at her from every side, that all but seeped out of the soil and rained down from the air, welling in through the doors and windows and through every cranny, and, gradually and inexorably, conquering the house and everything in it, things, people, livestock, and all. It seemed to her that, since she came to these backwoods, even her personal things had begun to exude a certain moldiness and rot and were slowly growing a patina of dirt which no rubbing or polishing could remove.

Very often she came back from her walks feeling shaken and quivering with fresh discouragement, because no sooner had she stepped out of the house than she came across a lame or mangy dog with a fearful and agonized look in his eyes, or a pack of street mongrels snarling over a lump of sheep's guts as they tore and dragged it all over the street. She went riding out of town and tried, from her high black horse, not to look at what was immediately around her. But even that was no comfort.

One day, after a brief spring shower, she rode out with a groom along the main road. As they left the town behind them, they met a beggar. The man, a sickly barefoot halfwit in rags, sprang out of the way of the riders and clambered up a steep path than ran above the road but parallel with it. In this way his feet were almost level with the face of the lady on the horse. For a moment her field of vision was filled entirely with the pair of huge, dirty, naked feet, slogging over trampled clay, the feet of a workman, old before his time, who could work no longer. She only glanced at them for a moment, yet in her mind's eye she would see those inhuman feet always: square, shapeless, gnarled, indescribably deformed by a lifetime of hard and endless plodding, dark and clotted with mud, with cracks like pine bark, crooked and lumbering as if they barely supported their own weight, feet whose stilted, maimed walk seemed to say with every step that the end of the road was near.

"Alas, a hundred suns and a thousand springtimes could do nothing to help those feet," Anna Maria thought suddenly at that moment. "Neither care nor food nor medicines could change or cure them. No matter what beauty there was, no matter how many blossoms came and went on this earth, those feet would only get yellower, uglier, more terrible!"

The thought haunted her wherever she went; the painful, monstrous vision did not leave her for days. Whatever she thought or set out to do was chilled and paralyzed beforehand by the realization: "*That* still exists!"

Of such things was Anna Maria's unhappiness compounded, and her anguish grew more acute in the knowledge that no one understood her feelings and repulsion or shared her longing for perfection and cleanliness. And in addition to this, and maybe for this very reason, she felt a gnawing need to talk about it and complained to everyone about the squalor of the town and the slackness of the servants, although she saw that no one understood her, no one was willing to help.

The parish priest at Dolats, the fat and coarse Fra Ivo Yankovich, listened to her plaints and bathos with an air of vacuous civility; then pretended to humor her as one humors a child, saying anything that came to his mind, declaring that people should bear their burden quietly and humbly and that, in the last analysis, even mud and filth "come from God."

"As for the rest, it has been said long ago: *Castis omnia casta* —to the pure everything is pure," the priest translated, with that perfunctory geniality which is characteristic of fat people and elderly clerics.

Afterwards Frau von Mitterer, cowed and disenchanted with everything, would remain indoors for days, shunning all contact with people and avoiding the sight of the town. She wore gloves all day long and sat in an armchair with a white dustslip that was regularly changed, allowing no one to come close when they spoke to her. In spite of all this she was haunted by the feeling that she was foundering in dirt and dust and foul odors. And when she couldn't bear it any longer, which happened often, she would get up and rush in to her husband, interrupting him in his work, reproaching him bitterly for having brought her here and demanding in tears that they leave this wretched, unclean country forthwith.

And this was repeated over and over again until force of habit began to have its effect or until a new mania replaced the old one.

In the Austrian Consulate itself, the chief factotum after the Consul-General was the interpreter and chancery secretary Nicholas Rotta. He had previously served at the quarantine station at Zemun, from where von Mitterer had brought him to Travnik.

He was a small hunchbacked man, although his hump did not protrude conspicuously; he had a powerful barrel chest and a large head, set well back between the hunched shoulders, on which a wide mouth, a lively pair of eyes, and graying, naturally crinkled hair were prominent. His legs were short and spindly and he wore either low boots with roll-down cuffs or silk stockings and flat shoes with large gilded buckles.

In contrast to his superior, von Mitterer, who was a mild and approachable man with a gentle melancholy manner in his dealings with people, this first assistant was highhanded and short-tempered with the Turks and Christians alike. His churlish silences were every bit as brusque, unpleasant, and insolent as his talk. Short and deformed though he was, he managed somehow to look down his nose at even the tallest man, twice as big as himself. From that strong head tilted back between the hunched shoulders, his dark eyes, with their heavy drooping lids, looked out on the world with an air of jaded insolence, a kind of weary contempt, as if they saw it from a great distance or a great height. But when he found himself in the presence of important or influential personages (and he knew exactly whether they were or not, or whether they merely appeared to be) and was translating their conversation, then the eyes looked down at the ground and became chary, patronizing, and remote, one after another.

Rotta spoke many languages: Travnichani had figured out somehow that he spoke ten. His greatest skill, however, lay not so much in what he said as in his ability to silence his opponent. He had a way of tossing back his head, scanning his opposite through slitted eyes, as if from a distance, and saying in a rude dry voice. "Well? What then? What then?"

These meaningless words, uttered in Rotta's particular manner, often disconcerted even the most forthright men, withered
and lamed even the best argument and evidence, took the wind
out of the most reasonable demands.

Only in César D'Avenat did Rotta find a match and a rival
worthy of himself. Ever since D'Avenat, even before their arrival
at Travnik, so effectively maneuvered with the commander at
Derventa to hold up the firman and the exequatur, forcing them
to languish there two whole weeks like any ragtag and bobtail,
he had acquired a stature in Rotta's eyes that was not to be
taken lightly. Nor did D'Avenat underestimate Rotta, whose
background he had thoroughly investigated among the merchants at Belgrade. The pair of them treated each other differently from the rest of the world. In their intercourse they always
adopted a light jovial tone that was supposed to convey a non-
chalant ease but which in fact served to mask a tense alertness
and a secret unease. They sniffed at each other like two animals,
sized each other up like a couple of thieves: sensing their own
kind right away but unsure as yet of each other's tricks and
methods.

Their talks, which usually began in French and affected a
cosmopolitan tone, liberally sprinkled with consular jargon,
turned now and then into lusty brawls in the juicy pidgin Venetian that was the lingua franca of the Mediterranean. At those
moments both interpreters tossed their genteel pretenses over-
board and came to verbal grips in Levantine style, forgetting
their rank and status, resorting to words of the earthiest kind
and to most explicit gestures and grimaces.

"Most Reverend Father, bless the humble servant of holy
Mother Church," D'Avenat would say with a deep bow, mocking
Rotta's relations with the Bosnian friars.

"As for you, my son," the Austrian would answer calmly, as
though reciting a part, "may the Jacobin devils bless you in
hell."

"You're an altar licker, admit it," D'Avenat would say.

"And wouldn't you like to lick them yourself, if the priests let
you? I can think of other things you'd lick too, only they won't
let you. They'll have nothing to do with the French. But I hear
you're opening a synagogue in a wing of the Imperial French
Consulate."

"No, we are not. Why should we? It's more amusing for us

to go to church at Dolats and watch His Excellency the Imperial-Royal Consul-General and his esteemed interpreter being altar boys to Fra Ivo."

"Why not? I can do that too."

"Yes, I know. You would do anything. But there's one thing you can't do—you can't grow any more."

"No, I can't, you're right," the hunchback said without batting an eyelid. "But I've stopped worrying about it since I got to know *your* bulk. Oh, when I think how long you're going to be when rigor mortis sets in! They'll have a job finding a coffin big enough so your feet won't stick out."

"Well, I hope to see you out first. And I'll spare no trouble or expense to get you a nice little box this size"—and D'Avenat spread his hands about a yard wide.

"Not yet, nothing doing. I don't feel a bit like dying. No chance of that as long as you're *not* my doctor."

"And a fat chance I'd ever be. Mark my words, the plague will be your doctor one of these days!"

"At least it won't charge a fee for killing me. True, it's not as efficient as you are. It lets a man live here and there, which is something you never do."

And so they went on until both broke out in grins, eyeing each other brazenly. These tête-à-têtes always took place unwitnessed and came to be a sort of respite and exercise for the two interpreters. And they wound up their conversation in French, once more polite and formal. And watching them take leave of each other with a low doffing of hats, the people of Travnik drew all sorts of conclusions about the long and friendly chat of these representatives of two great Christian powers.

With everyone else in town Rotta was always the same: insolent, dour, suspicious, matter of fact, and to the point.

Born at Trieste, Rotta was the twelfth child of a poor bootmaker, Giovanni Scarparotta, who had died an alcoholic's death. This twelfth child of his was born stunted, ugly, and with a hump; he was so sickly during the first months of his life that they kept a lighted candle over him and once even bathed him and prepared him for the funeral. But when the tiny, pale boy with the hump began to go to school, it was apparent that he was the brightest of all his family and would go further and do better than either his father or his grandfather. And while all the other brothers, big healthy boys, went to sea as sailors or learned crafts or took up those indeterminate jobs by which the

Triestinos manage to live as if they were real work, the boy hunchback went to work in the office of a shipping company.

Here the taciturn weakling, with large eyes and a sensitive mouth in a pale face, distributed mail and cut quills, and saw for the first time what the life of gentlemen was like, in spacious airy rooms, the life of well-bred folk in settled and comfortable circumstances, where voices were pitched low and the social round full of amenities, where food, clothing, and other daily needs were never in doubt but were taken for granted, where all thoughts and striving were on a level far above these, directed toward other, higher, more distant goals. The boy privately compared this life, which he was able to glimpse only in daytime on his rounds of the office, with the crowding, squalor, and poverty of his father's home, with the bickering, spite, and coarseness in his own family and among the neighbors. The comparison made him feel wretched. Now that he'd learned the existence of that other life, he could never again tolerate the abject poverty into which he had been born and in which he was supposed to spend the remainder of his life; and one night, just before dawn, after lying awake many hours with these thoughts, the boy threw off the rags in which he slept, which now filled him with unspeakable revulsion, and, kneeling on the floor, his face dissolved in tears, he swore, not knowing what or to whom, that he would either escape this life of his people or stop living altogether.

There, by his side, the horde of his brothers was fast asleep —younger and older, exhausted apprentices or unwashed, sunblackened loafers, covered with the same rags as himself. He felt no kinship or brotherly affection for them, but saw them as a pack of ugly slaves among whom he would choke, from whom he must run as soon as possible, forever, at any price.

From that day on, the boy with the hump turned his face wholly toward the better, higher life on the other side. He worked obediently and with his whole heart and soul, anticipating his master's wishes, learning, watching, listening, and strained desperately to find the key to that easier, finer life and to learn to wield it. A deep, powerful yearning to attain it and make it his own drove him forward; and from behind he was prodded, no less effectively, by an unforgiving hate of that other, hideous life in his parents' house and by his abomination of everything connected with it.

So much zeal and energy could not go unnoticed and unrewarded. The youth was gradually trained to do clerical work. He was given small assignments on the ships and with the authorities. He showed himself discreet, tireless, and possessing a flair for languages and a faultless handwriting. His superiors began to notice him. They gave him an opportunity to learn German and raised his salary. He took French lessons from a royalist refugee. The old gentleman, who was paralyzed and forced to maintain himself by tutoring, had once belonged to good and cultivated Parisian society; he instructed young Nicholas Scarparotta in a good many other things besides the languages, such as geography, history, and those other subjects that, in his words, constituted "knowledge of the world."

As soon as he had achieved this, the youth quite coolly and casually left his parents' home in the poor quarter and rented himself a modest but clean furnished room kept by a widow. It was his first decisive move toward that better world that was waiting to be conquered.

Little by little, he made himself indispensable in the company's offices, with the arriving ships, and in dealings with foreigners. He could express himself fluently and easily in five languages; he knew in detail all the procedures of the pertinent government offices throughout the Empire, and the titles of most officials. He memorized everything other people found it too much trouble to remember, but which they needed every minute of the day. And with it all he remained quiet and discreet, modest in his personal needs and demands, always ready to help, never in anyone's way.

That was how Major Kalcher, the commanding officer of Trieste, noticed him. The young hunchback had done him several favors and given him useful information about foreigners who came and went in the company's ships. And when the Major was transferred to Zemun, he asked the young man, a few months later, to come serve in the Zemun garrison command as interpreter and intelligence agent. The bootmaker's son, who had fled one kind of world and was trying to get a grip on another, saw in this call the writing of destiny and a welcome opportunity to remove himself physically from the scene of parental poverty, not many streets away from where he lived.

So the young man came to Zemun, where he soon distinguished himself by his skills and ambition. He crossed over to Belgrade on confidential errands and interviewed foreigners in the quarantine—he had lately learned Greek and Spanish as well. Here the son of the Triestine cobbler, determined to erase all trace of his origin, dropped "Scarpa" from his name and became "Rotta"; for a while he even signed himself "de Rotta." It was here too that he married a Levantine girl, daughter of an export merchant from Istanbul, who had come to visit some relatives at Zemun. Her father had been born at Istanbul, though his family originally came from Dalmatia; her mother was Greek.

The girl was pretty, quiet, plump, and brought a handsome dowry. It seemed to Rotta that the acquisition of such a wife was the final move needed to secure him a permanent foothold in the good life and that this would complete his long and tortuous climb, so full of sacrifice and privation.

Meanwhile, at this very point of his life, Rotta also began to realize that the sublime end of the road was not yet in sight, that the reward he had looked forward to was still out of reach. To this already faltering man life now revealed itself as an endless line tapering to infinity, with nothing permanent or secure about it, a spiteful recession of mirrors that opened and doubled back on themselves, stretching ever deeper and farther, to an illusory vanishing point.

He found he could not depend on his wife; she was lazy, often sick, careless with money, a problem in every respect. If Rotta had not so sharply and absolutely cut every link with the life of his childhood, he might have remembered the old Mediterranean saying which, as a boy, he had so often heard in his parents' house: *Chi vuol fare la sua rovina, prende la moglie Levantina*—"If you want to ruin your life, take a Levantine wife." The work at Zemun was neither as well defined nor as innocent as that at Trieste. He was given risky and unpleasant missions that taxed his nerves and consumed not only his days but nights as well, depriving him of sleep. The motley, coarse, and crafty multitude that swarmed over this important cross-road from Belgrade to Zemun, from Zemun to Belgrade, up and down the Danube, was baffling, unreliable, and very hard to deal with. There were sudden enmities, unexpected clashes, and underhanded vendettas. To survive, Rotta had to use the same methods. Little by little, his tone of voice took on the brittle edge of that dry insolence which is common to interpreters and kavasses in the Near East, and which is no more than an outward echo of inner desolation, of a lost faith in men, of the shedding of all illusions.

When their baby girl died a few months after birth, a mood of sullen recrimination filled the marriage. Quarrels sprang up between them which in no time at all exploded into noisy squabbling full of ugliness and brutality, not much better than the brawls he remembered from his childhood. In the end his wife left him, without regrets or a public scandal, and returned to Istanbul, which, they both agreed, she never should have left in the first place.

About that time it dawned on Rotta that if a man wanted to exchange the world he was born in for that other one he had glimpsed by chance and was drawn to with all his heart, the vows of a susceptible hunchback youngster, crying over his poverty in the depths of night, were not enough—and neither were twenty years of hard dogged work and single-minded service. What was even worse, the "new" world did not exist as a separate, clear-cut, stable entity which a man could grasp and make his own once and for all, as it had seemed to him in those first years; and likewise the "old" world of squalor and meanness that he had tried to escape by such prodigious effort was not nearly so easy or simple to shake off as he had shaken off his brothers and sisters and the rags of his parents' home; it accompanied a man, invisibly and fatefully through all his apparent changes and successes.

Although still in his thirties, Rotta began to feel cheated and tired before his time, like a man who had scattered his strength lavishly and had not got his just reward. Abstract reasoning was not in his line, yet he could not contemplate his life without feeling lonely and disheartened. Unable to face these thoughts, or himself for that matter, he threw himself entirely into the rough and turbid life of the frontier, where men coarsen and age long before they ought to. He became greedy and mercenary, threw his official weight about, was touchy to an extreme, quick to take offense, obtrusive, rude, superstitious, and inwardly afraid. His conceit struck people as out of all proportion, for he was proud not only of what he had achieved but also of the unseen efforts and human cost that had gone into the achievement. Yet even this vanity was not something he could depend on, since, in the nature of things, even the satisfaction derived from foibles and weakness ebbs away eventually. Having lost confidence in the purpose of further exertions, Rotta let himself drift downstream and confined his ambitions to leading a life without sickness and poverty, with a minimum of work and headaches, with as much gain, stability, and modest pleasure as was possible to get.

Like D'Avenat, the interpreter at the French Consulate, he learned to live with the Moslems, and got used to their customs and ways and to that barely human kind of life which was spent in endless companionship and also endless jealousy, in pecking and intrigue among themselves, against the common folk of all faiths, against strangers from any quarter.

Prematurely worn, he was now a gray-haired, sullen, self-centered hypochondriac, full of little fads and official pedantries. He suffered from imaginary illnesses, was afraid of spells and bad omens, hated the Church and everything connected with it. He felt lonely and thought with loathing about his wife and their life together, yet shivered at the mere thought of the filth and noisy penury he had left behind him in Trieste; he couldn't even bear to hear the name of his family mentioned. He saved passionately and became a compulsive hoarder, believing that this would make up, at least in part, for what was warped and amiss in his life, and that money was the only thing left which might, if only up to a certain point, lift up, protect, and save a man.

He was fond of rich food and good drink but was afraid of being poisoned; and besides being terrified of the expense, he feared that drink would make him talk and betray himself. The fear of poisoning was groundless, but it preyed on him very strongly; he made every effort to cure himself of the mania, which scared him as much as, if not more, than the actual possibility of poisoning.

In his younger days he had laid much store by dress and had got much pleasure out of astonishing people with the starched whiteness of his shirt and ruffles, with the lace on his chest and cuffs, with the color and number of his silk handkerchiefs, and the immaculate gloss of his shoes. He was now much less particular. The passion for thrift left little room for anything else.

The wealth he had gathered with so much effort and was watching over so jealously became merely a buffer against penury in his own mind. It was true, as the gossip had it, that he had once been a young fop with a hundred and one shirts and thirty pairs of shoes—his chests were still full of the stuff. And it was also true that his savings were in solid gold. But what good were these things when he was never for a moment free of the thought that a shirt slowly but surely frays at the hem, that shoes wear out at the heel, and soles grow paper-thin, that there was no safe place anywhere to hide the money? What was the use of it all? What was the good of twenty years of Spartan work and self-denial when neither money nor position nor clothes could turn one's fate around ("That bitch Fate," Rotta would tell himself in his bitter nightly monologues), when, lo and behold, everything kept right on splitting, fraying, wearing out; when through the holes and seam cracks of his footwear there kept staring at him, despite all affluence, visible to him alone, that embarrassing poverty which he thought he had left far behind him at Trieste, far away and forever?

His pathetic eagerness to protect and preserve his money was like a twin sister to his pathetic childhood eagerness for a farthing he never possessed; his present agony of thrift and stinginess was like the old agony of want and hardship. What good was it all? What was the use, when after so much pushing, futile running, and social climbing a man was back at the starting point; when the same meanness and coarseness crept back into his thoughts, though by another way, and the same vulgarity and corruption into his words and behavior; when, in order to keep what had been won, a man had to exert as much unpalatable effort as though he were still struggling with poverty? In short: what was the use of having possessions and becoming somebody when a man couldn't free himself of his fear of poverty, of his mean thoughts, of his rudeness of speech or shaky society manners, when a person's stark and grim beginning dogged his every footstep, while this fairer, better, quieter life kept fading away like an optical illusion?

And realizing that it all was in vain, that one's origins and early years were not to be escaped, Rotta threw his head back even more defiantly, moved around more haughtily, eyed the people around him with more contempt, saved more intensely, became a greater than ever stickler for order in his office, sterner and more demanding toward his juniors and all those who depended on him.

Under him, there were two subordinate officials in the Austrian Consulate-General.

The chancery clerk, Franz Wagner, was the son of a German immigrant from Slavonski Brod; he was light-haired and slight, obliging, a fiend for work, and gifted with a perfect handwriting. A small unassuming man, who dissolved in humility at a glance from his superiors, he yet harbored, just below the surface, a large quantity of that soft and controlled but bitter and deadly clerical spite which later, when he had risen in his career, he would vent on the head of some unfortunate junior, who was now perhaps still going to school. This Wagner was a major fly in Rotta's ointment. The two of them were always at cross purposes, like a pair of born enemies.

The bookkeeper, Peter Markovats, was from Slavonia. He was a tall noncommissioned officer, good-looking, with pink cheeks and black, faultlessly pointed mustaches; trim and carefully groomed, utterly absorbed in his good looks, content with himself, and unmoved by any other consideration.

It was no longer autumn, but the winter had not yet begun. It was the season, or rather unseason, which was neither autumn nor winter but worse than either, that freak of the year which can last days, sometimes weeks—days which are as long as weeks, weeks that seem longer than months. It meant rain and mud and snow; snow that turned to rain while still in the air, rain that became mud as soon as it hit the ground. At dawn, from behind the patch of clouds, a pale and listless sun would paint the east a wan rose; at the end of a gray day it would reappear again in the west as a sickly yellow glow, just before the grayness passed into the pitch-black of night. During the day, as at nighttime, the damp breathing of the sky and the soil mingled together in a smoke-thin drizzle that seeped through the town and pervaded everything; in the silent, inexorable alembic of the damp, solid things lost their shape and color, animals changed their temper, men thought and acted moodily.

The wind, soughing along the narrow valley twice a day, merely shifted the damp around and, by wafting sleet and a smell of wet woods as it went, brought in new waves of humidity; so the pools of dampness only nudged and overlapped one another and the raw, bone-chilling mountain mist merely replaced the stale, moldering kind in the town. The sod on both sides of the valley turned to bog, water welled out of the turf, rivulets gurgled downhill. Thin little streams, which till now had been invisible, swelled into torrents and roared tumbling down the slopes until, like a peasant crazed with drink, they bounded into the bazaar. And through the middle of the town the Lashva foamed and sang, high, silted, not to be recognized. There was no place one could hide from the din and clamor of all that water, or protect oneself from its cold sodden breath, for it reached into the inmost room and into every last bed; a living body could stave it off only with its own warmth. Even stone walls broke out in a cold sweat, wood became dank and slivery. Before this deadly, fetid onslaught everything shrank back into itself and tried to resist it as best it could; animal huddled to animal, seed lay quietly in the earth, trees dripped and grew numb with cold, bating their breath in the pith and down among the warm roots.

The local people, hardened and accustomed to it, bore it all quietly. They fed and kept themselves warm, each according to his ability, habits, and experience, the resources of his position and status in the community. The well-to-do did not leave their houses unless it was absolutely necessary, but slept and spent their days in heated rooms, warming their hands on the green tiles of earthenware ovens and waiting—waiting with a patience that comfortably outlasted even the longest winter and the foulest weather by at least one day. Not one of them feared that he would miss something or that someone else might take advantage of him or steal a march on him, since all of them vegetated alike, at the same pace and in the same conditions. Everything they needed was close at hand, under lock and key, in the cellar, in the attic, in the grain room, or in the larder, for they knew their winter and had not been caught unprepared.

With the poor it was the other way around. Days of this kind drove them out of the house, for they had not put in any winter stores. Even the man who in the summer was haughtily self-sufficient now had to go out and earn, borrow, or beg, to scrape something together and take it home. With their heads bowed, their muscles cramped, and their skin goosefleshy from cold, the poor wandered the streets for food and fuel; they covered their heads and backs with old burlap, folded at the top to make a cowl, and they wrapped, swaddled, and muffled themselves in odd rags, bundling their feet in leather, tatters, and even wood bark; they slunk under the house eaves and jutting balconies, walked gingerly around water puddles, jumped from stone to stone over the little runnels and shook the water off their feet like cats; they breathed into their chilblained hands or tried to warm them in their own crotch, chattering and moaning from cold. They worked, did errands, or begged, and the thought of food and fuel that these jobs might provide gave them the strength to endure every hazard.

In this way the people of Travnik got through the grim winters, which had been part of their life from birth.

But it was another thing for the foreigners whom chance had stranded in this narrow valley, which at this time of year was gloomy and full of damp and drafts, like a passage in a dungeon.

At the Residency, which was normally as carefree and bustling as a cavalry barracks, the damp brought in a sense of marooned isolation, like a disease. The Vizier's Mamelukes, for whom this was the first cold winter in their lives, shivered, grew sallow and listless, looking about them with the rueful and sickly eyes of tropical animals transported to a northern country. Many of them lay on their cots all day long, their heads wrapped in a coarse blanket, coughing and ill with longing for their distant and warm native land.

And even the animals which the Vizier had brought with him to Travnik, the Angora cats, the macaws, and the monkeys, stopped moving and screeching and amusing their master; they moped around and sat silent and waited huddling in a corner, for the sun to warm and cheer them.

The Secretary and the other worthies kept to their quarters, as if there were a flood outside. Their rooms had large earthenware ovens which were stoked from the corridor, and the servants now crammed them high with big logs of elmwood, which developed great heat and kept sizzling all through the night, so that in the morning fresh fires were built on the still glowing cinders of the night before. In these apartments, which were not allowed to cool off, it was pleasant, at daybreak, to hear the servants open the stove outside, rake out the ashes and pile in fresh wood, log after log. But even here, by the time the early dusk fell, a mood of pining spread and took hold. Men sought to throw it off by inventing games and diversions, by visiting one another, by conversation.

The Vizier himself began to lose his natural good humor and initiative. Several times a day he would come down to the twilit divan on the ground floor, where the walls were thick and the windows few and small, as the airier and brighter upper divan had to be abandoned in the battle against cold and was neither heated nor opened during the winter. Here he would call in a few senior intimates and try to kill time in conversation. He talked at great length about unimportant things in order to stifle his memories of Egypt, his thoughts of the future, and his yearning for the sea which troubled him even in his sleep. A dozen times a day he would remark scornfully to one or another of his people: "It's a fine country, my friend. A noble country! What sin have you and I committed to deserve it!"

And they would echo him with some coarse and unkind comment on the land and the climate. "Dog's own country!" the Secretary might say. "Enough to make the bears weep," would be the plaint of Yunuz Beg, the keeper of the arsenal and a countryman of the Vizier's. "I can see now they've sent us here to die,"—this from Ibrahim Hodja, a personal friend of the Vizier's who would lace his face in wrinkles as if he were really about to give up his ghost.

Vying with each other in their grousing, they managed to relieve at least some of their common tedium. And through all these conversations one could hear the babble of water and the hissing of rain, borne on a sea of damp that had been lapping at the Residency for days, seeping through every chink and crack.

When they were joined by Suleiman Pasha Skoplyak, the Vizier's Deputy, who made it a point to ride through the town several times a day, come rain or snow, they broke off their conversation and stared at him as if he were a freak.

In talking to his Deputy, a tough, unprepossessing Bosnian, the Vizier assumed an even and circumspect tone, but in the end couldn't help asking him in a half-joking manner: "In God's name, man, does this town often go through this kind of calamity?"

Suleiman Pasha answered gravely, in his accented Turkish: "It is not a calamity, Pasha, praise be to Allah. Winter has come as it should. When it is wet at the beginning and dry toward the end, we can count on having a good year ahead of us. Wait till the snow falls and the great frost takes over and the sun comes out. Then it'll be hard and crunchy underfoot, your eyes will be dazzled by the shimmer. It's a sweet and beautiful thing, as God made it and as it ought to be."

But the Vizier only shuddered at these new marvels, which his Deputy promised with so much enthusiasm as he rubbed his cracked, chilblained hands and dried his wet gaiters on the oven.

"Ugh, don't say that, my friend. Spare us a little if you can," the Vizier said in mock horror.

"But it's not like that at all. It's God's gift, truly it is. What use is a winter that's no winter?" The Deputy gravely stuck to his guns, impervious to the sly humor of these Osmanlis and quite unaware of their susceptibility to cold. He sat upright, cold and hard, among these shivering and chafing foreigners, who watched him with uncomfortable curiosity, almost as if he were responsible for the grim schedule of weather and yearly seasons.

And when the Deputy got up, wrapped in his ample red cloak, and left them to go riding through the icy rain along the soaking roads to his own quarters, they exchanged despairing and horrified looks; and as soon as the door closed behind him, they resumed their wisecracks and profanities about the Bosnians and Bosnia and the skies above it, until their abuse and cruel sarcasm brought some kind of comfort.

In the French Consulate too, life grew quieter and more secluded. Experiencing her first Travnik winter, Mme Daville tried to turn everything to good advantage; she made mental notes for the future and found a remedy and help for every problem. Wrapped in a gray cashmere shawl, brisk and active, she went around the huge Turkish house all day long, ordering and supervising work, finding it hard to communicate with the servants on account of the language and the lack of skill among the local domestic help, yet always managing to impose her will in the end and achieving more or less what she wanted. It was in this kind of weather that the defects and shortcomings of the house really came to light. The roof began to leak, the floorboards gave, the windows would not shut properly, the plaster crumbled, the stoves smoked. However, Mme Daville succeeded eventually in having it all repaired, patched, and put in order. Her chapped, perpetually red hands were now blue from cold but didn't pause a moment in their battle with waste, damage, and disorder.

On the ground floor, which was light and warm even if a little damp, Daville and his young Chancellor sat in the office. They talked about the war in Spain and the French authorities in Dalmatia, about the couriers who either failed to show up or came at the wrong time, about the Ministry which ignored their requests and petitions; but, most frequently of all, they talked about the despicable weather and about Bosnia and the Bosnians. They talked in low voices, reflectively, as people do when they are waiting for the servants to bring in the candles or call them to dinner, until, imperceptibly, the talk veered to general questions and took on an edge of dispute and disagreement.

It was the hour of the evening when the candles are not yet lighted and it is already too dark to read. Desfosses had just come back from a ride; for even in weather like this he seldom missed an opportunity to gad about the countryside at least once a day. His face was still flushed from the wind and rain, his short hair tousled and matted. Daville could barely conceal his displeasure with these outings which he regarded as dangerous to health and prejudicial to the dignity of the Consulate. Altogether he was irritated by this ambulatory and enterprising young man, by his lively curiosity and keen mind; while Desfosses, impervious to the harping undertone in the older man's voice and his kind of sensibility, kept on talking warmly about his discoveries and experiences during his rides through Travnik and its environs.

"Ah," Daville said with an impatient flip of his hand, "this Travnik and everything for a hundred miles around is nothing but a desert of mud populated by two kinds of poor devils, torturers and tortured, and it is our bad luck to have to live among them."

Staunchly Desfosses tried to prove to him that although the country was shut off from the world and seemed numb on the surface, it was far from being an out and out wilderness—it was, on the contrary, a place of variety, eloquent in its own way, and interesting in every respect. The people, it was true, were divided by their faiths, superstition-ridden, groaning under just about the worst government in the world, and for that reason unhappy and backward in many ways; but at the same time their native intelligence was remarkable, they had interesting qualities of character and some fascinating customs; at all events, a closer look at the causes of their backwardness and misery was eminently worthwhile. The fact that Messrs. Daville, von Mitterer, and Desfosses, being foreigners, found life in Bosnia irksome and unpleasant, was neither here nor there. The worth and importance of a country were not to be measured by how the consul of a foreign state happened to feel in it.

"Quite the contrary," said the young man. "I think there are few parts of the world *less* desolate and uninteresting. You only have to dig down one foot into the ground to find the tombs and relics of bygone ages. Every meadow here is a cemetery, and many times over at that. It's just one necropolis on top of another, an exact record of the birth and death of successive generations of various native races down the centuries, epoch after epoch, wave after wave. And burial mounds are proof of life, not wilderness. . . ."

"Oh well," shrugged the Consul, as if warding off a buzzing fly. The young man's predilection for dramatic phrases was something he could not get used to.

"And not only tombs, not only tombs! This afternoon, as I was riding out to Kalibunar, I came to a place where the rain had washed away a piece of the road. Down to a depth of about eight feet you could see as in a geological cross-section, layer upon layer of the earlier roads that used to traverse this very same valley. At the bottom there were heavy flagstones, remains of the old Roman road. Three feet above it was the cobbled crust of the medieval highway, and on top of that the gravel embankment of the present Turkish roadway, the one we use nowadays. So in this accidental profile I could read two thousand years of human history and three separate epochs that had buried each other. There you are!"

"Yes, yes, if you choose to look at things from that point of view," said Daville, merely in order to say something, for he was less interested in the words of the young man than in his cold, glittery brown eyes; as if he wanted to determine the secret of those eyes, the reason they looked at the world around them in that particular way.

Desfosses then told him about the remnant of neolithic settlements on the road to the village of Zabilye, where, before the rains set in, he had picked up some flint axe-heads and crude saws which might well have lain in the clay for tens of thousands of years. He had come across them in the field of a certain Karahodjich, a sullen and pigheaded old man, who wouldn't hear a word of anyone's digging or exploring anything on his land but waited angrily until the foreigner and his groom got out of his field and rode off in the direction of Travnik.

And on the way back to town, the groom had told Desfosses the story of the Karahodjich clan.

Some two centuries or more before, during a period of incessant wars, they had emigrated from these parts and settled down in Slavonia, in the vicinity of Pozhega, where they had acquired large tracts of land. A hundred and twenty years later, when the Turks were forced to abandon Slavonia, they too had to leave their rich estate near Pozhega and fall back on their smaller and poorer lands at Zabilye. Their family still kept a cauldron, or copper kettle, which they had taken with them as a reminder of the lost estate and lost lordship when, bitter and humiliated, and led by their ancestor Karahodja, they came back to Bosnia. On this cauldron, Karahodja had sworn them to a pledge: that they would never fail to answer a single war call against the Austrians and that each of them would do everything in his power to get back the lordship they had lost in Slavonia. And if, by some misfortune or God's design, the "Schwabes" dared to cross the river Sava, he swore them on oath to defend those fallow fields at Zabilye as long as they could, and, when they couldn't any more, to withdraw step by step, even if it meant falling back through the entire length of the Turkish realm, to the outermost frontiers of the Empire, the uncharted regions of China and Cathay.

As he was telling this to the young man, the groom showed him, in a plum orchard above the road, a small Turkish cemetery in which two slabs of white stone stood out. Those were the graves of the old Karahodja and his son, the grandfather and father of the old man who was still there by the picket fence, bristling angrily, sputtering something through his bared teeth, his eyes still flashing.

"So you see," Desfosses said, gazing at the dusk beyond the misted window, "I don't know which was more fascinating to me, those Stone Age relics dating back to Lord knows how many thousands of years before Christ, or that old man standing guard over the legacy of his ancestors, not allowing anyone to lay a finger on his field."

"Yes, I see, I see," Daville said absently and mechanically, amazed only at the scope of the young man's imagination.

Talking and pacing like this about the room, the two men stopped by the window.

Outside, the gelid twilight was closing in, but as yet no lights were burning anywhere. Only down at the bottom of the valley, beside the river itself, the glow from Abdullah Pasha's tomb trembled faintly. It was the taper that burned day and night above the Pasha's tomb; its weak flame could always be seen from the Consulate's windows, even before the other town lights were put on, or after they had been put out.

Standing here by the window, waiting for the darkness to grow deep and complete, the Consul and the young man had often talked about this "eternal light" and the Pasha whose taper they had come to accept as something familiar and permanent.

Desfosses knew its history as well.

This Abdullah Pasha had been a native of this country. He became rich and famous while still a young man. As soldier and governor, he saw a good deal of the world, but when they made him Vizier in Travnik, he died unexpectedly, still in his prime, and they buried him there. (He died, it was said, of poison.) Among the people, he left a memory of a mild and just rule. As one of the Travnik chroniclers described it, "During Abdullah Pasha's reign the poor knew no evil." Shortly before his death, though, he had willed his property to the imams of Travnik and to other religious institutions. He also left a considerable sum of money for the building of this fine mausoleum of good stone, while the income from his houses and tenant holdings was to ensure that a massive taper burned beside his tomb day and night. His vault was permanently draped with a green pall that bore the embroidered inscription in Arabic: "May the All-Highest light his tomb!" The sentence was composed by the learned imams, as an expression of gratitude to their benefactor.

Desfosses had managed to locate the testament of this Vizier and regarded it as an interesting document, typical of the people and circumstances. And now he was complaining that they wouldn't allow him to inspect it and copy it.

The conversation trailed off. In the short silence that followed, the deepening night outside gave voice to a drawn-out, indistinct song that was like a wail from some watery depth. It was a man's voice; he sang as he walked, then paused, then took up the song again after a few steps. As he went away, his voice trailed away little by little.

"Oh, that music! Heavens, that music!" moaned the Consul, whom Bosnian singing drove to distraction. With some impatience he rang the bell and ordered the candles to be brought in.

The man he had apostrophized was Musa the Singer, who passed down the steep alley every night. He lived in one of a cluster of houses hidden in the precipitous gardens on the hill above the Consulate.

Desfosses, who had informed himself about everything, also

knew the story of that drunkard and good-for-nothing who went home every night along this same alley, lurching and wailing snatches of his hoarse, drawn-out melody.

At one time, there had lived in Travnik an old man by the name of Krdzaliya. He was of humble origins and low reputation but very wealthy. He traded in arms—a business that paid very well, since those who needed arms didn't ask the price and paid anything that was asked, so long as they got their guns at the right time and place. He had two sons. The older worked with his father, while the younger, Musa, was sent to school at Sarajevo. Then, suddenly and unexpectedly, old Krdzaliya died; he went to bed hale and hearty and in the morning they found him dead. Musa dropped out of school and came back to Travnik. When they divided the property, it came to light that the old man had left a surprisingly small amount of ready money. All sorts of rumors began to circulate about the death of old Krdzaliya. Nobody would believe—and indeed it was hard to believe—that the old man had had no cash, and many people began to look with suspicion on the older brother and to advise Musa to go to court and demand his rights. Moreover, as they were dividing the little property that was left, the older brother tried to cheat and shortchange the younger. This older brother was tall and handsome, but one of those cold people whose eyes remain dark even when he is smiling. While the settlement was still in progress and Musa was vacillating between his natural disdain for money and the advice of the bazaar, things took an even worse and graver turn.

Both brothers fell in love with the same girl, a girl from Vilich. Both asked her hand in marriage. She was given to the older one. Then Musa disappeared from Travnik. There was no further talk of the dubious settlement between the brothers or of Krdzaliya's death. The older brother minded his business and increased what he had. Two years later Musa came back, changed, bearded, sallow, haggard, with the bloodshot, wandering eyes of a man who sleeps little and loves to drink. From that time onward, he lived on his piece of property, which was by no means small but was badly managed and neglected. And so with the years the handsome youngster and rich man's son, who had once had a beautiful voice and perfect pitch, turned into a haggard wretch who lived by his singing and only for drink, a silent, harmless tippler, whom children turned to look at. Only his famous voice remained unchanged for a long time.

But now even this voice was cracking as his health gave out and his inheritance melted away.

A servant brought in the lighted candelabra. Shadows played around the room briefly, then steadied. The windows suddenly filmed over with darkness. The voice of the drunken singer died away completely, as did the barking dog's that had answered him. Once again silence closed over everything. The Consul and the young man waited, each thinking his own thoughts, each privately wishing he could be far away from this room and have someone else to talk to.

Again it was Desfosses who broke the silence. He spoke about Musa the Singer and people of his kind. Daville interrupted him, saying that this noisy, brandy-swilling neighbor of his was not an exception but rather a true specimen of a society that was characterized mainly by brandy, idleness, and crudity of every kind. Desfosses denied this. There were such men in all communities, he maintained, and they performed a certain salutary function. People looked upon them with fear and regret but also with a kind of religious respect, much as the old Greeks revered *enlysion,* a spot that had been struck by lightning. And far from being typical of a community, they were considered to be exceptions, the lost ones. The existence of these outcasts and lone wolves, abandoned to their galloping ruin, served only to show how firm were the bonds and how implacably strict the laws of society, religion, and family in a patriarchal order.

And that was true, Desfosses went on, both of the Turks and of the rayah of all faiths. In such communities everything was interconnected, closely dovetailed, and all elements mutually supported and controlled one another. Each individual kept an eye on the community, and the community kept an eye on him. One household observed another, one street watched over the other, because everyone was responsible for everyone else, and all of them for everything; each man's destiny was bound up not only with the members of his own household and his relatives but also with his neighbors, coreligionists, and fellow citizens. In this lay the strength and also the slavery of these people. The life of a single cell was possible only in such a tissue, and the existence of the whole system only under such covenants. He who left the ranks and followed his own head and his own instincts marked himself as a suicide and came to grief sooner or later, beyond help and recall. Such was the law of these communities, laid down long before in the Old Testament. It was also the law of the world of antiquity. Marcus Aurelius had said somewhere: "No different from an outlaw is the man who shirks the obligations of a social order." And that was the law against which Musa had sinned, and the violated law and the injured community were avenging themselves and punishing him.

Once more Daville watched rather than listened to the young man, and he thought: "Well, tonight he seems bent on explaining and justifying all the horrors and ugliness of this country. Evidently he's now reached this chapter in his opus on Bosnia and feels compelled to lecture me—or anyone else for that matter. Perhaps all this just blew into his head right now. There now, this is youth, I suppose, this thing I see in front of me. Glibness, self-confidence, trenchant exposition, and the heady stuff of conviction. There's youth for you." Interrupting his reverie and the young man's discourse, Daville said: "My dear friend, I hope that we shall read all this in your book, but now let us see what happened to dinner."

At the table, the talk was confined to everyday things and happenings, and Mme Daville joined in with precise and factual comments. They talked mostly of cooking, which brought up memories of food and wine in various parts of France and comparisons with the Turkish style of diet; they regretted the lack of French vegetables, French wines and condiments. A few minutes after eight Mme Daville gave a short, muffled yawn. It was the sign that the meal was over, and shortly afterwards she withdrew and went to the children's room. In another half hour the Consul and Desfosses said good night to each other. With that the day was ended. The nocturnal side of Travnik life was beginning.

Madame Daville sat by the bed of her youngest child and knitted, nimbly and with concentration, in silence, with the intent air of an ant. It was the way she had eaten her dinner, and done all her other chores throughout the day.

The Consul was back in his study, sitting at his small writing table. In front of him was the manuscript of his epic on Alexander the Great. He had started this work long before and had been at it for years; progress was slow and sporadic, but he thought about it every day, often several times a day, against the background of everything he saw, heard, and went through. As mentioned before, this epic had become for him a kind of second reality, a better and more pliable one which he controlled at will, and which offered no trouble or opposition; in it he found inspired solutions for everything that was unresolved and unsolvable in himself and around him; in it, too, he sought consolation for everything that oppressed him and compensation for all the things which real life withheld or forbade him. Several times a day Daville took refuge in his "paper reality" and propped himself comfortably on some idea in the epic, like a lame man on his crutch. And conversely, as he listened to news of some new development in the war, or watched some incident or worked on some piece of business or other, he would often mentally transfer it to his epic. And by the simple expedient of pushing these things a few thousand years back in time, he would rob them of their bitterness and sting, so that, on the surface at least, they appeared easier and more bearable. This did not, of course, make reality any easier or advance the poem toward becoming a true work of art. But a good number of people have to lean on one kind of illusion or another, often stranger and more obscure than a work of poetry, with its clearcut subject, its rigid meter, and its precise rhyme.

This evening too, Daville set before him the fat manuscript in its green covers, like a man going through a motion that has become a habit. But ever since he had come to Bosnia and found himself enmeshed in consular dealings with the Turks, these evening hours had grown less and less productive, less and less satisfying. Images would not form, verses balked at the mold and emerged from it incomplete, rhymes would not spark one another, as they once had with a bright fire, but remained dangling, like some one-legged freak. Very often the green ribbons of the folder were not even untied and the manuscript served as a pad for little slips of paper on which the Consul jotted down his work program for the next day or something he'd forgotten to do during the day.

In those moments after dinner, all that had been said or done during that day rose up in his mind again and, instead of rest and distraction, brought on fresh exertions, reopening the worries that had already been worried over to excess. The letters that had gone out to Split, Istanbul, or Paris bobbed up in their entirety before his eyes; and all at once he could see, with remorseless clarity, everything that he had omitted to say or had said clumsily and redundantly. Blood rushed to his head from excitement and dissatisfaction with himself. The talks he had

had with people that day echoed in his ears again, down to the minutest detail, and not only the serious and important talks bearing on the business of service but also the trivial and niggling ones. He saw, clear as day, the person he had talked to, heard every undertone in his words; he saw himself too, and heard the poverty of his own words loud and clear, and also the enormous importance of the things which, for some baffling reason, he had failed to say. And there, on a sudden, appeared the cogent and forceful sentences which he ought to have spoken in place of the fey and bloodless words and answers he had in fact mouthed. So now he would rehearse them in solitude, knowing well that it was all in vain and too late.

A poem could not take wing in such a state of mind. Sleep tarried in the wake of such thoughts, and dreams became nightmares, even if he managed to doze off.

Tonight it was the buzzing of Desfosses's voice that filled the Consul's ears, talking as he did just before dinner. Suddenly he saw quite clearly how much youthful rant there was in those tales of threefold road layers from different centuries, of neolithic tools, of Karahodja and Musa the Singer, of the family and social order in Bosnia. Yet to all those flights of fancy of the young man, which, it seemed to him, would not stand up to the slightest touch of criticism, he had answered, like one paralyzed and spellbound, with a lame: "Yes, I see, I see, but . . ." What the devil did he see? he now asked himself. He felt ludicrous and humiliated, and at the same time cross with himself, for paying these meaningless rambles an attention they didn't deserve. When all was said and done, what sort of an important talk was it? With whom had he talked? Not with the Vizier or von Mitterer, but with a brash tenderfoot! A mere chitchat to pass the time! Still, the thought kept pecking at him, it would not be fobbed off. And just as it began to seem as if he might finally push it from his mind, he would suddenly jump up from the table and wheel around in the middle of the room, addressing himself with an outstretched hand: "I should've replied at once to his half-baked lecture with, 'The truth of the matter is as follows,' and put the young man in his place. Even on trifles, one ought to express one's opinion freely and fully, and then fire it away in the people's faces—let *them* worry about it afterwards! One should not bottle it up inside and have to wrestle with it later, as with a vampire." Yes, that's what he should've done but didn't; and he would probably not do it tomorrow or the day after or ever, not in his prattling encounters with the greenhorn or, for that matter, in his conversations with people of substance, for this kind of blazing revelation always hit him in the evening, after food and before going to bed, when it was too late, when the ordinary words of every day loomed as enormous and indestructible apparitions.

Brooding like this, Daville came back once more to his small desk by the curtained window; and still his thoughts followed him. In vain he tried to shake them off; he was quite unable to turn his attention to anything else. "Even that beastly singing is a point of interest to him, and he's quite willing to defend it," the Consul groaned to himself.

Aching to pursue his morbid hindsight and square his accounts with the young man, the Consul began to scribble hurriedly on the piece of white paper that should have been filled with a string of verses on the exploits of Alexander the Great. "I have listened to these people sing," he wrote without a pause, "and found that their songs too show the same morbid, barbarian frenzy which is to be found in every other activity of their minds and bodies. I have read somewhere in a travel account of a Frenchman who visited these parts and heard these natives more than a hundred years ago, how their singing is more akin to the howling of dogs than to human song. Whether the people have since changed for the worse, or whether the good old Frenchman never really got to know the country properly, I can't help feeling that the baying of a dog is much less sinister, certainly less savage, than the vocalizing of these natives when they are in a state of plum-brandy transport or simply seized by their furies. I have noticed how they roll their eyes whilst singing, and gnash their teeth and pummel the wall with their fists, so that it is hard to tell whether they are unhinged by too much brandy or simply venting a deep-seated primeval urge to yowl, wallow in self-misery, and flail about them blindly. And I have come to the conclusion that none of it has any connection either with music or singing, as this is understood by other peoples, but happens simply to be one of the ways in which they express their hidden passions and evil lusts, which otherwise, for all their wantonness, in the nature of things, they would not be able to articulate. I have also discussed this with the Austrian Consul-General. His soldierly indifference notwithstanding, he too has been horrified by this shrieking and ululation one hears nightly in the gardens and alleys and from the inns in the daytime. *Das ist ein Urjammer,* he said—and he translated it roughly as 'a dirgelike atavistic cry from the bottom of a primeval soul.' However, I can't help thinking that von Mitterer, as usual, errs in overrating these people. It is quite simply the frenzy of a wild race that has lost its innocence."

The narrow slip of paper was covered with writing. The last word, in fact, barely fitted into the bottom corner of the page. The zest of writing and the spontaneous ease with which words and analogies had come to his fingertips, had warmed him up, so that he felt something not unlike relief. Tired out, careworn, overburdened with duties which that evening seemed to him beyond his strength, with only his indigestion and insomnia to keep him company, he was sitting motionless and brooding over his manuscript when Mme Daville knocked on the door.

She was ready for bed. Under the white sleeping bonnet her face looked even smaller and more pointed. A moment before, she had made the sign of the cross over the sleeping children, tucked the blankets around them firmly, and had then knelt down and said the traditional evening prayer, asking God for a peaceful rest that night so that tomorrow she might get up alive and healthy "as I surely believe that I shall rise from the grave on the Day of Judgment." Now, with candle in hand, she put her head through the half-open door. "Enough for today, Jean. It's time to sleep."

Daville smiled and waved his hand to reassure her, then sent her off to bed. He remained alone with his papers until his eyes gave out and the written lines began to swim, until, at last, everything flowed together and became a dark simulacrum of the reality which by day seemed clear and understandable.

Then he rose from the desk, went up to the window, and, shoving the heavy drapes aside, looked out into the turbid darkness to see if the lights at the Residency or at the Austrian Consulate were still on, the last traces of that daylight reality. Instead, the misted windowpane confronted him with a reflection of his own lighted study and a blurred contour of his own face.

If anyone out there in the darkness, glancing up through the fog and the whispering curtain of rain, had looked up toward the French Consulate and seen that crack of light, he would never have guessed the morose content of this vigil of the sober, grave Consul who by day refused to waste a single minute on anything that was not factual, useful, or pertinent to his job.

.   .   .

The Consul was not the only one awake in that large house. Directly above his room on the first floor, three windows, curtained with Bosnian muslin, were alight. Here Desfosses sat over his own papers. His was another kind of vigil, inspired by reasons all its own; but he too was passing his night in a way he had not bargained for, one that was neither congenial nor pleasant. The young man was not fretting over what he'd said that day; on the contrary, five minutes after he had finished talking to the Consul, their conversation had dropped clear out of his mind. He was not feeling weary, or longing for peace, or worrying about the next day. But he was restless and choking with the unsatisfied desires of his youth.

On nights like these he was haunted by memories of women; and not just memories, but real women whose flashing smiles and white flesh would shatter the silence and the darkness like a cry and fill his spacious room. And he would remember too the great schemes, the bold and youthful schemes, with which he had set out from Paris and which were to take him far beyond this little provincial town in which he was now mired; he would see himself in some plush embassy or in Parisian society, in the kinds of places where one ought to be, cutting the sort of figure a man ought to cut.

That was how, night after night, his imagination teased his ambitions and his senses, only to betray and abandon him to the deathly Bosnian silence; and now the breath of this silence inflamed and tortured him. By day he could smother and elude it in work, in walks, and in conversation, but at night that was impossible except by struggle and effort, and these were becoming harder and harder, because the silence muffled, blotted, snuffed out, and overwhelmed even the little seeming life the town had; it swamped, engulfed, and saturated everything living and dead.

From the day he had left Split and had turned, on the heights above Klis, to have a last look at the gently rolling slopes down below and at the azure sea in the distance, he had not stopped feeling the clammy touch of this silence, or struggling with it.

He found it in everything around him: in the architecture of the house, which turned its true face to the courtyard and a mute, windowless back wall to the street; in the bearing of men and women; in their looks, which were eloquent because their lips were sealed. And even in their speech—when at last they condescended to speak—he got more sense from the pregnant pauses than from the words themselves. Both his ear and mind made him aware of how silence crept in between the words of their sentences, and between the letters of every word, like the ominous seeping of water through the bottom of a boat. He listened to their vowel sounds, so colorless and indistinct that the speech of little boys and girls sounded like helpless cooing that died away in silence. And even their singing, which sometimes rose up from the street or a courtyard, was no more than a long wail honeycombed with silence from the first bar to the last, so that the muted pauses were indeed an integral and most eloquent aspect of the song. And even the part of life that basked in the sun of daytime and could not be silenced or hidden away —a brief glimmer of physical beauty or a fleeting show of luxury—even that was sworn to concealment and silence and, with a finger on its lips, ran for safety and anonymity into the first doorway. Every living creature, even inanimate things, started at every sound, shied away from one's glance, and died from fear lest someone compel them to speak a word or call them by their right name.

Watching these men and women as they shuffled along, bowed, shrouded, and perennially mute, without a smile or gesture, he felt a much greater curiosity about their hopes and private agonies than about their workaday lives which were flattened and deadened to such an extent that they were lives only in name. In the end, because he thought about it constantly, he began to see examples and proof of his theory in almost everything. In the coarseness of their society, which was quite marked, and in the violence that convulsed it from time to time, he saw a fear of straightforward expression, a kind of crude and special form of silence. And even his own musings about these people (Where do they come from? How do they maintain their race? What are their goals? What do they believe in? How do they love and hate? How do they age and die?), even these seemed to slip, before he'd had a chance to develop and express them, into that vague indescribable pond of silence that encompassed him so completely, that filled everything around him and strove to deaden him in every fiber.

Indeed, the young man felt more and more clearly how the silence was beginning to erode and infect even him; how it filtered into his pores, subtly paralyzing his spirit and chilling his blood.

And the nights were the worst of all.

Now and then, it was true, some brittle and unexpected sound would ring out: the sharp crack of a shot somewhere on the outskirts of the town, a dog barking at some untimely passer-by, or at his own dream. It would ring out for only a second, as if to make the silence seem deeper still; instantly the void would close over it like a flood of bottomless, uncompromising water. It was a silence that destroyed sleep as effectively as an orgy of sound, that forced a man to sit up and feel how it threatened to liquefy, crumble, and wash him out of the ranks of conscious, living beings. Every night, as he sat like this beside the fast-dwindling candlelight, he seemed to hear the silence talk to him in her tongueless voice: "You won't be gadding about so foot-loose much longer, and look around you so proudly and flash your teeth and trumpet those fancy opinions and those loud, unequivocal words of yours. I will not have you here as you are. I shall break your back, drain the blood from your heart, force your eyes to the ground. I shall turn you into a bitter wild plant, vegetating in rocky soil on a windy height. Your French mirror, and the eyes of your own mother, will never again recognize you!"

And the voice that spoke to him was neither rasping nor mocking, but quiet and relentless; as it went on, he could feel it wrapping and shrouding him, as a foster mother wraps a foundling. It occurred to him that this silence was in fact another way of dying, the kind of death that took away a man's reason for living but left him the husk of life to live in.

But no one surrenders without a struggle or perishes without some attempt at defense, least of all a man of Desfosses's age, upbringing, and race. His youth and healthy nature sent out some fierce antibodies against this evil thing, as against some unhealthy climate. And even though it happened sometimes that the nights robbed him of strength and left his mind in a stupor, the morning would always rescue him, the sun would lift him up, water would refresh him, his inquisitive mind would sustain him.

This evening too he made a concerted effort and finally managed to wrest his thoughts from the silence and loneliness, to lift and rivet them to the living, audible, visible, and tangible aspects of everyday reality, and so protect himself from the quashing, smothering void that seemed bent on invading his consciousness, as it had invaded his room. He thumbed through his daily jottings, put them in order and amplified them. Slowly and laboriously his book on Bosnia was growing; made up almost entirely of "real reality." Everything in it was supported with evidence, shored up with figures and illustrated by examples. Shunning eloquence and high style, staying clear of generalizations, the pages slowly multiplied, dry, smooth, direct, and simple, a protective armor against this cunning and seductive Eastern silence which blurred, muddied, jellied, raddled, and numbed all things, which gave them a double meaning, too many meanings, and sometimes no meaning at all, until they melted away somewhere beyond the reach of eyes and reason, into some kind of deaf limbo, leaving one blind, tongue-tied, and groping, buried alive and cut off from the world, even though still in it.

When he had organized and copied the notes he had taken that day, he found himself once more face to face with the silence of the slow-ticking night. And now he too sat with his arms folded over his manuscript, borne away on his "nonfactual" reveries, until exhaustion glazed his eyes and the solid words of his sober prose began to dance on the paper like tiny phantoms in a mirage.

"Travnik! Travnik!" He rolled the word slowly over his tongue, like the name of a mysterious disease, or a magic formula that was hard to memorize and easy to forget. The more he repeated it, the stranger it sounded to him—two murky vowels, wedged between lifeless consonants. And yet the formula now encompassed more than he had ever dreamed the whole world could encompass. It was not simply a word, not just the cold dull name of a remote little town; it was not Travnik; it was now Paris and Jerusalem to him, the capital of the world and the center of life. So a man might dream from childhood on about great cities and celebrated scenes of action, but the actual and decisive battles for the survival of his personality, for the realization of everything he keeps instinctively hidden in himself, are fought wherever destiny happens to toss him, in Lord knows what cramped, nameless trap hole, without glamor or beauty, without judges or witnesses.

The young man rose absent-mindedly and went to the window. He drew the edge of the curtain and looked into the darkness, not knowing himself what it was he wanted to see in the unlighted, soundless night.

.   .   .

Through the void, full of a mist which may have been either rain or snow, it was impossible to see the usual weak glow of light behind the draped windows of the Austrian Consulate. But in that large house candles were burning and there were people sitting beside them, bent over papers and over their own thoughts.

The Consul's study was a long unpleasant room, sunless and airless, for its windows faced toward the high slope of the orchard. Consul-General von Mitterer had been sitting here for hours, beside a table littered with drafts and military manuals.

The fire in the stove was smoldering, forgotten; his long pipe lay on the table, burnt out; the room was cooling off rapidly. The Consul had thrown his service coat around his shoulders and was writing. Tirelessly he filled page after page of yellow draft paper. As soon as he had finished one sheet, he would warm his cold, numbed right hand over the candle flame and reach for a new, clean sheet; he would smooth it out with his palm, draw the first line, and then quickly fill it with the large angular writing that was typical of the officers and noncoms of the Imperial and Royal Army.

That evening after supper, as on many previous evenings and afternoons, Frau von Mitterer had wept, threatened, demanded, and implored the Colonel to write to Vienna to ask for a transfer from this unbearable wilderness. As always, the Colonel had tried to comfort his wife and explain to her that it was not as easy and simple as she imagined to ask for a transfer and run away from difficulties, that to do so might mean the end of his career, and not an honorable end at that. Anna Maria had overwhelmed him with reproaches, deaf to all his explanations, and had threatened in tears to take "her child" and leave Travnik, Bosnia, and him. In the end, to calm his wife the Consul had promised, as so often before, to write his application that very evening and, as so often before, had not kept his promise, for it was a decision he couldn't make lightly. He had left his wife and daughter in the dining room, lighted his pipe and withdrawn to his study, not to write the application for which he had no stomach, but to get on with the work which gave him satisfaction and regularly filled his evenings.

For ten consecutive nights von Mitterer had been working on a long report to the military authorities in Vienna, describing the location of Travnik from a strategic point of view. Using a great many diagrams and sketches, figures and useful facts, he was now outlining the fourteenth position that would have to be taken into account by a hypothetical army advancing along the Lashva valley toward Travnik, which had every intention of defending itself. In his preface to the large work, he had already said that he was embarking on the enterprise in the hope of giving the Chief of Staff something of possible value, and also because he wanted to "shorten the long evenings of monotony to which a foreigner in Travnik is condemned."

The evening indeed was wearing on, but very slowly, and von Mitterer wrote on diligently and without a breather. He described the Travnik fortress in the minutest detail, its origins, what was said and thought about it, its actual complement, the strength of its situation, the thickness of its walls, number of guns, arsenal stores, the possibility of supplying it with water and food. His pen scratched, the candles guttered, the lines of writing multiplied, regular and orderly, full of accurate figures and graphic detail, and the sheets kept piling up, the stack of them grew.

These were von Mitterer's best hours and this was where he liked to be most. Beside his candles and filled sheets of paper, enveloped in silence, he felt as if he too were inside an impregnable citadel, sheltered and protected, safe from quibbles and misunderstandings, his task clear-cut in front of him. Everything from his handwriting and style of expression to the ideas he expounded and the feeling that inspired him, seemed to link him to the great Imperial and Royal Army, to something solid, permanent, and secure on which a man could lean, in which he could lose himself with all his private worries and doubts. He knew and felt that he was not alone, not abandoned to chance. Above him there was a long line of superiors, below him ranks and subordinates. That bore him up and sustained him. Everything was threaded and bound together with countless rules, traditions, and customs, all unified in a pattern, unchangeable, constant, more enduring than an individual.

In a night and in a place like this, where men sought oblivion in their illusions, there was no greater happiness or a finer way of forgetting. And so von Mitterer penned line after line, page after page of his great report on the strategic position of Travnik and its environs, a report which no one would ever read and which, under the dust of archives and some unknown clerk's florid signature, would remain tied in its virgin file cover, unseen and unread for as long as the world lasted, as long as papers and writings lasted with it.

Von Mitterer wrote on. The night passed so quickly he could almost hear it soughing as it rushed by. The heavy service coat warmed his spine, his mind was alert, taken up with something that gave no pain and only calmed him, that sent the night hours flying, and left him tired but also with the quiet glow of a duty well discharged, and with a precious yearning for sleep.

Now, still writing, he hadn't begun to flag yet, his eyes were not yet bleary, the words did not dance yet. On the contrary, it seemed to him that between his neat written lines other lines were coalescing: neat regiments of men stretching out to infinity, in their shiny imperial uniforms and fine equipment.

As he wrote, he felt quietly exhilarated, as if he were working in the presence of the whole armed force, from the commander in chief down to the last Slavonian recruit. And whenever he paused, he would gaze long at his writing, not reading it but simply gazing at it, and forget the Travnik night and himself, his family, and his other duties.

From this pleasant half-dream the Colonel was wrenched by a sharp tattoo of footsteps in the long passage, approaching like a distant squall. The door flew open suddenly. Frau von Mitterer rushed in, loud and excited. All at once the room was filled with an electric charge and the air rained with disjoined, passionate words which she began pouring out right at the door and which mingled with the tapping of slipper heels on the bare floor. As she came closer, von Mitterer rose slowly; when she reached his desk, he was already drawn up to his full height. His happy, intimate hour faded without a trace. Everything darkened and vanished, lost all significance, value, and purpose. The manuscript in front of him shrank to a meaningless heap of paper. The glittering armed legions fell back in a rout, dissolving in a pink, silvery cloud. The tug of pain in his liver, which he had forgotten, came back with a vengeance.

Anna Maria stood before him glowing. It was a look of fury that trembled but did not see, a tremor echoed by every part of her face, her eyelids, lips, and chin. Her cheeks and the base of her throat were spotted crimson. She wore a peignoir of fine white wool, open at the breast and tied around the waist with a sash of cerise silk. On her shoulders was a small light shawl of white cashmere, joined across her breast and pinned with a large amethyst brooch in a gold frame. Her hair was gathered up and tied with a wide band of muslin, above which the hair spilled over in a teeming fountain of locks and curls.

"Joseph, for God's sake!"

That was how it always began: a preamble to a blustering fury and the tapping of heels all over the house, to shrill and ugly words that were unconnected and irrational, to baseless accusations, unwarranted tears, and morbid endless diatribes.

The Colonel stood with bated breath, like a cadet caught red-handed, knowing that the least word and slightest movement would only add fuel to the flames and bring on fresh outbursts.

"Joseph, for the love of God!" Anna Maria cried again, already choking with tears.

He did, now, move his hand feebly and with the best of intentions, and the storm broke over his head, lashing the objects around him, the manuscript on the table, through the chilly air that reeked of his cold pipe. His wife was in a rage. The wide sleeves of her white peignoir gusted through the room with such force that the candle flame bent now this way, now that; at times her fine strong arm, naked to the shoulder, would slice the air with a white flash. As her light shawl slid around loosely, the amethyst brooch kept shifting from one breast to the other. Tufts of hair escaped from the muslin fillet and arched over her forehead as if charged with static.

She poured out a torrent of words, now stifled and incomprehensible, now loud and mangled by sobs and sputtering. The Colonel did not listen to them, for he knew them by heart; he merely waited for them to grow quieter and less emphatic, which would indicate that the scene was nearing its close. For nobody, not even Frau von Mitterer, could possibly summon up that many thousands of words a second time, for a fresh outburst. For the moment, however, the bluster and fury raged undiminished.

She knew, she told him, that he wouldn't write the application for his transfer, even though, that very evening after supper, he had promised her that he would, for the umpteenth time. But she had come, all the same, to see this monster of a man with her own eyes, more cold-blooded than any hangman, more soulless than any Turk, to see him pore over his stinking pipe and scribble that stuff and nonsense which nobody ever read (and it was just as well they didn't!), only to gratify his mad vanity, the vanity of a misfit who didn't even know how to maintain and protect his family, his wife and child, who were pining away, dying a slow death, who . . . who . . .

But further outpouring was choked off by loud tears, accompanied by the fierce pummeling of two tiny but strong fists all over the table and the sheets of his manuscript.

The Colonel moved to put a gentle hand on her shoulder, but saw immediately that it was too soon, that the cloud had not yet discharged all it contained.

"Don't touch me, you jailer, you cold torturer . . . you beast without a soul and conscience. Beast, beast! . . ." Then a fresh torrent of words, followed by a stream of tears, a quaking of the voice, and a gradual abatement. She was still sobbing, but now she allowed the Colonel to take her by the shoulders and guide her to the leather chair. She slumped down with a deep sigh. "Joseph . . . oh dear God!"

It was a sign the outburst was over, that she was ready to listen to any explanation without talking back. The Colonel stroked her hair and assured her that he would sit down forthwith and write the application; he would phrase it firmly and unequivocally and have it copied and dispatched first thing tomorrow. He stammered endearments, made promises, and soothed her, dreading fresh outbursts and fresh tears. But Anna Maria was drained out and sleepy, grievous but silent and helpless. She let the Colonel take her to the bedroom, wipe the last tears from her eyes, put her to bed, tuck her in, and lull her to sleep with gentle, childish words of endearment.

When he returned to his study and put the candleholder on the table, he felt shivery and faint; the pain under his ribs on the right side had grown sharper. In these scenes, the worst moment for the Colonel was when everything was over, when he finally managed to calm his wife and then remained alone, each time with a clear realization that he could not go on living like this.

Once again the Colonel slung his greatcoat around his shoulders; it was heavy and cold, like something borrowed and strange. He sat down at the table, took a fresh sheet of paper, and began now, in earnest, to compose his application for a transfer.

Once more he wrote by the straight, unflickering candlelight. He cited the unblemished years of his previous service, pointed out that he was ready even now to give his best, but begged to be transferred from this post. He produced cogent arguments, demonstrating that "only a person without a family" could live and work in Travnik "under present conditions." Lines of regular writing formed again, but cold and dark this time, like the links of a chain, they failed to generate the bright effervescence of a moment before, the feeling of strength and belonging to a larger whole. He wrote as a beaten man would write of his weakness and shame, acting under inexorable pressure which no one could know or see.

The application was ready. Determined to send it off in the morning without fail, he now read it through a second time, as if it were his sentence. He read on, but his mind kept detaching itself from the dolorous text and returning to the past.

He saw himself as a pallid dark-haired lieutenant, sitting under a froth of lather before the officers' barber, watching the barber clip his thick hair and the fine regulation pigtail that was his pride and joy; shaving his head down to the scalp and getting ready to transform him, in suitable disguise, into a "Serbian lad" who would pass unnoticed in Turkish towns and the Serbian countryside and monasteries. He remembered his wanderings and his fears, the mishaps and troubles. He saw his return to the Zemun garrison, after successful reconnaissance, and heard the greetings of his comrades and the warm words of his superior officers.

He saw himself boarding a dugout on a dark rainy night, with two soldiers, and crossing the Sava and landing on the steep bank under the fortress of Kalimegdan, near the gates, to receive from his agent wax impressions of all doorkeys in Kalimegdan, the Belgrade fortress. He saw himself handing them over to his Major on his return, shivering with exhilaration and also with fever and exhaustion.

He saw himself in the mail coach on his way to Vienna—"a man who has made good" and is to receive a reward. He was carrying with him a letter from his commanding officer that described him in terms of the highest praise, as a "young officer who is as shrewd as he is fearless."

He saw himself . . .

There was a light noise outside in the corridor. The Colonel looked up in alarm, rigid in the anticipation of his wife's stormy footsteps. He listened—but everything was quiet. Some unimportant sound must have fooled him. But the images of a moment before had fled his memory and wouldn't return. He was confronted by the orderly lines of his writing, now lifeless and obscure to his bleary eyes. Where had he lost that young officer on his way to Vienna? Where were the freedom and daring of youth?

Heaving suddenly, the Colonel got up from the table, like a man gasping for a breath of relief. He went up to the window and parted the green curtains a little; but there, hardly a few inches from his eyes, the night rose up like a hulking wall of ice and darkness. Von Mitterer stood facing it, like one condemned, not daring to turn around and go back to the black handwriting of his application on the table.

Standing there and thinking of his transfer, he fortunately had no idea of how many more nights, how many autumns and winters, he would spend like this, caught between this dark wall and his worktable, waiting in vain for his application to be granted. For his letter would lie in the archives of the Geheime Hof-und-Staatskanzlei, together with his report on the strategic positions around Travnik, though in a different section. His application would reach Vienna quickly and punctually, and be referred to the proper official, a tired gray-haired *Sektionschef.* The man would browse through it one winter morning in his warm, high-ceilinged, bright office, which looked out to the Franciscan church, and would then draw an ironic red-pencil line under the sentence in which von Mitterer suggested that they replace him with *"einem familienlosen Individuum"*—a man without a family. He would write in the margin that the Consul must be patient.

For the *Sektionschef* was a placid man, a confirmed bachelor, a pampered lover of music and the arts who, from the cozy and secure heights of his position, could not possibly know or imagine the Consul's plight, or the kind of place Travnik was, or for that matter the endless variety of human predicaments and needs. A man like that would never, not even in his last moments, in the throes of death, find himself face to face with the kind of wall that von Mitterer confronted that night.

8

The year 1807 failed to keep a single one of the promises which Daville thought he had sensed in the balmy air of the previous autumn, as he rode above Kupilo. In truth, nothing was as likely to deceive a man as his own feelings of calm and pleasurable satisfaction at the course of events. They misled Daville too.

The year had hardly begun when he was stunned by the worst blow that could have been dealt him in his thankless job at Travnik. The surprise came in a quarter where he least expected it. D'Avenat found out, confidentially, that Mehmed Pasha was being replaced. A firman to that effect had not yet arrived, but the Vizier was already making secret preparations for departure, with all his effects and his entire retinue.

As D'Avenat explained it, Mehmed Pasha had no desire to await the firman at Travnik, but preferred to leave the town earlier, on some convenient pretext; he would simply not return. The Vizier knew well what happened in a Turkish town the day a courier rode in with an imperial firman decreeing the transfer of the incumbent Pasha and the appointment of a new one. He could almost see the arrogant Tartar mercenary who made his living on such errands and on the morbid curiosity of the bazaar and the lowest riffraff—made his living and enjoyed it. He could see and hear him rushing into the town, galloping like mad, cracking his whip and announcing, at the top of his voice, the name of the replaced and the newly appointed Vizier. *"Makhsul Mehmed Pasha, makhsul! Khazul Suleiman Pasha, khazul!"* (Mehmed Pasha is replaced! Suleiman Pasha is appointed in his place!)

The street crowd would glance up querulously, admiring him; they would argue about the Sultan's decision; they would be pleased, enthusiastic, sometimes riotous. Invariably they cursed the man who was leaving and praised the one who was to come.

It was the moment when the name of the outgoing Pasha was tossed to the idle street rabble like a piece of carcass to ravening dogs, with license to defile it without fear of punishment, and make obscene jokes over it, to flaunt their arrogance and feel heroes-for-a-day, without harm or damage. Little people, who would not have dared to lift their heads when the Pasha came riding by, suddenly popped up like some noisy avenging angels, even though the Pasha in question had done them no personal harm and wasn't even aware of their existence. Often, on such occasions, one might see a half-educated student or a bankrupt merchant rant away over a glass of plum brandy and pass thunderous judgment on the unseated Vizier, as though he himself had overthrown him in hand-to-hand combat; and he would thump his chest in an excess of emotion: "I'd sooner have lived to see this day, understand, than be given half of Bosnia!"

Mehmed Pasha knew that this had always been so, everywhere, that little nameless people always scrambled over the dead bodies of those who fell in the internecine struggle of the great. So it was understandable that he preferred to slip away.

Daville at once requested an audience. At this divan the Vizier admitted, in the strictest confidence, that he would indeed leave Travnik, on the pretext of making an early inspection tour of the forces being readied for a spring campaign against Serbia, and that he wouldn't come back again. From what the Vizier said, it transpired that he'd had word from a friend in Istanbul that the capital was in a state of anarchy and that a murderous intramural struggle was going on between the factions and individuals who, in May of the previous year, had overthrown Sultan Selim. The only point on which all were agreed was the need to banish everyone who showed even the slightest approval of the plans and reforms of the dethroned Sultan. In those circumstances, the accusation of the Bosnian begs that he was a friend of France and a follower of Selim's regime had fallen on eager ears. He knew that he had been replaced already. He only hoped that his friends' intercession had been effective enough to save him from exile, and that he might be given another pashalik far from Istanbul. In any case, he wanted to leave Travnik now, before the firman came, and as quietly as possible, so as not to give his Bosnian enemies an opportunity to gloat over his downfall and try to revenge themselves. Out on the road, somewhere in Sienica or Priepolye, he would then wait for the firman annnouncing his new appointment.

All this Mehmed Pasha conveyed to Daville in that vague oriental voice which, even in matters of the utmost finality, does not altogether preclude doubts or the possibility of change or surprises. The Vizier's face never lost its smile or, more accu-

rately, his perfect white teeth did not for a moment cease flashing in the crack between the beard and the thick, black, well-
groomed mustaches—as neither the Vizier nor the Consul had
any real ground for laughter.

Daville watched the Vizier, while listening to the interpreter,
and nodded politely, without being aware of it. In reality, the
Vizier's information had left him devastated. The cold and
queasy sensation in his innards, which, sometimes strongly,
sometimes faintly, attended all his visits to the Residency and
his every conversation with the Turks, now cut powerfully
across his abdomen like a blunt foreign body, impeding his
thoughts and speech.

In the recall of the Vizier from Bosnia Daville saw both a
personal setback and a considerable reversal for the French
government. Hearing Mehmed Pasha speak of his departure in
that studiedly casual way of his, he felt cheated, unappreciated,
and abandoned in this cold land, hemmed in by a scheming,
malicious, and baffling race whose thoughts and feelings would
always remain an enigma; a country where staying might also
mean "going," in more senses than one, where a smile was not
a smile, where "yes" did not mean yes any more than "no" meant
a final no. He managed to improvise a few sentences and tell
the Vizier how much he regretted his leaving; he expressed the
hope that the matter might still be settled favorably, and assured
him of his unshakeable friendship and the great esteem of his
government. He left the Residency with strong premonitions
about the future.

In that mood, Daville remembered the all but forgotten Sultan's emissary. The death of that hapless man, which had not
ruffled anyone's conscience, began to trouble him again, now
that it was shown to have been of some advantage.

At the beginning of the new year the Vizier quietly dispatched
the more valuable things of his household, and shortly afterwards left Travnik with his Mamelukes. The gleeful and vin-
dictive whispering that was beginning to grow louder among
the Travnik Turks could reach him no longer. The only one who
knew the date of the departure and saw the Vizier off was
Daville.

The parting of the Vizier and the Consul was cordial. On a
sunny January day, Daville and his interpreter D'Avenat rode
out about four miles beyond Travnik. In front of a lonely road-

side café, under an arbor sagging with the weight of snow, the Vizier and the Consul spoke warmly to each other for the last time.

The Vizier rubbed his cold hands and made an effort to keep smiling. "Give my greetings to General Marmont," he said in that peculiar warm voice which approximated sincerity in the way one drop of water approximates another, and which had a soothing and persuasive effect even on the wariest listener. "Please tell him, and all those who should know, that I shall remain a friend of your noble country and a sincere admirer of the great Napoleon no matter where destiny or circumstances happen to take me."

"I shall not fail to do it. I shall see to it," Daville said, moved to the quick.

"And to you, my dear friend, I wish good health, good luck, and every success. I am only sorry I shall not be at your side in the troubled hours which, I fear, you are bound to have with the barbarous and unenlightened Bosnian folk. I have entrusted your affairs to Suleiman Pasha Skoplyak, who will replace me for the time being. You may depend on him. He is rough and simple, like all Bosnians, but a man of honor in whom one can believe. Let me repeat, it is only on your account that I am sorry to leave. But that is how it must be. Had I wanted to be a tyrant and a head-chopper, I could have stayed on and brought these conceited, rattlebrained begs to their knees, once and for all, but I am not that kind and have no desire to be. That's why I must leave."

Shivering in the cold, pale and blue-lipped in his black cape that reached to the ground, D'Avenat translated quickly and mechanically, like a man who had learned all this by heart long before.

Daville knew perfectly well that what the Vizier had said was not, and could not be, entirely and completely accurate, but he was still touched by it. One aproaches every parting with a two-fold illusion. The person we are parting from—especially when, as in this case, it is likely to be forever—appears to us far more valuable and deserving of our attention than heretofore, and we ourselves feel much more capable of generous and selfless friendship than in fact we are.

Then the Vizier mounted his tall bay horse, disguising his lameness with quick, brisk movements. His big entourage followed after him. And when the two clusters of people—the

sizable one of the Vizier's, and Daville's tiny one—had gone
little more than half a mile apart, one of the Vizier's outriders
swerved sharply from the ranks, shot back like an arrow, and
swiftly overtook Daville and his escort, who had halted at that
moment. He reined in his panting horse fiercely and recited in
a loud voice: "The august lord Husref Mehmed Pasha once more
sends his high regards to the esteemed representative of the
great French Emperor. May all good wishes attend his every
step."

Surprised and somewhat taken aback, Daville took off his hat
with ceremonious flourish, whereupon the messenger galloped
back, at the same breakneck speed, to gain the Vizier's train
riding away on the snowy plain. In any intercourse with Orientals there are always some incidents of this kind that pleasantly surprise and stir one, even though it is understood that
they are not so much a sign of special attention and personal
regard as an integral part of an ancient and inexhaustible ceremonial.

From behind, the swaddled Mamelukes looked like women.
The horses' hoofs kicked up a snowy dust that billowed into
a pink and white cloud in the winter sun. As it rode on into the
distance, the band of horsemen dwindled steadily and the cloud
of snow dust swelled higher. In that cloud they finally vanished.

Daville rode back along the hard-frozen road that was barely
distinguishable from the rest of the snowy whiteness. The roofs
of solitary peasant homesteads, the fences and colewort patches
on the side, were under snow, noticeable only by their thin
skeletal outlines on the rolling whiteness. The shadows of rose
and gold were turning to blue and gray. The sky darkened to
pale indigo. The sunlit afternoon had quickly changed into a
winter twilight.

The horses stepped along smartly, all but mincing; small
icicles trembled on the frozen tufts of hair on their fetlocks.

Daville rode on, with a sensation of coming back from a
funeral. He thought about the Vizier from whom he had just
parted, and the thought had the quality of something irretrievably lost a long time ago. He remembered fragments of his
many conversations with him. He seemed to see his smile, that
beam of masking brightness that danced all day long between
his mouth and his eyes until, presumably, sleep snuffed it out.

He remembered the Vizier's protestations, up to the very last
moment, of his love for France and his esteem of the French.

·   ·   ·

Now, in the afterglow of the parting, he considered their sincerity. He thought he could see the Vizier's motives quite plainly, pure and divorced from the usual diplomatic flatteries. He thought he understood in a general way how and why foreigners loved France, the French way of life, and French ideas. They were drawn to them by the law of contrasts; they loved France for all those things they were unable to find in their own country, for which their spirit hungered unappeased; they loved her, and rightly, as a many-faceted image of beauty and harmonious rational life, which no momentary clouding can change or disfigure, an image which, after every eclipse and every flood, glows up afresh before the world as an indestructible force and a joy forever; they loved her even when they knew her only slightly, only superficially, or not at all. And there will always be many who will continue to love her, sometimes from the most contrary motives and impulses, for men will never cease asking and wishing something higher and better than what destiny has given them.

Yes, even he, now, was thinking of France, not as his own native land which he knew well and had always known, in which he had seen both good and evil, but of France as a marvelous far-off land of order and perfection of which men dreamed forever in the midst of coarseness and desolation. There would always be a France, as long as there was Europe. She would never disappear, unless in a certain sense (that is, in the sense of incandescent order and perfection) all Europe became a kind of France. But that was impossible. People were too different, too alien, and too remote from one another.

Here, by chance association, Daville remembered an incident with the Vizier the previous summer. The lively and curious Vizier had always shown an interest in French life and so one day he told Daville that he had heard a great deal about the French stage and would like to hear at least something of what was being shown in the French theaters, even if he could not see a real stage.

Delighted with the request, Daville had come back the very next day with the second volume of Racine's works under his arm, intending to read the Vizier some scenes from *Bajazet*. After coffee and pipes were served, all the servants withdrew; there remained only D'Avenat, who was to translate. The Consul explained to the Vizier, as well as he could, what a stage was, how it looked, and the task and purpose of the art of acting.

Then he began to read the scene in which Bajazet leaves his son Amurath in the safekeeping of the Sultana Roxana. The Vizier frowned, but kept listening to D'Avenat's dry translation and the Consul's feeling recital. But when it came to the dialogue between the Sultana and the Grand Vizier, Mehmed Pasha held up the reading with a hearty laugh and a wave of the hand.

"The fellow doesn't know what he's talking about," the Vizier said, weak with mirth. "Not since the world began did a grand vizier set foot in the harem and talk to the sultan's wives. That sort of thing is quite out of the question."

He kept laughing for some minutes, loudly, heartily, not hiding his disappointment, or the fact that the point and value of such entertainment was utterly beyond him. And he said as much openly, almost rudely, with all the tactlessness of a man reared in a different civilization.

In vain did Daville, vexed and hurt, try to explain the meaning of tragedy and the aims of poetry. The Vizier didn't stop waving his hand. "We too have all kinds of dervishes and holy beggars who spin out ringing verses by the mile. We give them alms, but it would never enter our minds to treat them on the same level with people of action and respect. No, no, I don't understand."

For days afterwards, Daville had thought of the episode as something unpleasant and offensive, as one of his private failures. Now, in retrospect, he was able to contemplate it more calmly, in a mellower light, like a man remembering a ludicrous incident that caused him disproportionate and unwarranted chagrin in his childhood. He only marveled that at a time like this he should remember such a trifle, out of so many grave and important things he had gone through with Mehmed Pasha.

Now as he moved along the snow-covered road, toward the snowbound town, after his farewell to the Vizier, everything fell into its proper place and struck him as understandable and rational. Disagreements were natural, failures unavoidable. And even his sad farewell to Mehmed Pasha now gave him a pang of another kind. He felt his loss as badly as before, but now a fear was added to it—a fear of new troubles and failures. All of it was muted and distant as yet, an inseparable aspect of a life in which, by some mysterious arithmetic, one made gains and sustained losses along the way.

With these thoughts, which impressed him as new and strange, but comforting for the time being, he rode quickly and made Travnik before nightfall.

The departure of Husref Mehmed Pasha was a signal for rioting among the Travnik Moslems. No one doubted any longer that the Vizier had escaped the wrath of the bazaar by cunning and stealth. It was also known that the French Consul had seen him out. This made the bitterness all the greater.

One could see now what was meant by a riot in a Moslem bazaar in a Bosnian town, and what such a riot looked like.

Year after year, the bazaar worked quietly and scrambled after a living, haggling, counting, and languishing in boredom, comparing one year with another, and all the while keeping its eyes and ears open, making mental notes of all that happened, buying news and gossip, spreading them in whispers from shop to shop, reserving its conclusions and avoiding any expression of its opinion. In this way, slowly and imperceptibly, the temper of the bazaar coalesced and took the shape of a common opinion. It was at first only a vague general mood, outwardly manifested in brusque movements and under-the-breath curses at no one in particular; then, by stages, it hardened into an opinion that was no longer kept secret; and finally it became a firm and definite conviction, about which it was no longer necessary to talk and which could only be expressed in deeds.

Imbued and linked together by this conviction, the bazaar whispered, braced itself, waited, as bees wait for the hour of swarming. It was impossible to follow the logic of these blind, furious, and usually ineffectual bazaar riots, yet they had a logic all their own, just as they had a technique all their own, obscure yet compounded of tradition and instinct. The only part that was clearly visible was the way they flared up, raged, and died away.

One day, which would dawn and begin like any other, the usual drowsy peace of the town would be broken, the shutters would come down and there would be an ominous scraping of doors and rattling of bolted stanchions in the warehouses. All of a sudden the bazaar folk would scramble from their habitual places, in which they had squatted for years without moving, neat and cleanly dressed, with their legs crossed, deigning to serve their customers, in their baggy trousers of fine cloth, their braided waistcoats and brightly striped long-sleeved shirts. This ritual movement of theirs and the muffled noise of closing doors and shutters were enough to send up the electrifying cry through the whole town and the countryside: "The bazaar's closed down!"

They were grave and fateful words; their meaning was plain to everyone.

The women and children would go down into the cellars. The more respectable bazaar people sought the safety of their houses, ready to defend them and perish on the threshold. And from the small coffeehouses and outlying quarters groups of poor Moslem folk came filtering in, people who had nothing to lose and stood to gain something in a riot or violent change. For here too, as in all outbursts and convulsions the world over, there were those who instigated and led a movement and others who carried it out and made it a reality. Materializing out of nowhere, one or two men would leap in front of the mob and spearhead it. As a rule they were noisy, violent, disgruntled cranks and have-nots whom no one had ever seen or known before and who, when the riot subsided, would vanish once more into the nameless squalor on the hillside outskirts from which they had emerged, or remain pining in some police jail.

And this would last a day, two, three, or five, depending on the place and circumstances, until something was smashed up or burned down, until someone's blood had spouted, or until the riot spent itself and petered out of its own accord.

Then, one by one, the shops would open again, the riffraff would melt away, and the bazaar people, ashamed and seedy-looking, grave and pale-faced, would resume their work and customary way of life.

Such, in general outline, were the origins, the evolution, and the end of a typical riot in a Bosnian town. The Travnik bazaar, like the Moslem landowners of Bosnia, had for years followed the efforts of Selim III to reorganize the Turkish Empire along new lines, dictated by the pressures and needs of contemporary European life. The bazaar made no bones about its suspicion and hatred of the Sultan's reforms, and often stated them openly in direct representations to the Sublime Porte and also to the local representative of the Sultan, the Vizier of Travnik. The bazaar never doubted that the reforms would profit only the foreigners and enable them to undermine and destroy the Empire from within. In the eyes of the Islamic world, and thus also in the eyes of Bosnian Moslems, the ultimate fruit of the reforms would be a decline of faith, loss of possessions, family, and life in this world, and damnation in the next.

As soon as it became known that the Vizier had left, ostensibly for the Serbian frontier, to inspect the positions and map a campaign, there set in that ominous silence which precedes eruptions of popular anger, and that conspiracy of looks and whispers which is unintelligible to an outsider. The outbreak was imminent and only waited for its appointed moment.

As usual, the outward cause of the eruption was incidental and trivial.

César D'Avenat had in his employ a messenger and confidential agent by the name of Mehmed, known as Whiskers, a strapping, broad-shouldered man from Herzegovina. All those who served in the foreign consulates were detested by the local Moslems, and this Mehmed more so than the others. That same winter Mehmed had married a young and pretty Turkish woman, who had come from Belgrade to visit her relations in Travnik. The young woman had been married in Belgrade to a certain Bekri Mustapha, who had kept a coffeehouse in a wooden cabin in Dorchole. Four witnesses, all of them Travnik Moslems, swore on oath that Bekri Mustapha had died of excessive drinking and that his wife was free. Thereupon the Moslem magistrate remarried the woman to Mehmed.

About the time of the Vizier's departure, Bekri Mustapha suddenly appeared in Travnik, dead drunk, it was true, but alive and looking for his wife. Drunk as he was and without any papers, he had no success with the magistrate at first. The coffeehouse keeper explained that he had spent eleven days traveling from Belgrade to Travnik, through snowdrifts and in bitter cold, which was the reason he had drunk so much brandy that he now found it quite impossible to sober up. But he was only asking for his rights: the return of his wife whom another man had made his own by trickery.

The bazaar intervened. Everyone felt that this was a very good opportunity to take it out on the hated Mehmed and his chief D'Avenat and the consuls and consulates in general. They all considered it their duty to help an honest Moslem defend his rights against these foreigners and their lackeys. As for Bekri Mustapha, who had arrived without a coat and decent boots in the depths of winter, bare as a skewer, feeding on raw onions and keeping himself warm on plum brandy, he was now suddenly lavished with warm clothes, fed, plied with drink and attention by the whole bazaar. Someone even made him a present of a short fur coat with a ragged fox collar, which he wore with much solemnity. Blinking and hiccuping, he went like that from shop to shop, borne along like a banner on the popular concern and sympathy, and demanded his rights in a louder voice than ever. He did not sober up, it was true, but that was no longer essential to the defense of his rights, since the bazaar had taken his case into its own hands.

When the magistrate firmly declined to restore the woman to the drunken man on his bare word, the bazaar went up in arms. The long-awaited riot had at last found its pretext and could burst forth openly and rage unimpeded. And burst it did—despite the fact that the winter days were not the best time for it and that these things usually occurred in the summer or autumn.

None of the foreigners could possibly have imagined the violence and scope of the mass hysteria that from time to time seized the population of these small towns, scattered and marooned among the mountain ranges. Even to D'Avenat, who knew the East but didn't as yet know Bosnia, it was all quite new and gave him, at times, real cause for concern. Daville shut himself up in the Consulate with his family and awaited the worst.

About an hour before noon on that winter day, the bazaar ground to a halt as if by a secret, invisible signal. The air was filled with the banging of shutters, gates, and door stanchions, echoing and re-echoing like the rumble and clap of a hail-bearing summer storm, as if stone avalanches were rolling down the steep slopes of Travnik from every side, with a thunderous sound, threatening to bury the town and every living creature in it.

In the hush that spread immediately afterwards, a few shots and wild cries rang out; then, beginning with a murmur that gradually swelled to a muffled roar, crowds of riffraff, street urchins, and underage youths began to collect. When the mob had grown to two or three hundred strong, they moved off, at first haltingly and then faster and more resolutely, in the direction of the French Consulate. They swung clubs and waved their arms. Most of their shouting was aimed at the Moslem magistrate who had married off Bekri Mustapha's wife and was otherwise known as a supporter of Selim's reforms and a Vizier's man.

One of the men, a stranger with a long mustache, cried out in a loud voice that it was the fault of people like the magistrate that nowadays a person of true faith didn't dare to lift up his head and that his children starved; he heaped words of abuse on the despised Mehmed, a lackey of the unbelievers and a pork eater, and urged the mob to grab him at once and clap him in irons, together with the magistrate who dispossessed true Moslems of their wives and gave them in marriage to other men, for a consideration, who in fact was not a real magistrate but a betrayer of faith, worse than any Christian priest. Another small pasty-faced man, a meek and diffident little tailor from the lower bazaar, out of whom ordinarily not a peep was ever heard in his own house, listened closely to the mustachioed speaker and then suddenly screwed up his eyes, jerked his head up high, and gave a hoarse savage yell of unexpected force, as if to make up for his long silence: "To hell with the priest-magistrate!"

This emboldened the others. Shouts and curses began to ring out against the magistrate, the Vizier, the consulates, and especially against Mehmed the Whiskers. Timid youths, not wishing to be left out of it, would rehearse their contribution by mumbling it under their breath, after which they would dart out in front, toss their heads up excitedly as if about to sing, and yell out the words they had rehearsed. Then, blushing, they would wait to hear their shout echoed, now faintly, now more loudly, in the murmur and approbation of the mob. So they encouraged and egged one another on, rousing themselves more and more to the pitch where every man felt free, within the limits of the riot, to shout and do whatever he pleased and to give vent to everything that troubled and oppressed him.

Suleiman Pasha Skoplyak, the Deputy Vizier, who well knew the meaning and the usual course of a Travnik riot, and never lost sight of his responsibility toward the Consulate, did the most sensible thing in the circumstances. He ordered the arrest of the consular messenger Mehmed and locked him up in the fortress.

The mob that spread out in front of the Consulate was furious to find that the building was shut off from the road by a wide courtyard and a big garden, so that the house was not even within a stone's throw. While the throng was making up its mind about the next move, someone shouted that Mehmed was being taken away through the back streets. The crowd surged uphill and ran to the bridge at the foot of the fortress. Mehmed was already inside, and the big mailed door had been bolted. Now a confused milling began. The majority turned back to town, singing, while others stayed on by the edge of the moat, looking up at the windows of the gate tower as if waiting for something to happen, and demanding, with loud shouts, the most hair-raising punishment and torture for the arrested messenger.

Now the bazaar—as empty as if a gale had swept it—filled with the rumble and cries of the idle crowd, whom Mehmed's arrest had only partially appeased. Suddenly these too died down and the men began to call and look at one another. Querulous heads swiveled in all directions. The mob was at that stage of boredom and flagging attention when it was willing to accept any diversion and change, whether vicious and bloody or good-humored and jocose. Presently all eyes became riveted on the steep lane that led down from the French Consulate to the bazaar.

Down the lane and through the scattered crowd came D'Avenat, solemn and armed, on his tall bay mare. Everyone stopped in amazement, rooted to the spot, and stared at the rider who went on his way calmly and without a care, as though he were followed by a detachment of cavalry. If one of the crowd had shouted something, anything, they might all have started yelling, milling, and shoving, and rocks would certainly have flown back and forth. But as it turned out, everyone first wanted to see what this intrepid consular dragoman was about, and where he was going, and only then join their voices to any abuse that might be hurled after him. The upshot was that nobody said anything and the mob stood around expectantly, without a common will or a clear purpose. D'Avenat made up for it by shouting himself, in a loud and stinging voice, as only a Levantine knew how, bending down in the saddle from one side to the other, as if herding a bunch of cattle. He was deathly pale. His eyes blazed and his teeth showed in a wide snarl.

"Were you bitten by a snake that you dare to lay a finger on the Imperial French Consulate!" he shouted, glowering at those nearest to him. And he went on: "Are you rioting against us, your best friends? Who put you up to it? Some drunken fool whose brain is soaked in Bosnian brandy? Don't you know that the new Sultan and the French Emperor are the best of friends?

That orders have come from Istanbul for everyone to respect the French Consul and honor him as a guest of state?"

A voice in the crowd muttered something unintelligible, but the mob failed to take it up. D'Avenat seized the opportunity and turned in the direction of the lone voice, addressing it pointedly, as if everyone else were on his side and he were speaking on their behalf. "How's that? What do you mean? You dare to stick your nose in something emperors have arranged and agreed between themselves, and spoil it? All right, let's look at the man who's inciting peaceful citizens to disaster! And get this through your thick skulls. The Sultan won't put up with it. If anything happens to our consulate all Bosnia will be scorched down to the ground and even the babes in their cradles will not be spared!"

A few voices were heard again, but scattered and halfhearted. The crowd backed away from the rider, who seemed to take his safe passage utterly for granted, and he rode like that the entire length of the bazaar, shouting angrily that he was going to see Suleiman Pasha and would ask him who was the master in this town; and afterwards—they could take his word for it—many of them would be very sorry indeed they'd listened to the advice of madmen and gone against orders from the highest quarter.

D'Avenat gained the bridge and crossed it. The furrow he had left in the mob behind him closed up again, but the men felt deflated and beaten, at least for the moment. They began to ask one another why they'd allowed the cocky infidel to ride through them unmolested, instead of squashing him like a bedbug. But now it was too late. The right moment had passed. The first gust had spent itself, the crowd had lost direction, it was at loose ends. It would have to start over again.

Later, taking advantage of their momentary faintheartedness and confusion, D'Avenat made his way back to the Consulate in the same daring and deliberate fashion; this time, however, he did not shout, but merely glared around brazenly and shook his head in a dire and meaningful way, as though he had just settled the matter at the Residency and knew exactly what was coming to them.

In point of fact, D'Avenat had tried to take a strong line with Suleiman Pasha and had met with little success. The Deputy Vizier refused to be shaken or intimidated, either by D'Avenat's threats or by the riot itself. Just as on a previous occasion he had defended the Travnik winter before the Vizier, maintaining that it was no calamity but, on the contrary, a necessity and a gift of God, so now he spoke about the riot in the same way. It was nothing to be alarmed about, was the gist of his message to Daville. The rabble had got up on their high horse, the tide was running. It happened from time to time. They would shout and brawl, and calm down again, and noise never harmed anybody. No one would dare to touch the Consulate. As for the case of the boy Mehmed, that was something for the Moslem courts to decide; they would question him, and if they found him guilty he would have to give up the woman. If he was blameless, nothing would happen to him. Everything else would remain as before, in good order, in its proper place.

This was the verdict Suleiman Pasha conveyed to Daville, speaking slowly in his mangled Turkish, which was heavily accented and laced with salty and obscure local idiom. With D'Avenat himself he refused to be drawn into a discussion, even though the interpreter tried hard to start one. He dismissed him like a Turkish servant, with the words: "There, remember well what I've told you and be sure to repeat it accurately to the good Consul."

Nevertheless the riot continued to spread. Neither D'Avenat's arrogance nor Suleiman Pasha's Turkish way of glossing over and minimizing had any effect on it.

Toward evening of the same day, an even larger and more wanton mob came down from the hillside slums and poured into the bazaar, to the delight of shouting young hoodlums. During the night some shady characters came up to the Consulate building. Dogs barked and the Consul's men kept watch. Next morning a crude hemp torch and a pail of tar were found, with which they had planned to set fire to the Consulate building.

The following day D'Avenat, fearless as ever, demanded and obtained permission to enter the fortress and visit the arrested messenger. He found him tied up in a dark cell, known as "the Well," reserved for those who had been condemned to death. The young man was indeed more dead than alive, as the Vizier's chief of police, not knowing the actual reason for the arrest, had ordered a hundred strokes of the bastinado, in any event. D'Avenat failed to get the young man freed, but found a way of bribing the guard and so easing his imprisonment.

To make matters worse for Daville, two French officers hap-

pened to arrive in Travnik at that time, on their way from Split
to Istanbul. For although these officer missions had long ceased
to be warranted and were, in fact, becoming harmful, and although Daville had for months implored Split not to send them,
at least not via Bosnia, where their presence inspired hatred
and odium among the people, it still happened from time to
time that groups of two or three officers set out in compliance
with some outdated order.

The riot confined these officers, like everyone else, to the Consulate building. But being tactless, haughty, and impatient, they
tried, right on the first day, to ride out into the surrounding
country in spite of the riot.

As soon as they left the Consulate and reached the streets
of the poor quarter, they were greeted by a hail of snowballs.
Street urchins ran after them, pelting them fiercely. Teenage
riffraff sprang from every gateway, flushed with excitement,
with hatred in their eyes, yelling and calling to one another.

"There's the Christian! Get him!"

"Hit the unbelievers!"

"You'll pay for it, dirty Christians!"

The officers watched them run up to the drinking fountain
and dip the snow lumps in water, to make them harder and
heavier. They were in a quandary. Spurring the horses on and
galloping away would be almost as bad as fighting the kids or
taking their savage pranks meekly. So they turned back to the
Consulate, fuming and humiliated.

And while the cries of the mob floated up from the bazaar,
a major in the Army Engineers, pining in the Consulate, wrote
as follows to his commanding officer at Split: "Just as well there
was snow, otherwise these young heathens would have showered
us with rocks and mud. I was beside myself with shame and
fury, and when the grotesque situation became unbearable, I
lashed out at the hoodlums with a stick. They dispersed for a
moment and then re-formed again and started to go after us
with still louder shouts. We barely got back to the town. The
interpreter at the Consulate assures me that it was a lucky thing
my stick did not hit a single child, as their elders would have
made us pay for it with our lives, since they are no better than
their children and surely put them up to it."

Daville tried to minimize the incident in front of the officers,
but was privately consumed with shame at having Frenchmen
witness his impotence and the humiliation in which he lived.

On the third day the bazaar opened up again. One by one the shopkeepers came, raised their shutters, squatted down in their usual places, and resumed business. They looked even stiffer and graver than before, somewhat sheepish and pale, like men after a night on the town.

It was a sign that things were quieting down. Idlers and urchins were still gathering, rambling around the town aimlessly, breathing on their frozen hands. Now and then someone would shout something against someone or other, but the cries got no response. As yet no one left the Consulate, except D'Avenat and a few servants on the most necessary errands; they were met with threats, snowballs, and an accasional shot fired in the air. But the riot had run its natural course. The French Consul had had a demonstration of what the people thought of him and how they felt about his presence in Travnik. D'Avenat's hated messenger was punished. They took his wife away but did not return her to Bekri Mustapha; she was sent back to her family. Bekri Mustapha himself promptly fell from the bazaar's grace. No one gave him another glance. As if they had just come to their senses, the people demanded to know who this drunken tramp was and what he was doing there. No shopkeeper would allow him to come near his platform or warm himself on his brazier. He wandered around for another few days and managed to get his brandy by selling, piece by piece, the clothes which the people had given him in the first flush of excitement. Then he vanished from Travnik forever.

So the riot ended of its own accord. But the difficulties with which the Consulate had to contend did not diminish; on the contrary, they grew bigger and multiplied. Daville stumbled over them at every step.

Mehmed the Whiskers was finally let out of jail, weak from the beatings and sullen over the loss of his wife. And while Suleiman Pasha, faced with Daville's sharp protests, had ordered the chief of police to tender apologies to the Consul for the arrest of the messenger and for the offensive shouting against the French and the attacks on the consular building, the chief, a proud and obstinate old man, announced firmly that he would sooner resign from service, and if necessary give the head off his shoulders, than traipse to the French Consul and beg his forgiveness. And there the matter ended.

The example of Mehmed the Whiskers struck fear into the rest of the consular staff. In the streets they were met with looks full of hate. The shopkeepers refused to sell them anything. Hussein, the Albanian kavass who was proud of his job, went through the bazaar pale with rage and stopped in front of the shops; but no matter what he asked for, the Moslem shopkeeper on his platform would tell him darkly that it was not available. The goods in question would be hanging there within an arm's reach, but when Hussein mentioned this to the shopkeeper, the man would either quietly inform him that the thing was sold or else growl: "If I tell you it's not available, then it's not available. For you it's not available."

Staples and groceries had to be procured secretly, through the Catholics and the Jews.

Daville could feel the hatred against him and the Consulate growing by the day. It seemed to him the time was not far off when this hatred would sweep him out of Travnik. It robbed him of sleep, immobilized his will, and lamed every decision before he ever made it. And the whole staff felt helpless against it, persecuted, thinly protected against the general hatred. Only their natural sense of shame and their loyalty to decent masters kept them from leaving the unpopular service of the Consulate. D'Avenat alone remained staunch and imperturbably cool. He was neither frightened nor thrown into confusion by the hate that was pressing closer and closer around the isolated Consulate. He remained unwaveringly faithful to his tenet: that one should cultivate, methodically and without scruple, those few who are at the helm of affairs, and treat the rest of the world with contempt and a firm hand, since the Turks were afraid of those who had no fear and shrank only from those who were stronger than themselves. Such a travesty of human life accorded entirely with his views and habits.

Worn out by the strain which the events of the last few months had thrown on him, chafing at the lack of understanding and the grudging support he received from Paris, from General Marmont in Split, and from the Ambassador at Istanbul, bewildered by the spite and mistrust with which the Travnik Moslems followed his every step and which, on the whole, summarized their attitude toward everything French, Daville felt a mounting sense of loss at Mehmed Pasha's absence. Lonely and fretful, he began to see everything in a special light, from an unaccustomed angle. All things became somehow magnified, terribly important, unnaturally complex and beyond help, almost tragic. The recall of the late Vizier, "a friend of the French," appeared to him not only a piece of bad luck affecting him personally but a proof too of the weakness of French influence in Istanbul, a conspicuous failure of French policy.

Privately he regretted more and more that he had taken on this appointment, which evidently was so tough that no one else had wanted it. He was particularly sorry that he had brought his family with him. He realized that he had made a mistake and was left with a bad bargain on his hands, and that chances were this place would cost him his reputation and the health of his wife and children. He felt himself helpless and harried at every step and so, of course, could not be persuaded that the future held anything better or more comforting.

All that he had so far heard and managed to find out about the new Vizier disturbed and alarmed him. They said that Ibrahim Halimi Pasha was a follower of Selim III, had even been his Grand Vizier at one time; but he had no great love of the reforms and was not a particular friend of the French. His utter and unconditional loyalty to Selim was well known, but that was the only thing that was known about him. Ever since the dethronement of Sultan Selim he too, they said, had been more dead than alive, and the new regime of Sultan Mustapha had first sent him to Salonica, as provincial governor, and soon afterwards to Bosnia, rather like a dead body being hustled out of sight. Rumor had it that he was a man of aristocratic origin and middling ability, left stunned by his recent fall from power and bitter over the unenviable post to which they were sending him. What possible good for the French cause, or for himself personally, could Daville hope for from such a Vizier, when even the clever and ambitious Mehmed Pasha had not been able to get anything done? So Daville awaited the new Vizier with trepidation, as one more piece of bad luck in the long spell of mishaps that his consulship in Bosnia had brought him.

Ibrahim Halimi Pasha arrived at the beginning of March, with a whole crowd of retainers and a caravan of luggage. He had left his harem at Istanbul. As soon as he had settled down and rested, the new Vizier received the consuls in a ceremonial audience.

Daville was the first one to be received.

This time too his ceremonial passage through the town elicited some abuse and threats (he had prepared his young Chancellor for it), but they were fewer and milder than the first time. A few loud curses and some unfriendly or derisive gestures were the only demonstration of the popular hatred of foreign consulates. Daville could not help gloating a little when he was informed that his Austrian rival, who was received the following day, had not fared very much better among the Moslem common folk.

The ceremonial that awaited Daville at the Residency was similar to the one arranged by the previous Vizier. The presents were richer and the service more opulent. The new Chancellor of the Consulate received an ermine coat, while Daville was again cloaked in sable. But what mattered particularly to Daville was that the Vizier detained him in conversation a good half hour longer than he did the Austrian Consul next day.

In other respects too the new Vizier was a genuine surprise for Daville—especially in his manner and appearance. It was as if Fate had wanted to play a joke on the Consul by sending him the exact opposite of Mehmed Pasha, with whom at least one could deal easily and pleasantly if not always successfully. (Isolated consuls are only too apt to see themselves abandoned by their governments and harassed by their opponents, and to regard themselves as men whom destiny has, so to speak, personally chosen to be the butt of her special malice.) In place of the youthful, lively, and affable Georgian, Daville found himself confronted with a ponderous, stiff, and cold Osmanli, whose visage repelled and inspired fear. Daville's conversations with Mehmed Pasha, even if they did not always yield what they promised, had nevertheless had a certain tonic effect on him, spurring him to further work and discussion. With this Ibrahim Pasha, it seemed to Daville, every talk was bound to leave one with a hangover of ill temper, depression, and quiet hopelessness.

He was like a ruin on two feet—a ruin without beauty or grandeur, or, to be exact, with a certain mortifying grandeur. If the dead could move, they might perhaps inspire the living with more fear and amazement, but they could hardly inspire more of that cold horror that freezes a glance, stifles words, and prompts the hand to draw back instinctively. The Vizier had a square bloodless face that seemed formed around a few deep wrinkles; a sparse beard that was colorless in a way all its own, like grass that withered long ago, flattened and blanched in the cracks of a rock. The face gave an odd impression of beetling under the pile of the turban, which was pulled down to his eyebrows and over his ears. The turban was artfully coiled from the finest silk, white with blushes of pink, with only the suggestion of an aigrette, embroidered in gold thread and green silk above his forehead. It sat grotesquely on his head, as if a strange hand had stuck it, in a hurry, in the dark, on a dead man who would never again adjust it or take it off but was destined to take it to his grave and rot with it. All the rest of the man, from his neck to the ground, was one compact block from which it was difficult to separate the arms, the legs, and the waist. It was impossible to guess what kind of body lived under that bundle of expensive fabric, leather, silk, silver, and braid. It might be small and frail, and then again it might be large and powerful. And most amazing of all, this heavy bulk of clothing and ornament showed itself capable, in the rare moments when it was not static, of unexpectedly swift and decisive movements, the kind one would expect of an alert younger man. At those times his broad, prematurely aged, and deathly face remained quite expressionless and immobile, while the corpselike figure and the mound of clothing gave every appearance of being propelled from inside by unseen cogs and springs.

All of which lent the Vizier a spectral aspect and inspired in his visitor mixed feelings of fear and aversion, of pity and discomfort.

Such was the impression which the personality of the new Vizier left on Daville at their first meeting.

With time, as he lived and worked with Ibrahim Pasha, Daville would get used to him, in fact make a friend of him, for he would realize that under the strange appearance was hidden a man who was not without heart or intelligence, a man who, though utterly crushed by misfortune, was yet not incapable of all those nobler emotions which his breed and his caste knew and allowed. But for the moment, judging from his first impression, Daville took a dim view of his future collaboration with the new Vizier, who reminded him of a scarecrow, though a luxurious one, ill-suited for the barren fields of this land, intended rather to frighten birds of paradise of exotic hues and shapes in some fantastic region.

In that hustle at the Residency, Daville also noticed a number of strange new faces. D'Avenat, who could no longer go in and out of the Residency as freely as during the regime of Mehmed Pasha—for he was now completely in the service of the French —nevertheless in time found new connections and ways of keeping abreast of things, of getting information about the Vizier, the chief functionaries, the relations between them, and the methods by which the more important business got done.

Partly from innate zeal, curiosity, and boredom, and partly also from an unconscious desire to emulate the old royalist ambassadors whose reports he loved to read, Daville strove to break through the veil of the Vizier's personal life, to glimpse the intimacy of his household and so, according to the notion of old-style diplomacy, learn the "temper, habits, passions, and inclinations of the ruler to whom we are accredited," in order to gain influence more easily and advance his wishes and designs.

D'Avenat, who regretted having to live in this Bosnian wilderness, instead of being in an embassy or in the service of some vizier in Istanbul, as befitted his talents and the opinion he had of them, was the ideal person to secure and deliver this information. With the audacity of a Levantine, the conscientiousness of a doctor, and the quick intelligence of a Piedmontese, he managed to learn and tell the Consul everything—dryly, matter-of-factly, and in full, with details which the Consul sometimes found fascinating, always useful, and often painful and disgusting.

Just as there was no resemblance between the two Viziers, so their adjutants too were completely different. The men whom Mehmed Pasha had brought and taken away with him had been, for the most part, young men, all professional soldiers more or less, in any case all good horsemen and hunters. There had been no outstanding personalities among them, who, by their physical or spiritual qualities, whether good or bad, might have stood out from the rest or particularly caught the eye. They had all been bluff and mediocre men, blindly devoted and obedient to Mehmed Pasha, and they were almost as alike to one another as the Vizier's thirty-two Mamelukes who, like some blank-faced dolls, were all of the same face and size.

Ibrahim Pasha's household was quite another matter. Here the number of people was greater, their types and appearance more varied. Even D'Avenat, for whom the world of the Turks held few secrets, sometimes asked himself in wonder where the Vizier could have picked up such a weird collection, why he dragged them around the world with him, and how he managed to keep them together. Ibrahim Pasha was not, as was the case with most viziers, an upstart of uncertain origin. Both his father and his grandfather had been high dignitaries and rich people in their own right. Their family had thus accumulated a large crowd of slaves, wards, confidants, and servants, adoptees, dependents, and relations of vague and uncertain kinship, hangers-on and parasites of every kind.

In the course of his long and active life and service the Vizier had had to use all sorts of people for a variety of purposes, and especially during the time when he was Grand Vizier to Selim III. Most of them had never left him, even though the job for which they had been employed no longer existed, but remained stuck to him like barnacles to an old ship, tied to his career and fortunes, or, more exactly, to his kitchen and treasury. A few of them were so old and infirm that they never ventured out in daylight and had to be tended in their little cubicles somewhere in the cellars of the Residency; they had, at one time or another, been in Ibrahim Pasha's employ and had performed some valuable service, which the Vizier had long forgotten and they themselves could only dimly remember. There were some who were young and perfectly fit, but had no clear-cut function and did very little work. A few had been born in Ibrahim Pasha's household, as their fathers worked there, and so they had grown up and would spend their lifetime in the household, for no visible reason and to no definite purpose. And the accretion did not lack its portion of spongers and the usual beggar dervishes. In short, D'Avenat did not overly exaggerate when, with his knowing smile, he referred to the Residency of the new Vizier as a "museum of freaks."

The Vizier took in all of these people without a murmur; he put up with them, dragged them around with him, and, with a patience bordering on superstition, endured their faults and their domestic intrigue and quarrels, feuds and bickering.

Even those who occupied posts of responsibility and did the work were mostly eccentrics, with a few normal everyday people between them.

The foremost among them, based on his importance and the influence he had on the administration, was the Vizier's Secretary, Tahir Beg, a man who enjoyed Ibrahim Pasha's full confidence and was his chief counselor in all affairs. He was sickly and peculiar, but an honorable man of unusual intelligence. Opinions about him were exceedingly divided, both at the Residency and in the town, but there was no doubt—and here the people of Travnik and the consuls were in agreement—that Tahir Beg was the brains of the Residency as well as the Vizier's "right hand and the pen in his fingers."

As was the case with every high Ottoman dignitary, he too had been preceded by a reputation, garbled and magnified in transit. The Ulema of Travnik—a body of scholars learned in the Koran—who were as numerous as they were full of envy, bit their lips spitefully and consoled themselves with the thought that he too was only a man and that "it is only the heavens above us to which nothing can be added and from which nothing can be taken away." And indeed, before Tahir Beg had come halfway to Bosnia, they had already managed both to inflate and disparage his reputation. Among those who had come from Istanbul and were spreading tales of Tahir Beg's intelligence and erudition, one man said that at school they still called him "the Well of Knowledge." So at Travnik he was immediately nicknamed "Well Effendi." Which was typical of the bluebloods and agas of Travnik, especially the educated and learned ones. For anything they did not have, did not know, or could not do themselves, they invariably found a bad word or a disparaging name. In this way they managed to participate in all things, even the most exalted, in which otherwise they could never share.

But when Tahir Beg reached Travnik, the people soon dropped the jeering nickname; it boomeranged on the Ulema, which had been too quick to invent it. Before the personality of the new Secretary every insult and every thought of ridicule withered of itself. After a few weeks the people already called him simply "Effendi," pronouncing that common title of respect with special emphasis. And although there were many effendis in Travnik at that time, literate and half-literate scribes, men who had learned the Koran by heart, theologians and hodjas, there was only one Effendi.

Learning, knowledge of foreign languages, and writing skill were in the tradition of Tahir Beg's family. His grandfather had been a lexicographer and writer of commentaries, his father First Secretary to the Porte, who ended his life as Reis Effendi —high religious dignitary of Islam. Tahir Beg might have followed his father's footsteps had it not been for the *coup d'état* which dethroned Sultan Selim and removed the Grand Vizier Ibrahim Pasha first to Salonica and then to Travnik.

Tahir Beg had only just completed his thirty-fifth year but he appeared much older. From being a precocious youngster he had become, almost without transition, a sickly, heavy, and prematurely aged man. His life and work reflected this. Today, after all he had gone through with Ibrahim Pasha during the latter's career as Grand Vizier at a most difficult time, and because of the illness which ate away more and more at his otherwise strong and well-made body, he was already a chronic invalid, who moved slowly and unwillingly and yet displayed an irrepressible will to live and an unusual vitality of spirit.

Had he known how to moderate himself or been willing to give up work, his physician at Istanbul might have perhaps cured him in the beginning. Now the peculiar disease had taken hold and become chronic, and Tahir Beg had resigned himself to the fact that he must live and suffer simultaneously. He had a permanent wound on his left abdomen which closed and reopened several times a year. This forced him to bend in the waist and walk slowly. In the winter and during the spring thaw he was racked with pains and insomnia, and had then to seek relief in alcohol and stronger sleeping draughts. In the absence of his Istanbul physician, Tahir Beg had to salve and dress his wounds himself; he suffered altogether quietly and in secret, never complaining or upsetting anyone.

It is true that among the numerous staff at the court of Ibrahim Pasha there was also a physician to the Vizier; he was Eshref Effendi, a witty old man who had long forgotten everything he once knew, let alone the medical skills with which he had never been too well acquainted in the first place. In his youth he had been something of an apothecary, but had spent half his life in the army, on the front and in camps, where he "cured" more by means of his kindness and indestructible good will than with professional knowledge and medicines. Ages before, Ibrahim Pasha had pulled him out of the army and taken him along wherever he went, more as a pleasant companion than a doctor. Once a passionate hunter, especially of wild duck, he was now virtually immobilized by rheumatism in his legs and mostly sat around in the sun or in a warm room, always wearing boots topped with woolen cloth. He was a lively man, witty and caustic, but loved and respected by everyone.

Naturally it would never have occurred to Tahir Beg to entrust himself to the professional mercies of Eshref Effendi, with whom otherwise he loved to converse and make jokes.

In a special chest, Tahir Beg kept a ready supply of bandages, wide and narrow ones, carefully rolled up, and also cotton wool, lotions, and balms. This was a finely wrought and cleverly designed little box, of a good and rare wood that became more good-looking the older it grew, the longer it was used. In that box Tahir Beg's grandfather had locked his manuscripts; his father had kept money; and he now stored his medicines and dressings.

On the days when he was sick, the Secretary had the servants prepare special hot water for him; he would then begin the long, painful, almost ritual treatment of bathing, cleansing, and bandaging. Alone, locked up, and with knitted brows, his facial muscles in a tense cramp, he would carefully wash his wound and apply the ointment and put on a fresh dressing. This often took him several hours.

Those were the secret and trying hours of the Secretary's life. Yet they also absorbed and washed away all the distress and rancor which he never spoke about. For after he had finally swabbed, bandaged, laced, and dressed himself, the Secretary emerged once more among his people, calm and strengthened and utterly transformed. On his cool, expressionless face the eyes burned with the old force and his thin lips quivered in a way that was barely noticeable. At such times nothing in the world was too difficult or too formidable for him, there were no questions that could not be solved, no men to be feared, no insuperable problems. The chronic, sore-infested invalid was stronger than healthy men, cleverer than the strong ones.

The feature which betrayed this man's real life and true strength was his eyes. At times they were large and shining, the eyes of a great man whose powerful intelligence raised him above the common; at times they narrowed and sharpened and became gold-specked, the bright eyes of an animal that is trap-wary, a marmot or a lynx, piercing and cool, showing no recognition or mercy; then again the excited, laughing eyes of a goodhearted but willful boy, sparkling with the natural charm and carefree innocence of youth. The whole of this man seemed to live in his eyes. His voice was hoarse, his gestures slow and sparing.

Of all the Vizier's assistants, Tahir Beg had by far the greatest influence on him. His advice was the most often solicited and was always listened to; to him were entrusted those troublesome and doleful problems which the Deputy Vizier often didn't even know existed. As a rule, he disposed of them swiftly, easily, and naturally, without too many words, with that golden glint in his eyes; and once the thing was settled, he would never refer to it again. He gave selflessly and generously of his knowledge and acumen, like a man who had more than enough and was used to giving, who needed nothing for himself. He was equally at home in Moslem law, military affairs, and finance. He knew Persian and Greek. He was a perfect calligrapher and had his own collection of verse which Sultan Selim had read and loved.

Tahir Beg was one of the few Osmanlis at the Residency who never complained about his exile in Bosnia, about the wildness of the land or the crudity of the natives. Privately he pined for Istanbul; more than any of his colleagues, he missed the luxury and joys of life in the capital. But like his wounds, he hid and "salved" his nostalgia out of sight, in the privacy of his room.

The direct opposite of Tahir Beg was the Treasurer, Baki—his irreconcilable but ineffectual opponent, known at the Residency as Kaki. He was a cripple in mind and body, a freak accounting machine, a man whom everyone hated and who did not ask for anything else. Force of habit, rather than need, had long made him indispensable to the Vizier. Although he never admitted this to himself, the Vizier, who ordinarily liked only quiet and gentle people, kept and tolerated this spiteful oddity in his midst from a kind of superstitious instinct, as though he were a talisman that attracted all hatred and evil to itself, from near and far. As Tahir Beg described it, he was "the Vizier's house snake."

Wifeless and friendless, Baki had for years been the keeper of the Vizier's accounts, a job he performed scrupulously and conscientiously in his own fashion, saving every penny with a morbid, tight-fisted obsession, defending it as it were from all comers, even the Vizier himself. His life, which in reality was joyless and devoid of any personal happiness, was devoted entirely to self-congratulation and the struggle against expenses, no matter whose, what kind, or in what department. Infinitely

and savagely malicious, he in fact derived no advantage from
his malice, since he needed nothing for himself and lived only
to indulge his malice.

He was a short and portly man, without beard or mustaches,
with a sallow, thin, and transparent skin that seemed to be
filled, not with muscles and bones, but with a colorless liquid
or with air. His yellow cheeks were bloated and sagging, like
two bags. Above them floated a pair of shifty eyes, blue and
clear like the eyes of small children, but always chary and suspicious. These eyes never laughed. His shirt and tunic were cut
low around the neck, which was swollen and ringed by three
deep creases, as on a fat anemic woman. All of him, in fact,
gave the impression of an oversized bagpipe that would collapse
with a loud hiss if one pricked it with a needle. His whole body
quivered with its own labored breath and shrank in fear from
any touch that was not its own.

Humor and relaxation were alien to him. He spoke little, not
a word more than he had rehearsed beforehand, or what he
considered necessary. He listened and paid rapt attention to
anything that concerned himself or what he regarded as his. If
he could have lived two lives, they would not have sufficed for
this preoccupation. He ate little and drank only water, for he
neither had teeth to chew with nor a stomach that could digest,
and the mouthful he saved was sweeter to him than the one he
ate. But since eating was unavoidable, he made the most of
every morsel, caressed it with his tongue and thought of it tenderly, for it was about to become part of his body.

This man always felt cold, no matter where he was or what
the season of the year. His sensitive skin and flabby body would
not allow him to dress as warmly as he should have. The chafing
of a seam or a hem made him sore; it could irritate and exas-
perate him to the point of self-pity. All his life he had been
looking for warm fabrics that were both light and soft, and he
dressed himself with an eye to comfort, in ample, loose, and
simple garments, regardless of style and public opinion. One of
his dreams was a dream of warmth. He dreamed of a small un-
furnished room that would be heated by an invisible fire from
all sides, evenly and constantly, and would yet be light, clean,
and full of fresh air. It would be a sort of temple to himself, a
heated tomb, but a tomb from which one could exert a mighty,
unceasing influence on the outside world, to one's own satisfaction and the undoing of everyone else.

For Baki was not only a ridiculous tightwad and an egocentric crank, but a slanderer, informer, and scandalmonger who had embittered many lives and caused not a few men to be separated from their heads. That was particularly true of the Treasurer's period of glory during Ibrahim Pasha's term as Grand Vizier, when he, Baki, had rubbed elbows with great dignitaries and had been at the center of events. "The man whose plate Baki upsets will never dine again," was what they said of him then. Yet even now, in this peripheral job of his, lacking his old connections and influence, an aging man more laughable than dangerous, he did not cease writing to various important people in Istanbul and, more from habit than anything else, informing them of anything he thought he had found out, slandering and casting suspicion on anyone he could. Even now he could sometimes spend an enjoyable night in this manner, hunched in a cramp over a piece of paper, as other people spend a night in jolly company or in the transports of love. And he did all this quite naturally, almost always without any personal gain, driven by an inner need, without shame, pangs of conscience, even without fear.

Every living creature at the Residency loathed this Treasurer, and he loathed them all in return, together with all the rest of creation. A fiend for thrift and bookkeeping, he refused to employ clerks and scribes. All day long he pored over money, muttering to himself as if in prayer, counting and making notes with a short blunt reed pen on odd scraps of paper which he had filched from other officials. He spied on the inmates of the Residency, beat and sacked the younger ones, pestered the Vizier with calumnies and denunciations of the senior officials, imploring him to stop and forbid waste and "extravagance." He fought against expenses and disbursements, against every pleasure and joy, indeed against every form of activity in general, and was inclined to lump together the articulate and enterprising people with the jolly and happy-go-lucky ones, and to look upon them all as idlers and dangerous spendthrifts.

In this battle of his against life as it is lived, there were a number of absurd and depressing incidents. He paid spies to tell him in what room the light was burning longer than necessary, he counted what people ate and drank, and took an inventory of the heads of onion in the garden as soon as they showed above the soil. In point of fact, all these measures cost more effort and money than the sum total of prevented waste.

(Tahir Beg jokingly suggested that Baki's zeal caused the Vizier more damage than all the indulgence and vices of the other officials put together.) Fat and short-winded as he was, he thought nothing of climbing down to the cellars or up to the attic to inspect the stores. He made lists of everything, marked everything, and kept an eye on everything, yet all of it melted away somehow. He waged a desperate campaign against the normal course of life itself and would have been happiest if he could have snuffed out the whole living world the way he snuffed out the needless candles in various rooms, with a moistened thumb and forefinger; and if then he could have remained alone in the dark beside this guttered light of life, gloating over the fact that they were all plunged in darkness, that at last they had stopped living, and therefore spending, whereas he was still alive and breathing, a victor and witness of his triumph.

He had a grudge against the rich because they had so much and because they spent and squandered, and passionately hated those who had nothing, those dark and perennial have-nots, that dragon with a million insatiable mouths. When the Residency people wanted to tease him, one of them would go to him and in the course of the conversation would say, in a compassionate voice and with a look of exaggerated sympathy, that so-and-so deserved attention "because he was poor." Like a machine that never fails, Baki would forget everything and leap from his seat, crying in his shrill voice: "What do you want with the poor? What are they to you? Let them sink if they have to. Am I God Almighty that I should turn beggars into rich people? Even He's given it up! He's fed up with them." He would drop his head and lower his voice in a sad caricature of the man who had spoken to him. "Because he's poor! And what if he is poor? Since when is it an honor to be poor or some kind of title that gives a man certain rights? You say 'He's poor' as if you were saying 'He's a hadji' or 'He's a pasha.'" Then he would raise his voice and peer into the man's face, sputtering with rage: "Why does he eat if he is poor? No one can eat as much as the poor. Why doesn't he eat less?"

He had nothing but praise for the native Bosnians who were simple and uncomplaining, whose poor were not impatient or demanding or aggressive like the poor of Istanbul or Salonica, who were content to spend their lives in quiet and anonymous squalor. He did not care for the people of Travnik because he had noticed that they were fond of ornament and that almost all of them, to a man, dressed well. He saw men wearing wide sashes and trousers decorated with silk braid, and women wearing shifts of heavy cloth and face veils embroidered with real gold; and that made him angry, because he could not explain to himself how these people got their money, why they bought such expensive and superfluous finery, and how they could afford to replace it, considering how fast the stuff wore out and was discarded. Such tangled speculations made him feel quite dizzy. And if, in talking to him, anyone rose to the defense of the Travnichani and took the line that it was a pleasure to see them in the bazaar, always so neat and well turned out, Baki would promptly jump at him. "Neat indeed! Where do they get the money for those fine clothes of theirs? Where? I ask you, where do these peasants get the money from?" And if the man continued in his praise of the townspeople and tried to justify their expensive taste in dressing, the Treasurer would get more and more stirred up. His blue eyes, so perplexed and at the same time so irresistibly comic, would suddenly turn a blustery purple and there would be a vicious glint in them. He would mince around on his short, invisible legs that were hobbled by too much fat, and wave his stubby arms like a crazed dervish. Finally he would find himself in the middle of the room, his feet astride, with outstretched arms, his pudgy fingers spread out like a fan, hissing and shrilling over and over again, in a sharp, breathless, piercing crescendo: "Where do they get the money? Where do they get it? Where—do—they—get—it?"

At this point, the man who had come to tease and infuriate him would go away, leaving the frantic Treasurer in the middle of the room, unanswered, like a man foundering without help and hope in that raging ocean of endless expenses and swirling accounts which make up this witless and miserable world.

The man who knew the Treasurer best and could tell the most stories about him was Eshref Effendi, the ailing physician to the Vizier. It was from him that D'Avenat learned most about the Treasurer.

Sitting out in the sun, with his high-booted legs stretched out in front of him, his long thin hands resting on his knees, veined and gnarled, Eshref Effendi spoke in his deep and rasping hunter's voice. "True, he's ridiculous now and no one takes him seriously any more. A pig wouldn't rub himself against him—but you should've seen him once. Even today you should not underestimate him. You say he's the color of parchment and his hands shake. That may be so. But you would be making a mistake if you thought that he hasn't long to live or that he won't harm and threaten everything living around him as much as is in his power. Yes, he's yellower than an old quince, but he has never been anything else. He was born yellow. For more than fifty years this *thing* has been crawling around God's world, coughing, sneezing, moaning, puffing, and blowing in all directions like a punctured bellows. From that first day when he soiled the mattress on which his mother had brought him into the world, he's been dirtying everything around him and suffering at the same time. He spent half his lifetime struggling with terrible constipation, and the other half with ghastly diarrhea and in racing across the yard with the water pot in his hand. But all that didn't stop him, any more than his chronic toothache, insomnia, eczemas, and hemorrhages could have stopped him, from rolling around like a little barrel and doing mischief, all kinds of mischief, to everyone and everything, with the speed of a snake and the force of a bull. I always protest when they talk of him as a miser. No, that's an insult to real misers. A miser loves money, or at least the thrill of miserliness, and is willing to sacrifice a good deal for it; but this one loves nothing and no one except himself, and loathes everything in this world, the living creatures as well as dead things. No, he's not a miser, he is a dry rot, the kind of noxious dry rot that eats through iron." Eshref Effendi finished his speech with a cryptic smile. "Oh, I know him, better than anyone, even though he never could touch me. You know, I've always been a hunter and nothing more. A free man. I could always stick people like him into my belt."

Besides these leading personages, D'Avenat managed to get to know other more important officials and to inform the Consul about them in great detail.

There was the thin, dark-skinned Deputy Secretary, Ibrahim Effendi, who was said to be incorruptible: a shy taciturn man, who was only concerned with his large brood of children and with the Vizier's files and records.

His life was a perpetual struggle with clumsy and irresponsible scribes, messengers, and mail carriers, and with the Vizier's papers which could never be got in order, almost as if there was a curse on them. He spent his days in a semidark room crammed with file boxes and shelves. Here there was a kind of order that only he understood. Whenever they asked him for a copy of some document or for an old letter, he became as flustered as if something utterly unexpected and unheard-of were happening; he jumped up, stopped in the middle of the room, clapped his hands to his temples, and tried to remember. All of a sudden the look in his dark eyes became a squint and he could see "two shelves simultaneously, on two opposite sides," as Eshref Effendi put it. All the while he would murmur the name of the document they had asked for, faster and faster, slurring it more and more, until the sound of it was no more than a long, indistinct humming through his nose. Then, just as abruptly, the humming would stop, the Deputy Secretary would lunge forward as if catching a bird, and pounce with both hands on some shelf or other. The letter in question was usually there. But if, as sometimes happened, it was not, the Deputy Secretary would return to the middle of the room and start his concentration act all over again, including the nasal hum and a second leap in another direction. So it went on until the thing was found.

The commanding officer of the Vizier's Guard was one amiable, scatterbrained Behdjet, a man of robust health, fat and lobster-faced, brave enough but an incorrigible dice player and lazybones. The two-dozen-odd foot soldiers and cavalry that made up the Vizier's motley bodyguard did not give Behdjet much trouble or much work. All in all, they solved the problem in such a way that Behdjet didn't have to worry about them much, or they about him. They played dice, ate, drank, and slept. The Guard captain's main and hardest task was having to battle the Treasurer, Baki, whenever the time came to squeeze the monthly pay out of him, or some special expense for himself or his soldiers, without lengthy palaver and undue delays. On those occasions there would be unbelievable scenes.

With his pettyfogging and quibbling the Treasurer managed to rouse even the placid Behdjet out of his equanimity, so much so that the latter pulled his knife and threatened to cut the skinflint of a treasurer into small pieces, "like for a kebab." And Baki, who was normally timid and weak, would defy Behdjet's naked knife in defense of his coffers, blinded with hate and revulsion against the spendthrift, vowing that before he died he would see Behdjet's head stuck on a pole, on that slope below the cemetery where the chopped heads of evildoers were displayed. In the end, the matter was closed with the captain's getting his money and coming out of the Treasurer's office laughing aloud, while Baki remained standing over his money chest, passing his fingers over the newly inflicted hole as though it were a wound; getting ready, for the hundredth time, to go to the Vizier and complain about the no-good thief of a captain who had been plundering his treasury and embittering his life for years. And he longed deeply and fervently, with all his Treasurer's soul, that he might live long enough to see the victory of right and order, and see too—really and truly see—that hollow and insolent head of Behdjet's leering down from a pole.

The post of Deputy Vizier was held by Suleiman Pasha Skoplyak, who, as we have seen, had occupied the same office under the previous Vizier. He was seldom in Travnik. And when there, he was much more accommodating and better disposed toward the Austrian than the French Consul. Nevertheless, this native Bosnian was the only man in the weird agglomeration at the Residency of whom one could say with reasonable safety that he intended to honor his promises and had the power and the skill to carry them out.

10

The consular era had brought ferment and unrest to this provincial capital. The immediate and indirect effects of it were that many men rose and many stumbled and fell; many would remember it for the better, others for the worse.

But what ever caused the barber's apprentice, Salko Maluhiya, son of a poor widow, to reap such a beating from the servants of the Moslem begs? Why was this mishap associated in his mind with the consular era, when he was not even remotely connected either with the consular officials or with the begs and notables or with the men of learning and the bazaar folk?

Salko's predicament was bound up with one of those life forces that throb inside us and around us, that give us wings and carry us forward, that paralyze and strike us down. It was this force, to which we give the abbreviated name "love," that prompted Salko the Barber to squeeze and scratch himself through the blackthorn hedge of the Austrian Consul's garden and climb a tree to get a glimpse of the Consul's daughter Agatha.

Like all true lovers, Salko neither showed nor talked about his love, but he found a way to gratify it, at least up to a point.

During his free hour at lunchtime, he crept unnoticed through the stables of the caravansary adjoining the Consulate, and from there, by a trap hole through which manure was removed from the stable, he gained a hedge from which he could observe the consular garden; in that garden, more often than not, was the Consul's daughter, to whom he was drawn by something bigger and more powerful than all the strength of his frail apprentice's body.

Between this hedge and the consular garden there was a strip of seedy-looking plum orchard, owned by the Hafizadich begs; looking across it, one had a clear view of the Consul's garden, laid out in the European style. Its paths were neat and the mole-hills smoothed away. In the middle, round and star-shaped beds had been dug and planted with flowers, and there were stakes crowned with globes of red and blue glass.

The whole area was sunny and well watered, so that whatever was sown grew quickly and to a great height, with abundant blossoms and fruit.

It was here that Salko the Barber saw the daughter of Herr von Mitterer. As a matter of fact, he had also seen her in the town, driving with her father. But that happened so seldom and was so fleeting that he hardly knew what to look at first: the Consul's uniform, the yellow high-polished open carriage, or the young miss, whose legs were always tightly bundled in a gray carriage rug with an embroidered crimson crown and a monogram. And now this same remote girl, the color of whose eyes he'd not yet had the luck to see, was there close at hand, for him to gaze at with impunity; moving all alone, unaware that anyone was watching her, through the garden in front of the low veranda which had been renovated and glazed that spring.

Hidden from men's eyes, crouching, with mouth half open and breath bated, Salko peeped stealthily through the fence. And the girl, believing herself quite alone, walked among the flowers, studied the bark of trees, hopped from one side of the path to the other, then paused and either glanced up at the sky or down at her hands. (Much as young animals pause in the middle of their play, not knowing what to do next with their bodies.) Then she would resume walking from one end to the other, waving her arms and clapping her hands, now in front of her, now behind her back. The gleaming stake balls of different colors

threw back a comical distorted image of her brightly clad figure, together with the sky and the greenery.

Salko forgot the world utterly and lost all sense of time, place,
and the existence of his own body. And it was only afterwards,
when he got up to go, that he would feel how numb his folded
legs had become, how sore were his fingers and nails, which by
then were full of earth and bark. And much later, back at the
shop, where he was often clouted for being late, his heart would
still pump hard in a disturbing way. All the same, the following
day he could scarcely wait to get through his frugal lunch and
leave the shop and slink through the caravansary stables toward
the fence of the Hafizadich plum orchard, trembling beforehand
at the possibility of being caught and at the joys that awaited
him.

One day—on a bright and quiet afternoon after a morning of
rain—the girl was not in the garden. The flowerbeds were wet
and the paths swept clean by the shower. Rain-washed, the glass
balls shone in the sun, gaily reflecting the scattered cotton wool
of clouds. Seeing that the girl was not there, and racked by
longing and impatience, Salko first climbed the fence and then
the old plum tree that grew alongside it, completely ringed by
a thick bush of alder. He peered out through the dense alder
foliage.

On the ground-floor veranda all windows had been thrown
open and the panes sparkled with the sun and the bright sky.
By contrast, the veranda's interior looked much cooler. Salko
took it all in at leisure. A red carpet on the floor, incomprehensible pictures on the wall. The Consul's daughter was sitting on
a small, very low stool. She had a large book in her lap, but
raised her eyes every other moment and gazed absently down
the veranda and out through the windows. This new attitude,
in which he had never seen her before, excited him even more.
The darker the shadows that fell on her, the more distant she
grew, the longer he felt he must gaze. He was terrified lest his
foot should slip or he should break a twig. He was numb with
happiness at seeing her so motionless, with a face that seemed
even paler and longer in the shadows; a premonition spread
through him that there was more to come, that something even
more exciting and extraordinary was about to happen, as strange
as the rest of that rainy day. He told himself that nothing was
going to happen. And what could possibly happen? And then
again, it might.

There now, she lay both her palms on the open book. His breath and mind stood still—it will, it *was* going to happen. And, true enough, the girl rose slowly and hesitantly, put her palms together and then opened them so that they were joined only by her fingertips. She gazed at her nails—now it was bound to happen! Suddenly she pulled her fingers apart, as if snapping something thin and invisible, looked down her dress, moved her arms away from her body and slowly began to dance in the middle of the red carpet. She tilted her head slightly, as if listening to something, and gazed at the tips of her shoes with lowered eyes. Her face was still, entranced; mirroring the shadows and lights of the rainy day as she moved.

And Salko, realizing that his premonition had come true, lost all sense of where and who he was, edged forward from the trunk of the tree to the outer branches, raised himself higher above the fence, and stretched out a little more every time she kicked a leg during her dance. He pressed his face hard into the young bark and didn't mind the tickling of the leaves. His whole inside danced and swooned. It was difficult to endure so much joy in such an awkward attitude. And the girl didn't stop dancing. As she repeated the same figure a second and a third time, a thrill of delight ran right through him, as if he were looking at something precious and long familiar.

Suddenly the tree gave a loud crack. The branch under him snapped and gave way; he felt himself sinking through the alder leaves, the branches switched and tore at him, he bumped hard twice, once with his shoulder, then with his head. He scraped through the hedge and into the garden of Hafizadich. He hit the fence first and from there tumbled to the ground between some moldy and worm-eaten boards that covered an irrigation ditch. The rotten boards gave way under his weight and he sank up to his knees in slime and mud.

When he lifted up his filthy scratched face and opened his eyes, he saw above him a maid from Hafizadich's scullery, an old woman with a wrinkled yellow face, like his mother's.

"Did you kill yourself, you little devil? What bad luck brings you to the ditch?"

But he only looked around him wildly, searching for a glimmer of that loveliness in which he had basked a moment before in his elevated place, before he toppled from it. He was listening to the old woman, without understanding her, when he saw,

with wide-open eyes, the servants of Hafizadich running with
sticks in their hands from the far end of the garden; but he
could not collect himself or grasp what had happened or what
those people wanted of him.

The frail, sad, and lonely little girl resumed her walking and
her artless games on the veranda and in the garden, knowing
nothing of what had just taken place because of her in the
neighboring garden, just as earlier she had not been aware that
anyone was watching her.

After the beating in the Hafizadich garden and the clouting
he got subsequently at the barber shop for coming back late,
Salko went to bed that day without supper. This was the usual
punishment meted out by his mother, a sallow woman, old before her time, whom poverty had worn out and made harsh and
shrewish. Thereafter the boy gave up stealing into other people's
gardens and clambering over fences and trees in quest of things
that were not for him. He stuck to his work and, paler and more
wistful than before, dreamed of the beautiful little foreign girl.
She now danced for him exactly as his heart and imagination
commanded, and he no longer risked the danger of falling into
a strange ditch and being caught and thrashed.

Yet even dreams of beauty must be paid for. Sometimes, as
he held the bowl of soap lather in his thin blue hands and stood
beside his fat master, busy shaving the pate of some effendi,
the older man would notice his vacuous look and indicate with
his eyes and a familiar gesture that he was supposed to pay attention to the master's razor and learn, instead of gaping, cretin-
like, into the blue yonder through the open shop door. The boy
would start, look nervously at the master, and then glue his eyes
to the razor. But a minute later his look would glaze over again
and his eyes, peeled to the naked bluish swath left on the effendi's pate by the master's razor, would see on it the garden of
paradise and a creature of exquisite beauty whose feet moved
with gazelle-like grace. Once again the master would notice his
mooning and deal out the first clout—with his free left hand,
on whose forefinger there would be a thick gob of used-up shaving lather. Then it would take all of Salko's skill to hold on to
the lather bowl while quietly absorbing the smack, for so much
depended on it. Otherwise the whacking became a rain of lather
and even the clay pipe came into play.

Such was master Hamid's system for curing his apprentice of

woolgathering, for coaxing sense into his head while shaking nonsense and idle thoughts out of it, and generally persuading him to keep his eyes glued to the work at hand.

However, that same life force which we mentioned at the beginning kept breaking to the surface like an underground stream, unbidden and unsuspected, welling up at different points and in different strengths and testing its power on an ever greater number of human beings of both sexes. And so it erupted even in places where there was no room for it and where, because of the resistance it was bound to meet, it could not possibly maintain its hold.

Ever since she came to Travnik Frau von Mitterer had been visiting and making gifts to the Catholic churches and chapels in the countryside. She did this not so much because she wanted to, but because the Colonel insisted, for he was anxious to increase his influence among the Catholic clergy and their congregations.

Vases of imitation porcelain were ordered from Vienna, and bargain candelabra and gilded twigs, all cheap and tasteless junk but a rare novelty in these parts. From Zagreb they obtained some embroidered brocade stoles and chasubles, made by the nuns of that city, which the Consul's wife donated to the monastery at Gucha Gora and to the priests of the village churches around Travnik.

But even on these errands, which were to serve a practical purpose beside pleasing God, Anna Maria could not keep a sense of proportion. As always, she was carried away by her passionate temperament which sooner or later was bound to twist everything she undertook, achieving the opposite of what she intended. By her zeal she very soon raised doubts among the Moslems, and alarmed and bewildered the friars and people of Dolats, who were mistrustful and apprehensive as it was. In making and distributing her gifts, she was capricious and unpredictable; she barged into the churches, rearranged the altar decorations to suit her taste, decided what was to be aired and laundered, which walls were to be whitewashed. The friars, who in any case abhorred innovations and disliked anyone's meddling in their affairs, even with the best of intentions, at first watched it all in amazement, and soon afterwards began to exchange glances and discuss it among themselves and plot active resistance.

To the chapel priest in the nearby village of Orashye, this

extraordinary zeal of Frau von Mitterer came to be a real temptation and danger. The chaplain, whose name was Fra Miyat Bakovich, was alone at the time, as his superior, whose name was also Fra Miyat but who was generally known as "the Carter," was away on business for the Order. The chaplain was a frail, nearsighted young man, given to daydreaming. He found it hard to bear his isolation and the bleak village life, and he had not yet firmly found his feet in the Order.

On this young chaplain Anna Maria descended with all the protective ardor of which she was capable, with that half-maternal, half-loverlike concern which so easily creates awkwardness and confusion even in more experienced and poised men. For a time in early summer she rode out to Orashye twice and three times a week, dismounted at the chapel with her escort, called the young priest out and gave him advice on how to order his church and his home. She meddled in his household, his daily schedule, and his church services. And the young friar gazed at her as if she were a marvelous and unexpected vision, too exalted and dazzling to be experienced without some pain. The narrow band of white lace around her neck, above the black fabric of her riding habit, shone as if it were made of light itself; to pupils that have never dared to look a woman straight in the face, it was blinding stuff. In her presence, the young chaplain shivered as in fever. And Frau von Mitterer looked with delight at those skinny, trembling hands and at the friar's face, while he died of shame at his own awkwardness.

And when she rode down the slope and away toward Travnik, the young chaplain sat devastated on the bench in front of the old parish house. In those moments everything seemed withered, lusterless, and dull to him, the village, the church, and his work. But next time, as soon as he caught a glimpse of the riders from Travnik, everything would shine and bloom once more. The confused trembling would start all over again, made more fevered by his desire to break free once and for all, as soon as possible, from that loveliness that so dazzled and ravaged him.

Luckily for the chaplain, Fra Miyat the Carter returned to the parish before long and the young man confessed himself thoroughly and wholeheartedly. The Carter was a husky energetic man of fifty, with a broad face, short upturned nose, and slanting eyes; experienced and tactful, witty and full of jokes, a learned and eloquent friar. He had no difficulty in sizing up the situation and divining the poor chaplain's predicament.

The first thing he did was to send the chaplain back to the monastery. And next time Frau von Mitterer rode up with her escort, instead of the embarrassed chaplain it was the Carter who came out to meet her. Smiling and relaxed, he sat down on an old tree stump and through a cloud of cigar smoke told the surprised Consul's wife, in reply to her suggestion about some church arrangement: "I wonder, madam, why you should want to break your legs on these rough village roads when the good Lord gave you every opportunity of sitting at home in complete ease and comfort. May the Lord give you long life, but you'd never be able to make order in these churches and chapels of ours, even if you spent all of the Emperor's treasury on them. Our churches are just like us—anything better wouldn't do. So if you have any gifts for our village churches, send them up with someone. We'll be delighted to have them, and you shall have God's own reward."

Offended, Frau von Mitterer tried once more to talk about the church and the parish, but Fra Miyat gave a humorous turn to all her remarks. And when she angrily mounted her black horse, the parish priest snatched the small friar's cap off his rumpled hair, made an impish little bow, and said in a voice both humble and bantering: "A fine horse, madam, good enough for a bishop."

Anna Maria never again visited the chapel at Orashye.

About the same time, the parish priest of Dolats approached Colonel von Mitterer in this matter. Since the Brothers looked upon the Consul as a friend and protector and didn't wish to offend him in any way, they chose the portly and lumbering but sly and clever Fra Ivo to intimate to the Consul in some way that the zeal of Frau von Mitterer was not convenient; he was to do it tactfully, so as not to offend either the Consul or his wife. Fra Ivo, whom the local Moslems called "Fox," and for good reason, accomplished this in very good style. He first explained to the Consul how, for fear of the Turks, the friars had to watch their every step and exercise particular care in meeting and being seen with other people, how welcome they found the gifts which Frau von Mitterer brought them, and how they would never stop thanking God for her and for what she gave. He wound up his long tale with a subtle unspoken hint, to the effect that they would be delighted to receive further gifts, but it might be better if Frau von Mitterer didn't deliver them personally and desisted from supervising their distribution and use.

However, Frau von Mitterer had already lost interest in churches and was disenchanted with the friars and their flocks. She burst in on the Colonel one morning and unleashed a hail of insults and harsh words on his head. The French Consul, she cried, was perfectly right to seek the company of Jews who were better educated than these Turkish Catholics. She came up to him and demanded to know whether he was a consul-general or a sacristan. She swore never again to set foot either in the Dolats church or in the parsonage.

That was how the young chaplain at Orashye was saved from what would have been an idle game to Anna Maria, but which for him might have been a grave trial. The incident also marked the end of Anna Maria's "religious period" in her life in Travnik.

The force we have been referring to all this time did not spare the French Consulate on the other bank of the Lashva, for she made no distinction between flags and sovereign emblems.

While Mme Daville was tending to her children on the ground floor of the "Dubrovnik Depot," while Daville pored over his long consular reports and knotty literary plans on the floor above them, the "young Consul" was struggling with his loneliness and with the desires which that state of mind breeds but cannot satisfy. He helped Daville in the chancellery and rode through the countryside, he studied the language and the customs of the natives and worked on his book about Bosnia. He did everything he could to fill his days and nights. And yet, when a man is young and still free from the worries of life, there remains enough vitality and time for yearning and loneliness and for those hour-long wanderings which only youth knows.

That was how the "young Consul" discovered Jelka, a young girl from Dolats.

We have seen how Mme Daville, after coming to Travnik, needed time and patience to gain the confidence of the Brothers and the sympathy of the Dolats folk. In the beginning, even the poor balked at the idea of giving their children in service to the French Consulate. But after they had got to know Mme Daville better and saw how many useful things the maids learned from her, the people eagerly volunteered to work for Madame Consul. All at once, there were several Dolats girls in the Consulate doing housework or learning the needlework which Mme Daville taught them.

During the summer months there would be three or four girls at one time doing needlework or knitting. They sat by the windows on the broad veranda, bent over their work and singing softly. Going in and out of Daville's office, Desfosses often passed the line of girls. They would then bend their heads even lower and their singing would falter and become ragged. Striding down the wide passage in his long-legged fashion, the young man often took a better look at the girls and spoke a word or two by way of greeting, to which they were usually too bashful to reply. Indeed, it was hard for them to know what to reply, because each time he said something different, usually a phrase he had picked up that day, which confused them quite as much as his open manner, his brisk movements, and his bold and clear voice. After a whole series of these encounters, under the strange logic that rules these kinds of relations, Desfosses came to be most impressed by the girl who dropped her head lowest when he passed by.

Her name was Jelka, and she was the daughter of a small shopkeeper who had a modest house, full of children, at Dolats. Her strong brown hair fell in a thick bang over her forehead and down to her eyes. An indefinable quality, which had something to do with the way she dressed and with her beauty, marked her apart from the other girls. The young man learned to recognize the glossy brown chignon and the firm white nape of her neck among the bowed heads of the other needleworkers. And one day, when he gazed a little longer at that bent neck, the girl unexpectedly lifted her head, as if his eyes burned her and she wished to escape them; and in doing so, showed him for a moment a fresh wide face, with shiny but gentle brown eyes, a firm and slightly irregular nose, and a strong though perfectly turned mouth with lips that were almost identical in shape and barely meeting. Surprised, the young man stared at the face and saw a faint quiver in the corners of the full mouth, as though she wanted to cry but was checking herself, while the brown eyes lighted up with a smile in spite of it. The young man smiled back and called out a phrase from his "Illyrian" vocabulary, the first one that came to his mind, since at that age and in that situation all words are fitting and meaningful. To hide her laughing eyes and her lips, with their faint quiver of intimated but nonexistent tears, the girl dropped her head again and once more presented him with her white neck under the brown bun of hair.

The scene was repeated several times in the next few days, like a private game between them. All games have a tendency to go on and perpetuate themselves, but the tendency becomes irresistible when the players are a young girl like this and a lonely young man, torn by desire. The trite phrases, the lingering glances, and the unconscious smiles thus come together and fuse into a solid bridge that virtually builds itself.

He began to think of her at night and in the morning when he woke up; he began to look for her, first in his thoughts, and then in actual reality, and to meet her more and more often, as if by chance, and gaze at her more and more pointedly. It was the time of the year when everything sprouted and burst into leaf and flower, and so she appeared to him as an aspect—a distinct flesh-and-blood aspect—of that rich, pullulating world of plants and trees. "She's a sapling," he told himself, like a man humming a refrain who knows neither why he is humming nor the meaning of the refrain. With that rosy skin and bashful smile of hers, and that trick of hanging her head like a flower nodding in the wind, she did, indeed, become associated in his mind with flowers and fruit, although in a deeper and special sense, which he didn't pause to examine—something like a materialized quintessence of fruit and flowers.

When the spring was well advanced and the garden was in leaf, the girls sat and worked outdoors. There they embroidered all through the summer.

If anyone wanted to find out about Travnik from two travelers, one of whom had spent the winter there and the other the summer, he would get two completely opposite views of the town. The first would say that he had lived in hell, and the other that he had been close to paradise. Places like Travnik, which are badly situated and have a trying climate, usually have a few weeks in the year which, by their beauty and delightful contrast, make up as it were for all the fickleness and hardship of the other seasons. In Travnik, this period falls between the start of June and the end of August, making the month of July a time of extraordinary glory.

When the last deep hollow has yielded up its puddle of snow, when the spring blizzards and rains have died away; when the winds have lost their bluster, cold and tepid in turns, now gusty and full of sound, now light and ruffling; when the clouds drift

up at last toward the high blurred edge of the sheer amphithea-
ter of the mountains that ring the town; when the balmy glitter
of leisurely days begins to roll back the night in real earnest and
on the slopes above the town the meadows take on a yellow
tinge, while sagging pear trees carpet the stubble fields with the
generous surfeit of their harvest, dropping down from its own
weight—that is when the short and lovely Travnik summer begins.

Desfosses cut short his excursions to the countryside and
spent many hours in the sloping garden of the Consulate, walking the same paths and looking at the same shrubbery as if
they were a wonder he had never seen before. And Jelka usually
managed to be there before the other girls, or lingered on when
they had gone. From the patch of level ground on which they
sat and worked, she went more and more often down to the
house for thread or water or a bite to eat. Now she and the
young man often met on some narrow path or other that was
hemmed in by thick greenery. She would lower her broad white
face, and he would smile and speak his "Illyrian" words, in
which the letter r sounded throaty and slurred and the accent
was always on the last syllable.

One afternoon they tarried a little longer on one of those little-
used paths that was lost in the foliage, where even the shadows
breathed heat. The young girl wore loose Turkish trousers of a
dove color and a tight-fitting waistcoat of pale blue silk with
a single button. Her ruffled shirt was pinned at the neck with
a silver brooch. Her arms, bare to the elbows, were young and
smooth and the skin on them had a rosy blush. The young man
took her by the forearm. The spot where he touched her blanched
at once, leaving a pale imprint of his fingers.

Her lips—pale rose, full-fleshed, completely and strangely
alike—curled up slowly in that imploring and, as it were, tearful smile, but a moment later the girl bowed her head and clung
to him, mute and giving like spring grass or the twig of a young
tree. "A sapling," he thought once again, but the weight pressing against him was a human being, a woman in a faint of tenderness, with a mind still struggling but already resigned to
heartbreak and submission. Her arms hung limply at her sides,
her mouth was half-open, the eyelids partly drawn, as in a
swoon. There she was, pressed into him, around him, fey with
the agony of love, with the ravishing promise of love and the
shadow of horror that came in its wake. Clinging, numbed,

struck down, she was the image of utter surrender, helplessness, defeat, and despair, and of rare greatness too.

Throbbing with his own blood, the young man exulted in his happiness and an irrepressible sense of triumph. Yes, that was it! Had he not always felt, and said in so many words, that this poor, barren, and God-forsaken country was actually a land of untold bounty? And here, now, one of its hidden beauties was reaching out for the light of day.

The steep, green, and flowering slopes seemed to bloom all over again and the air was filled with an unknown, intoxicating breath which—it seemed now to him—had been coursing in this valley all the time, hidden just below the surface. The secret wealth of this dark squalid land suddenly took shape and became visible to the naked eye, and all at once one discovered that the stubborn silence hid within itself this fitful, quickening breath of love which melted alike the last moan of resistance and the joy of surrender, that its mute and forever blank visage was no more than a mask beneath which there glowed fountains of light, crimson with the sweetness of young blood.

Near them, there was a thick and gnarled old pear tree, uprooted and lying athwart the steep slope like a sofa. Rotted away at the lower end, it was still sprouting new branches along the upper trunk. They leaned on it, then sank down, embracing; first the girl, then he on top of her, against the broad trunk of the pear tree, as on a bed laid ready for them. She was still unresisting, making no sound or movement, but when the young man's hands slid downward and gripped her soft middle between the waistcoat and the trousers, where there was only her shirt, the girl pulled away to free herself, straining over backwards, like the branch of a fruit tree ready to snap back when they bed it down at harvest time. He never even felt her thrusting him away; and he suddenly found himself standing on the path once again, not knowing when or how it happened. The girl was kneeling at his feet, with her hands clasped and her face turned up to him, almost as if she were praying. Blood had drained out of her cheeks, her eyes were liquid with tears. She spoke words which he did not recognize but which at that moment were clearer to him than his own mother tongue: imploring him to be human and to spare her, not to ruin her, since she herself didn't have it in her to withstand this thing which had taken hold of her with all the force of death, which was even more dire and irreparable than death itself. She pleaded with him, on his mother's life and by all that was dearest to him, and kept repeating in a voice suddenly hoarse with emotion and urgency: "Don't, don't . . . !"

Conscious of the thudding of blood in the veins of his neck, the young man tried to collect himself and grasp the meaning of the unexpected turnabout, accomplished with such lightning speed. He asked himself in amazement what it was that had suddenly wrenched this swooning woman from under him and rooted them both in this ludicrous posture: he roused and on his feet, like a heathen scourge conqueror; and she on her knees at his feet, her fingers laced in supplication and her moist eyes lifted up to his face, like a saint in a holy picture. He wanted to pull her up from the ground, circle his arms around her again, and lay her down on the leafy bedstead of the fallen pear tree; but he had neither the strength nor the daring for it. Everything had suddenly changed, in a baffling fashion.

He didn't know how or when it had happened but he could see plainly that this submissive girl, pliant as a reed, had in some astonishing way passed from the "vegetable world," of which she had been a part until then, into an altogether different realm; that she had cunningly escaped under the sure protection of some stronger will which he was unable to challenge. He felt himself cheated, outplayed, sorely disillusioned. He was overcome by shame, then infuriated, with her, himself, with the whole world. He bent down and carefully raised her up from the ground, mumbling a word or two. She was still limp and docile, yielding to every movement of his arm as she had done a little while before, but she continued to implore him with looks and words to take pity on her and spare her. He no longer thought of embracing her. Frowning, studiedly polite, he helped her rearrange the folds in her trousers and pin the silver brooch at her throat, which had come undone. Then, just as abruptly and inexplicably, the girl ran off down the slope toward the Consulate building.

The young man passed a few unquiet days. He was constantly haunted by a sense of bewilderment, by the helpless fury and shame of those moments in the garden. In his thoughts he kept harking back to the question: what came over him and the girl, and what had happened, exactly? And he tried, just as stubbornly, to push it out of his mind and not to remember the brief encounter on the deserted garden path. But now and then he told himself with a sheepish grin: "Yes, yes, you're certainly a model lover and a fine psychologist to boot. For some mysterious reason you go and get it into your head that she's part and parcel of the plant world, a pagan symbol of the country, an undiscovered treasure waiting only to be gathered up. So you condescend to bend down. And once you're down there, everything changes all of a sudden. She's on her knees like little Isaac about to be sacrificed by Abraham, only an angel flies down in the nick of time and snatches him from the jaws of death. Because that's exactly what she looked like. And you did Abraham to perfection. Congratulations! Now you're starting to play real live tableaux on Biblical subjects, with deeply moral and devout motives. I congratulate you!"

And only long rides in the hillside woods around the town could restore him to something like equanimity and turn his thoughts in other directions.

For some days he was tormented by his frustrated desire and youthful vanity, and then that too ceased. He began to calm down and forget. He still saw the needleworkers as he passed through the garden, and Jelka's lowered head among them, but he no longer stopped or felt embarrassed; he would call out to them gaily and speak a word or two that he had learned and memorized that day, and then pass on with a smile, brisk and without a care in the world.

However, one evening about this time, he added a sentence to his manuscript on Bosnia, in the chapter devoted to the types and racial characteristics of the Bosnian people: "The women are well built as a rule and many of them have conspicuously fine and regular features, beautiful bodies, and a white skin that is dazzling to the eye."

11

It seemed as if nothing in this country was immune to sudden, startling changes. Everything, at any moment, might become the opposite of what it seemed to be. Daville was beginning to reconcile himself to the unpleasant fact that he had lost Mehmed Husref Pasha, a lively and openhanded man on whose cordial reception, understanding, and at least token help he could always depend, and that in his place he now had to deal with the cold, unbending, and lugubrious Ibrahim Pasha, who was as hard on himself as on others, from whose stony countenance it was hard to wheedle a good word or a human emotion.

This impression of his had grown stronger since his initial contact with the Vizier; moreover, everything he had learned about him from D'Avenat added fresh substance to it. Very soon, however, Daville was forced to conclude that his interpreter, for all his realistic and expert approach, was actually a one-sided judge of men. It was true that in ordinary business and the routine intercourse of workaday life his judgment was penetrating, pitilessly accurate, and dependable. But as soon as he was faced with subtler and more complex problems, his indolence and disregard of moral issues led him to generalize, oversimplify, and make snap judgments. So it was in this case.

After his second and third audiences, the Consul discovered that the Vizier was not as remote as he had seemed at first sight. Above all, the new Vizier also had his "favorite topic of conversation." In his case it was not the sea, as with Mehmed Husref Pasha, or some other lively and positive subject. For Ibrahim Pasha the starting and finishing point of every conversation was the fall of his master Selim III, and his own personal tragedy which had been closely bound up with that fall. From this point, his views fanned out in all directions. They even shadowed and colored all that was happening in the world around him; and viewed thus, it was natural that the world should appear dark, troubled, and without hope.

Still, the Consul was heartened by the discovery that the Vizier was not simply a "physical freak and a spiritual mummy," and that there were topics and words that moved and stirred him. What was more, the Consul realized with time that this hard and somber Vizier, whose every conversation was a lecture on the worthlessness of all existence, was in many respects a better and more trustworthy man than the flashing, volatile, and ever-smiling Mehmed Pasha. The way in which Daville listened to his pessimistic judgments and general discourses pleased the Vizier and inspired his confidence, for it was to his taste. He never talked as long or as confidentially either to von Mitterer or to any other personage, as he came more and more to talk to Daville. And the Consul, in his turn, grew fonder and fonder of these meetings in which the pair of them wallowed avidly in the manifold troubles of this imperfect world and at the end of which he would usually extract some small concession, which had been the purpose of his visit to the Vizier in the first place.

The conversation usually began with a tribute to Napoleon's most recent success on the battlefront or in the field of international politics; but the Vizier, obeying his natural compulsion, moved at once from cheerful and affirmative topics to grave and unpleasant ones—England, for example, her toughness, ruthlessness, and acquisitive drive, against which even Napoleon's avenging genius was helpless.

From there it was only a step to a general discourse on the problems of ruling people and telling them what to do, on the thankless job of those who ruled and gave orders, on how public affairs tended, more often than not, to fly off at a tangent and double back on themselves, contrary to the wishes of high-minded men and the clear but unenforceable laws of morality. At that point, he would pass on to the fate of Selim III and his followers. Daville would listen with mute attention and deep sympathy as the Vizier's words took on a note of pathetic zeal: "The world is determined not to be happy. People can't stand a sensible government or a noble-minded ruler. Goodness in this world is like a naked orphan. May the All-Highest guide your Emperor, but I saw with my own eyes what happened to my master Sultan Selim. There was a man whom God had blessed with every good quality of mind and body. He slaved away and burnt himself out like a candle for the happiness and progress of the Empire. Clever, gentle, and righteous, he never had an evil or treacherous thought, never dreamt what depths of malice, duplicity, and bad faith men harbored in themselves; and so he laid himself wide open and no one could save him from it. Spending all his strength in the discharge of his sovereign duties and leading a pure life such as hadn't been known since the times of the caliphs, Selim did nothing to defend himself from the attacks and treachery of evil schemers. That explains why a mere detachment of Jamaks, the scum of the army, led by a mad rabble rouser, could force such a ruler from the throne and shut him up in the Serai, in order to wipe out all his far-seeing plans for pulling the Empire out of its rut and apathy and to place on the throne a shallow, sensual wretch who surrounded himself with boors, drunkards, and professional traitors.

There, that's the kind of politics the world dotes on. And how few people there are who can see that, and even fewer who are able and willing to prevent it!"

From this topic he would pass on to Bosnia and the conditions under which he and the Consul had to live there. The minute he turned to Bosnia and the Bosnians the Vizier's language and word pictures became exceedingly sharp and dismal, and here Daville found himself listening with genuine compassion and real understanding.

The Vizier was inconsolable over the fact that the news of Selim's fall had overtaken him at a moment when, at the head of his army, he was about to push the Russians out of Wallachia and Moldavia, with success almost in his grasp. Thus at one stroke the tragedy robbed the Empire of the best of Sultans and him, Ibrahim Pasha, of a great victory that was as good as won, only to cast him suddenly, a humiliated and broken man, into this remote and poverty-stricken land.

"You can see yourself, my noble friend, where we are and the kind of people I have to contend and put up with. It would be easier to run a herd of wild bison than these Bosnian begs and chieftains. They are wild, wild, wild. They're brainless, rude, and uncouth, but touchy and puffed up at the same time, headstrong but nothing inside the head. Believe me when I tell you, these Bosnians have no feeling of honor in their hearts and no sense in their heads; they fall over one another with their quarrels and intrigue and that's the only thing they know and can do. And with these people I'm supposed to go and put down the uprising in Serbia! That's been the story of our Empire since they removed and banished Sultan Selim, and God alone knows what we're going to do next."

The Vizier's voice died away in silence and his hollow eyes, which only despair could light up now, glowed up weakly, like tarnished crystals, on his impassive face.

Framing his words carefully, Daville broke the silence: "But if things were to change at Istanbul by some lucky turn of circumstances, and you were reinstated in the office of Grand Vizier . . ."

"Oh, even then!" said the Vizier, who that morning took particular pleasure in painting the future in the bleakest of colors. "Even then," he went on in a dull voice, "I would be dispatching firmans that no one would carry out. I would be defending the country from the Russians, the English, the Serbs, and every other kind of blight. I would be trying to save something that's almost impossible to save."

At the end of such talks the Consul would usually state the purpose of his visit, which might concern a permit for the export of grain to Dalmatia, some frontier dispute or the like, and the Vizier, still deep in his bleak reveries, would give his approval without much thought.

At other times the Vizier would speak of different things during the audience, but always in the same glum tone of quiet hopelessness and disillusion. He talked of the new Grand Vizier, who hated him and envied him because he had been more fortunate in the previous wars, and who for that reason kept him in suspense and withheld the equipment and the intelligence he needed in the campaign against Serbia. Or he would give Daville the latest news about his predecessor in Travnik, Husref Mehmed Pasha, whom the same Grand Vizier had exiled all the way to Keser.

All this so filled and burdened the Consul's head that, in spite of the fact that he usually accomplished his mission successfuly, he returned home as if poisoned and could not eat his supper and would spend the night dreaming of calamities, exiles, and misery of all sorts.

All the same, Daville was glad that in the Vizier's incurable pessimism he had found, momentarily at least, a point of contact with the man; it was like a narrow, isolated strip of no man's land on which the two of them could meet as man to man, in that crude Turkish world that was devoid of a spark of understanding or a vestige of humanity to which he, a luckless foreign consul, might respond. At times it seemed to him it would need only a little effort and a little leisure for a real friendship and a close human relationship to spring up between him and the Vizier.

And just then some incident would occur that would show up, all at once, the impassable distance between them, that revealed the Vizier in an entirely new light, a worse and more deplorable person than D'Avenat had pictured him in their conversations. And once more Daville would be thrown into utter confusion, robbed of the hope of ever finding in these parts "one spark of humanity" that would live longer than a fear or outlast a smile or a glance. The Consul would then tell himself, in wonder and despair, that the harsh school of the East knew no recess and

went on forever, that in these lands there was no end to surprises, just as there was no true moderation, no steadfast judgment, no lasting value in human relationships.

One could not tell or foresee, even approximately, the next
move these people were likely to make.

One day the Vizier unexpectedly summoned both consuls at
the same time, which had never happened before. Their two
processions met at the gate. The divan had the air of a special
occasion. The courtiers whispered and buzzed. The Vizier was
cordial and dignified. After the first coffee and chibouks, the
Secretary and the town mayor also appeared and took their
places modestly. The Vizier told the consuls how his Deputy,
Suleiman Pasha, had crossed the river Drina the week before
with his Bosnian troops and had routed a very strong and well-
equipped Serbian force, trained and led by "Russian officers."
He ventured to hope that as a result of this victory there would
be no Russians left in Serbia, which in all probability would
mean the end of the whole rebellion. It was an important victory, said the Vizier, and the moment was obviously close at
hand when quiet and order would be restored in Serbia. Knowing that the consuls, as good friends and neighbors, would be
delighted to hear this, he had called them to share his pleasure
at the good news.

The Vizier fell silent. As if that were a signal, a group of
pages entered the audience hall almost at a trot. A reed mat was
spread across the vacant part of the great hall. They brought in
several baskets, sacks of goat hair, and greasy black sheepskin
bags. They quickly untied and opened these containers and
began to empty them on the outspread mat. While this was
being done, the servants brought the consuls lemonade and
fresh chibouks.

A great big heap of severed human ears and noses began to
grow on the mat—an indescribable heap of wretched human
flesh, salted and blackened in its own dried blood. A cold and
sickly reek of damp salt and curdled blood spread through the
audience hall. Then, out of the baskets and sacks, they took
several hats, belts, and bandoleers with metal eagles on them;
and from other bags they pulled out red and yellow pennants,
narrow and gold-tasseled, with a picture of a saint in the middle.
These were followed by two or three icons, which hit the floor
with a dull thud. Finally they carried in a sheaf of bayonets
tied with bark rope.

These were the trophies of the victory over the rebel Serbian army "which the Russians had organized and led."

Someone unseen on the fringe of the gathering said in a deep, praying voice: "Allah has blessed the arms of Islam!" All those present echoed it with an indistinct murmur.

Daville, who would not have expected a scene like this even in his dreams, felt his stomach heave and the lemonade turn acrid on his tongue, threatening to burst through his nose. He forgot his pipe and could only stare at von Mitterer, as if expecting rescue and an explanation from him. The Austrian was himself pale and bowed, but as he had long been used to surprises of this kind, he was the first to find words and congratulate the Vizier and the Bosnian army on their victory. Anxious not to appear to lag behind his rival, Daville suppressed his fear and revulsion and spoke a few sentences in honor of the victory, adding his wishes for the continued success of imperial arms and peace in the Empire. He said this in a somewhat wooden voice; he seemed to hear each one of his words clearly, as if another person spoke them. Everything was duly translated. Then, once again, it was the turn of the Vizier. He thanked the consuls for their good wishes and felicitations, saying that he deemed himself well blessed to have them beside him at a moment when, with considerable emotion, he beheld these arms which the faithless Muscovites had shamefully left behind them on the battlefield.

Daville forced himself to look at the Vizier, whose eyes indeed had lighted up and glowed at the corners like crystals.

A barely audible murmur passed through the divan. The audience was at an end. Seeing von Mitterer's eyes riveted on the mat, Daville too screwed up courage to cast a glance at the trophy heap. The lifeless objects of leather and metal seemed dead twice over; abandoned and pitiful, they lay there like something that had been disinterred and brought into the light of day after centuries. The indescribable mound of severed ears and noses lay still; around it was a scattering of salt, black as earth with the soaked-up blood and mixed with the chaff of grain sacks. All of it gave off a cold, rancid, trailing odor.

Daville looked several times at von Mitterer, and then back at the reed mat in front of him, secretly hoping that the whole thing would vanish like a bad dream; but each time his eyes came to rest on the same objects, defying belief yet real and inescapable in their lifelessness.

"Wake up!" Daville thought quickly. "Wake up and shake off the nightmare, get out into the sun, rub your eyes and get a breath of fresh air!" But there was no awakening; this sordid horror was the bedrock of reality itself. This was the kind of people they were. Such was their life. This was what the best of them did!

Once more nausea welled up in Daville's throat and he felt his eyes dimming. Still, he managed to take his leave politely and go home with his suite as if nothing had happened. Once there, instead of sitting down to lunch, he went and lay on his bed.

Next day Daville and von Mitterer met again. Not asking who owed a visit to whom, they all but rushed into each other's arms, as if they hadn't seen each other in ages. They kept shaking hands and looking into each other's eyes like two shipwrecked men. Von Mitterer had already checked up on the true facts of the Turkish victory and on the origin of the trophies. The arms had been seized from a Serbian column, while the pennants and everything else were taken in a brutal massacre which the exasperated and unemployed troops had wreaked on a congregation of Bosnian peasants somewhere in the vicinity of Zvornik, during a religious feast.

Von Mitterer was not a man given to reflection and there seemed to be no point in discussing the thing further. But Daville fretted himself sick over the last audience, asking himself over and over again: "Why the lies? Why this useless, almost infantile pretense? What is the real meaning of their laughter and of their tears? What is behind their silence? And how can the Vizier, with his lofty notions, and that seemingly honorable Suleiman Pasha and the wise Tahir Beg organize such a thing and lend their presence to these exhibitions which bear the ghastly stamp of another, lower world? Which is their true face? Which is real life and which calculated play-acting? When are they lying, when are they speaking the truth?"

And besides his physical revulsion he felt himself tormented by the gnawing realization that he would never be able to find a rational standard for judging these people and their actions.

This kind of soul-searching was even more painful and harder to take when it involved some point of French interest—in other words, Daville's personal pride and official zeal.

Through his agents Daville kept in constant touch with the

Turkish garrison commanders on the Austrian frontier. Every plundering foray by these garrisons, even the smallest, or even an intimation that a foray was being mounted, forced the Austrians to send their troops into the territory and maintain them there. Making full use of his connections, Daville thus tried all he could to weaken the Austrian army's strength and to perpetuate the tension along the Austrian-Bosnian frontier.

Outstanding among these garrison commanders was the captain of Novi, Ahmed Beg Cerich. Daville knew him personally. He was quite a young man, who had taken over his father's command after the latter's death. He was voluble and impetuous. Ahmed Beg burned with a desire to gain glory in fighting on the frontier which his forebears had crossed and plundered so often. He boasted indiscreetly of his ties with the French and sent threats and insulting messages to the Austrian commander on the other side, signing them: "From Ahmed Beg Cerich and the French Emperor Napoleon."

In keeping with the tradition of the frontier commanders, he hated and despised the Vizier, seldom came down to Travnik, and refused to obey orders and instructions from anyone.

The Austrians succeeded, through their people at the Porte, to blacken Ahmed Beg's name and expose him as a traitor in the pay of the French. It was a faster, cheaper, and more efficient method than battling for years with the young and ebullient captain along the frontier. The trap was well laid. A decree sentencing Ahmed Beg to death was sent to Travnik, with a reprimand to the Vizier for tolerating such captains and letting the Porte find out about their treason from other sources. The choice was laid down very plainly: Either the offending captain would be removed and disposed of or a new Vizier would be sent to Travnik.

It was not an easy thing to lure Ahmed Beg to Travnik, but the Austrians were helpful even here. The captain was tricked into believing that the French Consul would like to see him and talk to him. The moment he got to Travnik he was arrested, put in irons, and thrown into the fortress dungeon.

Daville now had an opportunity to see the Turkish terror at work, to find out what lies and force could do when combined, and what powers he was up against in this town of the damned.

Already the morning after Ahmed Beg's arrest, a gypsy was hanged below the cemetery and the town crier announced pointedly that he had been hanged "because he invoked God's mercy

on the captain from Novi" when the latter was being led to
the fortress. It was the same as condemning the captain to
death. All at once, everything and everybody began to quail with
that blind, cold fear that from time to time descended on Travnik and Bosnia, halting and freezing all life and even thought
for a few hours or days, thus enabling the power which inspired
it to carry out its will swiftly and without interference.

All his life Daville had loathed and avoided everything that
was dramatic. He found it hard even to imagine that there could
be only one solution to a conflict, the tragic one; this ran coun-
ter to his whole nature. Yet now he was embroiled, indirectly,
in a real tragedy that was beyond unraveling and solution. In
the excitable state he was in, trapped in these mountains, confused and harried now for almost two years by difficulties and
troubles of every kind, Daville felt himself more entangled in
the affair of the captain from Novi than in fact he was. What
pained him especially was that the captain, according to D'Avenat, had been lured to Travnik in his name, so that the hapless
man might imagine that the French Consul had been an ac-
cessory to his misfortune.

After a sleepless night he decided to seek an audience with
the Vizier and to intercede for the captain, in a discreet and
moderate way, so as not to cause him more harm. The talk with
the Vizier revealed a totally new face of Ibrahim Pasha. This
was not the Ibrahim Pasha with whom, only a few days before,
he had conversed, as with a close friend, about the disorders
of the world and about the need for harmony among intelligent
men of high ideals. As soon as he mentioned the captain, the
Vizier grew cool and distant. Impatiently, almost in wonder, the
Vizier listened to his "noble friend," whom, evidently, life had
not yet taught that conversations were conversations and business was business and that everyone had to bear his appointed
burden alone and deal with it as best he could.

Summoning all his wits, Daville tried to be resolute, persuasive, and trenchant, but he himself was aware that his mind
and will were languishing and ebbing, as in a dream, and that
some irresistible flood tide was sweeping the handsome smiling
captain away. He even dropped Napoleon's name a few times,
asking the Vizier what the world would say when it learned that
a distinguished high officer was given capital punishment simply
because he was thought to be a friend of France and had been
falsely accused by the Austrians. But every word of Daville's

was swallowed up instantly, without recall, in the silence of the Vizier.

At length, the Vizier said: "I thought it would be safer and better to hold him here until the hue and cry against him has died down; but if you wish, I shall send him back to his garrison and let him wait there. However, Istanbul shall have the last word."

It seemed to Daville that none of these obscure phrases had any connection with the captain's fate, or with his own agitation, but he could not get anything more out of the Vizier.

He also called on Suleiman Pasha, who had just come back from Serbia, and on Secretary Tahir Beg, and was amazed and stunned to be greeted with the same silence and the same gaze of pained astonishment from them. They looked at him as if he were wasting his breath on something that had long been over, and irretrievably lost, although politeness required that his speech should not be interrupted but should be heard with patience and sympathy to the end.

On the way back to the Consulate, Daville asked his interpreter what he thought about it. D'Avenat, who had translated all three interviews that morning, said unexcitedly: "After what the Vizier said it is clear that nothing can be done for Ahmed Beg. It is a lost cause. It will be either exile to Anatolia, or something worse."

Blood rushed to the Consul's head. "How do you mean? Didn't he promise to send him back to Novi at the very least?"

For a moment the interpreter let his red-rimmed eyes rest on the Consul's face; then he said in a dry, flat voice: "How could he send him back to Novi, where the captain would have a hundred ways of saving himself and defying him?"

The Consul had the impression that the tone and the eyes of his interpreter too had something of that impatient wonder which had so rattled and offended him when he spoke with the Vizier and his assistants.

Once again, the Consul had to endure a sleepless night, with its creeping hours, its sense of utter loss that sharpened his realization of impotence and sapped his will to defend his cause. He opened the window, as if seeking help from outside. He inhaled deeply and stared into the darkness. Out there somewhere was the grave of the gypsy who'd had the bad luck to meet the captain on the bridge before the fortress and had called out "*Merhab*"—God be with you—in a humble and timid voice, for, gypsy though he was, he had not the heart or the effrontery not to greet the man who had once done him a great favor. Out there too was the young captain, lost, without justice or good reason. As if the darkness were easier to see by than the beguiling light of day, Daville now plainly saw his own helplessness and the captain's fate.

During the Revolution in Paris and in his war years in Spain he had seen many deaths and disasters, tragedies of innocent lives, and fatal misunderstandings; but he had never yet seen, in this way, so close at hand, a man of honor foundering headlong under the pressure of events. In this kind of environment, where morbid circumstances, blind chance, caprice, and base instincts were the order of the day, it was evidently possible for a man, singled out accidentally by someone's accusing finger, to find himself swept into the whirlpool of events and to drown without help. And now this handsome, strapping, wealthy captain was suddenly caught up in this kind of vortex. He had done nothing which frontier commanders had not done all their lives as far back as anyone could remember, but he, as it happened, found himself snarled in a tangle of events that was to kink and knot itself into a lethal rope.

It was by accident that the Austrian frontier commander, in advancing his proposal to destroy the young captain of Novi, had met with ready understanding among his superior officers; it was by accident too that the Austrian authorities happened just then to attach great importance to keeping peace on the frontier; that Vienna sent a strongly worded demand to an official at the Porte, who was in their pay, asking that the captain be removed; that this unknown high official, being very anxious at that moment not to jeopardize his Austrian income, exerted strong pressure on the Vizier at Travnik; and that Ibrahim Pasha, discouraged and intimidated for the rest of his life, handed the matter over to the harsh and implacable town Major, who thought nothing of destroying an upright man, and who, in his turn, happened at that moment to be casting about for a strong deterrent example that would illustrate his power and strike fear into the notables and frontier commanders.

Each one of these personages acted independently and for himself alone, without any reference to the person of the captain; but working as they did, all together, they drew the noose tight around the captain's neck. All unwittingly and quite by accident.

Such was the fate of the Consul's unlucky protégé. As he peered into the humid darkness, Daville began to grasp more clearly what he had been unable to grasp that morning from the impatient silence and those amazed looks at the Residency.

And on the other side of Travnik, on the farther bank, as it were, of that same darkness, sat Colonel von Mitterer, still awake in a pool of untroubled light, penning his report on the case of Ahmed Beg Cerich to his superior. He took care to underline his own contribution to the downfall of the captain from Novi, without undue embellishment, so as not to upset the commanding officer in Croatia and all the others who had worked on this case. "The restless and ambitious captain, a great enemy of ours, is at this moment lying in irons in the local citadel, under a grave indictment. The way things stand, he is not likely to keep his head. From what I have learned, the Vizier is determined to make short work of him. While I cannot work openly and make special efforts toward that end, you may rest assured I shall do nothing do discourage them from wringing his neck once and for all time."

Next day at dawn, the captain from Novi was shot dead in his sleep and buried the same morning in the cemetery between the highway and the Lashva River. The town was given to understand that he had attempted escape while they were taking him to Novi and that the guards had to fire after him.

Daville lived in a slow fever and all but collapsed from lack of sleep and fatigue. Yet the moment he closed his eyes he felt that he was alone in the world, surrounded by a conspiracy of the forces of hell, that he was fighting them with the last of his strength, with fading senses, in thick fog and on slippery ground.

He was kept awake by the thought that he must write a report without delay, in three copies, one each to Paris, Istanbul, and Split. He must sit down and write, describing his intervention with the Vizier as a dramatic struggle for the prestige of France, and blaming his lack of success on unfortunate circumstances.

For a time, the death of the captain of Novi afflicted Daville like a sickness, but then he began to convalesce. When he rose up from it he said to himself: "You came to this country at a bad time and now you can't turn back. Try to bear in mind always that you cannot measure the actions of these people by your own standards and according to your own sensibility, for this is the surest way of going under in a very short time." With this resolution he went back to work once more. And times being what they were, new anxieties soon pushed the old ones into oblivion. New tasks and instructions arrived for the Consul. Realizing that his superiors did not attach the same significance to the death of the captain of Novi that he did himself in his isolation and bewilderment, Daville too made an effort to erase this defeat from his consciousness and silence the nagging questions raised by it. It was not easy to forget the ruddy girlish face of Ahmed Beg, with its flashing teeth and the clear brown eyes of a mountaineer and the smile of a man who was afraid of nothing. Nor was it easy to forget that silence of the Vizier's, before which the Consul had felt powerless and humbled, incapable of defending his rights and the cause of his country. And yet, under the avalanche of new problems that kept growing by the day, he could not help forgetting even that.

The Vizier suddenly became his old self again. He resumed inviting Daville and was cordial to him, he did him various favors and talked to him as usual. Daville cultivated this peculiar friendship of his. They came to spend more and more time in intimate conversation, which the Vizier often monopolized for his pessimistic soliloquies but in which Daville always managed in the end to push through some petty consular business for which he had come. There were days when the Vizier himself took the initiative and asked the French Consul for a chat on some pretext or other. In this respect Daville far outclassed his rival von Mitterer. The Austrian Consul was received only when he asked for an audience and the Vizier talked to him briefly, in a politely cool and official manner.

Not even the fact that Napoleon's peace treaty with Russia had caused widespread disappointment and strong anti-French feeling in Istanbul could for long affect the relationship between the Vizier and the Consul. As always with the Turks, the change of mood was sudden and the surprise complete. When the Vizier first got the news of the treaty from Istanbul, he cooled off immediately. He stopped inviting Daville for a chat; and when the latter asked for an audience, he talked to him dryly and curtly. But all this lasted only a short while and, as always, ended in an abrupt about-face. The Vizier relented for no visible reason, and the friendly discourses and small mutual attentions were resumed once more. If the Vizier felt like carping on Napoleon's latest move, that too served only as a take-off for joint melancholy reflections on the impermanence of human relation-

ships. Daville put the blame for everything on England; and
Ibrahim Pasha had loathed the English as much as the Russians
ever since the day when, as Grand Vizier, he had watched the
English navy force an entry into the Bosporus.

After a while Daville began to take these surprises in stride
and grew accustomed to the ebb-and-flow pattern in their relationship.

Von Mitterer's attempts to gain the Vizier's ear with gifts and
to squeeze Daville out remained fruitless. He obtained an ele-
gant carriage from Slavonski Brod and presented it to the Vizier.
It was the first genuine, luxuriously appointed fiacre Travnik
had ever seen. The Vizier accepted the gift with thanks, and the
townspeople trooped to the Residency to have a look at the black
and shiny lacquered coach. However, the Vizier showed no great
enthusiasm for it, and von Mitterer felt deeply humiliated by
the fact—which he kept out of his official reports—that Ibrahim
Pasha never once sat in the carriage and rode out in it. The
fiacre was left standing in the middle of the courtyard of the
Residency, a cold, resplendent, and unwelcome gift.

About the same time Daville, whose funds were considerably
more modest and whose influence with his government was
nowhere as great as von Mitterer's, managed to obtain from
Paris, as gifts for the Vizier, a small telescope and an astrolabe,
an instrument for observing the position and altitude of stars
on the horizon. The Consul was hard put to explain the proper
use of the telescope, indeed it looked to him as if some parts
were missing or defective; but the Vizier accepted the gift with
his usual grace. To him, in any case, all objects were dead and
meaningless and he valued them only in relation to the person
or the intent of the person who gave them. But the telescope
served to launch them on a fresh discussion of celestial bodies
and the human fortune that is written in the stars and of the
changes and catastrophes which they foretell.

In that first year of his rule at Travnik the Vizier suffered a
grave new blow that almost crushed him, if indeed he needed
any more crushing.

Some time during the summer the Vizier had set out with a
large escort toward the Serbian frontier on the river Drina. He
intended, by his presence there, to encourage the Bosnian troups
to stay put as long as possible and to keep them from dispers-
ing, ahead of time, to their winter quarters in Bosnia. Chances

were he might have succeeded in this, but at Zvornik news reached him of a new *coup d'état* at Istanbul and of the tragic death of the former Sultan, Selim III.

The courier who brought the details of all that had taken place at Istanbul at the end of July, not knowing that the Vizier was at the front, had come first to Travnik; from there he was immediately dispatched to Zvornik. Through the same courier, Daville sent the Vizier a box of fresh lemons from Dalmatia, with a few friendly lines that made no allusion to the recent events at Istanbul but which were clearly intended as a token of attention and sympathy toward the Vizier in the misfortune that had overtaken his master. When the same courier returned to Travnik, he brought a letter from the Vizier thanking Daville for the gift and saying only that a gift from a sincere friend was a great joy and that "the Angel of Light guides the steps of the gift giver." Daville, who realized only too well what a heavy blow Selim's terrible death was for the Vizier, stood amazed and thoughtful over the cordial, all but serene letter. It was one of those baffling surprises that a person meets with in the Orient. There seemed to be no connection whatever between the man's actual inner life and his written words.

The Consul's wonder would have been still greater if he could have seen the Vizier right after he got the news from Istanbul. The tents of the Vizier and his suite were on a strip of level ground below an abandoned mine. Here, even on sultry summer nights, the air was always cool, because all night long a steady breeze wafted the freshness of water and brook willows through the narrow valley. The Vizier at once retired to his tent and allowed no one except his nearest and most loyal friends near him. Tahir Beg gave orders that everything should be made ready for the return to Travnik, but the Vizier's condition made it impossible even to think of an immediate start on such a rough journey.

Having received the bad news with an expressionless face, the Vizier, without a glance at those present, and with the same unruffled calm, intoned a Koran prayer for the dead and invoked the peace of Allah on the soul of the man he had loved more than anything or anyone in the world. Then, with that slow step of a phantom in the deep of night, he walked to his tent and, as soon as the heavy flap had closed behind him, fell like a log on the cushions and began to tear off his equipment and his dress like a man who is choking for air. His old manser-

vant, a mute since birth, tried in vain to undress him and cover
him, but the Vizier would not allow himself to be touched, as
if every touch, even the lightest, gave him inexpressible pain.
He pushed away the glass of sherbet with a convulsive movement. Then, like a stone hurtled from a great height, he lay
with his eyes shut and his lips pressed together. The color of
his skin changed rapidly: from yellow to green and then to
an earthy brown, in a sudden access of gall. He lay dumb and
unmoving like this for several hours. It was only toward evening
that he began, first to moan softly, and then to make long, monotonous groaning sounds, with rare and brief intermissions.
If anyone had dared to come near the tent, he might have
thought that some weak foolish lamb, born only the day before,
had strayed into the tent and was bleating for its mother. But
except for the Secretary and the old manservant no one was
allowed to come near or even to see and hear the Vizier from
a distance.

For a whole day and night the Vizier lay like this, refusing
all help, not opening his eyes, making that throaty, drawn-out
monotone sound of a subdued animal wail: "E-e-e-e . . . !"

It was only at dawn of the second day that Tahir Beg managed to bring him around and coax him to talk. Once the spell
was broken, the Vizier quickly came to himself; he dressed and
became his old self again. It was as if in putting on his clothes
he also put on his habitual stiffness and recovered his old sparing movements. Even the greatest calamity found nothing more
to change in him. He gave instructions for an immediate departure, but was obliged to travel slowly, in short stages, from
one camp site to another.

When the Vizier returned to Travnik, Daville sent him, by
way of welcome, another box of lemons, but did not ask for an
audience, as he thought it wiser to let the grief-stricken man
decide about it himself; yet he was most anxious, all the same,
to meet him and hear him so as to tell his Ambassador in Istanbul about his impressions of Selim's former Grand Vizier
and his comments. Daville was doubly pleased with his shrewd
decision when he learned that the Austrian Consul had at once
asked for an audience and had been received, but in a cool and
unfriendly manner, and that the Vizier had refused to say a
word in answer to his queries about the events at Istanbul. A
few short days later, Daville reaped the fruits of his wise restraint.

The Vizier invited the French Consul on a Thursday, ostensibly to inform him, after his visit to the front, about the course of operations against the rebels in Serbia. He received him warmly and did, in fact, begin by talking of what he had seen at the front. To hear him describe it, it was all rather trivial and without significance. The undertone of contempt in his deep dull voice seemed to apply equally to the insurgents and to the Bosnian army that was sent against them.

"I saw what I had to see, and now my presence in those frontier districts has become unnecessary. The Russians who helped the rebels to carry out the operations have left Serbia. What remains now are the disgruntled, misguided bands of peasantry. It is beneath the dignity of the Ottoman Empire that a former grand vizier should be directly involved with them. These are poor devils, bickering among themselves, who will bleed each other and then fall at our feet. One should not dirty one's hands there. . . ."

In admiration, Daville gazed at this statue of grief that was lying with such imperturbable dignity. What the Vizier had said was in utter contradiction to reality, but the calm and dignity with which he said it were themselves a potent and undeniable reality.

"There you are!" Daville's old reflection rose up in his mind, while the interpreter was winding up his translation. "There . . . the course of life doesn't really depend on us at all, or at least very little, but the way we react to events does depend on us to a great extent, so there's no point in wasting one's strength and diverting one's attention."

Very shortly after the Vizier's contemptuous reference to the Serbian rebellion and the Bosnian army that was supposed to have crushed it, the conversation turned automatically to Selim's death. Here too there was no change in the Vizier's voice or expression. It was as if all of him were saturated with a fatal grief that permitted no shading or modulation.

For a while they were alone in the great divan on the first floor. Even the chibouk bearers had vanished at a secret signal. There were only the Vizier and the Consul and between them, on a slightly lower level, bent forward over his crossed legs, with folded arms and downcast eyes, D'Avenat, who seemed to have shrunk down to a bare voice, a quiet monotone, almost a whisper, in which he translated for the Consul.

The Vizier asked Daville if he knew the details of the tragedy

at Istanbul. The Consul told him he did not, but would like to
know them as soon as possible, since all Frenchmen were distressed over the death of so sincere a friend and so remarkable
a ruler as Selim had been.

"You are right," the Vizier said pensively. "The Sultan—may
he rest in peace and enjoy the splendors of paradise—truly
loved and esteemed your country and your Emperor. All right-
thinking and noble-minded people, without distinction, have lost
a great friend in him."

The Vizier spoke in a low hushed voice, as if the dead Sultan
lay in the next room, and confined himself to actual facts and
details, as if deliberately avoiding the main and gravest aspect
of the matter.

"No one who didn't know him well could possibly have any
idea of what a loss it is!" said the Vizier. "He was a many-sided
man, consummate in every field of endeavor. He sought the company of learned men. He even wrote himself, under the name
of 'Il Khani'—Inspired—and his verses were a joy to those who
could appreciate them. And I can remember the poem he composed on the morning he ascended the throne. 'Allah's grace has
accorded me the throne of Suleiman the Magnificent,' was how
it began, I think. But his real passion was architecture and
mathematics. He personally collaborated on the reforms of the
administration and the tax system. He went around the schools,
questioned the students, and distributed rewards. He climbed
the buildings with an ivory ruler in his hand and supervised the
methods of work, the quality and cost of the structure. He wanted
to see and know everything. He loved work and was healthy in
body, strong and nimble, and no one could match him with a
sword or a lance. I have seen him with my own eyes cut three
rams with a single blow of his sword. They must have taken
him by surprise, by some ruse, when he was unarmed, because
with a sword in his hand he was afraid of no one. Ah, he was too
noble, too trusting, too gullible!"

The only way one could tell that the subject was a dead man
was the Vizier's use of the past tense in speaking of his beloved
master. Apart from this, either from fear or superstition, he
never so much as mentioned the death and the disappearance
of the Sultan.

He spoke fast and absently, as though he wanted to outrace
another conversation inside himself.

D'Avenat translated quietly, trying to remain as unobtrusive as possible with his voice and presence. Once, near the end of the translation, the Vizier started all of a sudden, as if only just discovering and noticing the interpreter, and turning toward him with his whole body, slowly and stiffly, like a statue manipulated by unseen hands, fixed his terrible ghoul-like eyes, the eyes of a stone man, on the interpreter, whose voice quailed and whose spine bent still lower.

That was the end of the conversation for that day. The Consul and his interpreter came out as if emerging from a funeral chamber. D'Avenat was deathly pale and there were beads of cold sweat on his forehead. Daville was silent all the way home. But he put down the spectral movement of that living statue as among his most fearsome experiences at Travnik.

Nevertheless, the death of the former Sultan Selim also helped to create a stronger bond between the Vizier and the Consul, who was a good listener and knew how to show interest in the doleful talks of the Vizier, with restraint and discretion.

Several days later, the Consul was summoned to another audience. Ibrahim Pasha had received further news from Istanbul, from a servant who had witnessed the death of Selim, and he evidently wished to tell the Consul about it.

The Vizier's outward appearance gave no clue of what had gone on inside him during those last ten days, but one could see from his talk that he had begun to reconcile himself to the loss and was learning how to live with his pain. He now spoke about that death as something that was finished and done with.

In the next fifteen days Daville met the Vizier three times; twice in the divan, and once when they went to the Vizier's new foundry to watch the casting of new field guns. Each time Daville came with an agenda of petitions and items of current business. Everything was settled quickly and almost always in his favor. Immediately afterwards, with a grim and passionate eagerness, the Vizier turned to the subject of Selim's tragic death, the causes and details of that event. His need to talk about it was great and compulsive, and the French Consul happened to be the only person he thought worthy of such conversation. By asking a tactful question now and then, Daville helped and encouraged him, while demonstrating his sympathy; that was how he learned the full details of the last act of Selim's, and in fact the Vizier's own, tragedy. And he could see that the Vizier felt a strong need to dwell on these details at great length.

The movement supporting the dethroned Sultan Selim III had

been spearheaded by one Mustapha Bariaktar, one of the best commanders in the army, an honest but impulsive and illiterate man. He set out from Wallachia with his Albanian troops and marched on Istanbul, planning to overturn the unworthy government and Sultan, Mustapha, and then to free Selim from his imprisonment at the Serai and reinstate him. He was acclaimed all along the route and at last came to Istanbul, where he was greeted as victor and liberator. He managed to reach the Serai and penetrate the outer courtyard, but here the guards succeeded in shutting the strong inner gate in his face. It was then that the brave but simple and clumsy Bariaktar made a fatal mistake. He began to shout and demand the immediate release of the dethroned but lawful Sultan, Selim. Hearing this and realizing that Bariaktar was master of the situation, the stupid but cunning and brutal Sultan Mustapha ordered the immediate execution of Selim. A slave woman betrayed the luckless Sultan, who had just knelt for his afternoon prayer when the Chief Eunuch and four of his assistants entered the apartment. For a second they hesitated in confusion, then the Chief Eunuch threw himself on Selim, who at that moment was bowed over his knees and touching his forehead to the prayer rug. The other eunuchs helped their Chief, one seizing the arms of Selim, the other his legs, while a third chased out the servants with a drawn knife.

The Consul felt a cold shiver run down his spine. Listening only with half an ear, he imagined suddenly that he had a madman before him and the Vizier's inner mind was even stranger and more deranged than his weird exterior. D'Avenat translated with difficulty, omitting words and skipping whole sentences. "He is mad, there could be no doubt about it!" The Consul told himself. "He's mad!"

Imperturbably the Vizier went on with his tale, in a kind of intonation, as though he were not talking to a man beside him but carrying on a private dialogue. His account grew more and more precise, detailed, and meticulous, as if that were of tremendous importance, as if he were weaving a spell and by that spell hoped to save the Sultan who was no longer to be saved. Driven by his mysterious but irresistible need, he was bent on repeating aloud everything he had heard from the escaped witness, everything that now oppressed his mind. Clearly he was determined to relive the days of his own temporary insanity. It was a kind of obsession, the cause and center of which was the fall of Selim III, and he gained at least some partial relief from his agony by baring the whole drama to a well-disposed stranger.

Daville could picture the fatal tussle in the Serai only too vividly; against his will, he was obliged to follow it in all its grisly details, which made him shudder afresh every other moment.

In the struggle which took place, the Vizier went on, Selim managed to wrench himself free and send the fat Chief Eunuch reeling to the floor with a powerful blow. He stood in the middle of the room, flailing out with his hands and feet. The Negro eunuchs went at him from all sides, ducking his blows as well as they could. One of them had a strung bow and was trying to catch his victim's head in it, to garrote him with the bowstring. "He had no sword—if he'd had it, it would have been a very different matter," the Vizier repeated sorrowfully. Selim was so intent on warding off the bowstring that he lost sight of the fallen Chief Eunuch. The fat and powerful Negro rose to his knees unobserved and with one lightning movement caught the straddled Selim by his testicles. The Sultan cried out in pain and bent down so low that his head was level with the sweaty and blood-smeared face of the Chief Eunuch. At this short range he could not swing back and hit the man, who rolled about on the carpet and didn't let go of his victim. One of the slaves took advantage of that moment and succeeded in throwing the bowstring over Selim's head. His hands clutched a few more times at his neck, but weakly and helplessly, then all of him grew limp and folded, first at the knees, then in the waist, then the neck, and he slumped down against the wall and remained hunched like that, half-sitting, twitching no more, as if he had never lived and defended himself.

The corpse was immediately laid on a carpet and carried in it, as in a stretcher, to Sultan Mustapha. Outside, Bariaktar was banging at the closed gate and shouting impatiently: "Open up, you bitches and sons of bitches! Let out the true Sultan or there won't be a head left among you!"

His Albanians were shouting and yelling, as if to give more force to his cries, and were about to break down the heavy doors.

At that moment one of the long narrow windows, cut in the wall on both sides of the gate, opened slowly. The shutter, which was rust-bound and overgrown with moss and lichen, was raised up with difficulty. A rolled-up mat appeared on the half-apron window; out of it slid an almost naked corpse which fell down with a thud on the white mosaic floor of the courtyard. The first to run up was Bariaktar. Before him lay the dead, bareheaded, bruised, and purple-faced Sultan Selim. It was too late for everything. Bariaktar had got what he wanted, but there was no value or point to his victory. Evil and madness had carried the day over good and reason. Vice remained on the throne, disorder in the government and the state.

"Such, monsieur, was the end of the noblest sovereign of the Ottoman Empire," concluded the Vizier, as if waking up, eased, from the trance in which he had spoken till then.

When Daville came home after this conversation, he reflected that no one was ever likely to know how dearly he paid for his small successes and for the concessions he obtained from the Vizier. Even D'Avenat was subdued and could find no words.

12

The year 1808 was evidently to be a year of losses and misfortunes of all kinds. Instead of that humid season, "which is neither autumn nor winter," Travnik was visited by an early and bitter cold wave at the start of November. At this time one of Daville's children suddenly fell ill.

This middle son of Daville's was in his third year and had up till then been robust and thriving, in contrast to his younger brother who had been born at Split during the journey out and had always been delicate. When the child first sickened his mother treated him with herb tea and household medicines, but when he lost strength rapidly even the staunch Mme Daville lost her confidence and self-possession. They began to call in doctors and all those who styled themselves doctors and were regarded as such by the world. The Davilles were able to see then what health and sickness meant for these people and what life and falling ill amounted to in this country.

The doctors were: D'Avenat, who was on the staff of the Consulate; Fra Luka Dafinich, from the monastery at Gucha Gora; Mordo Atias, a Travnik druggist; and Giovanni Mario Cologna, the accredited doctor of the Austrian Consulate. The attendance of the last had an official character, for he solemnly announced that he "came, on the instructions of the Austrian Consul-General, to place my professional skill at the disposal of the French Consul-General." Almost immediately, there was disagreement and conflict between him and D'Avenat, both on diagnosis and the course of treatment. Mordo Artias kept quiet, while Fra Luka wanted to go back to Gucha Gora for some special herbs.

In reality these Travnik physicians were upset and at a loss, for they had never had to treat such a small child. The range of their skill did not include, as it were, the two extreme ends of the human span. In these countries small children died or lived by the whim of chance, just as very old people died away or stretched out their lives a little longer. It was all a question of the children's or old people's power of resistance, the care they received from those around them, and, in the last instance, of the will of fate which neither medicines nor doctors could alter. For that reason, creatures such as these, who have either not lived long enough to grow strong or have lived too long to keep their strength, were not a proper subject for cures and doctors' care. And, except for the fact that in this case prominent people in high positions were involved, not one of the doctors would have bothered about this tiny human being. As it was, their visits were more an expression of attention toward the parents than of actual concern for the child. In this there was hardly any difference between Fra Luka and Mordo Atias on the one side and D'Avenat and Cologna on the other, for even these two foreigners were by now quite steeped in the ideas and customs of Eastern countries. And besides, their knowledge went neither further nor deeper than that of the other two.

Faced with this situation, Daville decided to take his child all the way down to Sinj, where there was a good and well-known French army doctor. The Travnik "physicians," true to their ideas, were unanimous in firmly opposing this bold and unusual decision, but the Consul stuck to it.

In the cold weather, which was rapidly worsening, and along icebound roads, the Consul set off accompanied by a kavass and three grooms. He himself carried the sick child in his arms, well wrapped up.

The strange caravan started from the Consulate at dawn. They had hardly crossed the Karaul Mountains when the child died in his father's arms. They spent the night in an inn with

the dead child and turned back to Travnik the following morning. They reached the Consulate at dusk.

Madame Daville had just put her baby son to bed and was
whispering a prayer "for the ones on the road" when she was
startled by the clatter of horses and knocking at the gate. She
went limp and remained rooted to the post, waiting there until
Daville came into the room, carrying the bundled child in his
arms as tenderly and carefully as he had taken him. He laid
the dead child down, threw off the great black cape that still
radiated the chill of outdoors, and then put his arms around
his wife who, stunned and frozen rigid, kept whispering the
last words of the prayer that, a moment before, she had offered
for the safe return of her infant.

Cold and sore from a two-day ride, Daville could barely stand
on his feet. His arms, which had been holding first the sick,
then the dead child in the same position for many hours, were
in a painful cramp. But now, forgetting all this, he embraced
her frail body with a wordless tenderness that expressed his
infinite love of her and of the child. He closed his eyes and let
his feelings sweep over him: it seemed to him that by forgetting
his exhaustion and overcoming his pain in this way, he was still
carrying his child toward recovery and health, that the child
would not die as long as he bore it like that across the world,
in pain and anguish. And all the while this creature in his arms
kept weeping softly and quietly, as only a brave and selfless
woman can.

Desfosses stood a little way behind them, dazed and superfluous, looking on in astonishment, unable to understand this
sudden transformation of a plain, ordinary man.

Next day, in sunny weather and a dry frost, little Jules-
François-Amyntas Daville was buried in the Catholic cemetery.
The Austrian Consul, his wife and daughter came to the funeral
and later went to the French Consulate to offer their sympathies. Frau von Mitterer offered her help and talked with a good
deal of emotion about children, illnesses, and death. Daville
and his wife listened quietly and gazed at her with dry eyes,
like people to whom every word of consolation is welcome but
whom, in reality, no one can help and who expect no help from
anyone. The conversation turned into a long dialogue between
Frau von Mitterer and Desfosses and finally ended in a long
monologue from Anna Maria about fate.

Anna Maria was pale and solemn. Shocks and upsets were

her true element. Her brown hair tossed and shook itself into restless curls. Her great eyes lit up her pallid face with an unnatural brilliance, which in turn brought out the gray depths of the eyes, so that it was difficult to look at them for long and without flinching. Her face was round and smooth, her neck without a wrinkle, her breasts those of a full-blown girl. In this circle of death and sorrow, between her careworn, pasty-faced husband and her frail, tongue-tied daughter, she seemed to shine and dominate all the more with her strange and dangerous beauty. Desfosses couldn't take his eyes off her slender firm hands. The skin of these hands was of a marble whiteness; but when they moved, bent, and waved, the whiteness took on a dull pearly sheen, as if mirroring the faint dance of an invisible, pure white flame. Something of that white gleam stayed in his eyes the rest of that day. And when he next saw Anna Maria in the church at Dolats, where Requiem was read for the little departed one, his first glance went out to her hands. But this time both were in black gloves.

After a few unquiet days, the old life was resumed. Winter closed all doors and drove the people into their warm houses. Once more, communication between the two consulates ceased. Even Desfosses cut short his outings. His talks with Daville before lunch and supper had grown mellower and more cordial, and turned mostly on the kind of topic that precluded a difference of opinion. As usually happens on the days immediately after a funeral, they avoided talking of the loss and death of the child, but since the thought of these could not be exorcised, they spoke a good deal about the child's illness, then about health and sickness in general, and more particularly about the cures and doctors in this difficult country.

Countless and various are the surprises that await an Occidental who is suddenly thrown into the East and forced to live there, but one of the biggest and most disturbing surprises is manifest in the problem of health and sickness. To a man of the West the life of the body is suddenly revealed in an altogether new light. The West too knows sickness in various forms, each with its own terror, but they are something to be fought and alleviated, or at least kept out of sight of the healthy and cheerful workaday world, through special efforts of the community, by convention and by the established traditions of social life. Here in the East, on the other hand, sickness is looked upon as something not in the least exceptional. It makes its appearance and runs its course alongside health, and takes turns with it; one can hear it and feel it at every step. Here a man treats his illness as naturally as he eats, and he suffers as naturally as he lives. Sickness is the other, heavier half of life. Epileptics, syphilitics, lepers, hysterics, morons, hunchbacks, lame ones, stammerers, blind men, cripples, all swarm in broad daylight, creep and crawl, begging alms or else brazenly silent, flaunting their hideous deformities almost with pride. And it is just as well that the women, especially Moslem ones, veil and hide themselves, for otherwise the number of sick one meets would be twice as great. Daville and Desfosses were invariably reminded of it when they saw some peasant coming down a steep country road on his way to Travnik, leading his horse by the bridle, with a woman jogging on it, all shrouded up in her garments, like a bundle of unknown pain and sickness.

And it is not only the poor who fall ill. While sickness here is the lot of the poor, it is the scourge of the rich too. On the compost pile of affluence, as of poverty, there blooms the same flower: sickness. Even the Vizier's Residency, when one has looked at it closer and got to know it better, is in this respect not very different from the poverty and squalor one sees in the streets on market days. If the ways of suffering are different, the attitude to sickness is the same.

During the illness of Daville's child, Desfosses had got to know all four of the Travnik physicians. They were, as we have seen, D'Avenat, Cologna, Mordo Atias, and Fra Luka Dafinch.

We have already got to know D'Avenat as interpreter and temporary official at the French Consulate. Even when he was still in Mehmed Pasha's service, he had not practiced much as a doctor. In common with many other foreigners, he had used the title of "Doctor" as a kind of credential for doing a variety of other work in which he showed greater skill and knowledge. He was happy and content now in his new position, which he liked and which suited his talents. In his youth, it seemed, he had done some medical study at Montpellier, but he lacked all the usual prerequisites for a career of medicine. He had no love for people and no confidence in nature. Like the majority of Occidentals who for one reason or another stay on in the Orient and grow used to life among the Turks, he had become infected with a profound pessimism and a sceptical view of life. The healthy and sick halves of mankind were to him two worlds without any real connection. He looked upon recovery as a temporary condition, not as a bridge from human sickness to human health, for in his opinion there was no such bridge. A man was born, or fell sick, and that was his lot in this life; all the other miseries, like pain, expenses, treatments, doctors, and other sad things, were no more than a natural counterpart of it. For that reason he much preferred to have to do with healthy people than sick ones. He had a revulsion toward the very ill and was apt, in some ways, to look upon a long confinement as a personal insult, for he felt that invalids of this kind ought to make up their minds—go one way or the other; that is to say, join the healthy or the dead.

On the rare occasions when he had treated the Turkish masters he used to serve, he had done it not so much by relying on his knowledge and his more or less "neutral" medicines, as by projecting a very strong will and by his ruthless daring. He flattered his influential patients skillfully, praising their strength and stamina, encouraging their vanity and the will to resist disease, or deprecating, by suggestion, the illness itself and its importance. This came to him all the more easily because he was used to flattering them as wholesomely and persistently when they were well, though in different ways and for other purposes. Very early in his career he had grasped the importance of flattering patients and the power of intimidation, and had understood the impact which a kind or a sharp word can have on them when spoken at the right moment and in the right place. Rude and inconsiderate with the great majority of people, he saved all his attention and all his kind words for the mighty and the great. In this he was extraordinarily deft and bold-faced.

Such was D'Avenat's way as a doctor.

His complete opposite was Mordo Atias, a small taciturn Jew, who owned a store in the lower bazaar where he sold not only medicines and treatment prescriptions but everything from eyeglasses and writing materials to potions for childless women, wool dyes, and good advice of all kinds.

The Atiases were the oldest Jewish family in Travnik. They had lived there for more than a hundred and fifty years. They had built their first house outside the town in a narrow and damp gulley, through which flowed one of those nameless streams that run down into the Lashva. It was a gorge within the Travnik gorge, almost entirely sunless, humid, and full of torrential pebbles, overgrown on all sides with alder and clematis. Here they were born and died, generation after generation.

Later they managed to leave this damp, twilit, and unhealthy spot and to move up into the town, but all of them retained something of their earlier home, for they were all stunted and pale, as if they had grown up in a cellar; they were silent and retiring, they lived modestly, all but unnoticed, although with time they grew prosperous and even rich. And there was always one of the family who dealt in medicines and doctoring.

Of all the Travnik doctors, and those who were considered as such and were called to the Consulate in that capacity, there was least to be said about Mordo Atias. And what indeed was there to be said about a man who himself hardly said a word, went nowhere, did not associate with anyone, did not ask for anything, but looked only after his business and his home? All of Travnik and the surrounding villages knew Mordo and his medicine shop, but that, at the same time, was all they knew about him.

He was a small man, all but hidden in a beard, mustaches, bushy eyebrows, and side locks, dressed in a striped kaftan and baggy blue trousers. As far back as the family could remember, their ancestors had been doctors and apothecaries while they still lived in Spain. They continued to ply these skills as exiles and refugees, first at Salonica and then at Travnik. Mordo's grandfather, Isaac the Doctor, had died here in Travnik, one of the first victims of the great plague in the middle of the last century; his son had taken over the practice and had passed it on, some twenty years before, to Mordo himself. The family had preserved books and notes of some of the well-known Arab and Spanish physicians, which the Atiases had taken with them when they left Andalusia as exiles and had passed down from generation to generation like a secret treasure. For more than twenty years Mordo had been sitting on his little shop platform, day in and day out, except on the Sabbath, with his legs crossed under him, hunched forward, his head bowed, always busy with customers or working on his powders, herbs, and potions. The shop, which resembled a wooden box, crammed from top to bottom, was so low and narrow that Mordo could lay his hand on everything without having to get up from his place. He sat like this summer and winter, always the same, wearing the same kind of clothes, his mood always the same; a huddling bundle of silence that neither drank coffee nor smoked tobacco nor took part in the bazaar jokes and gossip.

A customer would come by, a sick man or someone from a

sick man's family, and would lean on the edge of the narrow platform and state his complaint. Mordo would then pronounce his diagnosis, mumbling through invisible lips behind the thick bush of mustache and beard; he would give the person his medicine and tell him the charge. It was impossible to draw him into a conversation. Even with sick customers, he said no more about their ailments than was absolutely necessary. He would listen to them patiently, and gaze at them with mute lackluster eyes out of that forest of hair, among which there wasn't a single gray one as yet, and to all their tales of woe he would answer always with the same staple sentences, of which the concluding one would be: "The medicine is in my hand but health is in God's." This put an end to any further conversation and signaled the customer to take the stuff and pay for it or else "kiss and leave it."

"Yes, yes, I'll take it. What can I do but take it? If it was poison, I'd take it," wailed the patient, who felt the need of talking and complaining as much as he needed medicines.

But Mordo was not mollified. He wrapped the prescription in blue paper, set it down before the patient, and busied himself with the work he had put aside when the customer appeared.

On market days a crowd of peasants and their women would collect in front of Mordo's shop. One of them would sit on the wooden platform and carry on a whispering dialogue with Mordo, while the others stood in the street and waited. They came for medicines or brought herbs to sell. They chatted quietly, bargained, explained, went, and came back. Only Mordo remained in his place, motionless, cold, and silent.

Especially loud and hard to please were the older peasant women who came to buy spectacles. They would begin by spinning a long tale of how until lately they'd had no difficulty threading even the thinnest needle, but ever since last winter, after a cold or something, their eyes had started to blur and now they could hardly see what they were knitting. Mordo would look at a woman in her late forties, whose sight was naturally beginning to fail; he would study the width of her face and the thickness of her nose, then take a pair of tin-rimmed spectacles out of a round black box and put them on the woman's nose. The woman would first look at her hands, turning them palms upward, and then at a ball of wool which Mordo would give her. "Can you see? Or can't you?" he would ask through his teeth, saving his voice.

"I can see, I can see well. It's wool, but it looks far away somehow, as if it's down there at the bottom of the street," the peasant woman said with hesitation.

Mordo produced another pair and asked, "Better?"—economizing on words.

"It's better. Then again it isn't. There's a kind of fog before my eyes, like smoke . . . like something . . ."

Unruffled, Mordo pulled out a third pair, the last size he had. The woman would have to see with these and buy them or else "kiss an' leave them." There could be no further discussion with Mordo, for love or money.

Then it was the turn of the next patient, a gaunt, pale, and rawboned peasant from the mountain village of Paklarevo. In his inaudible voice and Spanish accent, Mordo demanded to know what hurt him.

"Here in the middle, there's something like a hot coal . . . may it never happen to you . . . and it hurts, hurts . . ." said the peasant, indicating his chest with a finger. He would have wanted to go on talking about the pain, but Mordo broke in drily, with faulty syntax but in a tone of authority: "There nothing to hurt. Cannot hurt in that spot."

The peasant tried to explain that the pain was exactly in that spot, but moved his finger a little to the right as he did so. "Yes, it hurts. . . . How can I tell you? The pain goes this way . . . it starts here, then it moves over, if you'll excuse me, all the way over . . ."

Eventually the sick man gave way a little, Mordo gave way a little, and they reached agreement about the spot where the pain was more or less located. Then Mordo asked him in a curt and businesslike manner whether he had any rue in his garden, and told him to bray the herb in a mortar, add a little honey, and sprinkle the mixture with the powder which he would give him; he was then to roll the mixture into three little balls between his palms and swallow them before sunrise. "And so every day for eight days, from Friday to Friday. Pain and illness will pass. Give me two groschen. Good luck to you."

The peasant, who until that moment had been trying to memorize the instructions with unconscious mouthing and rolling of his eyes, suddenly forgot everything, even the pain which had caused him to come, and clutched at the part of his coat where he kept his linen bag with money. Now began the slow pulling out, with many sighs and much reluctance, and the act of untying, counting, and finally paying with a sigh of real pain.

And then Mordo sat once more, unmoving, diminutive, in a huddle with the next customer, while the peasant slowly left the bazaar behind him and set out along the bank of a stream toward his village eyrie of Paklarevo. On one side of his chest there was the pain that never let up; on the other, in his pocket, there was Mordo's powder wrapped in blue paper. And through his whole being there cursed another, separate pain as it were, the pain of regret for the money, which now seemed to him like money thrown out, the pain of distrust and fear, lest he may have been cheated. He kept on walking like that, straight into the sunset, utterly listless and bent, for there was no creature as sad and bewildered as a peasant who was sick.

But there was one visitor to whom Mordo talked longer and more intimately, with whom he didn't mind losing a few minutes and an extra word or two. That was Fra Luka Dafinich, better known as "the Doctor." Fra Luka used to work and live on the best terms with Mordo's father David, and for twenty years now he and Mordo had been inseparable friends and confidants. When, as a younger man, he had served in the country parishes, he used to come to Travnik as often as he could and first visit Mordo at his shop, before going to the parish priest at Dolats. The Travnik bazaar had long become used to seeing Mordo and Fra Luka huddling and whispering together, or browsing through herbs and medicines.

Fra Luka was born in Zenitsa, but he entered the monastery at Gucha Gora when still a child, after plague had wiped out his entire family. Here, except for short intervals, he had spent his entire life among medicines and medical books and instruments. His cell was filled with pots, earthen jars, and boxes, and the walls and rafters were hung with sheaves and bags of dried herbs, twigs, and roots. On the window sill was a large bowl with leeches in clear water, and a smaller one containing scorpions in oil. By the sofa, which was covered with an old, stained, burned, and patched rug, there was a brazier of baked clay; a pot of herbs cooked on it constantly. In the corners and along the shelves there were hunks of rare woods, small and large stones, animal skins and horns.

But with all that the cell was always clean, well aired, pleasant, and smelling mostly of juniper berries or mint tea.

On the wall there were three pictures: Hippocrates, St. Aloysius Gonzaga, and the portrait of an unknown medieval knight in armor, with a visor and a great plume on his head. Where Fra Luka got this picture from, or what he saw in it, no one had ever been able to find out. Once when the Turks were inspecting the monastery and, having found nothing objectionable, came across this picture, they were told that it was the portrait of some sultan or other. An argument developed as to whether it was possible and proper to make pictures of the sultans, but as the picture was quite faded and the Turks were uneducated, the matter was left at that. Those pictures had hung there for over five decades and, as they had not been very clear to begin with, with time they faded completely, so that St. Aloysius now resembled Hippocrates, and Hippocrates the "Sultan," and the "Sultan," poorly engraved on some cheap kind of soft paper, no longer resembled anything; and only Fra Luka could still make out his sword and his helmet with anything like certainty and see his fighting visage of fifty years before.

When he was still a young student of divinity, Fra Luka had shown an eagerness and a gift for medical knowledge. Seeing this and knowing how much the people and the brothers themselves needed a good and skillful doctor, the monastery superiors sent the young man to the medical school at Padua. But the following year, at the first change in the monastery council, the new opposing party of superiors decided that this was unsuitable for Fra Luka and too expensive for the Order, and they recalled him to Bosnia. When in the third year the original council was re-elected once more, they sent the young friar to Padua for a second time, to complete his medical studies. But a year later the opposition was returned to the council, they canceled everything that had been put into effect earlier, and, among other things, out of spite, ordered Fra Luka to come back from Padua to Gucha Gora.

With the knowledge he had gained and the books he had managed to collect, Fra Luka had then settled down in this cell and continued to study and gather medicines with passionate devotion and to heal people lovingly. This passion had never left him and this love had never grown cold.

All was peace and order in this cell, around which the tall, nearsighted, thin "Doctor" moved without making a sound. Fra Luka's thinness had become a byword throughout the province. ("There are two things even the most learned Koran scholars cannot tell: what the earth rests on and what Fra Luka's habit hangs on.") On this towering and fleshless body there sat an

upright, lively, and fine head, with blue eyes that had a vague
look of transport and vacancy, with a thin wreath of white hair
on a well-formed skull, and a delicate rosy skin that was sprin
kled with tiny bluish bloodbursts. He had remained active and
nimble right up to his old age. "That man doesn't walk, he
flashes by like a saber," one of the guardian Brothers said of
him; and in fact this man with the smiling eyes and darting
but inaudible movements never sat still. His long, wizened, but
immaculately clean fingers were busy all day long with countless small objects, scraping, knocking, smearing, tying, making
notes, rummaging among the boxes and shelves. For to Brother
Luka nothing was without significance, unnecessary, or dis-
pensable. Under those thin fingers and the smiling, nearsighted
eyes everything sprang to life, became articulate, and clamored
for a place of its own among the medicaments or, at least,
among the staple or unusual items.

Having observed the herbs, minerals, and living beings around
him, and their changes and movements, day after day, year after
year, Fra Luka became more and more firmly convinced that in
this world as we see it only two things existed—growth and
decay—intimately and inseparably bound up with each other,
eternally and everywhere in action. All phenomena around us
were merely different phases of that endless, complex, and everlasting ebb and flow; mere figments and fleeting moments which
we arbitrarily set apart, designated, and called by precise names
like health, illness, and dying; none of which, in fact, existed.
Only growth and decay existed, in different states and different
perceptions. And the whole art of healing consisted in recognizing, seizing, and using the forces that surged in the direction of
growth, "as a sailor makes use of winds," and in avoiding and
removing the forces that worked for decay. Wherever a man
succeeded in catching hold of the forces of growth, he recovered
and sailed on; where he failed to do it, he sank, quite simply
and without appeal. And in the great and invisible account book
of growth and decay one force was carried from one side of the
ledger to the other.

Such was his view of the world in the over-all; in detail it
was, of course, far more difficult and involved. Every living
creature, every plant, every disease, every season of the year,
every day, and every minute, each again had its own growth
and its own decay. And all of it was dovetailed together, linked
in endless obscure ways, all of it functioned and bubbled, pulsed

and streamed, day and night, deep inside the earth and all over it, high up in space and beyond the planets, all obeying the single, twofold law of ebb and flow which was so hard to grasp and follow.

All his life Fra Luka had been hopelessly bewitched by this vision of the world and by the sublime harmony which man could only guess at, which he at times succeeded in turning to his advantage, but which he could never master. What was a man in his position to do, one to whom all this had been revealed and who was destined to labor away on a hopeless task beyond anyone's grasp, the quest of medicine and the curing of sickness, God permitting . . . ? Which part of this picture should he scoop up and memorize first—this incandescent vision that sometimes opened out before him in a flash, clear, intelligible, and near at hand, within his grasp, and at other times grew dim and became a witless swirling, like a blizzard in a pitch-black night? How could he find his way in that ravishing hide and seek of dazzling light, in that seeming welter of tangled, contrary influences and blind forces and elements? How was he to gather up at least some significant threads and tie the effects to the causes?

This was Fra Luka's only worry and his chief preoccupation, besides the priestly and monastic duties of his Order. It was what made him so rapt and distracted, so haggard and thin like a strung wire. It was why he lavished so much zeal on a stalk of grass or a sick person, no matter where he found them, no matter how they looked or by what name they called themselves.

Fra Luka firmly believed that there were as many healing forces in nature as there were diseases among humans and animals. Each one exactly corresponded to its opposite, down to the last atom and molecule. These were profound calculations, not to be measured or solved; but, by the same token, there was no doubt in his mind that they were exact, that somewhere at the infinite vanishing point out of human sight they worked out to a perfect equation. And these healing forces were to be found, as the ancients taught, *"in herbis, in verbis, et in lapidibus"*— in herbs, in words, and in stones. Privately Fra Luka held the bold conviction—although he wouldn't admit it to himself— that every change for the worse in the human body could be reversed, at least in theory, since the illness and its cure had a common beginning and lived side by side, though apart, often infinitely far apart from each other. If the physician succeeded in joining them, the illness fell back; if he did not succeed, the illness overwhelmed and destroyed the organism in which it had taken hold. No failures and disappointments could shake this secret belief of his. With this silent conviction, Fra Luka approached every medicine and every patient. It was true that he perpetuated this inexplicable faith of his by quickly and firmly forgetting, like many a doctor, every patient who died or whom he failed to cure, while remembering every successful cure as far back as fifty years.

Such was Fra Luka Dafinich, the Doctor. He was an ardent and incorrigible friend of the ailing part of humanity. Among his friends he counted the whole of nature, and had only two enemies: friars and mice.

The business with the friars was an old and long story. Generations of them came and went and they differed from one another in many respects, but in one thing they were in accord: they underestimated and deprecated Fra Luka's medical skill. Ever since they had sent him to Padua as a student and then recalled him, and later shuttled him back and forth once more, he had lost all hope of ever finding some appreciation or help among his Brethren. Once the Guardian of the monastery, Fra Martin Dembich, known as Dembo, described Fra Luka's relations with other Brothers in these terms: "You see this 'doctor' of ours? When he prays aloud to God, in the choir with the other Brothers, he's not thinking the same thing as they. They may be saying the same prayer, but here's what *he* is thinking: 'O God, put some sense into the heads of these no-good Brothers and soften their hearts, so that they will not hinder me at every step in the good and useful work I am doing. Or, if you can't grant that—seeing how the heads of these Brethren may be too hard even for the hand of God—then at least fortify me with holy patience that I may be able to bear with them such as they are, without hatred or an evil word, and that in their illness I may be able to help them with my skill, which they despise and criticize.' And the friars pray and think like this: 'O God, enlighten our Fra Luka, cure him of his grievous affliction, cure him of medicines and his passion to cure. Blessed be all the little pains Thou visitest upon us (since one has to die of something!), only take Thou, take off our necks this man who wants to cure us of them.'"

To Dembo, who was witty, forceful, and a merciless tease, though an excellent Superior and a model monk, Fra Luka had for many years been the subject of endless tales and jokes. And yet he too, like so many others, was fated to die in Fra Luka's arms. But even at that last moment, when he was grimacing with pain, Dembo chuckled and told the assembled Brothers, while laboring for breath: "Brothers, all the accounts of the monastery are in order, the credit as well as the cash. The Vicar knows all the particulars. Bless you all and remember me in your prayers. Remember, two things did me in: my asthma and my doctor."

So mocked Dembo, exaggerating even on his deathbed.

But all that was long before, "in Dembo's time," when Fra Luka was younger and sprier and those of his generation were still living; today very few of them were still alive, for he had entered his eighty-first year on St. Ivo's day this summer. He had long forgiven the Brothers for not letting him stay longer at Padua, for not ever giving him as much as he needed for books and experiments; and they, in the course of time, had let up teasing him about his unusual way of life, his medical passion, and his fraternizing with Mordo Atias. To this day Fra Luka regularly went to Travnik, sat down with Mordo on his shop platform, and exchanged information and experiences; bartering herbs and roots for sulphur or lapis lazuli, since there was no one who could dry lime flowers or preserve osier herb, St.-John's-wort, or yarrow like Fra Luka. But the Brothers had long become accustomed to this "friendship between the Old and New Testament."

What used to be the greatest irritant to the Brothers and a frequent cause of dispute—his visiting and healing the sick outside the monastery—was now held down to a minimum. Once this had been a source of constant embarrassment to the Order and the only cause of serious discord between Fra Luka and the monastery superiors. And even then it was not Fra Luka who had sought patients in the mundane community, especially not among the Turks, but the Turks themselves who had asked for him, sometimes calling and begging him to come but more often ordering him and sending the police to get him.

These visits of Fra Luka's caused him and his monastery a good many headaches, trouble, and harm. It happened sometimes that they called him and begged him to treat a sick Moslem or a Moslem woman, and later both he and the monastery would be blamed if the patient took a turn for the worse and died. And even when the treatment was successful and the pleased family lavished gifts on Fra Luka, there would be some stupid and evil-minded Turks who would accuse him of entering a Turkish house. Invariably there were witnesses to prove that the friar had been called and had come in a good and decent cause, but until that was proved and set right and the complaint was thrown out, the monastery went through a good deal of trouble, fear, and expense. So the Brothers forbade Fra Luka to go and see a case in a Moslem house until that house obtained a permit from the authorities, in which it was clearly stated that they were calling him of their own free will and that the authorities had nothing against it.

There were plenty of cases when the treatments were successful and pious and grateful people showered gifts and thanks on Fra Luka and the monastery. A certain beg, one of the humbler village begs but a stouthearted and influential man, whom Fra Luka had healed of an old wound below the knee, would say to the friar whenever he met him: "As I get up on my feet in the morning, yours is the first name I mention after Allah's."

And as long as he lived, this beg defended the monastery and the friars and, when they needed him, acted as their witness and guarantor.

Another wealthy Moslem from Turbe, whose wife Fra Luka had saved, did not speak of it to anyone (since one did not talk of women), but every year after the Feast of the Assumption he sent the monastery a big jar of honey and a sheepskin with the instructions "to give it to the priest who cures the sick."

But there were also contrary cases of black ingratitude and diabolical spite. The monastery would long remember the case of Mustay Beg Miralem's daughter-in-law. The young woman suffered some kind of seizure and began to act in a restless, possessed fashion; she screamed, tossed, and gnashed her teeth day and night, or else lay on the bed all day long, speechless and unmoving, refusing to look at anyone or eat anything. The people in the house tried everything they were advised to do, but nothing helped, neither sorcery nor hodjas nor talismans. And the woman wasted away by the day. In the end, her father-in-law, old Miralem himself, sent to the monastery for "Brother Doctor."

When Fra Luka arrived, the woman was in a state of near collapse for the second consecutive day, her body all contorted; and no one could move her out of her dark silence. At first she wouldn't even turn her head. But a moment later, opening her eyelids just a little, she caught sight of the friar's heavy sandals, then the hem of his cassock and the white cord which the friars tie around their waists, and then her gaze traveled slowly and sullenly up the long lean figure of Fra Luka, and it took quite some time until she came up to his gray head and met his smiling blue eyes. At that moment the woman suddenly burst into laughter—unexpected, uncontrollable, mad laughter. The friar tried to calm her with words and gestures, but in vain. As he came out of Miralem's house he could still hear that terrible laugh echoing from the ground floor behind him.

Promptly the next day the police took a manacled Fra Luka to jail. The Guardian of the monastery was informed that old Miralem had accused Fra Luka of casting an evil spell on his daughter-in-law, with the result that for two days now she had been in a spasm of laughter and drove the whole house crazy. The Guardian denied it and maintained that a doctor's duty was to treat and cure if he could, and that spells and charms were against the religious laws of the Brotherhood. At the same time he bribed the officials left and right, five groschen to one, ten to another, though it was for nothing. He was told only that the "Doctor's" case looked very bad, as the young woman had stated that the friar had secretly given her a drink of "something black and thick like axle grease" and had twice struck her on the forehead with a long cross, and that since then she hadn't been able to stop that laughter which was a constant racking agony.

Just as everything began to look grim and hopeless, they suddenly broke Fra Luka's irons and let him go as if nothing had happened. It seems that on the fourth day the young woman had calmed down and then burst into silent copious tears. She called her father-in-law and her husband and told them that she had vilified the friar in her fit of madness; she admitted that he had given her no medicines of any kind and did not have a cross on him, but had merely raised his arms over her and prayed to God according to his own law, on account of which she was now feeling better.

So the affair died down. For a long time afterwards, however, the Brothers were very cross with Fra Luka. Fra Miyo Kovachevich, who was Guardian at the time and had had the most trouble and worry over Fra Luka's case, told him later in the refectory before the assembled Brothers: "Now listen to me, Fra Luka. Either you take those harebrained Moslem hussies off my back or I'm going to run off into the forest and you take these and carry on both as doctor and Guardian. We can't go on like this." Angrily, in all seriousness, he held out the monastery keys.

But peace was restored and the incident was forgotten. All that remained was the Guardian's entry in the monastery ledger, under "fines and expenses":

> On January 11 the police officer came with manacles and a warrant declaring that Fra Luka Dafinich, the doctor (ill-starred was the day when he became one!), had given the wrong pills to Miralem's daughter-in-law. . . . Paid in fines, to the judge and the cashier: 148 groschen.

And even in later years there were frequent difficulties with Fra Luka's medical practice. The Brothers usually forgot them after a while, but the monastery ledger did not. In the column of fines, bribes, and expenses, there was many a note on Fra Luka.

> Because Fra Luka treated a Turk . . . 48 groschen.
> On account of the doctor . . . 20 groschen.

Here, somewhere, an entry was made at last of the number and date of the order by which the monastery superiors placed a total ban on "Any praying over a Turk or Turkish woman whatsoever, or giving any medicines whatsoever," even if they had a permit for it from the Turkish authorities. And immediately underneath there was a new fine entry:

> Because Fra Luka did not go to see the patient . . . 70 groschen.

And so it went on, year in and year out.

Twice during Fra Luka's long life Travnik was laid waste by the plague. The people fell sick, died, took to the mountains. The bazaar closed down and many houses were left desolate forever. The most intimate ties loosened, conventions were swept away. In both epidemics Fra Luka proved his great worth as a fearless doctor and member of his Order. He went through the plague-stricken quarters, treated the sick, heard confession and administered communion to the dying, buried the dead, helped and counseled those who survived. The Brothers fully acknowledged this and his reputation and fame as "Doctor" were recognized even among the Moslems.

But when a man lives a long time he is apt to outlive everything, even his good works. The epidemics and catastrophes were succeeded by good and quiet years; things changed and were forgotten, they blurred and faded away. And through all this, the successes and the misfortunes, the praise and the abuse, the temptations and the victories, Fra Luka alone remained the same, unchanged and constant, with his look of preoccupation, his thin smile and lightning movements, with his faith in the mysterious interdependence of medicines and illnesses. Because he knew no other life but that of medicine and pharmaceutical work, as far as he was concerned everything in the world had its place and *raison d'être*—sickness as well as harm, the Guardian's anger as well as misunderstandings and calumnies. In the last analysis, even being arrested was undoubtedly some sort of blessing, except for those unpleasant irons on one's feet and the nagging worry that back there at the monastery the herb potions might spoil and the leeches die out, or his Brothers in Christ might scatter and mix up the sprigs and packets of his botanicals.

And yet whenever these "inveterate opponents" of his, the friars, at whom sometimes, though only for a moment, he grumbled to himself—whenever any of them fell ill, Fra Luka nursed them and cared for them with selfless devotion, and advised them and worried over them when they were well. As soon as one of them had the slightest cough, Fra Luka would set a pot of herbs on the brazier and personally carry the hot aromatic brew to the patient's cell and force him to drink it. Among the Brothers there were a few cholerics and eccentrics, waspish, grumpy old "uncles" who wanted no part of the "Doctor" or his medicines, who drove him out of their cells or else jeered at him and his treatments; but Fra Luka refused to be put out or turned back. He passed over the jokes and insults as if he didn't hear them, doggedly insisting that they follow his treatment and look after themselves; he begged them, argued with them, and bribed them to take the medicine which he had compounded with so much trouble and often at so great a cost.

There was one among the old "uncles" who loved plum brandy in excess of his allotment and beyond what was considered good and useful for physical health and spiritual well-being. The old man had a bad liver but wouldn't stay off drink. Fra Luka, who in his book of prescriptions also had a formula under the heading "to make drinking hateful," went to a lot of trouble to try to cure the old friar, but without success. Every day they would go through the same argument.

"Forget about me, Fra Luka, and get busy with those who

want to be cured and for whom there *is* a cure," the uncle would grumble.

"Come, come, sick one, use your head. There is help for everybody. Mother earth has a cure for every man."

And Fra Luka would sit by the ailing and churlish old uncle who had never, even when he was in better health, cared much for books or learning, and he would produce texts and expatiate at great length on the bounties of the earth and her marvelous benevolence toward mankind: "Did you know that Pliny calls the earth *'benigna, mitis, indulgens, ususque mortalium semper ancilla'*—kindly, gentle, patient, ever at the service of mortals? That he wrote, 'She bringeth forth healing herbs and ever laboreth in man's cause'? See, that's what Pliny says. And you keep repeating, 'There's no cure for me.' Of course there is, and we have to find it."

The old man's answer was a bored frown. He dismissed both Pliny and the potion with a wave of his hand, but Fra Luka would neither be brushed off nor foiled.

And when he could not cure him with his medicines and soothe him with quotations, he then brought him, secretly and under the guise of medicine, a dram or two of plum brandy from which the Guardian had cut him off completely, and so eased his suffering at least a little.

Moreover, Fra Luka didn't confine his nursing to the Brothers who were in the monastery. For those scattered in the outlying parishes he wrote out yellow slips of paper in his microscopic hand and bound them into thin little booklets. These little volumes, known as "medicals," were then copied over and distributed through the villages and parishes. They contained alphabetical lists of folk medicines, interspersed with instructions on hygiene, popular superstitions, and useful household hints and advice. For example: how to clean a hassock of candle wax dripping; or, what to do about wine that is turning vinegary.

Here, among the prescriptions for jaundice and "fever not caused by gall," there were notations from Italian sources on "How Experts mine Ore in the Indies and other Places," or "How to Make the so-called Vermouth Wine, which is a tonic for the Intestine." All the knowledge and the facts which Fra Luka had culled and gathered in the course of years, from the hoary *Compositiones Medicamentorum* down to Mordo Atias's formulas and old wives' brews, were contained in these little brochures. Yet here too Fra Luka met with ingratitude from his Brothers and many disappointments. Some were careless in making copies, while others, either from ignorance or lack of attention, perverted or dropped out single words and entire sentences; and there was a third lot who filled the margins of certain prescriptions with scornful remarks about the medicines and even the "Doctor" himself. But Fra Luka laughed at these remarks when he came across them; and then consoled himself with the thought that this labor of his on the "medicals" was nevertheless of far greater use to the people and to the Brothers themselves than the hurt he suffered from the inattention and lack of appreciation of his Brothers.

There was one other, though much less obdurate, thing that made Fra Luka's work difficult—the mice. The ancient and sprawling monastery building truly abounded in mice. The Brothers maintained that Fra Luka's cell, resembling as it did Mordo's pharmacy, with its fats and balms and concoctions of every kind, was the main reason that the building teemed with mice. On his side, Fra Luka complained that due to the age of the building and the disorder in the cells the mice had become firmly ensconced, which was why they now played havoc with his medicines and why he was powerless against them. The battle of the mice had with time become a harmless mania with him. He wailed and complained more than was warranted by the actual damage. He locked things away from them and hung his medicines on the ceiling beams, and he thought up a hundred tricks for outsmarting his invisible enemies. He dreamed of getting a large metal box in which he could store all the more valuable things under lock and key, fully protected from the mice, but hadn't the courage even to breathe of such a purchase and expense before the Brothers or the Guardian. And he was inconsolable when the mice did, in fact, eat up the rabbit fat which he had so carefully prepared and cleansed in several waters.

He kept two mouse traps in his cell at all times, a large and a small one. Every night he set them up meticulously, baiting them with a sliver of smoked ham or a gob of wax from the remnant of a candle. And in the morning, when he got up to go to chapel prayers, he usually found both traps empty, though still set, and the wax and ham eaten up. But when sometimes the mouse did get caught and he was awakened by the snapping of the trap door, he would get up from bed, walk around the frightened mouse, and shake his finger and his head at him.

"Ahaaa! What now, you little wretch? Wanted to do mischief, did you? Well, look at yourself now!" Then, barefoot as he was and wrapping the habit loosely around his middle, he would carefully pick up the trap, carry it into the long gallery as far as the stairs, open the small trap door and hiss: "Out with you, you little sneak! Out, out!"

The panic-stricken mouse would dart down the few steps, then straight across the courtyard floor and into the woodshed which was stacked with logs at all seasons of the year.

The Brothers were familiar with this mouse-catching system of Fra Luka's; they teased him often and said that the "Doctor has for years been trapping and releasing the same mouse." Fra Luka firmly denied it and cited long chapter and verse to prove that over a twelve-month period he had caught a good many of them, large, small, and medium-sized ones.

"Come, come," one of the older Brothers told him, "I heard that when you let the mouse out, you open the trap door and say to him: 'Get out and run to the Guardian's room. Run!' "

"Ooh, you tempter, what a tongue you have! What'll you think of next!" laughed Fra Luka, defending himself.

"I didn't think it up, Doctor Effendi, they've heard you, the ones that gad about the gallery in the dead of night the way you do."

"Go on, tempter. Stop it, will you."

And the others were usually quick to join in. "If I were you, Brother, I would catch him and dunk him in boiling water, trap and all, and then see if he came back," a younger friar said with tongue in cheek.

At this Fra Luka always grew very agitated. "Go on, you wretch, think what you're saying. What boiling water? Is that the talk of a Christian?" the "Doctor" would fly at him.

And even half an hour later, after all the banter and other conversation, he would turn to the young man, his voice brittle with reproof: "Boiling water, eh? Look at him! One of God's creatures into boiling water—really!"

And that was how Fra Luka contended with his adversaries, big and small, while nursing, feeding, and defending them. It filled his long and happy life.

The fourth doctor who came to the Consulate during the illness of Daville's son was Giovanni Mario Cologna, the accredited physician of the Austrian Consulate-General.

It would seem now that we erred when we said of Mordo Atias that he was the one of whom least could be said among the four doctors of Travnik. In reality, no more could be said of Cologna than of Mordo. The reason for it, in Mordo's case, was that he never said anything, whereas Cologna talked too much and constantly modified what he said.

He was a man of uncertain years, of uncertain origin, nationality, and race, of uncertain beliefs and views, and of equally uncertain knowledge and experience. About the whole man there was, in fact, very little that lent itself to clear definition.

According to his own account, he was born on the island of Cephalonia, where his father had been a well-known doctor. The father had been a Venetian, though born in Epirus, and his mother had come from Dalmatia. Cologna had spent his childhood with his grandfather in Greece and his youth in Italy, where he had studied medicine. His adult life had been spent in the Levant, in Turkish and Austrian service.

He was tall but uncommonly thin; he walked with a stoop, bent and loose in all his joints, so that at any given moment he could either contract and fold up, or else unwind and extend himself, as on hidden springs; which, in fact, he did constantly whilst talking, now more, now less. This long body was topped by a regular head, always restless, almost entirely bald, with a few long wisps of lusterless flaxen hair. The face was clean-shaven, the eyes were large, brown, and always unnaturally shiny under the thick bristling gray brows. In the large mouth there were a few big yellow teeth which clattered slightly as he talked. And not only his facial expression, but the whole appearance of the man kept changing all the time, in a way that was hard to believe. He was capable, in the course of a single conversation, of transforming his appearance completely several times over. Under the mask of a feeble old man there would sometimes flash out—was it yet another mask?—the image of a forceful, self-assured man of middle years; or—a third mask? —that of a pert, fidgety, lanky youth, who has grown out of his clothes and doesn't know what to do with his hands and feet, or where to look. The expressive face was always in motion and betrayed the feverishly rapid play of his brain. Depression, reverie, outrage, sincere enthusiasm, naïve delight, pure unruffled joy, succeeded one another with amazing swiftness on this regular and unusually mobile face. In keeping with it, his large mouth, with its scant and infirm teeth, poured out words, a spate of them, rich and pregnant ones, words that were angry, bold, kindly, sweet, and rousing. And they were words of Italian, Turkish, modern Greek, French, Latin, and "Illyrian." And the ease with which he changed his facial expressions and his movements was also apparent in his switching from one language to another, in his mixing and borrowing of words and whole sentences. In reality, the only language he knew well was Italian.

He did not even sign his name always in the same way, but wrote it differently on different occasions and at different periods of his life, depending on whose service he was in and what kind of work he did, whether scientific, political, or literary— *Giovanni Mario Cologna, Gian Colonia, Joannes Colonis Epirota, Bartolo cavagliere d'Epiro, dottore illyrico.* The nature of what he did, or claimed to do, under these different names changed even more frequently and thoroughly. In his basic convictions Cologna was a man of his time, a *philosophe*, a free and critical spirit, purged of all prejudice. But that did not prevent his studying the religious life, not only of the various Christian churches, but Islamic and other Eastern sects and faiths. And for him to study meant identifying himself for a period of time with the object of his study, enthusing over it, at least for the moment, as his sole and exclusive belief, and rejecting all that he had previously believed and all that heretofore had moved him to enthusiasm. He had an extraordinary mind, capable of strange flights, but made up of elements which readily fused with their environment and had a tendency to link and identify themselves with whatever lay around them.

This sceptic and *philosophe* had seizures of religious ecstasy and spells of practical piety. He would then go to the monastery at Gucha Gora, pester the friars, ask to be allowed to do spiritual austerities with them, only to discover that they hadn't enough zeal or theological acumen or devout fervor. The monks at Gucha Gora, who were genuinely pious but simple hardy people, had, in common with all Bosnian friars, an ingrained loathing of bigoted chest-beating, exalted zealots, and all those who hang on to God's coat tails and "lick the stones of the altar." The old "uncles" used to bridle and grumble, and one of them has even left a written record of how spurious and distressing they found this mundane doctor "who professes to be a great servitor of the Catholic Laws, hearing Mass every morning and performing all manner of Devotions." Nevertheless, because of his connection with the Austrian Consulate, and out of the respect they had toward von Mitterer, the friars could not altogether shake off the latter's Illyrian doctor.

But Cologna did the same with the Orthodox monk Pakhomi, and frequented the Orthodox homes of Travnik, in order to see their religious customs, to hear the service and the ritual chanting, and to compare them with the Greek service. And with the headmaster of the Moslem school, Abduselem Effendi, Cologna carried on learned discussions about the history of the Islamic faith, for he was not only well grounded in the Koran but was familiar with all the theological philosophic currents from Abu Hanif to Al Gazali. At every opportunity, too, he would shower the other members of the Travnik Ulema with quotations from Islamic theologians, of whom in most cases they had never heard. In this he was tireless and unrelenting.

And the same chameleon quality seemed to animate the man's character. At first sight, he impressed everyone as tractable, pliant, and acquiescent to a degree that was embarrassing. He would invariably accommodate his own opinion to that of the person he was talking with, and would not only adopt the latter's viewpoint but also surpass him in vehemence of expression. But then again, just as often, he would suddenly and quite without warning take up daring positions against everything and everyone and would defend them doggedly and well, with his whole being, regardless of the cost and danger to himself.

From his youth on Cologna had been in the Austrian service. This was perhaps the only thing in which he had been consistent and steadfast. He had spent a certain time as personal physician to the Pasha of Scutari and Janina, but even then he had kept up his connections with various Austrian consuls. Now he was attached to the Consulate of Travnik, not so much for his reputation as a doctor as on account of those old ties, his linguistic proficiency, and his knowledge of local conditions. In fact, he was not a member of the Consulate staff but lived separately and was registered with the authorities merely as a doctor under the protection of the Austrian Consulate.

Von Mitterer, who had no aptitude for fantasy and no understanding of philosophy, and whose knowledge both of the language and the country far exceeded Cologna's, was hard put to decide what to do with this unwanted co-worker. Frau von Mitterer had a physical revulsion toward the Levantine and declared excitedly that she would die sooner than accept a medicine from the man's hands. In conversation she would refer to him as "Chronos," because to her he resembled the symbolic figure of Time—though a Chronos without a beard, whose hands held neither the mortal scythe nor the sand-filled hourglass.

Such was the life this doctor without patients led in Travnik. He lived away from the Consulate, in a ramshackle house on top of an abandoned stone quarry. He had no family. A single servant, an Albanian, ran his whole household, which was frugal and eccentric in every respect, in its furnishings, its food, and its daily program. He spent a good deal of time in vain attempts to find someone to converse with who would not grow bored and run away, or poring over his books and notes which encompassed the sum total of human knowledge, from astronomy and chemistry down to military skills and diplomacy.

This man without roots and equipoise, who nevertheless had a pure heart and an inquiring mind, had one morbid but great and selfless passion: to delve into the mystery of human thought wherever it might appear and whatever direction it took. He catered to this passion with his whole being, immoderately, without any clear objective or reserve of any kind. All the religious and philosophical movements and endeavors in the history of mankind, without exception, fascinated his mind and lived and hobnobbed inside it, clashing and overlapping one another like waves on the sea's surface. Each one was equally close to him and equally remote; with each he was able to agree and identify himself for a certain time, while he was occupied with it. These inner intellectual adventures were to him a real world; in them he enjoyed real inspirations and profound experiences. But at the same time they marked him apart and estranged him from people and society, and brought him in conflict with the logic and common sense of the rest of the world. Thus, what was best in him remained unnoticed and inaccessible, while the sides of him that could be observed and sensed put everybody off. Even in another, less taxing environment, a man like this could not have won a fitting place for himself or any real respect. Here, in this town and among these people, he was fated to be unhappy and to seem odd, ludicrous, suspicious, and futile.

The friars considered him a maniac and a scatterbrain, the townspeople a spy or else a learned fool. Suleiman Pasha Skoplyak said apropos of this doctor: "The biggest fool is not the man who cannot read but the man who believes that everything he reads is true."

Desfosses was the only one in Travnik who did not shun Cologna and had the desire and the patience to talk with him from time to time, unreservedly and at length. However, the upshot of this was that Cologna was accused in the Austrian Consulate of being in French service.

It was hard to tell just what Cologna's medical competence and interests consisted of, but it was certain that they were among his least worries. In the glare of the philosophical truths and religious illuminations which swept and washed through him without pause, human needs and pains, even life itself, did not represent anything of particularly great importance or deep meaning. To him illness and changes in the human body were merely one more incentive to exercise his mind, a mind that was condemned to perpetual ferment. Because his own links with life were rather tenuous, he could not begin to appreciate the meaning of blood ties to a normal man, of bodily health, or the problem of whether an individual lived a shorter or a longer life. The fact was that as far as Cologna was concerned, in questions of medicine too, everything started and ended with words—a flood of words, animated exchanges, disputes, and often in abrupt and complete changes of opinion about a given disease, its causes, and methods of treating it. It goes without saying that very few people would have thought of calling or asking for such a doctor unless they were quite desperate. One might say that the main professional occupation of the garrulous doctor was his standing quarrel with, and passionate dislike of, César D'Avenat.

Having studied in Milan, Cologna was a follower of the Italian school of medicine, while D'Avenat, who despised and took a dim view of Italian doctors, maintained that the University of Montpellier had centuries before beaten and surpassed the school of Salerno, which was considered antiquated and passé. Cologna did, in fact, glean his wisdom and his many aphorisms from that great miscellany *Regimen Sanitatis Salernitanum*, which he jealousy kept hidden under lock and key and from which he lifted and liberally distributed verse maxims on physical and mental hygiene. D'Avenat, on the other hand, drew his sustenance from several volumes of lecture notes by celebrated professors at Montpellier and from the great classical manual *Lilium*

Medicinae. But the wellspring of their differences lay not so much in books and professional knowledge, which they had very little of, but in their Levantine compulsion to bicker and vie with each other, in the obduracy common to their profession, in the boredom of Travnik life, and in their own personal vanity and intolerance.

Cologna's attitude to human illness and health—if, in his case, one might speak of a single and unvarying attitude—was as uncomplicated as it was futile and hopeless. Cologna looked upon life as "an active state constantly gravitating toward death and approaching it slowly and by degrees; and death is the final resolution of the long illness which we call life!" But these patients, whom we call people might live longer and with proportionately fewer distresses and pains if they followed proven medical advice and the golden rule of moderation in all things. Pains, as well as premature death, were merely natural results of breaking that law. Three doctors were indispensable to man, Cologna was want to say: *mens hilaris, requis moderata, diaeta* —a serene mind, moderate rest, and proper diet.

Such were the principles on which Cologna treated his patients, and the patients were neither better off nor worse off for them; either they died when they wandered too far from the line of life and approached the line of death, or they improved, which is to say, threw off their pains and disorders and came back within the purview of the beneficial rules of Salerno—a process which Cologna made easier and expedited with an occasional Latin couplet from among those thousands of useful couplets which were so easy to memorize but so difficult to observe in practice.

This, in brief, was the "Illyrian doctor," the last of the quartet of doctors who, each in his own fashion, waged a hard and hopeless struggle against disease and death in the valley of Travnik.

13

Christmas, the holy day of all Christians, came to Travnik too, with its share of worries, memories, solemn and nostalgic thoughts. This year it was the occasion for renewed relations between the consuls and their families.

Things were particularly lively at the Austrian Consulate. These were the days in which Frau von Mitterer went through her phase of goodness, piety, and family devotion. She scurried around, getting up presents and surprises for all. She locked herself in the room and decorated the Christmas tree; she practiced old Christmas carols on the harp. She even thought of going to the midnight Mass at the Church of Dolats, remembering Christmas Eves in the churches of Vienna, but Fra Ivo, to whom she had sent one of the Consulate clerks to inquire about it, had reacted so sharply and rudely that the clerk had not dared to repeat his answer to the Frau Consul; nevertheless, he managed to convince her that in a country like Bosnia such things had better be left alone. Frau von Mitterer was disappointed, but went on with her preparations at home.

Christmas Eve was a great success. The whole of the small Austrian colony was gathered around the tree. The house was warm and brightly illuminated. Pale with excitement, Anna Maria gave each one his present, wrapped in fine paper, tied with gold string, and decorated with sprigs of juniper.

Next day there was a luncheon to which Daville, his wife, and Desfosses were invited. Also present were the parish priest of Dolats, Fra Ivo Yankovich, and the young vicar from the monastery of Gucha Gora, Fra Julian Pashalich, deputizing for the Guardian, who was sick. He was that giant, irascible friar whom Desfosses had met in the inn at Kupres when he first arrived in Bosnia, and whom he later met again on his first visit to Gucha Gora.

The big dining room was warm and aromatic with cakes and the scent of pine wood. Outside, a new carpet of fine powdery snow sent up a white glow. A reflection of this whiteness fell over the richly laden table and sparkled on the silver and the crystal. The two consuls wore their gala uniforms; Anna Maria and her daughter were in light fashionable dresses of embroidered muslin, with high waists and wide sleeves. Only Mme Daville struck a note of contrast in her black mourning dress, which made her look even thinner. The two friars, both tall and heavy men, wearing their best habits, completely covered the chairs they sat on and looked like two brown haystacks in the midst of a brightly hued group.

The meal was sumptuous and good. Polish vodka, Hungarian wines, and Viennese sweets were served. All the food was well seasoned and spiced. Frau von Mitterer's imagination was evident in everything, down to the tiniest details.

The friars ate heartily and in silence, daunted occasionally by the unfamiliar dishes and the exquisite little spoons of Viennese silver which disappeared like children's toys in their huge hands. Anna Maria often turned to them, encouraging them and pressing food on them, fluttering her sleeves, tossing her hair, and flashing her eyes, and they wiped their thick peasant mustaches and looked at this fair, vivacious woman with the same quiet wonder as they did at the unfamiliar food. Desfosses could not help noticing the natural dignity of these two simple men, their alertness, their discretion, and the politely unequivocal way in which they declined to eat and drink things they did not like or weren't used to. And their awkwardness in manipulating the forks and knives and the gingerly manner in which they approached each dish were not in the least crude or laughable but rather dignified and touching.

The conversation grew more animated and louder, and was carried on in several languages. At the end the Brothers firmly declined both the dessert and the Dalmatian fruits. Anna Maria was taken aback. But the thing was soon smoothed over with the arrival of coffee and tobacco, which the friars received with unconcealed satisfaction, as though it were a kind of reward for all they'd had to endure up to that point.

The men withdrew for a smoke. It so happened that neither Daville nor Desfosses were smokers; but von Mitterer and Fra Julian more than made up for it by spouting fierce clouds, while Fra Ivo generously helped himself to snuff and mopped his whiskers and his pink double chin with an enormous blue kerchief.

It was the first time that von Mitterer had invited his rival and his friends together and that the consuls had met in the

presence of the friars. It seemed as if Christmas had ushered
in a period of festive cease-fire, as if the death of Daville's boy
had mellowed or at least deferred the antagonism and com-
bativeness of the two men. Von Mitterer was pleased to have
set the stage for an observance of such generous sentiments.

But at the same time the occasion gave everyone present an
excellent chance to air his "politics" and display his personality
in the most winsome light. Speaking blandly and unemphatic-
ally, von Mitterer sketched out, for Daville's benefit, the extent
of his influence with the Brothers and their flock, and the
Brothers corroborated him by nodding and with occasional remarks. Partly from obstinacy, partly from the habit of duty,
Daville put on the air of Napoleon's representative, and this
"imperial" attitude, which accorded so little with his true nature,
made him appear stiff and gave a false coloring to his whole
personality. The only one who spoke and behaved naturally and
did not seem forced was Desfosses, but as he was the youngest
he kept quiet most of the time.

The Brothers, insofar as they talked at all, complained about
the Turks, about fines and persecution, about the vagaries of
history, their lot, and more or less about the world in general,
with that strange and characteristic gloating that creeps into
the voice of every Bosnian when he talks about grave and hopeless things.

In company such as this, where everyone tried to say only
what he desired to be known and spread further, and confined
himself to hearing only what he needed and what the others
tried to conceal, it was natural that conversation could not get
going or take on a cordial, unstudied tone.

Like a good and tactful host, von Mitterer did not allow the
talk to veer to topics that might evoke a dispute. Only Fra Julian
and Desfosses managed to draw apart and start a somewhat
livelier discussion of their own, as old acquaintances.

The Bosnian friar and the French youth had felt sympathy
and respect for each other ever since their first meeting at Kupres. Subsequent meetings in Gucha Gora had only brought them
closer. Being young, healthy, and cheerful, they set to talking,
and even sparring in a friendly way, with obvious relish, innocent of second thoughts or personal vanity.

Drawing a little apart and gazing through the steamy window
at the bare trees that were dusted with fine snow, they talked
of Bosnia and the Bosnians. Desfosses asked for facts and in-

formation about the Catholic population and the work of the friars, and then offered his own impressions and experiences up to that time, in a calm and sincere voice.

The friar could see right away that the "young Consul" hadn't squandered his time in Travnik but had mustered a good deal of information about the land and the people, even about the native Catholics and the activities of the Brothers.

They both agreed that life in Bosnia was uncommonly hard and that the people, regardless of their denomination, were poor and backward in every respect. In his attempt to explain and find reasons for this state of affairs, the friar was apt to put the whole blame on the Turks, maintaining that there could never be any improvement until these countries freed themselves from Turkish rule and replaced it with a Christian regime. Desfosses was not satisfied with this interpretation and looked for causes in the Christians themselves. Their subjection to the Turks, he said, had produced certain characteristics of behavior in the Christians, such as furtiveness, mistrust, mental turpitude, and fear of every innovation, all work and all movement. These habits, ingrained through centuries of unequal struggle and constant fighting for survival, had become second nature to the people of these parts and had hardened into permanent traits of character. Created under the pressure of necessity, they were today, and were likely to be in the future, great obstacles to progress, a bad legacy of a distressing past and a formidable defect that would have to be rooted out.

Desfosses didn't hide his amazement at the obstinate way in which not only the Moslems but the Bosnians of all faiths resisted every influence, even the best, every novelty and sign of progress that was eminently feasible in the present circumstances and which depended on them alone. He pointed out the laming effect of such Chinese rigidity, such withdrawal from life at large. "How could this land possibly settle down and evolve some kind of order," he queried, "and become at least as civilized as its nearest neighbors, when its people are more divided than any in Europe? There are four different religions existing side by side on this narrow, mountainous, and barren strip of land. Each one is exclusive and rigidly separated from the other three. All of you live under one sky and by the same earth, yet each one of the four groups claims a spiritual home in the remote world outside, in Rome, in Moscow, in Istanbul, in Mecca, in Jerusalem, and God knows where else—but not in the place where they are born and die. And each one believes that its own progress and welfare cannot be achieved without harming and setting back the other three communities, and, conversely, that the other three can only advance at its own expense. And each one has made intolerance the highest virtue and looks for its salvation to the outside world, each from a different direction."

The friar heard him out with the smile of a man who believes he knows a thing or two and has no need of authenticating and enlarging his knowledge. Evidently determined to contradict Desfosses at all costs, he went on to say that, considering their circumstances, his people could only live and survive the way they were, unless they wanted to turn renegades, become depraved, and perish.

Desfosses replied that a people, if they were to adopt a healthier, more rational way of life, did not necessarily have to give up their faith and their ritual. And, in his opinion, it was precisely men like the friars who had the possibility and the duty of working to that purpose.

"Ah, *mon cher monsieur,*" said Fra Julian with that geniality peculiar to men defending an untenable premise, "it's easy for you to talk about the need for material progress and about healthy influences and Chinese rigidity, but if we had been less rigid and had opened our doors to all sorts of 'healthy influences,' my good parishioners Peter and Anthony would today be called Mohammed and Hussein."

"Allow me, but there is no need to go to extremes right away —or to be stubborn about it."

"Well, what are you to do? We Bosnians are pigheaded people. Everybody knows that—we're famous for it," said Fra Julian in the same tone of complacency.

"Forgive me, but why do you care how you look in other people's eyes, or what people think and know about you? As if that were of any importance! What matters is how much a person gets out of life and what he makes of himself, of his environment, and his children."

"We have preserved our viewpoint and no one can boast of having forced us to change it."

"But Father Julian, it's not the viewpoint that matters but life. A viewpoint is meant to serve life, but what *is* your life here?"

Fra Julian was just opening his mouth to produce a quotation, as was his habit, but the host interrupted their conversation.

Fra Ivo had got up. Flushed with good food, and acting a little like a monsignor, he held out his heavy fat hand to everyone; wheezing and puffing, he announced that it was winter, there was a snowstorm, that it was a long way to Dolats and they had better get started if they wanted to get there by daylight.

Desfosses and young Fra Julian were sorry to part.

While they were still at the table, Desfosses had now and then glanced at the white restless hands of Frau von Mitterer. As often as he saw that pearly luster of her skin reappear unchanged in the same places of her arm, whenever she made a movement, he had shut his eyes momentarily, feeling that between him and that woman there was a kind of steady current which no one could possibly know about or see. Her uneven, high-pitched voice cascaded through his ears all the time. Even the rather hard accent with which she spoke French had appeared to him not as a defect but as an unusual attraction peculiar to her. With a voice like that, he had thought then, one could speak any language in the world and to every man it would sound as near and intimate as his own mother tongue.

Before the party broke up, the talk turned to music and Anna Maria showed Desfosses her *Musikzimmer,* a small light room with very little furniture, several silhouette portraits on the walls, and a large gilded harp in the middle of the floor. Anna Maria complained that she'd had to leave her clavichord in Vienna and had only been able to take along her harp, which was now a great comfort to her in this wilderness. With that she stretched out her arm, which fell bare to the elbow, and languidly passed her fingers over the strings.

In those few chords, plucked so casually, the young man seemed to hear the music of the spheres rippling down over the leaden silence of Travnik, heralding days of opulence and delight in the midst of barrenness.

He stood on the other side of the harp, saying in a low voice how much he would love to hear her play and sing. But she reminded him with a mute glance of Mme Daville's mourning and promised to do it another time.

"You must promise to come out for a ride as soon as the weather improves. Do you mind the cold?"

"Why should I mind?" she answered slowly from the other side of the harp, and her voice passing through the strings impressed the young man as an intimation set to music.

He looked deep into her brown eyes, with a glow somewhere in their depths, and he imagined that even there he could see a promise beyond understanding.

Meanwhile, in the next room, von Mitterer had managed to convey to Daville, in a perfectly natural and casual fashion, in the greatest confidence, as it were, that the relations between Austria and Turkey were going from bad to worse and that Vienna had been obliged to take serious military measures not only along the frontier but in the interior as well, since it counted with the possibility that Turkey might attack them during the coming summer.

Daville, who had learned of the Austrian preparations and, in common with the rest of the world, believed that they were aimed not at Turkey but at France—Turkey being only a pretext—found in this declaration of von Mitterer's fresh confirmation of his belief. Daville pretended to believe the Colonel's words, while speculating how soon he might have a courier available to report this intentionally dropped indiscretion as one more proof of the hostile designs of the Vienna government.

As the guests were leaving, Anna Maria and Desfosses repeated in front of everybody that they would not let winter interfere with their riding and that they would go out on horseback as soon as the weather turned dry and sunny.

On the evening of that first day of Christmas, the inmates of the French Consulate did not linger long around the supper table. By tacit agreement they all wanted to withdraw to their rooms as soon as possible.

Madame Daville was depressed and could barely hold back her tears during supper. This had been her first venture into the outside world since the death of her child and now she was suffering from the effect of this first contact; for it had shaken her and brought back once more a poignant sense of anguish and loss which the silence of her retirement had already begun to heal. In her most troubled moments she had vowed that she would control her tears and suppress her grief and would offer her child, together with her own pain of bereavement, to God as a sacrifice. But now the tears welled unchecked and the pain was as strong as on the first day, before she had made the vow. She wept and at the same time begged God to forgive her for not being able to keep her vow, made in a moment when she had overestimated her strength. And she cried without restraint, doubling up with the pain that tore at her innards more terribly than the pangs of birth.

In his study Daville wrote his report on the conversation with the Austrian Consul, well pleased that his premonitions, "in this humble corner of world politics, from this bleak observation post," had turned out to be correct.

Desfosses had not even lighted his candles but was pacing up and down his bedroom with long steps and pausing by the window from time to time, seeking out the lights of the Austrian Consulate on the other side of the river. The night was opaque and deaf, there was nothing to see or hear outside; but the young man was pulsing with light and sounds. Whenever he stopped and closed his eyes, the darkness and the silence would coalesce into sound and light, and both would become Anna Maria. Her words spread a radiance and that glow at the bottom of her eyes spelled, as it did in the afternoon, the quiet and somehow significant words, "Why should I mind?"

To the young man, the whole world had suddenly become eclipsed by a towering harp, and he fell asleep lulled by the hypnotic, Dionysian music of his own trembling senses.

14

At last there came dry and sunny days when it was possible to go riding despite the cold. As they had agreed at Christmas, the riders from both Consulates met on the frozen road that goes through Kupilo.

This road seemed to have been made for excursions on horse-back. Even, straight, and well drained, more than a mile long, carved out of the steep slopes at the foot of Karauldjik and Kayabasha, it ran alongside the Lashva, but high above the river and the town which lay in the valley below. At its farther end it became slightly wider and rougher and began to fork out into rutty country roads, which continued farther uphill to the villages of Yankovichi and Orashye.

The sun rises late in Travnik. Desfosses, accompanied by a groom, rode along the sunlit road while beneath him the town still lay in shadow, under a blanket of smoke and mist. Puffs of vapor came from the riders' mouths and rose like a haze from thc animals' croups. The hard-frozen ground threw back a muffled echo of the clattering hoofs. The sun was still among the clouds, yet the valley was slowly filling with a rosy light. Desfosses rode in fits and starts, now at a slow walk so that it seemed as if at any moment he might stop and dismount, then again at a brisk canter, leaving the groom on his sluggish dun horse almost a gunshot's distance behind him. That was how the young man whiled away the time as he waited for the moment when he would catch a glimpse of Anna Maria and her escort somewhere on the road. For those who are buoyed up by youth and driven by desire, even the boredom of waiting and the exasperation of uncertainty are part and parcel of the great delight which love holds out for everyone. The young man waited in trepidation but also with an absolute conviction that in the end all his fears—Is she ill? Have they stopped her from coming? Did anything happen to her on the way?—would be proved groundless, for in affairs of the heart everything was good and favorable except the ending.

And every morning, in fact, as the sun teetered over the jagged rim of the mountains and doubts and questions came flocking to his head on a mounting note of wonder, Anna Maria would inevitably appear in her black costume and a long skirt *à l'amazone,* as if poured and cast in one piece onto her side-saddle on the tall black horse. Then both would rein in and come close to each other, as naturally as the sun rose above them and the day grew lighter in the valley. Even from a distance of a hundred yards the young man imagined he could see, with perfect clarity, the way her hat à la Valois blended, as no other woman's did, with the sweep of her brown hair into one indivisible whole; and he could see too her pale face in the morning freshness and the eyes still dusty with sleep. ("Your eyes look as if you haven't slept enough," he would tell her each time as soon as they met, giving the words "not slept enough" a bold and pointed meaning, at which she would drop her eyes and show her eyelids, glistening with a bluish shadow.)

For a while, after their greeting and the first exchange of words, they would remain stationary; then they would separate and after a short ride meet again, as if by accident, and ride on part of the way side by side, talking quickly and eagerly, only to part once more and again meet further on and resume their chatter. They owed these maneuverings to convention and to their station of society, but inwardly they did not part even for a second, and as soon as they came together they picked up their conversation of a moment before with the same delight. To their escorts and to anyone who might watch them casually, they both looked as if they were mainly concerned with their horses and their riding, and their encounters seemed accidental and their talk innocent, for it was mostly about the road, the weather, and the pace of their horses. No one could have known the contents of that wisp of white vapor which fluttered like a restless little flag now from her lips, now from his, then broke off and scattered, to unfurl once more on the cold air, livelier and longer than before.

And when the sun reached the nethermost point of the valley and all the space above it turned pink for a moment, and the half-frozen Lashva began to smoke as though invisible fires were smoldering all through the town, the young man and the woman took lingering and cordial leave of each other (it is when they part that lovers betray themselves most easily!), and then descended, each at his end of the road, toward the town under the snow and hoarfrost.

The first one who noticed that there was something afoot between young Desfosses and the handsome Frau von Mitterer, ten years his senior, was Colonel von Mitterer himself. He knew his wife well and thought of her as a "sick child." He knew her sudden enthusiasms, her "wanderings" as he called them, and could easily foresee the evolution and their ending. Thus the Colonel saw at once what was happening with his wife and could tell in advance the whole course of the affliction: the first kindling of the imagination, the enthusiasm with Platonic overtones, dismay at the coarse male desire for sensual contact, panic, flight, despair—"everyone desires me and no one loves me"—and, at last, oblivion and the discovery of new objects for enthusiasm and despair. Likewise it didn't take much insight to gauge the intentions of this tall young man who had been wrenched from Paris, dumped in Travnik, and set before the beauteous Frau von Mitterer, the only civilized woman for a hundred miles around. What the Colonel found difficult and vexing this time was the question of his position and attitude toward the French Consulate.

The Colonel had himself set the pattern of relations with the rival Consulate and its staff—for himself as well as his family and his colleagues; from time to time these relations were re-examined, adjusted, and changed, as a watch is wound and adjusted, to conform to the instructions of the Ministry and to the over-all situation. This was a grave and difficult matter for him, because his military sense of exactitude and his conscientiousness as an official were stronger and better developed in him than any other sentiment. And now, with her conduct, Anna Maria might change and unbalance those relations to the detriment of the service and the Colonel's official reputation. This particular problem had never before been raised by her "wanderings," and for the Colonel it was a new, hitherto unknown burden that his wife placed on him.

Even though he was only a tiny flywheel in the works of the great Austrian Empire, the Colonel, by dint of his position as Consul-General in Travnik, knew that his government was making military preparations, counting on a new coalition against Napoleon, and that the deployments, insofar as they could not be hidden, were made to appear as if they were directed against Turkey. But the Colonel had explicit instructions to soothe the Turkish authorities and in fact to convince them that these preparations could in no way be construed as warmongering against Turkey. At the same time, he was receiving ever stricter and more frequent orders to keep an eye on the activities of the French Consul and his agents, and to report back everything in the minutest detail.

From all this it was not hard for the Colonel to conclude that in all probability there would be an early rupture of relations with France, a new alliance, and war.

So it went without saying that the Colonel was discomfited by his wife's infatuation and by the lovers' rides in the middle of winter, before the eyes of the world and the servants. But he also knew that it was no use talking to Anna Maria, for rational arguments usually elicited the opposite reaction from her. He saw that there was nothing else for it but to await the moment when the young man would reach out for Anna Maria as a woman, and she would, as on all earlier occasions, shrink back in disgust and despair and the whole thing would snap off by itself, for good and ever. And the Colonel fervently wished that this moment would come as soon as possible.

Nor did these outings and trysts with Frau von Mitterer escape the notice of Daville, who, even in normal circumstances, was inclined to regard his "talented but somewhat bouncy" colleague with a jaundiced eye. And since he too had decided ideas on the point of his own and his staff's relations toward the Austrian Consulate, he found these encounters no less inconvenient. (As often happened in many other matters, Daville's wishes on this point coincided with von Mitterer's.) But he too did not know exactly how to stop them.

In his attitude toward women Daville had, since his youth, shown a strict discipline of mind and body. This discipline was as much the product of a stern and sound upbringing as of congenital "cold blood" and weak imagination. Like all such men, Daville had a feeling of superstitious fear about all irregular and messy affairs of this kind. Even as a modest and abstemious young man in Paris and in the army, he had always kept a kind of guilty silence during the wild and loose talks of other young men. And now it would have been easier for him to express his displeasure and admonish young Desfosses on virtually any other count than on a question involving a woman.

Besides, Daville was afraid—yes, that's the right word: afraid —of his young colleague. He was afraid of his restless, alien, but keen mind, of his varied and disorderly but far-ranging knowledge, of his carefree attitude and his levity, his intellectual curiosity, his physical strength, and especially his utter lack of fear of anything. This was the reason that Daville too marked time and looked for a suitable, circumspect method of warning the young man.

Meanwhile the month of January passed and February once again brought damp and foggy days with deep mud and slippery roads, which put a stop to what neither Daville nor von Mitterer had dared or known how to stop. Riding was no longer feasible. Desfosses, it was true, went out even in weather such as this, foot-slogging through the countryside in his high boots and brown cloak with a collar of otter pelt, freezing and tiring himself to the point of exhaustion. But Anna Maria, her temperament and inclination notwithstanding, could not leave the house in such weather; like an angel banished from the heavens, half-sad, half-smiling, and somehow ethereal, she gazed at the world with her big eyes "dusty with sleep," and walked absently past the other members of the household as if they were lifeless shadows and harmless ghosts. She spent the greater part of the day at the harp, running unsparingly through her abundant repertory of German and Italian songs, or losing herself in endless improvisations and fantasias. Her strong and warm, though occasionally unsteady, voice, in which the threat of tears and sobs was never far below the surface, filled the small room and spread to the other parts of the house. From his study the Colonel could hear Anna Maria singing, as she accompanied herself on the harp:

> *"Tutta raccolta ancor*
> *Nel palpitante cor*
> *Tremente ho l'almar."*

> My soul trembles still
> All gathered into my
> Fluttering heart.

Listening to that voice of passion and bold feelings, he shuddered with helpless hatred against that world, incomprehensible to him, from which all his domestic unhappiness and his bitter shame welled unceasingly. He dropped his pen and clapped his palms over his ears, but still he could hear, from the first floor below him, as from a mysterious depth, the haunting voice of his wife and the trickling and strumming notes of her harp. They came from a world which was the reverse of all that was sacred, important, and near to the Colonel. This music, it seemed to him, had haunted him ever since he could remember, it would never be silent; faint and tearful though it was, it would outlast him and everything that lived: armies and empires, order and justice, duties and conventions, and would still moan and trickle over all of them in much the same way, like a thin spout of water singing above the ruins.

And the Colonel took up his pen again and went on with the report he had started, writing at feverish speed, to the time of the music which rose up from below, feeling that it was all quite unbearable and yet had to be endured.

Elsewhere their daughter Agatha was also listening to the singing. On the warm, light veranda, the "winter garden" of Frau von Mitterer's, the little girl was sitting in her low chair on the red carpet. In her lap she held, unopened, the new issue of *Almanac of the Muses*. Its pages were full of wonderful new pieces, in prose and verse, of an edifying nature, and she had tried to force herself to read them, but in vain; something painful and irresistible compelled her to listen to her mother's voice coming from the music room.

The frail little creature, with intelligent eyes and a bald unwavering gaze, diffident and taciturn since childhood, had an
inkling of many things that were as yet obscure to her but which
she felt to be grave and somehow fateful. For years now she
had been dimly aware of the relations within the family, had
quietly observed her father, mother, servants, and family friends,
and been disturbed by glimmerings of knowledge that were
baffling in themselves but which added up to sorrow, ugliness,
and vexation. She felt more and more ashamed and shrank back
into herself, yet there too, within herself, she found new reasons
for embarrassment and withdrawal. When they were still at
Zemun she had had a few playmates among the officers' daughters and her life, besides, had been filled with school, with fierce
worship of the nun-teachers, and a hundred small worries and
joys. But now she was utterly alone and left to herself, a prey
to her restive years, alone between a kind ineffectual father and
a stormy incomprehensible mother.

Listening to her mother's singing, the girl hid her face behind
the copy of the *Almanac,* dying of inexpressible shame and a
strange apprehension. She pretended to read, but in reality she
listened with closed eyes to the song which she knew well from
her childhood years, hating and fearing it as something which
only grownups understood and permitted themselves, but which
was horrid and intolerable all the same and made mockery even
of the loveliest of books and the best of thoughts.

The opening weeks of the month of March were exceptionally
warm and dry, more like the end of April, and were an unexpected boon to the riders from the consulates. Waiting and encounters started afresh on the high straight road above the
valley, with exhilarating gallops over the soft earth and yellow
flattened grass, through the mild but fresh air of a premature
spring. Once more the consuls began to worry, each for himself,
and to consider ways of foiling the equestrian idyl without causing a sharp dispute.

According to the information reaching both consuls, a clash
between the government at Vienna and Napoleon was inevitable.
"Relations between the two countries are developing in the opposite direction from those affectionate relations being cultivated, as all the world can see, on the bridle path above Travnik," Daville told his wife, permitting himself one of those intra-
family jokes which husbands are wont to indulge in before their
wives, at little or no cost of intellect or strain. But the joke was

also a rehearsal for what might very well be the opening gambit in a man-to-man confrontation with young Desfosses on that distasteful topic. Things really couldn't go on much longer as they were.

In the meantime, the demon called "quest of a knight," which sent Anna Maria in pursuit of young, gifted, and forceful men, and which caused her to reel back just as violently the moment the knight, a man of flesh and blood, showed human desires and appetites, this demon intervened here too, and simplified matters for both Daville and von Mitterer—if, indeed, in the case of the latter, one could at all speak of things being simplified. What was bound to come, did come: the moment when Anna Maria, disenchanted, recoiling, and feeling sick, dropped everything and ran and hid herself in her room, overwhelmed by a sense of loathing toward herself and the whole world, rent by thoughts of suicide and by the urge to vent it all on her husband or anyone else for that matter.

The unusually warm last week of March quickened the course of events and brought them to a head.

One sunny morning the level road between the bare thickets echoed once again to the clatter of horses. Both Anna Maria and Desfosses were exhilarated with the beauty and freshness of the morning. Each in turn would spur his horse into a gallop, then they would meet again farther along the road and, excited and panting, exchange glowing words and broken sentences whose meaning and import were clear only to themselves; which, in turn, sent their blood coursing even faster, stirred as it was with riding and the incandescence of the day. Anna Maria would whip her horse in the middle of a conversation and streak down to the far end of the road, leaving the excited young man in the middle of a sentence; then she would come back at a walk and the conversation would be resumed. This game tired them both out. Like the experienced riders they were, they spurred their horses apart, then met again and parted once more, like a pair of balls that constantly attracted each other and crisply bounded apart. The game increased the distance between them and the escorts. Their grooms and kavasses rode slowly on their small ponies and stayed aloof from the game of the gentlefolk. They did not mingle with each other but waited in separate groups until their masters had spent their energy and had enough, after which they could then return to their homes.

Racing like this, each on their own, the young man and woman met at one moment at the end of the level road at a spot where it veered suddenly and became rocky and rutted. On this curve there was a small copse of pines. In the sunlit morning the trees looked like a shapeless black mass and the ground beneath them was russet and dry with the fallen needles. Desfosses quickly dismounted and suggested that Anna Maria dismount too and take a closer look at the wood which, in his words, reminded him of Italy. The word Italy had an immediate effect on her. Dismounting, she hooked the bridle rein on her arm and walked onto the smooth carpet of rust-hued pine needles, shakily, for her legs were numb from riding.

They entered the wood, which grew thicker and closed in behind them. She found the going difficult in her boots, and held the long skirt of her black riding habit in one hand. She stopped and hesitated. The young man spoke up, as if to exorcise the deep silence of the forest and reassure both himself and her. He drew a comparison between the wood and a temple, or something of that order. Between the words there was emptiness and silence, filled with his short hot breath and the quickening thumps of his heart. The young man then slung both their reins over a branch. The horses stood quietly, their muscles quivering.

Then he drew her, stumbling, another few steps to a hollow where the pine trunks and trailing branches completely hid them from view. She drew back and slipped, awkward and frightened, on the thick layer of pine needles. And before she could get free or say anything, she saw the flushed face of the young man quite close to her own. There was no more talk of Italy and temples. Those great red lips were bearing down on hers, now quite wordless. She paled, opened her eyes wide as if she had suddenly awakened, wanted to push him away and run, but her knees gave way under her. His arms already circled her waist. She moaned like someone who was being killed quietly, defenseless. "No! Not this!" She rolled up the whites of her eyes, then let go of the hem of the long skirt which she had been clutching up to that moment, and grew limp.

Gone was the familiar world of words and walks, of consuls and consulates. Gone too was the pair of them, in this convulsive, knotted bundle on the thick matting of pine needles that crackled under them. Embracing the swooned woman, the young man cuddled and caressed her as if with a hundred invisible arms. The wetness of his lips mingled with her tears,—for she was crying—and with blood, for somehow her mouth had begun to bleed. And still they did not separate; indeed they were no longer two mouths but one. But this embrace of a young man gone wild and a woman in a trance didn't last even a full minute. Anna Maria suddenly started, her eyes widened even more, as if staring into a terrifying abyss; she came to herself and, in a sudden access of strength, angrily thrust the impassioned young man away, pounding at his chest with both her little fists, hysterically, like an infuriated child, crying with each blow: "No, no, no!"

The great rapture, in which everything had gone down in limbo, was shattered. Just as they had not been conscious of sinking to the ground, so now they were unaware of being back on their feet. She was sobbing with fury and jabbing at her hair and hat, while he, rattled and clumsy, brushed the dry pine needles from her black habit, gave her back her whip, and helped her to clamber out of the hollow. The horses were standing where they had left them, shaking their heads.

They regained the road and mounted before their escorts could notice that they had ever dismounted. As they were parting, they looked more flushed than usual and he blinked in the glaring sun. Anna Maria was quite transformed. Her lips were now so blanched that they were almost lost in the bloodless face, and there was a new, suddenly "awakened," look in her eyes, with two black circles in the place of pupils, into which it was even more difficult to see than into the erstwhile deep gleam. Her whole face was puffed up, with an ugly expression of rage and endless loathing of herself and everything around her; it suddenly seemed aged and neglected.

Desfosses, who in other circumstances did not easily lose his presence of mind and his cool native confidence in himself, was genuinely bewildered and felt ill at ease. He realized that this was no longer bashfulness or the usual society woman's fear of embarrassment and scandal. He suddenly felt himself to be lower and more defenseless than this strange woman whose peculiar temper and fretting heart were a world in themselves, in which she could exist all by herself.

It all seemed so changed and chaotic, everything about him and inside him, even the dimensions of his own body.

And so the winter riders, those tender lovers from the high road to Kupilo, parted forever.

. . .

Von Mitterer saw at once that the relationship of his wife and the new would-be knight had reached, as so often before, the critical point of reversal, and that domestic storms were about to begin. And in fact, after two days of complete withdrawal, without food or company, the scenes began with the usual groundless reproaches and imprecations ("Joseph, for the love of God . . .!"), which the Colonel had anticipated and quietly resolved to endure to the end, like all the earlier ones.

Soon Daville too noticed that Desfosses no longer went out riding with Frau von Mitterer. This suited him perfectly, for it relieved him of the uncomfortable duty of having to speak about it to the young man and telling him that all intimate contact with the Austrian Consulate must be broken off. The fact was, all reports seemed to point to a new straining of relations between Napoleon and the Vienna Court. Daville read these reports with alarm, as he listened to the strong south winds of March howling around the house.

During that time the "young Consul," sitting in his warm room, choked with rage at Anna Maria and, still more, at himself. He tried in vain to understand her behavior; but no matter what explanations he found, they all left him with a feeling of disillusion, of shame and wounded vanity, and, what was more, with the sharp pain of desire aroused and left unslaked.

He remembered too—now that it was too late—his uncle in Paris and the advice this uncle had given him one day when he saw him at the Palais Royal dining with an actress who was known for her eccentric ways. "I see that you've grown up and become a man," the old gentleman had told him, "and that you're beginning to break your neck like the rest of them. Well, that's how it has to be, and will be, I suppose. Let me give you just one piece of advice: keep away from foolish women."

The good and wise uncle often haunted his dreams.

Now that the affair had fizzled out in such a silly and ludicrous fashion, he saw clearly, like a man shaken awake, the moral repugnance of his "entanglement" with the middle-aged and eccentric Frau Konsul, to which his momentary lapse of self-control and his boredom at Travnik had driven him.

And now he went back in his memory to last summer's *tableau vivant* in the garden with Jelka, the girl from Dolats, whom he had all but forgotten; and several times that night he jumped up from the table or sprang out of his bed, with the blood rushing to his head, his eyes filmed over, and his whole being filled to bursting with shame and rage at himself—emotions which youth can experience every bit as devastatingly as its passions. And, standing in the middle of the room, he cursed himself for having acted like an idiot and a boor; and at the same time he never ceased to analyze the reasons for his lack of success.

"What sort of country is this? What kind of atmosphere?" he asked himself then. "What kind of women are these? They look at you meekly and submissively, like flowers in the grass waiting to be plucked, or else with burning eyes (through the strings of a harp), enough to melt your heart. And when you give in to that pleasing look the first lot drop to their knees, twisting the whole thing around by a hundred and eighty degrees, and beg you in such a fainting voice and with such a sacrificial look that you feel sick to your heart, everything suddenly becomes mean and depressing, and you lose all interest in living and loving. And the other lot put up a fight as if you were a bandit and start swinging like an English boxer."

That was how, on the floor above Daville and his sleeping family, the "young Consul" searched his soul and wrestled with his private anguish, until he got the better of it and the anguish, like all torments of youth, began to fade into oblivion.

15

The news and instructions from Paris, which Daville had been getting with considerable delay over the last few days, showed that the great war machine of the Empire was once more on the move, this time against Austria.

Daville felt personally threatened and embroiled. It seemed to him a personal calamity that this lava should be rolling toward these very parts which contained his own small sector and where he had great responsibility. The vexing urge to do something and initiate some kind of action, and the crippling fear that he might make a mistake or leave something undone, never left him now, not even in sleep. The calm and *sang froid* of young Desfosses irritated him more than usual. To the young man it seemed natural that the imperial army should wage war somewhere or other and he saw no reason in this whatever to change his manner of life or way of thinking. Daville fairly trembled with suppressed anger as he listened to the glib phrases and *bon mots* that presumably were the fashion of the young men of Paris, and which Desfosses employed when speaking of the coming war, without respect or enthusiasm, but also without doubt in its victorious outcome. They filled Daville with instinctive envy and sharpened his distress at having no one to talk to ("to exchange fears and hopes") about the war and everything else, on a level and in a spirit that were close and peculiar to himself and his generation. Now more than ever the world seemed to him to be full of snares and jeopardy and of those shapeless thoughts and fears which war spread over the land and wedged among the people, particularly those who were advanced in years or weak and tired out.

Daville felt at times as though he were losing his breath and dropping with fatigue, as though for years he had been marching alongside a dark and soulless column with which he could no longer keep in step, and which threatened to walk over him and crush him if he so much as knelt down and stopped marching. Whenever he was left alone, he would heave a deep sigh and say quickly in a low voice: "Ah, dear God, dear God!" He spoke the words without being aware of them, not connecting them to what was happening around him at that moment, for they were part of his breath and sigh.

How was one to avoid staggering from exhaustion and the giddy rush that had been going on for years, yet how was one to chuck everything and abandon all further effort and endeavor? How was a man to see clearly or understand anything in the general and incessant scramble and confusion, and then again how was he to march through fatigue, convulsions, and uncertainty toward some new, vanishing, nebulous horizon?

It seemed only yesterday that he had listened with excitement to the news of the Austerlitz victory, with its promise of hope and settlement; only this morning that he had written his verses about the Battle of Jena; only a little while ago that he had read bulletins of the victory in Spain, the entry into Madrid, the sweeping of the English troops clear out of the Iberian Peninsula. The echo of one campaign had scarcely died down and already it was mingling with the tumult and fury of new events. Were the laws of nature really to be changed by force, or was everything to be smashed on their rocklike constancy? Sometimes it looked as if the first might happen, sometimes the second; yet there was no clear conclusion. The spirit grew numb, the brain refused to function. In this state and mood he kept marching along, together with other millions of people; he worked and talked, trying his best to keep in step, to do his part, not showing or breathing his oppressive, wretched doubts and confusion of soul to anyone.

And now, here it was beginning all over again, down to the last detail. He received *Le Moniteur* and *Journal de l'Empire*, containing articles that explained and justified the need for the new campaign and forecast its certain success. (While he read them, Daville had no doubt that that was how things were and how they ought to be.) Then days and weeks would follow in which he debated with himself, doubted, waited for something to happen. (Why war again? How long would it last? How would all this affect the world, Napoleon, France, and Daville himself and his family? Would their luck hold out this time, or would they live to see their first defeat, a harbinger of the end to come?) But later there would be a bulletin of new successes, with the names of cities occupied and countries overrun. And finally a total victory and a victorious peace, with new territorial gains and new promises of a general reconciliation, which in fact would never take place.

Then, together with all the rest, and perhaps louder than the rest, Daville would celebrate the victory and talk about it as though it were a self-understood thing, in which he too had played a part. And no one would ever see or know those sickening doubts and trepidations which victory had dispelled like mist and which he was now trying to forget himself. For a short time, but only a very short time, he would deceive even himself, but soon the imperial war machine would give another heave and he would begin another private game with himself, identical with those he had played before. And all of it was sapping and whittling him down and made for a life that seemed peaceful and orderly to the naked eye, but which in fact was an unbearable torment and went sorely against his deeper grain and the whole of his real being.

The fifth coalition against Napoleon was formed during that winter and was made public, suddenly, in the spring. As he had done four years before, but even more swiftly and daringly, Napoleon's answer to the treacherous attack was a lightning strike at Vienna. Now even the uninitiated could see why the consulates had been opened in Bosnia and what purpose they were meant to serve.

All contact ceased between the French and the Austrian at Travnik. Their household staffs did not greet one another, the consuls avoided meeting each other on the street. On Sundays, during the high Mass in the church at Dolats, Mme Daville and Frau von Mitterer and her daughter sat far apart from one another. The two consuls paid court to the Vizier and his staff more assiduously than before and intensified their cultivation of the friars, the Orthodox priests, and leading citizens. Von Mitterer broadcast the proclamation of the Austrian Emperor, Daville the French bulletin of the first victory at Eckmühl. Couriers overtook and crossed one another on the road between Split and Travnik.

General Marmont wanted at all cost to take his Dalmatian troops and join up with Napoleon's main army before a decisive battle took place. He therefore asked Daville for information about the districts he would have to pass through on his way north, and kept sending him fresh instructions. This trebled the volume of Daville's work and made it increasingly burdensome, expensive, and complex; all the more so as von Mitterer watched his every step and, being an experienced military man and past master of frontier intrigue and jockeying, used every conceivable trick to prevent General Marmont's passage through the provinces of Lika and Croatia. As the number and gravity of Daville's tasks mounted, so did his energy, his resourcefulness, and his will to fight. He managed, with the help of D'Avenat, to discover and organize all those who from sentiment or self-interest were against Austria and willing to work in that direction wherever they could. He sent appeals to the Turkish fortress commanders along the frontier, especially to the captain of Novi, the brother of the unfortunate Ahmed Beg Cerich, whom he had been unable to save from death in the Travnik prison; he encouraged them to foray into the Austrian territory and offered them money and equipment for the sallies.

Von Mitterer, through the friars at Livno, sent news and proclamations into Dalmatia, which was under French occupation, kept in touch with the Catholic clergy in northern Dalmatia, and helped to organize resistance against the French.

All the paid agents and volunteer workers of the two consulates scattered in various directions and their activity began to make itself felt in a general unrest and in frequent clashes. The friars stopped all intercouse with the people at the French Consulate. In the monasteries prayers were offered for the victory of Austrian arms over the Jacobin hosts and their godless Emperor, Napoleon.

The consuls visited and received people with whom ordinarily they would never be seen, they distributed gifts and bribed generously. They worked day and night, not sparing their strength or wasting too many scruples on the means they employed. In this the Colonel had many more things in his favor than Daville. True, he was a tired man, ground down by troubles and ill health, yet to him this way of life and struggle was nothing new and it accorded with his experience and training. Faced with orders from the higher authority, the Colonel soon forgot himself and his family and slid into the well-worn rut of imperial service, jogging along without joy or enthusiasm but also without a second thought or futile arguments. Besides, the Colonel knew the language, the country, the people, and local conditions and had no difficulty in finding sincere and selfless helpers wherever he turned. All this was nonexistent in the case of Daville, who was forced to work under all manner of handicaps. Even so, his sense of duty, his alertness of mind and innate Gallic fighting spirit sustained him and goaded him to keep in the forefront of the race; not only that, but he managed to give as good as he got.

Despite all this, if things had depended only on the two consuls, their relations would not have been quite so bad. The worst elements were their petty officials and clerks, their agents and servants, who observed no limits in their intrigue and blackening of each other. They were carried away by their official zeal and personal vanity as a huntsman is carried away by his passion, and they forgot themselves so far that in their eagerness to humiliate and squeeze each other out they degraded and lowered themselves in the eyes of the rayah and the gloating Turks.

Both Daville and von Mitterer saw clearly how damaging this reckless and unsparing tug of war between them was to both camps and to the prestige of Christians and Europeans in general, and how undignified it was for the two of them, the only representatives of civilization in this barbarian wilderness, to grapple and wrestle in front of these people who hated, despised, and misunderstood them both, and to call on these same people to be their witnesses and judges. Daville, who was in a weaker position, felt this especially. He decided, through the intermediary of Cologna, who was regarded as an unofficial person, to draw von Mitterer's attention to this and to propose to him that they both curb their overzealous co-workers a little. Cologna would be contacted by young Desfosses, since the interpreter D'Avenat was not on speaking terms with the old doctor. At the same time, through his devout wife and by other feasible means, he wanted to influence the friars and to indicate to them that, as the representatives of the Holy Church, they were sinning when they gave their exclusive and one-sided endorsement to one of the embattled sides.

To show the Brothers how groundless were their accusations about the godlessness of the French regime and in order to place them under greater obligation, he hit on the idea of asking them for a permanent paid chaplain for the French Consulate. Through the parish priest of Dolats he sent a letter to the bishop of Foynitsa. When he received no reply, it fell to Mme Daville to approach Fra Ivo and convince him personally what a good and fitting thing it would be if the friars were to assign one of the Brothers as chaplain and were to modify their attitude toward the French Consulate in general.

One Saturday afternoon Mme Daville went to Dolats, accompanied by an "Illyrian" interpreter and a groom. She had carefully chosen a weekday, when there would be evening Benediction in the church, rather than a Sunday when there was a throng of people and the parish priest was busy.

Fra Ivo received Madame Consul very civilly, as always. He told her that the bishop's reply had arrived "that morning" and he was just getting ready to send it on to the Consul-General. The reply was negative, for much to their regret, in these difficult times when they were poor, persecuted, and few in number, they did not have enough friars even for the immediate needs of their flock. Moreover, the Turks would be only too apt to look upon such a chaplain as an agent and a spy and would take it out on the Order as a whole. In short, the bishop was very sorry not to be able to grant the French Consul's request and begged him to understand his position, etc., etc.

So wrote the bishop, but Fra Ivo made no bones of the fact that even were he able and allowed to do so, he himself would never permit a chaplain of their Order to serve in one of Napoleon's consulates. Madame Daville tried, in her mild-mannered way, to correct his opinion; but the friar, in his carapace of fat, remained unbending. While freely acknowledging his personal respect toward Mme Daville, for her sincere and undoubted piety (the Brothers, in general, had much more respect for Mme Daville than for Frau von Mitterer), he nevertheless stuck to his viewpoint obstinately. He accompanied his words with a rather fierce lopping motion of his huge hand, which sent an unwitting shudder through Mme Daville. It was obvious that his instructions were clear, his attitude set, and that he had no desire to discuss it with anyone, least of all with a woman.

After reassuring her once more that he would always be at her service for any spiritual needs but that, in all other respects, he must stick to his viewpoint, Fra Ivo left her and went into the church, where Benediction was about to begin. That day, for some reason, there were quite a number of friars and visitors at Dolats and this gave Benediction a special air of solemnity.

If she could have followed her own impulse, Mme Daville would have returned home right away, but considerations of duty required that she stay for Benediction, lest anyone get the idea that she had come only to talk to Fra Ivo. This normally poised woman, who was not given to excesses of feeling, was upset and offended by the parish priest's reaction. The unpleasant conversation had been all the more disagreeable as due to her upbringing and her temperament she had always kept aloof from such general problems and public affairs.

Now she stood in the church beside a wooden pillar and listened to the muffled and yet ragged chanting of the friars, who were kneeling on both sides of the altar. Fra Ivo was saying Benediction. Portly and lumbering though he was, he yet managed, whenever necessary, to bend down lightly and nimbly on one knee and then straighten up again in one swift, unbroken movement; but Mme Daville still had a vivid mental picture of his huge hand in its cutting gesture of refusal, and of his eyes, hard with pride and obstinacy, as he had looked at her interpreter during their talk just now. Never before in France had she seen that look either on a priest's or a layman's face.

The Brothers sang the Litany of the Virgin in a soft chorus, in their peasant voices. A deep voice took the lead: *Sancta Maria.* And they all replied hoarsely, in unison: *Ora pro nobis.* The voice went on: *Sancta virgo virginum . . .* *Ora pro nobis,* the other voices answered all together. The praying voice continued to call out the attributes of Mary with a long drawl: *Imperatrix Reginarum . . . Laus sanctarum animarum . . . Vera salutrix earum . . .*

And after each one, the chorus echoed in a ringing monotone: *Ora pro nobis.*

Madame Daville would have wanted to join in and pray the familiar litany, which she had once listened to in the drafty cathedral choir of her native Avranches, but she could not forget the conversation of a little while before or push away the thoughts which mingled with her prayer.

"We all say the same prayers, we are all Christians and of the same faith, and still there are such gulfs between us," she thought, still seeing in her mind's eye the fierce stubborn look and the cutting hand movement of this same Fra Ivo who was now singing litanies.

The chanted catalogue went on undiminished: *Sancta Mater Domini . . . Sancta Dei genitrix . . .*

Yes indeed, one knew that these gulfs existed, together with all the other enmities between peoples, but it was only when a person went out into the world and felt them in his own life that he truly realized how great they were, how deep and unbridgeable. What sort of prayer should one pray that could fill up and erase all these gulfs? Her mood of dejection told her that there was no such prayer; but at this point her mind stopped short, helplessly bewildered, and she whispered quietly, joining her barely audible voice to the steady chant of the friars which kept recurring like a wave, over and over again: *"Ora pro nobis!"*

When vespers were finished, she humbly took the benediction from that same hand of Fra Ivo's.

Outside, in front of the church, she found Desfosses and his groom waiting, beside her own escort. He had been riding through Dolats, and when he found out that Mme Daville was in church he decided to wait for her and accompany her back to Travnik. She was glad to see the familiar, cheerful face of the young man and to hear the sound of her mother tongue.

They rode back to town along the broad, dry road. The sun had set, but the whole countryside was still bathed in a luminous, reflected yellow light. The clay surface of the road looked red and warm, while the new foliage and the flower buds on the undergrowth stood out against the dark bark, as if they were made of light itself.

Beside her walked the young man, flushed from exercise, and chatting away with a good deal of animation. Behind them was the sound of the grooms' footsteps and the stomping of Desfosses's horse, which one of the servants was leading by the rein. The murmur of the litanies was still in her ears. Now the road began to slope downhill. The roofs of Travnik loomed ahead, with thin blue smoke above them, and the sight of them brought back the reality of ordinary life with its needs and tasks, far removed from her dismal thoughts, doubts, and prayers.

About the same time Desfosses had his talk with Cologna.

He went to see him one evening, around eight o'clock, accompanied by a kavass and a groom carrying a lantern. The house stood on one side of a steep rise, enveloped in a damp mist and thick darkness. Unseen waters from the spring of Shumech filled the night with a purl. This sound of water was muffled and transmuted by the darkness and magnified by the silence. The path was wet and slippery; in the meager, flickering light of the Turkish lantern it looked as new and unfamiliar as a forest glade trodden by human feet for the first time. The gate to the house appeared just as mysterious and unexpected. The threshold and the ringed doorknockers were illuminated, but everything else was in darkness; shapes and dimensions of objects stretched away into the night, defying identification. The door gave out a hard, hollow sound when the kavass knocked. The noise struck Desfosses as somehow rude and out of place, almost a physical pain, and he winced at the man's excessive zeal, which seemed to him boorish and uncalled-for.

"Who's knocking?" The voice came from above, more like an echo of the kavass's banging than a question in its own right.

"The young Consul. Open up!" shouted Ali, the kavass, in that unpleasant, needlessly sharp voice in which young people are apt to talk to one another in the presence of a senior.

Male voices and the gurgle of water from afar—it was all like some casual and unexpected cries in a forest, without a known cause and without a visible effect. Finally there was the rattle of a chain, the creaking of the lock, and the noise of a latch. The gate opened slowly and behind it there stood a man with a lantern, pale and drowsy, wrapped in a shepherd's coat. Two lights of unequal intensity illumined the sloping courtyard and the low dark windows of the ground floor of the house. The two servants' lanterns vied with each other to light the ground at the young Consul's feet. Bemused by this interplay of voices and flashing lights, Desfosses suddenly found himself before the wide, open door of a large ground-floor apartment, which was full of smoke and the heavy reek of tobacco floating on the moldy air.

In the middle of the room, by a large candelabrum, stood Cologna, tall and stooping, dressed in a weird assortment of Turkish and European garments. On his head was a small black cap, from under which peeped long, sparse tufts of gray hair. The old man bowed deeply and spoke resonant greetings and compliments in that peculiar language of his which might have been either corrupt Italian or half-learned French, all of which sounded glib and stilted to the young man, empty conventions that were not only devoid of cordiality and genuine respect but lacked even the normal conviction a speaker might be expected to put behind his words. And then all at once everything he had encountered in that low-ceilinged, smoky apartment—the reek and the appearance of the room, the figure and the speech of the man—coalesced into a single word, so quickly, so vividly and clearly that he all but said it out aloud: age. Melancholy, toothless, forgetful, lonesome, earth-bound old age, which corroded, travestied, and embittered all things—thoughts, sights, movements, and sounds—all things, even light and smell themselves.

The old doctor ceremoniously offered the young man a seat but remained standing himself, explaining that he was merely observing an old Salernian rule: *Post prandium sta*—After a meal one should stand.

Desfosses sat down on a hard armless chair, but was filled with a sense of physical and mental superiority which made his mission appear easy and simple to him, almost pleasant. He began to speak in that tone of smug confidence which young men so often adopt in conversing with old men who seem to them outdated and at the end of their rope, quite forgetting that bodily infirmity and slowness of mind are often accompanied by vast experience and hard-won skill in handling human affairs. He delivered Daville's message to von Mitterer, trying to make it appear for what it was, namely a well-meant suggestion in their common interest and not a sign of weakness or fear. He concluded and was pleased with himself.

Cologna hastened to assure him that he was honored to have been chosen as an intermediary, that he would pass on the message conscientiously, that he fully appreciated the intentions and shared the opinion of M. Daville. He agreed that his own background, profession, and convictions made him the most suitable person for such a role.

Now, evidently, it was Cologna's turn to be pleased with himself.

The young man listened to him as he might have listened to the babble of water, gazing absently at his regular, long face with its lively round eyes, bloodless lips, and teeth that moved as he spoke. Old age! thought the young man. The worst of it was not that one suffered and died but that one grew old, for growing old was a malady for which there was no cure or hope; it was a long-dragged-out death. Except that the young man did not think of aging in terms of a common human destiny, which included his own, but as an affliction that was peculiar to the doctor alone.

And Cologna said: "I don't need too many explanations. I understand the Consul's situation, as I understand the situation of every enlightened man from the West whose fate it is to live in these parts. For a man like that, living in Turkey means walking the sharp blade of a knife or roasting over a slow fire. I know it too well, for people like me are born on the knife's edge and we live and die on it. And in this fire we grow and burn ourselves to a cinder."

Through his musings about age and growing old, the young man began to listen with more attention and to grasp the doctor's words.

"No one knows what it means to be born and to live on the borderline between two worlds. What it means to know and understand the one and the other and yet be unable to do anything that might help them explain themselves to each other or bring them closer together. What it means to love and hate either, to waver between the two and imitate now one now the other. To have two homes and yet none, to be at home everywhere and yet remain a stranger forever. In short, to live crucified, but as victim and torturer at one and the same time."

The young man listened in amazement. These were no longer empty phrases and compliments; it was as if a third man had joined in the conversation and was now holding forth. Before him stood a man with flashing eyes and long thin arms outspread, demonstrating how one lived torn between two conflicting worlds.

As often happens with young people, Desfosses could not help feeling that this conversation was not entirely adventitious, that

it was somehow, in a special and intimate way, bound up with
his own thoughts and with the book which he was preparing to
write. There weren't too many opportunities in Travnik for conversations of this kind; he felt pleasantly stimulated and in his
excitement began to ask questions, then to make observations of
his own and describe his own impressions.

He spoke as much from inner necessity as from a desire to
prolong the discussion. But there was no need to prompt the
old man to talk. He never as much as wandered from his main
theme. Although, here and there, he was brought up short for
want of a French phrase and substituted an Italian one, he
spoke like one inspired, almost as if he were reading from a
prepared text: "Yes, these are the miseries which torment the
Christians in the Levant and which you people from the Christian West will never be able to understand fully, just as the
Turks cannot understand them. Such is the fate of a man from
the Levant, for he is *poussière humaine*, human dust, drifting
wearily between East and West, belonging to neither and pul-
verized by both. These are people who speak many languages
but have no language of their own, who are familiar with two
religions but hold fast to neither. They are victims of the fatal
division of mankind into Christian and non-Christian; eternal
interpreters and go-betweens, who carry within them so much
that is unclear and inarticulate; they are good connoisseurs of
the East and West and of their customs and beliefs, but are
equally despised and suspected by both. To them can be applied
the words written six centuries ago by the great Jelaleddin, Jelaleddin Rumi: '. . . For I cannot tell who I am. I am neither a
Christian, nor a Jew, nor a Parsee, nor a Mussulman. I am neither of the East nor of the West, neither from dry land nor
from the sea.' They are like that. They are a small mankind
apart, stumbling under a double load of Eastern sin, that ought
to be saved and redeemed a second time, though no one can
say how or by whom. They are a frontier people, bodily and
spiritually, from that black and bloody dividing line which
through some terrible, absurd misunderstanding has been drawn
between man and man, all creatures of God, between whom
there should not and must not be any such lines. They are the
pebble between the land and the sea, condemned to eternal
swirling and pull. They are the *third world*, a repository of the
curse and damnation which the cleaving of the earth into two
worlds has left in its wake. They are . . ."

Excited, with shining eyes, Desfosses watched the transformed old man who, with his arms flung out so that he resembled a cross, vainly searched for words and then suddenly wound up in a broken voice: "It is heroism without glory, martyrdom without rewards. But at least you who are our kinsman and believe in the same God, you people of the West who are Christians by the same grace that we are, at least you should understand us and accept us and lighten our burden."

The doctor dropped his arms with an air of utter hopelessness, of anger almost. There was no vestige left of that queer, elusive "Illyrian doctor" Desfosses had known. Here stood a man who thought his own thoughts and expressed them forcefully. Desfosses burned with the desire to hear and learn more; he had quite forgotten his own feeling of superiority of a little while before and the house he was in and the business on which he had come. He knew that he had sat there far longer than he should have or had intended to, but he didn't get up.

The old man's eyes were on him with a look full of unspoken emotion, as though he were watching someone who was moving away out of reach and whose going saddened him. "Yes, monsieur, you may understand this life of ours, but to you it's only an uncomfortable dream. You're living here now, but you know it's only for a time and sooner or later you will go back to your country, where conditions are better and life has more dignity. You will rise up from this nightmare and walk with your head high once more, but we never shall, for to us it's the only life."

Toward the end of the conversation the doctor grew more and more subdued and queer. Now he too sat down, quite close to the young man, leaning toward him in an attitude of the most intimate confidence and motioning him with both hands to keep quiet, almost as if, by an inadvertent word or gesture, he might frighten and scare away something fragile, precious, and timid that was there, like a bird, on the floor at their feet. Staring fixedly at a spot on the carpet, he spoke in a whisper, yet also in a voice that was warm and soft with an inner sweetness. "In the end, when all is truly and finally said and done, everything is nevertheless good and works out for the best. It is true that here everything seems to be out of joint and snarled up beyond hope. 'Un jour tout sera bien, voilà notre espérance' —One day everything will be all right, that's our hope, as your philosopher has said. And it is hard to visualize it any other way. For, in the last instance, are my thoughts, which are good

and right, worth any less than someone else's identical thoughts
in Rome or Paris? Simply because I've conceived them in this
mountain gorge known as Travnik? Certainly not. What is to
prevent my thoughts from being jotted down and appearing between the covers of a book? Nothing! And even if things seem
to be disjointed and chaotic, they are nevertheless linked together and interdependent. Not a single human thought, no
enterprise of the mind, is ever lost. All of us are on the right
road, we shall all be amazed when we meet eventually. And we
shall meet and understand one another, no matter how scattered
we may be now or how far we may have strayed. That will be a
happy meeting indeed, a glorious surprise that will save us all."

The young man had trouble following the doctor's premise,
but he was eager to hear him talk on. And Cologna did go on,
in the same confidential tone of joyful excitement, even though
what he said was at times not immediately pertinent. Desfosses
nodded his approval, grew excited himself and now and then,
unable to hold back, threw in some observations of his own. He
told the old man about his discovery on the road at Turbe, where
the telltale layers under the road's surface clearly indicated various historical epochs—the same story he had once told Daville,
without much success.

"I know you look around you and notice things. You are interested in the past as well as the present. You know how to
look," said the doctor approvingly. And, like a man divulging a
secret of hidden treasure and letting his smiling eyes insinuate
more than words can encompass, the old man said in a low but
dramatic voice: "Next time you go through the bazaar, stop by
the Yeni Mosque. There is a high wall around the whole area.
Inside, under huge old trees, there are graves and no one can
remember any longer whose they are. But the people still remember that once upon a time, before the Turks came to the
country, the mosque used to be the Church of St. Catherine.
And they believe that the sacristy stands to this day in one of
the corners of the mosque and that no one can open it. If you
look a little closer at the stones in the ancient wall, you will see
that they were taken from Roman ruins and tomb monuments.
And on one particular stone that has been built into the wall of
the mosque enclosure you can read quite clearly several neat
and regular Roman letters from a text fragment: 'Marco Flavio
. . . optimo . . .' And deep down below, in the hidden founda-

tions, there are great big blocks of red granite, the remains of a much older cult, the former shrine of the god Mithras. On one of these blocks there is a mysterious relief, in which one can make out the young god of light killing a powerful wild boar in full flight. And who knows what else is hidden in those depths, under those foundations? No man can tell whose endeavors may be buried there or what traces may have been wiped out forever. And that is just one little plot of land, in this remote little town. Where are all the countless other great settlements the world over?"

Desfosses stared at the old man, expecting further confidences, but here the doctor suddenly changed his voice and began to speak much louder, as though any outsider were now allowed to hear what he was saying: "You understand, all these things are fitted one into another, bound together, and it is only to the outward eye that they appear lost and forgotten, scattered about and lacking a master plan. They all stretch away, quite unconsciously, toward a single goal, like rays converging on a distant, unknown focus. One should bear in mind that it is expressly written in the Koran: 'Perhaps one day God shall visit peace upon you and your adversaries and create friendship between you. He is mighty, gentle, and merciful.' So there's hope, and where there's hope . . . you understand?"

His eyes brightened with a meaningful, triumphant smile, the purport of which was to hearten and reassure the young man, and with his palms he outlined a round form in the air in front of his face, as if he wanted to show the closed circle of the universe.

"You understand?" the old man repeated meaningfully, with a touch of impatience, as though he considered it needless and redundant to search around for words to express anything so obvious and certain, anything so near and familiar to him.

And having said it, his whole tone changed again. Once more he rose, thin and erect, bowed unctuously and spoke sonorous hollow words, telling the young man how honored he felt by his visit and by the mission entrusted to him.

That was how they parted.

On his way back to the Consulate, Desfosses walked absently in the pool of light which the kavass's lantern splashed in front of him. He no longer heard or noticed anything around him. He thought about the eccentric old doctor and his lively, hopscotch kind of reasoning, and tried to collect and organize his own thoughts which crowded back to his mind in a wild, unexpected merry-go-round.

16

The news reaching Travnik from Istanbul grew more confused and disturbing. Neither Bariaktar's successful *coup d'état* nor the tragic death of Selim III had produced the stability everyone had hoped for. The year was hardly out when there was another revolution and Mustapha Bariaktar was killed.

The upheavals and changes in the distant capital were echoed in the remote province, though much later, in a distorted fashion that was almost a caricature, like something in a trick mirror. Fear, discontent, economic insecurity, and wrath that could find no outlet racked and poisoned the Turks in the towns and cities. They felt themselves betrayed from inside and threatened from outside, like a people with a vivid premonition of an earthquake that brings a havoc of change. Their instinct for survival and self-defense drove them to action and gestures of protest, but circumstances denied them the means of action and barred all avenues of recourse, so that their energy swirled around uselessly and spent itself in the wind. In the crowded little towns between steep mountains where different faiths and conflicting interests were thrown together quarter to quarter, tempers grew brittle and created a mood in which anything was possible, in which blind forces were bound to clash and furious outbreaks certain to follow one after another.

In Europe at this time battles were being fought on a scale of horror and intensity that had never been seen before, whose effects on history could not yet be grasped. In Istanbul there was one *coup d'état* after another, sultans came and went, heads of grand viziers rolled in the dust.

Travnik was astir. As every spring, under standing orders from the capital, an army was being raised against Serbia; the hubbub and clamor as usual greatly exceeded the results. Suleiman Pasha had already left with his small but disciplined force. The Vizier was to march off any day. Ibrahim Pasha, in fact, had no precise idea of the campaign plan or the size of the army he was supposed to lead. He moved off because he could not do otherwise, because he had received a firman to move and because he hoped that by his presence in the expedition he would induce the others to do their duty. But the Janissaries did not submit kindly to muster and marching orders and used every conceivable dodge to keep out of it. While some were being called up, the others quietly vanished; or else they simply provoked a brawl and a riot, under cover of which they melted away discreetly and returned to their homes, while on the muster roll they were officially on their way to Serbia.

Both consuls made every effort to gain the most comprehensive information about the Vizier's intentions, about the number and quality of the troups under his command, and about the true situation on the Serbian battlefront. Both they and their assistants wasted their days in this activity, which at times seemed to them complex and tremendously important and at times futile and meaningless.

As soon as the Vizier followed Suleiman Pasha to the river Drina, leaving all authority and responsibility for public order with the weak and timid town Mayor, the Travnik bazaar closed down, suddenly and unexpectedly, for the second time. In reality it was a continuation of the previous year's riot, which had never guttered completely but had gone on simmering under a sullen silence, waiting for an opportune moment to flare out anew. This time the fury of the mob vented itself on the Serbs who had been caught in various parts of Bosnia and brought to Travnik on the suspicion that they were in touch with the rebels in Serbia and were plotting a similar uprising in Bosnia itself. But their rage was directed just as much at the Turkish authorities, who were accused of weakness, corruption, and betrayal.

Feeling that the new uprising in Serbia was a threat to all they held dearest and nearest, and that the Vizier, like all the other Osmanlis, failed to protect them as he should have, and that they themselves had no will or energy left to defend themselves, the Bosnian Moslems fell into the morbid excitability typical of a threatened class and avenged their impotence with barren and pointless acts of cruelty.

Almost every day captured Serbs were brought in, first in twos and threes, then in groups, sometimes by the dozen—bound and exhausted men from the Drina and the border country, charged with grave but unspecified offenses. There were townsmen and priests among them, but the majority were peasants. No one bothered to examine the charges or pass proper judgment. Day by day they were tossed into the raging Travnik bazaar as into the crater of a flaming volcano, and the bazaar became their executioner without due process or trial.

In spite of Daville's warnings and entreaties Desfosses went out and saw the gypsies torture and kill two men in the middle of the livestock market. Standing on an elevated spot behind the backs of the mob, who were completely engrossed in the spectacle before them, he could watch unnoticed and have a clear view of the victims, the hangmen, and the spectators.

The victims were a couple of tall swarthy men who might have been brothers, so alike they were. As far as one could make out from the remnants of their dress, which had been ripped and tattered during the journey and at the hands of their captors, they were from a small town. They were caught, it was said, at a moment when they were trying to smuggle into Serbia, in hollowed-out walking sticks, some letters from the Catholic bishop of Sarajevo.

Tumult and commotion reigned in the market square. Armed guards brought in the two accused, who were barefooted and bareheaded but wore coarse woolen trousers and torn soiled shirts. The guards tried to clear the space necessary for the hanging. The gypsy hangmen were slow to unwind the rope. The seething crowd heaped as much abuse on the two unfortunates as on the guards and the gypsies, they swayed this way and that, threatening to stampede and sweep away victims and executioners alike.

The two bound men, their long necks bared, stood upright and rigid, with similar expressions of astonished disbelief and distress on their faces. They showed neither fear nor bravery, neither indifference nor any strong emotion. From the expression on their faces they were merely two *worried* men, oppressed by thoughts of some remote anxiety, wishing only to be left alone so that they might think it over more quickly and with greater concentration. It was as if the pushing and noise around them were not connected with them in any way. They merely blinked their eyes and bowed their heads from time to time, as if wishing to shut out the milling and the din that kept them from giving all their attention to their main worry. They sweated profusely and on their foreheads and temples knotted veins stood out in throbbing relief; and since, being bound, they could not wipe their sweat, it ran in glistening rivulets down their sinewy, unshaven necks.

At last the gypsies managed to untangle their ropes and approached one of the condemned men. He backed away a little, but very slightly, and then stood quite still and let them do with him as they wanted. At the same time, the other man shrank back unwittingly, as though he were invisibly tied to the first. Here Desfosses, who had watched it quietly thus far, turned sharply on his heel and went into the nearest street. He thus did not see the worst and the most dreadful part.

The two gypsies now fetched the rope around the neck of their victim but did not hang him; instead they stepped back and each began to tug and pull his end of the rope tighter. The man started to gag and roll his eyes, to jerk his legs, to double up from the hips and thrash like a puppet on a twitching string.

The crowd begun to shove and sway. Everybody wanted to get closer to the scene of the torture. The first movements of the man in the noose produced excitement and a delighted response from the mob, who shouted, laughed, and mimicked his jerks with their own. But when his gagging became a deathly convulsion and his thrashing quickened to a macabre dance of pure horror, those nearest to him began to turn and edge away. Doubtless they had wanted to see something unusual, not quite knowing what it would be, hoping perhaps to find some relief for themselves and an outlet for their vague but deep and real feeling of discontent. They had long hoped and yearned to see their enemy hounded down and punished. But the scene being enacted in front of them was pain and torture for them too. And so, startled and full of fear, they began to avert their heads and turn away. But the great mass of people behind them, who had not been able to see the sight, surged powerfully and pushed those in the front ranks closer and closer to the scene. And these, in turn, aghast at being so near to the agonizing spectacle, turned their backs to the execution and tried desperately to break through and escape, flailing around them in a frenzy as if they were running from a blaze. Not knowing what possessed them and unable to under-

stand their panic-stricken behavior, the men behind them hit
back and pushed them again toward the spot from which they
were trying to escape. So in addition to the slow strangulation
and the monstrous performance of the dying man, a general
crush and fist-fighting broke out all around, with a whole chain
reaction of individual clashes, brawls, and fights. The ones
who were squeezed from all sides and could not swing and
return the blows, clawed and pulled at one another, spat, cursed,
and glared in one another's demented faces with utter incom-
prehension and with all the hatred they had stored up for the
condemned men; while those who, horror-struck, tried to get
away from the choking men, pushed with all their might and
used their fists unsparingly and in grim silence. Still others
continued to swarm from all sides toward the place of execution and they were in the majority, shouting at the tops of their
voices. Many were so far away that they saw nothing either of
the torture or of the fighting that had broken out in the middle;
and they laughed, borne on the surging wave, not realizing
what horror was being enacted in their vicinity, and jeered
and sent up the kinds of shouts one always hears in a packed
and heaving mob of people. There was a mingling, clashing,
and overlapping of different voices and cries—cries of anger,
surprise, horror, loathing, fury, banter, and joking—blended
with those nameless, inarticulate shrieks and grunts which
emanate from any crush of the human mass, from pushed-in
stomachs and pressed lungs.

"Hooo, ho!" cried some young ruffians in unison, hoping to
stir up the mob even more.

"Heave-ho!" replied the others, pushing in the opposite direction.

"Whom are you trying to knock down? Have you gone mad!"

"Mad, mad! He's mad!" shrilled someone in a demented
voice.

"Hit him! Don't be sorry for him! He's no brother of yours!"
someone chipped in from far back, grinning, thinking it was
all a joke.

There was a scuffle and stomping of feet, followed by loud
blows. Then voices again.

"Hey . . . d'you want more? Do you?"

"Hey, you there in the cap!"

"Are you pushing? Come over here and I'll ask you again."

"You're just patting him, man. Give him a good one on the head!"

"Stop, will you! Stop!"

Throughout this time only the ones in front, or those watching from elevated places around, had a full view of what was happening in the square. The two strangled men had fallen down unconscious, first one and then the other. They were sprawling on the ground. Now the gypsies ran up, tried to prop them up, splashed water on them, punched them with their fists, and scratched them. As soon as the men came to and raised themselves up on their feet, the torture was resumed. The noose was tightened again and the rope pulled taut, and again the two men jerked and gurgled once more, only this time with less strength and for a shorter time. And once more the spectators out in front turned away and tried to leave, but the dense throng wouldn't let them through and pushed them back, cursing and flailing and forcing them to face the sight they wanted to escape.

A slight little Moslem student with a faun's face was taken with a fit but could not fall to the ground. Wedged and borne along by the swaying mass of bodies, he remained in an upright position, although unconscious, his head thrown back and dangling, his face the color of chalk, his lips frothing.

The torture was repeated three times and each time the two men quietly got up and offered their necks to the rope for a fresh strangling, obediently, like two people who were anxious to do everything in their power to have the matter proceed smoothly; both were calm and collected, calmer than the gypsies or any of the spectators—just bemused and worried-looking, with so pronounced an air of worry about them that even the agony of strangulation did not altogether drain their faces of that expression of dark and distant woe.

After they failed to bring them around the fourth time, the gypsies went up to the fallen men, who lay on their backs, and kicked in their ribs methodically and so finished them off.

Then they gathered their rope and coiled it fist over elbow, waiting for the crowd to thin out so that they could get on with their work. Glancing around uncertainly, between movements, they puffed greedily and nervously at the cigars that someone had given them. They seemed to be equally resentful of the witless throng milling around them and of the two lifeless bodies that lay there, still and lost, in the thick and shifting forest of feet of the curious mob.

A little later the corpses of the two victims were slung on a special gibbet, on a wall below the cemetery, so that they could be clearly seen from all sides. Their bodies had straightened out once more and they looked again as they used to, long and thin, like a pair of brothers. They seemed as light as if they were made of paper. Their heads had become smaller, as the rope bit sharply under their chins, squeezing away the flesh of the jaws. The faces were still bloodless, but not blue or distorted like those of men who are hanged alive; their legs hung together and the feet were turned up as if they had been running.

That was how Desfosses saw them when he came back about noon. One of them had the sleeve of his dirty shirt torn off at the shoulder and the piece of cloth flapped raggedly in the weak breeze.

With his jaw set, firmly decided to see even this with his own eyes, shaken and yet solemn and deliberate, the young man looked at the two dangling bodies.

The grave and solemn mood stayed with him for a long time after; it was still on him when he returned to the Consulate. Daville now appeared to him a confused little man, panicking over trifles; D'Avenat seemed crude and ignorant. All of Daville's timorousness now struck him as childish and irrelevant, and all his remarks as either anemic and bookish or else niggling and much too officious. He realized that he could not possibly talk to either of them about this, after witnessing what he had with his own eyes, after his deep and inexpressible emotional experience. And after supper, still in the same mood, he made an entry in his diary on Bosnia in which, faithfully and matter-of-factly, he described "the way death sentences are carried out among the rayah and the rebels."

People began to grow accustomed to bloody and hideous sights. They were quick to forget the last one and eagerly cast about for something new and different. They picked a new place of execution on a hard patch of level ground between the *han* and the Austrian Consulate-General. Here the Vizier's executioner Ekrem set up a chopping block; the heads were afterwards stuck on poles and raised in the air.

Tears and consternation filled the house of von Mitterer.

Anna Maria rushed to her husband, crying, "Joseph, for God's sake!" Her voice rose and fell with her tears; she called him Robespierre and began to pack her things and get ready to flee. Afterwards, exhausted, her emotions spent, she fell into her husband's arms, sobbing like a desolate queen who has been sentenced to the guillotine and is awaiting the executioner's knock on the door. Little Agatha, frightened and unhappy, sat on her low stool on the veranda and wept silent, inconsolable tears, which von Mitterer found harder to bear than all the scenes his wife made.

The hunchback interpreter Rotta, pale from excitement, scurried back and forth between the Residency and the police, threatening, bribing, demanding, and imploring that they stop the beheadings in front of the consular house.

That same evening ten more Serbian peasants from the border country were brought to the square and executed by the light of torches and lanterns, to the whooping and catcalls, hostling and jeers of the assembled Moslems. The victims' heads were again raised up on poles. All through the night the Consulate could hear the snarling of ravenous street dogs that collected almost immediately. They could be seen in moonlight as they jumped at the poles and tore lumps of flesh from the severed heads. It was only next day, following the Consul's visit to the town Mayor, that the poles were taken down and there was no more killing on that spot.

Daville did not leave the house and heard only the muted and distant roar of the mob from time to time; but D'Avenat kept him accurately informed about the course of the riot and the series of executions in town. When he learned of what was happening in front of the Austrian Consulate, he at once forgot all his fears and reserve; and, not consulting with anyone or stopping to ask himself whether it was in keeping with international custom or in the interests of the service, he sat down and wrote a friendly letter to von Mitterer.

It was one of those moments in the life of Daville when he knew, clearly and exactly, without any of his usual hesitation, what he had to do and was bold enough to do it.

The note, naturally, contained allusions to Bellona, Goddess of War, and to the "rattle of arms" that was still in progress between their two countries, and to the devoted service that each of them owed to his Sovereign.

"And yet," wrote Daville, "I do not believe I shall offend

your sensibilities or be remiss in my duties if, by way of exception in these exceptional circumstances, I send you these few lines. With bitterness and loathing, and equally victimized by these barbaric excesses day after day, my wife and I, well aware of what is taking place at your very doorstep, beg you to believe that we are thinking of you and your family at this difficult time. As Christians and Europeans, despite all that separates us at the moment, we would not wish you to remain without some word of our sympathy and consolation at a time like this."

No sooner had he dispatched the letter in a roundabout way to the Consulate on the other bank of the Lashva, than he began to experience doubts as to whether he had done well or not.

On that same day of summer, when von Mitterer received Daville's letter—it was July 5, 1809—the Battle of Wagram was just beginning.

During the most beautiful days of July, Travnik was in the grip of complete anarchy. A contagious, rampaging madness drove people out of doors and spurred them to commit unbelievable and monstrous acts they had never dreamed of committing. Incidents developed without rhyme or reason, following the logic of blood and warped instincts. Situations arose by the merest of accidents, from a single shout or from the banter of young men; they swelled in a way no one could foresee and ended as unexpectedly, or else they simply broke off in the middle for no visible reason. A group of boys would be going in one direction, with a single purpose in mind, and on the way, having come across some other, more exciting sight, they would drop everything and give it their most passionate attention, as if they had been rehearsing for it for many weeks. The passion of these people was a mystery. Each one felt a burning desire to do his bit for the defense of his faith and of good order and longed, with utter conviction and in holy indignation, to participate not only with his eyes but also with his hands in the torture and slaughter of traitors and bad characters who were responsible for all the ills of the land and for every personal misfortune and woe. People went to the beheadings as if going to a shrine where health was restored miraculously and every grief eased for certain. Everyone wanted to produce a rebel or a spy and to assist personally in his punishment and in the choice of a suitable spot and method of execution. They bickered and fought over it, throwing all their ardor and resentment into these arguments. Around some condemned and roped wretch one often saw a dozen poor Moslems waving their hands excitedly, quarreling and wrangling as if a goat were about to be sold. Boys hardly out of their swaddlings called out to one another and dashed around out of breath, clutching their slipping pants and trying to dip their toy knives in the blood of the victims, so that later, in their own quarter of the town, they could brandish them and scare the smaller fry younger than themselves.

The days were sunny and the skies cloudless, the town blessed with greenery, water, early fruits and blossoms. At night the moon shone with a glassy, cool, and limpid light. But night and day the bloody carnival went on, in which they all sought one and the same thing and yet no man could understand another or even recognize himself.

The unrest was general and caught up everyone like an epidemic. Hatreds long stifled broke out anew and old vendettas came to life again. Innocent people were caught up in them and there were fatal misunderstandings and cases of mistaken identity.

The foreigners in both consulates never left the house. The kavasses brought them news of everything that went on. The only exception was Cologna, who couldn't bear the loneliness of his damp house. The old doctor could neither sleep nor work. He came to the Consulate as usual, although he had to make his way through raging mobs and past the places of execution that sprang up now here, now there. They all noticed that he was in a state of constant agitation, that his eyes burned with a fevered brilliance, that he was apt to tremble and stammer. The mindless tide that was eddying through the valley drew the old man as a whirlpool draws a stalk of straw.

One day about noon, as he was returning from the Consulate, Cologna came across a large group of Moslem rabble in the middle of the bazaar, leading a fettered and bruised man. He had ample time to turn into one of the side alleys, but the crowd exerted a morbid and irresistible fascination for him. As soon as he came a few steps closer, a hoarse voice called out from the center of the mob: "Doctor, doctor, don't let me die, for God's sake!"

As if spellbound, Cologna walked up close and focused his nearsighted eyes on the man—a Catholic from Foynitsa, by the name of Kulier. The man shouted disconnectedly, not knowing

what to say first, begging them to let him go as he was innocent. Glancing around the crowd to find someone he might talk
to, Cologna met several bloodshot stares. Before he could open
his mouth or do anything, a tall man with a hollow colorless
face detached himself from the group and thrust himself in
front of the doctor. "On your way! Go on," he said. His voice
shook with a smoldering rage, which broke through his feeble
pretense of restraint.

Had it not been for this man and his voice, the old doctor
might have gone on and abandoned the man from Foynitsa, for
whom there was no help, to his fate. But the voice drew him
on like a deep dark body of water. He wanted to say that he
knew this man Kulier as a loyal citizen, to ask what he had
done and where they were taking him, but the tall Moslem
would not let him speak.

"For the second time, on your way," the Moslem said in a
raised voice.

"No, you can't do that. Where are you taking him?" the doctor said.

"If you want to know, I'm going to hang the dog, like the
other dogs."

"How's that? Why? You can't go around hanging innocent
people. I'm going to call the Mayor."

Cologna was beginning to shout too, not realizing what he
was letting himself in for.

Now there was a muttering in the crowd. From a couple of
minarets, one quite near and the other some way off, the muez-
zins were calling out the hour of prayer and their voices broke
over the crowd in a strained, double-pitched howl that rose and
fell on the air. The onlookers began to join the swelling crowd.

"Now that you've come along to defend him," the tall man
cried, "I think I'll string him up on this here mulberry tree."

"You'd better not. You can't! I'm going to call the guards. I'll
go to the Mayor. Who are you?" The old man cried shrilly
drawing breath between sentences.

"I'm someone who's not afraid of you. Get out of my sight
while your skin is still in one piece."

The mob began to surge and shout. More people from the
bazaar gathered around them. During the squabble the tall man
paused after each sentence and looked at them sideways, to see
if they were with him. They looked back at him, without moving, but with obvious approval.

The tall Moslem went up to the old mulberry tree by the roadside, followed by Cologna and the mob. They were all shouting and waving their arms. Cologna himself never stopped shouting, but no one would listen to him or let him finish.

"It's an effrontery! Banditry! Crime! You're spitting on the Sultan's good name. You bastard Turks!" screamed the doctor.

"Shut up or you'll hang right alongside him!"

"Who? I? You dare to touch me, you dirty barbarians!" All of Cologna's joints seemed to loosen up and he swung out wildly and kicked around him. He and the tall man were now the focus of all jostling. The man from Foynitsa was pushed aside, forgotten.

The tall Moslem jerked himself up and, his upper body askew, called to his people in a taunting voice: "You heard him, didn't you? Fouling the Faith and the men of God!"

The milling and shoving around Cologna grew more intense.

"Who? The Faith? What man of God?" cried Cologna. "I know more about Islam than you do, you illegitimate Bosnian! I am . . . I am . . ." Cologna went on shrilling as he twisted around, sputtering and beside himself.

"Up with him! Hang the infidel dog!"

In the frantic crush and pulling Cologna's words came through indistinctly, like a gagging sound. ". . . Moslem . . . I'm a Moslem, better than you! . . ."

At that point some of the men from the bazaar stepped in and rescued the doctor from the mob. Three of them were now prepared to stand witness that the old man had twice loudly and clearly averred his willingness to embrace the pure Faith, and as such had become inviolate. They now escorted him home, with as much attention and as solemnly as if he were a young bride. And it was high time too, for the old gentleman had lost all self-control and was trembling all over, gibbering and stammering disconnectedly.

The startled and disappointed men who had brought in Kulier and had been his accusers, judges, and executioners, now let him go and sent him staggering on his way home to Foynitsa.

The rumor went around quickly that the physician of the Austrian Consulate had become a Moslem. Even in this town, which had gone stark crazy, where each new day dawned madder than the one before and where scenes were enacted quite beyond description or belief, the news of the doctor's conver-

sion hit the people like a bolt from the blue. As none of the
Christians dared to go out in the streets, it was impossible to
question it or verify it. The Austrian Consul sent a servant to
Fra Ivo Yankovich in Dolats, but the canon received the news
with scepticism and promised to come to see the Consul as
soon as the riot abated a little, perhaps even the next day. In
the late evening, at the Consul's request, Rotta went out to
Cologna's house along the steep cobblestone road. Half an
hour later he was back, silent and ashen as never before. He
had been scared to death by unknown men who looked wild
and bristled with arms and shouted to his face: "Get yourself
converted, infidel, while there's still time!" They carried on like
drunks who had gone out of their minds. But what he had seen
at Cologna's had shaken him much more.

Having barely managed to get himself admitted into the
house, from which some perfectly calm and unarmed Turks
had just issued, he had run into the doctor's manservant, the
Albanian, in a state of excitement. The hall was in disorder
and the doctor's voice could be heard inside the room.

The old man was pacing up and down in acute agitation; his
face, usually bloodless and dun-colored, was lightly suffused
and his jaw trembled. Out of slit eyes, as though he were looking into the distance and could see only dimly and distinguish
with difficulty, he gave the interpreter a long, hard stare that
was anything but friendly. And as soon as Rotta mentioned that
he was coming from the Consulate-General to find out what
had happened, Cologna interrupted him excitedly.

"Nothing happened, nothing at all. And nothing's going to
happen either. I don't want anyone to worry about me. I'll look
after myself. Here I stand and defend myself like a good soldier." The old man paused, abruptly tossed back his head and
pushed out his chest, then said with a catch in his breath:
"Yes, here I stand. Here, here!"

"Yes, of course, stand . . . stand, Herr Doktor," mumbled
the timid and superstitious Rotta, suddenly bereft of his composure and self-assurance. As he spoke he took a step back and,
keeping his eyes on the doctor, groped behind him with a shaking hand for the doorknob, repeating all the while: "Yes, do
stand, please."

Relaxing his stiff and chesty posture, the old man presently
leaned toward the cowed Rotta, with a much gentler, almost

confidential expression. His wizened old face, or rather his
eyes, lighted up with a knowing, triumphant smile. As though
communicating an important secret, he said quietly, over a
wagging finger: "Aleikhiselam says: 'Like blood doth Satan
spread through the human body!' But Aleikhiselam also says:
'Verily shall ye see your Master as ye see the moon at the full
cycle.'"

At that he wheeled around, suddenly assuming a grave and
pained air; while the interpreter, whom it would have taken
much less to frighten to death, used the moment to open the
door noiselessly and slink like a shadow into the hall, without
greetings or leave-taking.

Outside the moon was already up. Rotta hurried through the
side alleys, dodging the shadows and feeling as if the ghouls
were at his back. And when he got home and went in to the
Consul he still could not pull himself together or give any co-
herent account of what had happened to Cologna and what the
story was about his conversion. He could only repeat obstinately that the doctor had gone off his head; and when the Consul wanted to know rather more in detail how the madness outwardly manifested itself, he kept saying: "Mad, mad. Anyone
who talks about God and Satan like that must be mad. You
should have seen him. You should have seen him."

By the end of the evening the news had gone around the
town that the doctor of the Austrian Consulate had declared
his intention to embrace Islam and that he would be initiated
on the following day in all due solemnity. However, it was
fated that the ceremony should never take place and that the
actual truth of the old doctor's "conversion" should never see the
light of day.

A day later, another rumor raced through the town, with
even more lightning speed than the first, that Cologna had
been found dead that morning on a garden path near a stream,
in that ravine at the foot of the cliff on which his house stood.
The top of the old man's head was bashed in. The Albanian
manservant could not explain when and how the doctor had
left the house in the night and how he had fallen over the
precipice.

Informed of the doctor's death, the parish priest at Dolats
came down to Travnik to see for himself and to arrange the
funeral. Risking an attack by the wandering mobs, Fra Ivo

reached the doctor's house but did not tarry too long. Despite his great size and weight, he scrambled nimbly and quickly down the steep road before the sticks and pickaxes of the roused Moslems who would not let him as much as peep into the house. The hodja had already taken charge of the corpse, since the three citizens had confirmed that the doctor, of his own free will, had three times publicly declared his willingness to be received into the Moslem faith and that even now he was a truer True-Believer than many a so-called Moslem in the bazaar of Travnik.

And Rotta, hearing of the doctor's death, rode up to the house with his kavass Ahmed, but finding only a few busy-looking Turks in front of the doctor's home, he came straight back to the Consulate. The kavass remained for the burial.

Had the times been different, or at least a little quieter, had the key people at the Residency been in town, the spiritual and temporal authorities would have intervened, the Austrian Consulate would have acted with more decision, Fra Ivo would have cajoled the officials and the more influential Turks, and the affair with the hapless Cologna would have been settled in a clearer fashion. But in the present state of anarchy and mob rule no one was inclined to listen to anyone or understand anything. The hysteria, which just then had begun to show signs of slackening, found something new to feed on; it seized on the corpse of the old man as a welcome trophy and would not let it go without bloodshed and more broken heads.

The doctor was buried before noon on a green slope of the Moslem hillside cemetery. Although the bazaar was still closed, a great many Moslems left their houses to participate in the funeral of the physician who had turned Moslem in such a strange and unexpected way. Especially numerous were the armed riffraff, who had wanted to hang him only the day before; grave and solemn-faced, they avidly took turns at carrying the litter, so that the shrouded body of the doctor on the bier slid continuously over a great number of eager masculine shoulders in quick succession.

Thus the great riot came to an end with an exciting and unforeseen climax. The arrests and killings of Serbs ceased. Once more the town relapsed into that seedy, shamefaced mood when men are anxious to forget as quickly as possible all that has happened; when the swirling throngs of the worst and noisiest shouters and bullies ebbs away to the distant periphery, like flood water receding to its original bed; when the old order returns and, for a time at any rate, strikes everyone as better and more bearable. Once again, silence closed over Travnik, oppressive and uniform, as though it had never been ruffled.

Return to normalcy was hastened by the return of Suleiman Pasha Skoplyak. The presence of his authoritative voice and his skilled hands made itself felt right away.

Immediately after his arrival, he summoned the leading citizens and demanded to know what had become of the peaceful town and its law-abiding inhabitants. He stood before them, tall, weatherbeaten, wearing the same austere dress he had worn during the campaign, his lean, muscled chest thrown out like a greyhound's, his hard blue eyes unflinching, and questioned and scolded them like children. Having spent six weeks on a real battlefield and a fortnight on his estate at Kupres, he now gazed sternly at these pale tired men who had suddenly sobered up, and asked them bluntly since when the bazaar had taken it upon itself to be the judge and executioner, who had given them such authority, and where their wits had been in the last ten days.

"I am told the rayah got up on their hind legs, they were unruly and full of mischief. That may be so. But one should remember that the rayah have no spirit of their own, they breathe through their masters. You know that very well. It's always the masters who turn bad first, the rayah merely follows. And once the rayah get up on their hind legs and have it their own way, that'll be the end of it. There'll be no rayah left, and who's going to do your work then?"

Suleiman Pasha spoke in the tone of a man who until yesterday has dealt in grave and difficult matters, of which these people, with their narrow parochial minds haven't the slightest idea, but which he must try to explain to them as best he can.

"Allah, praise and honor to Him, gave us two things—land and the power to do justice. And here, you go and squat on your cushions and leave justice in the hands of the rabble and a few bastard Moslems—how long do you suppose the villagers will put up with it? The peasant's business is to work, the aga's to keep an eye on him, because grass needs the dew and the sickle, both. You can't have one without the other. Look at me"—he turned to the man nearest him, not without pride—

"I am fifty-five years old, but before I sit down to supper tonight I will have visited all my fields around Bugoyno. Believe me, there are no worthless and disobedient tenants on my estate."

And indeed his long neck and sinewy arms were deeply burned by the sun and as rough as those of a day worker.

None of the assembled men knew how to reply to that. Each one longed to be out of his sight as soon as possible, to forget all that had taken place and to be forgotten himself.

As soon as the riot subsided, von Mitterer set about investigating the mystery of Cologna's conversion and his strange death. In doing so he was not prompted by any concern for Cologna himself, whom for some time now he had regarded as unpredictable and an embarrassment to the service. Having known him well, von Mitterer thought him quite capable of declaring himself for Islam in a moment of heated argument; and it was just as plausible and possible that he might have committed suicide or lost consciousness and fallen into the ravine in a moment of great emotional stress. Moreover, now that the riots had abated and things were beginning to look different and people were revising their opinions and attitudes, it was not an easy task to try to get to the bottom of something that had taken place in altogether different circumstances, in a climate of widespread madness, blood-letting, and turmoil.

Von Mitterer was nevertheless compelled to take these steps for the prestige of the Empire and in order to prevent further attacks on imperial subjects or members of the consular staff. And Fra Ivo urged him to do it for the sake of the Catholic community, which wanted to know the truth of Cologna's alleged turncoat behavior and his funeral.

Suleiman Pasha, who from the very first had been the only one in the Residency sympathetically inclined toward von Mitterer and had always been more open and cordial with him than with Daville (with whom he had to converse through an interpreter, and whose face he did not like), tried to oblige him. But at the same time he advised him in all sincerity not to make matters more acute by pursuing them too far.

"I know that it is your duty to intervene for one of your own imperial subjects," he said to the Consul in his cool, reasonable, and deliberate manner, which everyone, himself not excluded, was apt to consider infallible. "I realize that you cannot do otherwise. Only, is it a good thing to tie the reputation of the

Empire to every imperial subject that comes along? There are many kinds of men, but there's only one reputation of the Empire."

And Suleiman Pasha went on discussing, in a dry and impersonal voice the prospects of settling the matter in a way that would be satisfactory to all.

As for the question whether Cologna had in fact been converted or not, the best course would be to leave the matter alone altogether, since the whole thing had been so chaotic that one could not tell the day from the night, let alone one religion from another or a real Moslem from a convert. To put it quite bluntly, the person under discussion had been the sort of man whose conversion could not be regarded either as a grave loss to the Christian faith or a special gain for Islam.

On the subject of his obscure death, so soon after his obscure conversion, this would bear even less scrutiny. Dead men tell no tales, but a man who has taken leave of his senses and does not watch where he is going is, of course, likely to slip and stumble. Indeed, this would seem to be a realistic interpretation and would not offend anyone. And what useful purpose would now be served by exploring other possibilities on which no sufficient light can ever be thrown and for which the Consulate would never obtain the kind of satisfaction it had in mind?

"And how can I now find and round up all those tramps and morons who wanted to play the Turk and dispense justice around Travnik?" said Suleiman Pasha. "No more than you can resurrect and interrogate the late doctor now lying in the Turkish cemetery. Who can make amends now? Is it not better to leave things as they are and give our attention to more sensible business? I know well how you feel, it's the way I would have felt myself. I shall order an inquiry into the death of the physician, which will show that no one is to blame really. We shall have a detailed report drawn up, with all the witnesses and the evidence. And you will forward it to your superiors, so that there will be no further argument either on your side or ours."

Von Mitterer had to agree that this solution, if not the best, was the only possible one in the circumstances. All the same, he requested and received from the office of the Vizier copies of the relevant instructions and depositions which, as far as distant Vienna was concerned, might give the impression that

the Consulate had acted and received due satisfaction and in-
demnity. Together with Rotta's memorandum on his last meeting with Cologna, the material stood a fair chance of placating
Vienna, representing the case as an unfortunate accident of an
unbalanced man, and saving the Consul's face. Privately, however, von Mitterer was none too pleased with the course of the
affair or with himself.

Pale and lonely, in his twilit study, von Mitterer thought
about it all and felt himself disarmed and helpless in the face
of a whole maze of conflicting circumstances, in the midst of
which he was doing his conscientious and devoted best to per-
form his duty and was straining beyond his strength, while
realizing clearly that all was hopeless and in vain. The Colonel shivered, even though outside the evening was heavy with
the heat of July, and felt at times as though he too were swooning and teetering on the edge of an unknown ravine.

17

This second and more hideous riot was not connected in any
way with the French Consulate. On the contrary, it had centered, in its later stages, around the Austrian Consulate and
its physician Cologna. Nevertheless, the inmates of the French
Consulate had spent some anxious days and sleepless nights.
Save for a couple of brief outings by Desfosses, no one had
dared even to appear at the window during that time. As for
Daville, the second riot oppressed him worse than the first, for
this was excitement of a kind that no man can ever take in
his stride, one that, on the contrary, he finds harder and harder
to bear the more often it is repeated.

As during the first riot, Daville had thought of fleeing Travnik and saving himself and his family. Shut up in his room, he
was torn by agonizing thoughts and imagined the darkest possibilities; but in front of the servants and the chancellery staff,
even in front of his wife, he took great pains to keep his
thoughts and his real mood strictly to himself.

Yet even this common tribulation failed to bring the Consul
and his senior assistant closer together. He would talk to Des-

fosses several times a day (being confined to the house, they met oftener than before), but the conversation brought him neither relief nor peace of mind. In addition to all his other worries, doubts, and disappointments, Daville had to remind himself every so often that he was living with a stranger and was separated from him by an unbridgeable abyss of ideas and habits. Not even the young man's undeniable finer traits— his courage, his unselfishness and presence of mind, which came to the fore conspicuously in difficult moments like these —could mollify Daville. For it is in the nature of things that we take and judge the good qualities of a man only when they are offered to us in a form molded to our own ideas and inclinations.

As he had always done, Daville looked with scorn and distaste at what was happening around them, interpreting everything in terms of native malice and the barbarous ways of life of these people, and was concerned only with maintaining and protecting the French interests. Desfosses, on the other hand, with a detachment that appalled Daville, analyzed all phenomena around him and tried to discover their causes and to clarify them by induction and also in relation to the circumstances that had spawned them, regardless of the advantage or disadvantage, friendship or hostility, that he or his Consulate might momentarily gain from them. This cold and disinterested objectivity of the young man's had always puzzled Daville and annoyed him, all the more so as he couldn't help seeing in it a clear sign of the young man's superiority. In the present circumstances, he found it even more unpleasant and oppressive.

Every talk they had, whether official, semiofficial, or private, elicited from Desfosses a wealth of analogies, free-ranging associations, and coldly objective conclusions, while on the Consul's side it produced only irritation and offended silence which the young man did not even seem to notice.

This son of a well-to-do family, in many ways so gifted, behaved intellectually like a millionaire—he was whimsical, bold, and prodigal. In the workaday routine of the Consulate he was of no great use to Daville. Although it was the young man's job to make clean transcripts of the Consul's reports, Daville avoided giving him this work. While still drafting it, he already squirmed at the thought that the youth, whose mind seemed to have a hundred eyes, would judge the report coldly and critically as he copied it. Even as he resented his self-consciousness, Daville could not help wondering after every other sentence how they would appear in his Chancellor's eyes. So in the end he preferred to write and make fair copies of his more important reports himself.

In short, in all this work, and more crucial still, in all his inward uncertainties over the larger events set in motion by Napoleon's new expedition against Vienna, Desfosses was no help to him at all and was often a burden and a hindrance. The difference between them was so great and of such a nature that they were unable even to share their common good fortune. When toward the middle of July, about the time the riots were quelled, the news reached Travnik of Napoleon's victory at Wagram and, shortly afterwards, of the truce with Austria, Daville perked up with one of his periodic moods of good humor. He felt that everything had gone off pretty well and was satisfactorily concluded. The only thing that spoiled his sense of well-being was the indifference of young Desfosses, who showed no exhilaration at the success, just as he had shown none of the doubts and fears that preceded it.

It hurt and puzzled Daville to see the young man always with the same knowing noncommittal smile on his face. "As if he had a life subscription to victories," was the way Daville described it to his wife, having no one else to complain to and unable to keep quiet any longer.

Once more the Travnik summer drew to an end in a blaze of warm, rich days—days that were considered the finest and best by those who lacked nothing, and least burdensome by those who had to struggle alike in winter and summer.

In the month of October 1809, peace was concluded at Vienna between Napoleon and the Austrians, creating the new Illyrian provinces that included Dalmatia and Lika, regions that were in Daville's sphere of activity. A Governor-General and an Intendant-General arrived in Ljubljana, the capital of the new Illyria, with a whole staff of police, customs and revenue officials, who were to organize the administration and, more particularly, establish trade and communications with the Levant. Earlier, General Marmont, the commander in chief of Dalmatia, who had gone to Wagram in time to join the battle, had been appointed Marshal. And now Daville, contemplating all these developments around him, experienced the melancholy but not unpleasant feeling of one who has contributed to the victory and glory of others and has himself been left in the shadow, without glory or rewards. He rather liked the sensation, and it helped him to bear his troubles at Travnik, which no victory could do much to change.

A nagging question still remained, one that tormented him now as it always had, one he had never dared to admit or confide to anyone: Is this at last the final victory and how long will the peace last? To this query, on which depended not only his own peace of mind but the future of his children, he could find no answer either in himself or around him.

At a particularly solemn audience Daville acquainted the Vizier in some detail with Napoleon's victories and the provisions of the Peace of Vienna, with special reference to the territories in the close neighborhood of Bosnia. The Vizier offered him congratulations on the victories and spoke with satisfaction of the fact that their good neighborly relations would continue and that henceforward, under French rule, there would be quiet and order in the lands around Bosnia.

But the words "war," "peace," and "victory" had a dead and remote sound on the Vizier's lips. He delivered them in a cold hard tone of voice, with a stony expression on his face, as if he were talking of things in the distant past.

The Vizier's Secretary, Tahir Beg, with whom Daville spoke the same day, was much livelier and more talkative. He asked questions about the situation in Spain and wanted to know the details of the administrative structure in the new Illyrian provinces; it was apparent that he wished to inform himself and compare notes professionally. Yet all his amiable garrulity and shrewd questioning revealed no more than had the Vizier's mute, leaden indifference. One gathered from the general temper of his talk that he could as yet see no end to warfare and to Napoleon's conquests. And when Daville pressed him for a clearer statement, the Secretary sidestepped a direct reply and parried, with a shrewd smile: "Your Emperor has won. Everyone sees the victor in a blaze of light, or, as the Persian poet says, 'The victor's face is like a rose.' "

As usual, Daville was left vaguely discomforted by the peculiar smile that never faded from the Secretary's face, and that gave a diabolical slant to his eyes and made him almost squinty. And after every conversation with him Daville felt bewildered and somehow cheated; instead of indicating some

solution or answer, the talk would raise new questions and
fill him with alarming uncertainties. And at that the Secretary
was the only person in the Residency willing and able to talk
business.

As soon as the peace treaty was signed, contact between the
two consulates was re-established. The consuls called on each
other and wordily expressed their precarious joy at the peace
just concluded; the effusiveness served to hide their embarrassment over all the petty tricks they had played on each other
over the last few months. Daville tried hard not to offend von
Mitterer by putting on an air of "victor," while at the same
time enjoying the advantages that victory had given him. The
Colonel spoke cautiously and made his points like a man who
was unwilling to dwell on the uncomfortable present and who
expected a good deal more of the future. Both hid their true
opinions and real fears under a veil of desultory small talk—
a frequent recourse of older people who still hope for something from life, yet are well aware of their helplessness.

Frau von Mitterer had not yet exchanged visits with Mme
Daville and had been lucky so far in avoiding Desfosses, who,
of course, had been "dead" for her since the spring, laid to
rest in the large necropolis of her previous disenchantments.
Throughout the time of Napoleon's campaign against Vienna
she had remained stubbornly and aggressively "on the side of
the great and incomparable Corsican, with all my heart," and
had thus poisoned her husband's days and nights, for he could
not, even in the privacy of his bedroom, bear to listen to such
indiscreet bravado without a stab of pain at every thoughtless
word.

That summer Anna Maria had a sudden recurrence of an
old passion: her love of animals. Her morbidly exaggerated
pity for beasts of burden, dogs, cats, and cattle kept breaking
out at every step. The sight of bony laboring small oxen,
wearily putting one spindly leg in front of another while a
black cloud of flies whined and settled on the tender flesh
around their eyes, could throw Anna Maria into a nervous
crisis. Carried away by her passionate nature, she championed
these animals no matter what the place of the circumstances,
without any moderation or compunction, and so, of course,
courted new disappointments. She collected lame dogs and
mangy cats, and nursed them and looked after them. She fed

the birds, even though they were gorged with the bounty of summer. She chided the peasant women for carrying chickens slung over their shoulders, strung by the feet and hanging head downward. She halted overladen carts and overburdened horses in the streets of the town, demanding of the peasants that they reduce the load, salve the sores of the animals, repair the worn harness that was causing them, or loosen the girth that was cutting into their flesh. But in this country such demands were unprecedented and led to difficulties, for no one could understand them; they were bound to end in ridiculous scenes and embarrassing incidents.

One day, in a steep alley, Anna Maria came across a big cart piled high with sacks of grain. A team of oxen labored in vain to pull the enormous load up the hill. The men then brought an underfed horse, harnessed it at the head of the oxen, and began to drive them up the slope with loud shouts. The farmer walked beside the oxen and took turns whipping their bony flanks and beating them across their soft muzzles, while the horse was switched mercilessly by a hefty Moslem from the neighborhood, stripped to the waist and deeply tanned, a certain Ibrahim Zhvalo, one of the lowest men in town, a drunken cart driver who occasionally doubled as a hangman and so deprived the gypsies of their income.

The oxen and the horse in front could not be goaded to pull together, and the farmer ran back every other moment to brace the wheels with a stone. The animals panted and quivered. The cart driver swore hoarsely and volunteered the opinion that the left ox was malingering and did not pull at all. They started once more, but the ox on the left stumbled and fell to his knees; the one on the right and the horse pulled on. Anna Maria screamed, ran up and tearfully began to importune the cart driver and the peasant. The latter pushed the stone under the wheel and stared in astonishment at the foreign lady. But the Moslem Zhvalo, bathed in sweat and furious at the ox which was only pretending to pull, turned in a rage toward Anna Maria, wiped the sweat off his forehead with the hooked finger of his right hand and shook it to the ground, cursed poverty and those who allowed it to exist, then, gripping the whip in his left hand, walked straight up to Anna Maria. "Get out of my sight, woman, and don't you start making trouble, or, by God, I'll—" Saying this, he sliced the air with his switch. Anna Maria saw his face close above hers, twisted in a snarling grimace, full of pockmarks, scars, sweat, and dust, a vicious and angry but above all a tired face, almost in tears from exhaustion, like that of a runner who has just won a race. At that moment her groom ran up in alarm, pushed the frantic driver aside and took Anna Maria home, weeping aloud in helpless fury.

For two days Anna Maria shivered whenever she thought of that scene and tearfully demanded of her husband that he punish those men for their cruelty and for insulting the wife of a consul. At night she would suddenly start from her sleep, jump out of bed screaming, and try to ward off the vision of Zhvalo's face.

The Colonel did his best to calm his wife with soothing words, although he knew there was nothing to be done. The sacks of oats the men had carted were for the Vizier's stable. Zhvalo was a person without any standing and a complaint against him would accomplish nothing; bringing action against him could only debase one. And, in the last analysis, it was all the fault of his wife, who, as she had so often done on other occasions, had meddled in things that were not her business, in an ill-advised manner, and who even now, as usual, was deaf to all reason and explanation. So he comforted her as best he could, promising her everything, as he would a child, and stoically put up with the reproaches and abuse which she hurled at him, in the hope that she would forget her obsession.

Meanwhile there was news at the French Consulate. Madame Daville was in the fourth month of her pregnancy. Outwardly unchanged, small and frail as ever, she moved quietly and nimbly around the big house and the garden of the Consulate, preparing, stocking up, anticipating, and giving orders. This fourth child was giving her more trouble than the previous ones. Yet all these chores, and even the physical discomforts of pregnancy, helped to soften the pain of losing her little boy so suddenly the previous autumn. Although she never spoke a word about it, he was constantly in her thoughts.

Young Desfosses was spending his last days at Travnik. He was only waiting for the first courier to arrive from Istanbul or Split on his way to Paris, in order to set out with him. He had been recalled to the Ministry and had already been notified that he would be sent to the Embassy at Istanbul before the end of the year. The outline of his book on Bosnia was complete. He was glad that he had got to know this country and was happy to be able to leave it. He had fought against its silence and endured many hardships and now, serene and undefeated, he was departing.

Before his departure, on the Feast of the Assumption, he visited the monastery at Gucha Gora with Mme Daville. Monsieur Daville did not accompany them, as the relations between the Consulate and the Brothers had become very strained. Indeed, they were more than strained: the struggle between the French Imperial Government and the Vatican was at its peak just then. The Pope had been banished, Napolean excommunicated. For months now, the Brothers had not come near the Consulate. And yet, thanks largely to Mme Daville, the friars at Gucha Gora received them both very cordially.

Desfosses could not help admiring the Brothers' subtle flair for separating their personal duties toward the guests from the public obligations of their calling and their stern concept of duty in general. Their attitude was a fine balance of reserve and offended dignity that was in keeping with their position, and just the right amount of friendliness demanded by the laws of ancient hospitality and that simple humanity which reaches beyond the clashes of the moment and transient circumstances. Indeed, there was a little of everything in their manner, in nice proportions, and all of it blended together into a smooth, rounded whole and was conveyed with the utmost poise, with an air of ease that lent their gestures and facial expressions a thoroughly relaxed and natural look. One could hardly have expected so much composure and such an innate sense of proportion from these coarse, harassed, and quick-tempered men with their bristling whiskers and ridiculous clean-shaven round heads.

Once more he saw the piety of the Catholic peasantry and had a close look at the life of the Franciscan Order, "Bosnian version"; once more he talked and argued with *monsieur, mon adversaire*, Fra Julian.

It was a fine and warm festival day at the best time of the year, when fruit was ripe and the foliage still green. The huge whitewashed monastery church quickly filled with peasants in their clean holiday clothes, in which white was predominant. Just before High Mass began, Mme Daville went inside. Desfosses remained in the plum orchard with Fra Julian, who happened to be off duty. They walked up and down, talking.

As always when they met, conversation turned to the relations between the Church and Napoleon, then to Bosnia, to the work and role of the Brothers, and the lot of Bosnians of all persuasions. All the windows of the church were open and from time to time they could hear the tinkle of the altar boys' bells and the deep old-man baritone of Brother Superior, intoning passages of the Mass.

The two young men enjoyed arguing as healthy children enjoy a game. And their discussion, conducted in bad Italian and full of naïve, challenging statements and obstinacy for its own sake, went around and around in a circle and kept coming back to the starting point.

"I don't expect you to understand us," was the friar's answer to most of Desfosses's remarks.

"But I do think," protested Desfosses, "that in all this time I've got to know your country pretty well. Contrary to other foreigners, I have tried to understand the hidden values as well as the shortcomings and backwardness which a stranger is so quick to notice and so quick to condemn out of hand. So you must allow me to tell you that I find the attitude of your Order often hard to understand."

"And I tell you that you can't possibly understand."

"But I do understand, Fra Julian. The point is that what I see and understand I cannot approve. This country needs schools, roads, doctors, contact with the outside world, work, and enterprise. I know that you won't be able to realize and achieve these things as long as the Turks are here and the communications between Bosnia and Europe are what they are. But still, you're the only educated class here and you ought to prepare your people and prod them in that direction. Instead of which, you take the side of the reactionary European powers and their feudal policies and want to align yourselves with the part of Europe that's living in the past and must perish. And this puzzles me, because your people are not fettered in traditions and class prejudices and should, on the face of it, take their place among the free and enlightened nations of Europe."

"Enlightenment won't do us any good unless we also have faith in God," interrupted the friar. "Even in Europe this enlightenment won't last any length of time. But while it lasts, it can only bring upheaval and misfortune."

"You are wrong, my dear Fra Julian. Wrong from the bottom

up. A little more upheaval here wouldn't do you any harm.
You can see that the people of Bosnia are divided into three,
even four religions—divided and at one anothers' throats. All of
them together are cut off from Europe—that is, from the world
and life at large—by an impassable wall. Watch out, or you
may find yourself committing the historical sin of not having
grasped this, of leading your people in the wrong direction, of
not getting them ready in time for what is undoubtedly their
due and birthright. Among the Christians of the Turkish Empire one hears more and more talk of freedom and liberation.
And really, one day freedom is bound to come to these countries. But you know the old saying, it's not enough to become
free, it's much more important to deserve freedom. Getting rid
of the Turkish rule won't help you much unless you have
modern education and liberal ideas. In all these centuries your
people have become so much like their oppressors that they
will gain very little if the Turks should go away one day,
leaving them not only with their own weaknesses as a subject
people but with a legacy of Turkish faults as well—idleness,
intolerance, violence, and the cult of brute force. What kind of
liberation would that be? You would not deserve freedom and
wouldn't know how to enjoy it. You would be the same as the
Turks, who don't know anything but slavery and how to en-
slave others. There's no doubt that one day your country will
join the European family, but it might very well happen that
she will do so divided and weighted down by a legacy of
prejudice, habits, and tendencies which have become outdated
everywhere else and which, like some malevolent ghosts, will
stand in the way of her normal development and make of her
an antiquated curiosity, an easy target for any comer, just as
today she is for the Turk. I think your people deserve better.
You can see for yourself that no nation, no country in Europe,
would think of basing its future progress on religion—"

"Exactly, that's the whole tragedy," Fra Julian broke in.

"No, it's a tragedy to live as you do."

"When you live without God and betray the faith of your
ancestors, that's tragedy. Whereas we, with all our mistakes
and flaws, have remained true to it. You can say about us,
'Multum peccavit, sed fidem non negavit'—He sinned much
but did not deny his faith."

Fra Julian was pleased with his quotation. Presently the
young men's argument came back to where it had started.

Both believed firmly in what they were saying, but neither made himself very clear or listened to what the other said.

Desfosses had stopped by an old plum tree that was gnarled and covered with thick green lichen. "Did it never occur to you," he said, "that one day when the Turkish Empire falls and abandons these parts, these people under the Turkish yoke, calling themselves different names and professing different faiths, will have to find some common ground for their existence, a broader, better, more sensible and humane rule of life—"

"We Catholics have had this rule a long time—the Credo of the Roman Catholic Church. We don't need any better rule."

"But you know, not all your compatriots in Bosnia and the Balkans belong to that Church. And you never will—all of you together, that is. No one in Europe associates any more on that basis, don't you see? You ought to be looking for some other common denominator."

They were interrupted by the swelling chorus of peasant song coming from the Church. Timid and ragged at first, then waxing stronger, mixed female and male voices rang out in unison, in a droning peasant monotone: "Ha-a-il, Bo-o-dy of Je-e-su-us." The singing grew in volume. The massive, squatting church without a belfry, roofed in a dark-colored wood and slightly askew all the way from the apse to the façade, began to roar and echo like a ship casting off, her sails billowing in the wind, a crew of unseen singers on its deck.

They both stopped talking for a moment. Desfosses wanted to know the words of the hymn which the congregation was singing with so much pious enthusiasm, and the friar translated it word for word. Its general meaning reminded him of the ancient Church hymn:

"*Ave verum corpus natum*
De Maria virgine . . ."

While the friar was searching for words to render the second verse, Desfosses followed his efforts absently; he was in fact giving all his attention to the doleful, simple, grave, and crude melody that reminded him now of the united bleating of an enormous flock of sheep, now of the soughing winds in a dark forest. And at the same time he asked himself whether it was possible that this shepherd's dirge reverberating through the squat church could be expressing the same idea and the same faith as the singing of the well-fed, learned canons or the pale seminary students in the French cathedrals. "This is *Urjammer*, a howl of primeval misery," he said to himself, remembering Daville's and von Mitterer's opinion of Musa's song, and instinctively he walked deeper into the plum orchard, trying to escape the melody like someone averting his head from an unspeakably sad scene.

There, at a distance from the church, Desfosses and the friar resumed their conversation, swapping arguments in which each one stuck to his original position.

"Ever since I came to Bosnia," said Desfosses, "I've asked myself how it is that you Franciscans, who've had some schooling and have seen something of the world outside, who are at bottom good men and genuine altruists, do not have a broader, freer outlook and fail to grasp the needs of the age. How is it that you don't feel the human urge to gather your people together and seek with them a saner, more dignified kind of life?"

"With Jacobin Clubs, for instance?"

"My dear Fra Julian, Jacobin Clubs have been out of date for a long time, even in France."

"No, they've been absorbed in the ministries and schools."

"And you here don't even have schools, or anything else for that matter. And one of these days, when civilization catches up with you, you won't know any more how to take it. You will be torn apart, bewildered, a shapeless mass without a head or a goal, lacking every organic link with the rest of mankind or with your own countrymen or even with your closest fellow-citizens."

"But still believing in God, monsieur."

"Believing, yes, believing! Do you think you're the only ones who believe in God? Millions of people do, you know. Everyone in his fashion. But that doesn't give anyone the right to stand aside and shut himself off in a cocoon of unhealthy pride, turning his back on humanity, often even on his neighbor next door."

Groups of people began to come out of the church, although the peasant singing still went on like the rhythmic rolling of a bell that was growing fainter and fainter. Madame Daville also appeared and brought their endless discussion to a halt.

They had lunch in the monastery, where Fra Julian and Desfosses continued their dickering at the table. Then they took leave of each other, forever, parting the best of friends. Madame Daville and the young man started back for Travnik.

Daville took Desfosses to an audience with the Vizier, to pay his respects and take his leave. He thus saw Ibrahim Pasha once more. The Vizier was gloomier and more ponderous than ever; he talked in a deep hoarse voice and rolled his words slowly, moving his lower jaw to and fro as if grinding them. His tired, bloodshot eyes gazed at the young man with an effort, almost crossly. One could see that his mind was a world away, that he had trouble understanding this youth who was saying good-bye and moving off in God knew what direction, that he did not particularly care if he understood him and only wanted to be rid of it all as soon as possible.

But the official visit to the Austrian Consulate was brief and went off well. The Colonel received him with a sort of melancholy dignity, but kindly, and regretted that Frau von Mitterer was unable to see him on account of a severe and persistent migraine.

Taking leave of Daville was a more difficult and wearisome matter. In addition to written reports, the young man was to take with him a number of verbal messages that were complicated and ambiguously worded. As the day of his departure drew near, the messages were modified and qualified over and over again, and expanded with fresh recommendations. In the end the young man had no clear idea of what he was supposed to say about life in Travnik or the work of the Consulate, as Daville filled his head with endless complaints, requests, observations, and remarks, some of which were intended for the Minister in person, some for both the Minister and his Department, some only for Desfosses, and some for the world in general. The labyrinthine subtlety and pedantic hedging of these innumerable messages numbed the young man and caused him to yawn and think of other things.

On the last day of October the Chancellor left Travnik in a freezing, unseasonable blizzard, like the one in which he had arrived. Travnik was not a town that gradually floated out of sight on the horizon; it sank abruptly into its hold and vanished. It dropped like that out of the young man's consciousness too. The last he saw of it was the fortress, squat and vaulted like a helmet, and a mosque and a minaret next to it, straight and slender like a plume. On top of the sheer cliff to

the right of the citadel, he could barely make out the large
abandoned house in which he had once called on Cologna.

As he passed along the good level road toward the Tombs,
young Desfosses thought about the old doctor, about his fate,
and about the strange conversation they had had that night
long ago: "You're living here now, but you know that sooner or
later you'll go back to your own country, to a better and finer
life. You'll wake up and throw off this nightmare, but we never
will, for it is the only life we know."

As on that night when he had sat next to him in the smoke-
filled room, he felt again that breath which hovered around the
doctor—like some great and mysterious excitement—and heard
his warm and intimate whisper: "In the end, when all is truly
said and done, everything is still for the best and all things
find their good and just solution."

That was how Desfosses left Travnik, remembering, of all
things, only the luckless "Illyrian doctor" and thinking of him
during a few brief moments. But only a few moments—for
youth spends little time on memories and does not linger long
on the same thoughts.

18

From the very first, life in the French Consulate had been
centered in the family. It was a true family life, the kind that
depended so much on the wife, a life in which the living
reality of family sentiment overcame all changes and shocks, a
life of births, dying, troubles, joys, and a beauty unknown to
the outside world. This life reached out beyond the confines
of the Consulate and achieved what no other thing could possibly achieve, no force, no bribe, no persuasion: it brought the
inmates of the Consulate closer to the people of the town, at
least to some extent, and this in spite of the hate which, as we
have seen, was still felt against the Consulate as such.

Already the year before, when the Daville family had lost
their child so suddenly, there was hardly a house in town that
did not know every detail of the sad event and did not take a
lively and sympathetic interest in it. And for long months

afterwards, during Mme Daville's rare visits to town, people on the street still turned to look after her with a feeling of wistful compassion. Moreover, the domestic help and the women of Dolats and Travnik—especially Jewish women—had spread tales of the harmonious family life and the "golden touch" of Mme Daville, her deftness, her thrift, her housekeeping, and the cleanliness of her home. Even in Moslem houses, where no one ever mentioned the foreign consulates without spitting to avert the evil eye, everyone knew in detail how Madame Consul bathed her children before putting them to bed, what frocks they wore, how their hair was combed, and the color of ribbons used in tying it.

So it was natural that Mme Daville's pregnancy and delivery were a matter of close and anxious concern to the women of all households, almost as if she were an old friend and neighbor. They speculated about the "month" she was in and the way she carried her "burden," whether she had changed noticeably and how she planned to do her lying-in. It then became apparent what great and important things birth and motherhood were in the life of these people, a life that was otherwise starved of joy and change.

At the appointed time the old woman Matishichka came to the Consulate; she was the widow of a respected but insolvent merchant and was considered the best midwife in the whole of Dolats. The old woman, who attended all the deliveries among the well-to-do families, embellished even more Mme Daville's reputation as mother and housewife. She described in detail the order and all the neatness and beauty of the house, which was "cleaner than paradise," it smelled so sweet and was heated and lighted down to the last corner; she reported about the Consul's wife, who even at the very last moment, in her labor pains, gave orders and instructions from her bed, with a mere "nod of the eyes," and about her piety and unbelievable patience under pain; and finally, about the Consul's solicitude which was so full of love and yet dignified, which you would never find among the local husbands. For years to come old Matishichka would talk about it to young expectant mothers when they became too excited from fear and pain, and would cite the example of the French Consul's wife to shame them and calm them down.

The child which was born at the end of February was a girl.

Messages of congratulations began to pour in from the

homes of Travnik and Dolats, proving anew that the people, though not yet reconciled to the existence of the Consulate, did feel closer to the Daville family. Housewives from Dolats arrived, all rustling and pink-cheeked, in fur-lined jackets of satin, solemn and waddling like ducks on ice. Behind each one came a frozen page-boy, an apprentice of her husband's, stepping gingerly, his ears tingling with cold and a runny "icicle" forming under his nose, which he could not wipe off as his outstretched hands were full of wrapped gift packages. A number of the begs' wives also sent their gypsy maids with presents to inquire about the health of the Consul's wife. The gifts were displayed in the birth chamber—copper trays of *baklava*, stacks of fruitcakes, like miniature firewood, embroidery and rolls of silk linen, demijohns and flasks of plum brandy and mulled wine, stoppered with a few leaves of a window plant.

As once before, after the death of Daville's little son, Frau von Mitterer now took a lively interest in the event. She brought as a gift for the newborn a lovely and costly Italian gold medallion, studded with flowers of diamond and black enamel; and stayed on to tell its complicated and touching history. She came back several times during those days and seemed to be a little disappointed that everything went off so easily and smoothly, with no dramatic developments or cause for excitement. She sat by Mme Daville's bedside and chatted long and disjointedly about all that was in store for the little creature, about the women's lot in society and about fate in general. From her high white pillows, Mme Daville, small and pale, gazed at her and listened without appearing to understand.

But the biggest and finest birthday present came from the Vizier—a huge ornamental bowl full of sweets, tied first with silk ribbons and then covered with a length of orange-red Brusa brocade. The bowl was carried by several boys, preceded by an official from the Residency. They had carried the bowl like this all the way through the bazaar, just before noon.

D'Avenat, who sooner or later knew about everything, learned in due course about the trouble they had had in getting the bowl out of the Residency. The difficulties had started with the Treasurer. As always, Baki had tried to spare expenses and to cut the size of the Vizier's gift. They started to choose bowls and consulted about the type of wrapping to go with it. The Vizier had ordered that the sweets be sent in the largest bowl that could be found in the Residency. Baki first tried to convince him that there was no need to make a present at all, since this was not a custom among the "Franks," but when that didn't help he went and hid the largest bowl and substituted a smaller one; but the servants of Tahir Beg found it. The Treasurer gave them a tongue-lashing, in a voice that was choked with fury: "Go and get a larger one still! Give them the whole courtyard, why don't you! Give it all away, make presents, ruin us all!" When he saw them selecting a covering from the finest piece of material, he screamed again, threw himself on the floor, lay on the fabric, and wrapped the ends around him. "No, no, you don't! I won't give it to you! Robbers, wastrels! Why don't you give away your own!"

They could hardly separate him from the precious material, which they proceeded to wrap around the bowl. They left Baki still wailing like a wounded man, cursing all the consuls and consulates on earth, all births and nursing mothers and the idiotic custom of birthday presents, and his own sorry Vizier who no longer knew how to defend and preserve the little that was left but listened to his mad spendthrift of a Secretary, who scattered money and presents left and right, on Moslems and unbelievers alike.

The child in the French Consulate was christened a month later, at the first letup in the cold weather that gripped the town at the very end of the winter that year. The baby girl was named Eugénie-Stéphanie-Annunziata and recorded in the Register of Births in the parish of Dolats on March 25, in the year 1810, the day of the Feast of the Annunciation.

That year—a year of peace and high hopes—brought everyone at least a partial fulfillment of his desires and expectations.

At long last von Mitterer received clear instructions on how to comport himself vis-à-vis the French Consul. ("On private occasions with politeness, even cordiality, but in public, before the Moslems and the Christians, you are to refrain from any demonstration of friendliness and maintain a certain dignified distance and reserve, etc., etc.") Armed with the directive, von Mitterer went about it more easily and a little less self-consciously. The only cramping element was Anna Maria, who never bowed to anyone's instructions and set her own standards of conduct and discretion.

The bethrothal and marriage of the Austrian Princess Marie Louise to Napoleon were matters of passionate concern to Anna

Maria. She followed every detail of the ceremonies in the Vienna newspapers, knew the names of all personages who took part in them, and memorized every word allegedly said on those occasions; and when she read somewhere how Napoleon, unable to wait for his bride at the prearranged spot, had rushed off incognito, in a plain carriage, to meet her and had burst into her coach somewhere along the open road, Anna Maira wept with enthusiasm and rushed like a whirlwind into her husband's study to tell him how right she had been all along in judging the Corsican as an unusual man and a unique example of greatness and sensitivity.

Although it was Holy Week, Anna Maria visited Mme Daville, to tell her all she had learned and read and to share with her the admiration and wonder she felt.

April had brought some unusually sunny days and Mme Daville was putting them to good use in the garden. Work around the flowers and the vegetable patch was the duty of Mundjar, a deaf-mute, who had been their gardener from the first year. Madame Daville was so used to him that she found it quite simple, with signs, facial expressions, and finger movements, to work with him in perfect understanding on everything relating to the garden. And not only that, but the same language of signs enabled them to "talk" about other things, the events in the town, the gardens in the Residency, the Austrian Consulate, and especially about the children.

Mundjar lived with a young wife in one of those poor huts at the foot of Osoye. Their place was clean and orderly, the woman was strong, handsome, and a good worker, but they had no children. This was a bane of their life. When the Daville children came to watch him at work, he often couldn't take his eyes off them and watched them longingly. Always clean, quick and nimble-handed, he kept right on digging like a mole as he smiled at them with his deeply sunburned, creased face—the special, inimitable smile of those who cannot speak.

Wearing her wide-brimmed garden straw hat, Mme Daville would stand by as he dug and supervise the manuring, crumbling hard clods of soil with her fingers, preparing a special bed for a rare species of hyacinth she had managed to obtain that spring. When they told her that Frau von Mitterer had come to visit her, she took the news as though it were an interruption of nature or freak weather, and went in to change.

In a sunny warm alcove, where even the windows and walls

were draped in white, the two consuls' wives sat down to exchange many pleasantries and fine sentiments. Anna Maria supplied both in abundance, for her eloquence and intensity of feeling all but mesmerized Mme Daville. The main topic was the Emperor's marriage, about which Frau von Mitterer knew every last detail. She knew the exact number and rank of the persons present in the church during Napoleon's wedding rites, the length of Marie Louise's imperial mantle, which was held up by five real queens and was made of heavy velvet, nine feet long, embroidered with bees in thread of gold, the same ones the Barberini family use in their coat of arms, a family which, as is well known, has given the world a great many Popes and statesmen, who in turn, as is well known . . .

Frau von Mitterer's talk drifted further and further into the hoary past and ended with cries of enthusiasm that were less pertinent than they were heartfelt. "Oh, aren't we fortunate to be living in these great times, even if we're not always aware of them, and don't appreciate their true greatness?" said Anna Maria and embraced Mme Daville, who submitted to it without protest, as she could not turn away or ward it off. Madame Daville had always been content to get along without imperial weddings and historic particulars, as long as her children remained healthy and everything in her home was in good order.

Then came the tale of the dashing Emperor who, like any ordinary traveler, dressed only in a simple uniform, raced down the road at breakneck speed and stormed into the carriage of his imperial bride, throwing all protocol to the winds.

"Oh really . . ." said Mme Daville, who could not quite see the point of the story or its reference to greatness, since her natural inclination would have been to see the bridegroom wait for the bride in a place duly selected for the purpose and not to upset the arrangements.

"Ah, it was magnificent . . . simply magnificent!" sighed Anna Maria and flung the light cashmere shawl from her shoulders. Her enthusiasm had made her feel quite warm, although she wore only a thin rose-colored dress that was much too light for the time of the year.

Madame Daville would have liked, if only out of courtesy, to say something equally nice and pleasant to Frau von Mitterer, so as not to be thought lacking in enthusiasm. But the whims and ways of rulers and great personages were to her strange and remote things, of which she had only the vaguest idea and on which she hardly knew how to comment, even if she had been willing to lie and pretend. Still, in order to say something at least, she told Anna Maria about her plans for a new type of very showy hyacinth, indicating, not without zest, how striking they would look in four rows of different colors down the middle of the whole garden. She showed her the boxes that contained the lumpy, rough, brown tubers of the future hyacinths, divided according to the color of flowers.

In a separate box she had the bulbs of a particularly choice variety of white hyacinth that a courier had brought from France, of which she felt especially proud. A strip of these was to be planted diagonally across the four other beds so as to tie them in a white band. No one here in Travnik had ever seen such a fine variety, nor such color, smell, or size. She spoke about the trouble she had had in procuring this treasure and added at the end that, taken all in all, the whole thing was quite inexpensive.

"Oh, oh!" cried Anna Maria, still in the throes of her wedding excitement. "Oh, isn't that magnificent! We shall have Imperial Hyacinths in the wilderness! Oh, *chère madame,* let us christen this variety and name it 'Wedding Joy' or 'Imperial Bridegroom' or . . ."

Enraptured by her own words, Anna Maria thought up a whole series of new names, and Mme Daville agreed to all of them automatically, as if she were talking to a child whom it was better not to contradict if the conversation was ever to come to an end.

After this their talk was bound to falter. When two people converse, one word usually sparks another and together they light a flame, but here the words missed one another and went off in different directions. It could hardly have been otherwise. Anna Maria thrilled to things that were remote, strange, and outside her life; Mme Daville only to what was near and intimately bound up with herself and her family.

In the end—and this was how every conversation with Mme Daville always ended—her children came in to meet the visitor and say good morning. They were boys, two of them; the baby girl, still only two months old, having just been fed and warmly wrapped, slept in her crib of white tulle.

The eight-year-old Pierre, slight and pallid in his dark blue velvet suit and white lace collar, was pretty and demure like an altar boy. He led in his younger brother Jean-Paul, a sturdy robust child with blond locks and pink cheeks, who had been born at Split and had just turned three.

Anna Maria did not like children, while Mme Daville could not imagine anyone's being indifferent to them. Time spent in the company of children filled her with a sense of desolation and boredom. These soft, childish bodies that were still growing repelled her as something unformed and immature and gave her a feeling of almost physical queasiness and ineffable fear. She was ashamed of this feeling (she herself did not know why) and tried to disguise it with sweet words of endearment and playful cries, which was her stock approach to children in general. But in herself, deep inside, she shrank from children and feared them, those little people who stared at one with their big new eyes, in that unflinching, quizzical way of theirs, as if in cold, dispassionate judgment—or so at least it seemed to her. As a rule she broke away from those long childish gazes and dropped her eyes, which never happened to her with the grownups, perhaps because the grownups were either easier to bribe and cajole into assent or were more willing accomplices to one's weaknesses and vices.

And now Anna Maria felt the same boredom and queasiness in front of the Daville children. In default of genuine delight in these little people, she kissed them passionately and loudly, summoning the necessary enthusiasm from her inexhaustible surfeit of transport over the imperial wedding in Paris.

When she finally took her leave, she marched down the path between the newly dug flowerbeds to the tune of the wedding march, while Mme Daville and her astonished children watched her from the threshold of the doorway. She turned once more at the garden gate and, with a wave of her hand, called that they must see each other more often now, and talk some more, much more, about the lovely, lovely, and great things that were happening.

This soaring mood of his wife struck Colonel von Mitterer as being out of keeping with the directive he had received, but he and the whole household were happy that Anna Maria had found a distant, harmless, and more or less steady object for her enthusiasm. For a whole year Travnik and the petty, tedious life of the Consulate ceased to exist for Anna Maria. She seemed to forget about wanting her husband to transfer and lived entirely in a cloud of imperial married bliss and peace on earth and mystical visions of universal harmony. This was reflected in her talk, her bearing, and her music. She knew the names of all the ladies in waiting of the new Empress of France, the value, shape, and quality of all the wedding presents, and Marie Louise's way of life and her daily program. She followed the career of the divorced ex-Empress Josephine with sympathy and understanding, so that even her need to cry from time to time was now focused on a remote but worthy target, which meant that the Colonel was spared many a trying moment.

Life in the French Consulate that year passed off without excitement and dislocation. Toward the end of summer Daville sent his oldest son to a *lycée* in France. At his recommendation, D'Avenat's son was also accepted as a state scholar and sent off to Paris.

D'Avenat was overjoyed and immensely proud, but being dry and burnt out like a cinder, he was incapable of showing and articulating his joy like other people; he trembled in his whole body as he thanked Daville, assuring him that he was ready to lay down his life for the Consulate whenever necessary. So great was his love for his son and his longing to secure for the boy a better, finer, and worthier life than he himself had had.

As the year wore on, monotonously and peacefully, and nothing untoward happened, one had every reason to call it a good year.

There was peace in Dalmatia, the frontiers were mercifully quiet. The Residency was becalmed. The consuls met during the holidays as heretofore, avoiding cordiality and more intimate contact, and watched each other closely on working days, though without excessive zeal or spite. The people of all faiths slowly grew accustomed to having the consuls around. Seeing how the troubles and difficulties with which the consuls had had to contend so far had not been enough to drive them from Travnik, the people reconciled themselves and began to collaborate and reckon with them in business and include them in their workaday existence.

So the life of the town and the consulates flowed on placidly, from summer to autumn and from winter to spring, with no other changes save the usual ones brought about by the daily round and the march of the seasons.

But the chronicle of quiet and happy years is brief.

19

The same courier who, in the month of April 1811, brought to Travnik the newspapers announcing that a son had been born to Napoleon who was to bear the title King of Rome, also brought von Mitterer an order that recalled him from Travnik and placed him at the disposal of the Ministry of War. Here, then, was the rescue which the Colonel and his family had been awaiting these past years. And now that it was here, it all seemed rather simple and self-evident; and like most rescues, it came both too late and too soon—too late because it could not change or mitigate all they had gone through while waiting to be rescued, and too soon because, like all uprooting, it raised a host of new problems (moving, money, further career prospects), to which so far no thought had been given.

Anna Maria, who in the last few months had settled down wonderfully and become much quieter, burst into tears—for, like most people of her temperament, she was prone to cry from sickness as well as cure, from yearning as well as its fulfillment. It was only after a stormy scene with the Colonel in which she blamed him for all those things which by rights he ought to have blamed her for (had he been so inclined) that she gathered enough strength and purpose to begin packing.

A few days later the new Consul-General, Lieutenant-Colonel von Paulich, who till then had commanded a frontier regiment at Kostaynitsa, arrived to take over from von Mitterer.

The entry of a new Austrian Consul, on a sunny April morning, was a colorful and impressive event, even though the Vizier did not send a particularly large escort to meet him. Tall and youthful-looking, riding a fine horse, von Paulich drew all eyes and aroused curiosity and grudging admiration even in those who would never be caught admitting it. And not only he, but his retinue too, was exceptionally well got out, spruce and trim, as if they were on parade. Those who saw him told those who happened to be away from the bazaar at the time what a handsome, upstanding fellow the new Austrian Consul was ("Infidel though he is!").

And when, two days later, he and von Mitterer passed in a

ceremonial procession on their way to a reception at the
Vizier's, an unexpected miracle occurred.

The people actually watched the procession, stared at the
new Consul, and turned to gaze at him long after he had passed.
The Moslem women looked from behind their window grilles,
the children clustered on fences and walls, but no voices were
raised, not a single disparaging word was heard anywhere,
even though the Moslems in the shops along the way remained
impassive and dour as ever.

Such was the public reception of the new Consul. And the
same thing happened again on the return trip from the Residency.

Earlier von Mitterer had told von Paulich how both he and
his French colleague had been treated on their first arrival in
Travnik a few years back, and he was now disappointed at the
change. In a huff that was more than a little tinged with envy,
he filled the new Consul's ears with details of the abuse he
himself had been exposed to at the time. He spoke of it rue-
fully, with an undertone of reproach in his voice, as if he, von
Mitterer, had by his humiliation, smoothed the way for this
pleasant passage of his successor.

But the new Consul, in fact, was a type of person before
whom all roads seemed to open up smoothly.

Von Paulich came from a rich Germanized family in Zagreb.
His mother had been an Austrian from Steiermark, from the
prominent family von Niedermayer. He was thirty-five years
old and strikingly handsome. He was tall, fine-complexioned,
with a small brown mustache over his mouth, large eyes in
which a pair of dark blue pupils shone with a steady light,
and a shock of naturally wavy hair that was cropped and
combed in military fashion. The whole man radiated a cool,
self-possessed, almost monkish air, without, however, a trace
of those inner conflicts and strife that so often leave their
tortured imprint on the visage and bearing of monks. This
exceptionally handsome creature seemed to move and live, as
it were, in a sort of icy armor, behind which all sounds of a
personal life and human weakness and needs faded and grew
inaudible as in a shell. His conversation was like that too—
factual, affable, and quite impersonal; and so were his deep
voice and the smile that sometimes played over his regular,
white teeth and flitted over his stony face like frosted moonlight.

This imperturbable man had once been the precocious child of a comfortable family, developed beyond his years and gifted with a remarkable memory, one of those exceptional school-boys who turn up once in a generation, to whom studies are no problem whatever and who can cram a two-year course into one scholastic year with the greatest of ease. The Jesuit fathers, with whom this unusual boy was studying, quickly saw that he was developing into one of those perfectly rounded, command-ing personalities who stand like cornerstones at the base of their Order. At the age of fourteen, however, the boy turned his back on the Order, betrayed the hopes of the Jesuits, and showed an unexpected interest in a military career.

His parents encouraged him, especially his mother, whose family had a strong military tradition. And so, from a boy who amazed his humanities teachers with the quickness of his intel-ligence and the extent of his knowledge, he progressed to a lanky, bluff cadet with an apparently brilliant career ahead of him, then to a young subaltern who did not drink or smoke, had no love affairs, no trouble with his superiors, no duels, and no debts. His company was the best kept and the best outfitted, he took the lead in all examinations and drills, yet without any of that visible zeal which follows ambitious men in their climb like a harsh shadow.

After he had completed all courses and passed first in all examinations, von Paulich again startled his superiors by opt-ing for service on the frontier, a domain usually reserved for officers of inferior qualifications and middling ability. He learned the Turkish language, familiarized himself with the territory and methods of work, with the local people and conditions. And when von Mitterer's repeated pleas for a transfer finally came to the attention of his superiors, von Paulich was luckily available as the "familienloses Individuum" (man without a family) for whom the Colonel had appealed so fervently from Travnik.

And now von Mitterer, weary and intimidated by life's mul-tiplicity, could sit back and observe this young man and his extraordinary professional ways. Under his eyes and hands, it seemed, every job became transparently clear and was settled easily and simply, at the proper time and in its proper place, so that there was no crowding or confusion, no pressure or delay. Every piece of work was liquidated smoothly and thoroughly, like an account without outstanding balances. And the man himself seemed to stand above and outside everything, inscrutable and hard to reach, and took part in the work merely as a brooding presence and an energy that supervised, instructed, and made decisions. He was quite innocent of those doubts and irresistible waverings, those partisan sentiments and idiosyncrasies, all those emotional shadings that lie athwart the business of men and so often baffle, upset, and immobilize one, even sometimes warp the task itself in an undesirable way. He was not hampered by any of these—or at least so it seemed; the man functioned like a disinterested higher spirit or like unfeeling nature herself.

Moving the household strips a man's life bare in all its intimate details. Von Mitterer had the opportunity to observe and compare his own moving out (which he would have best liked not to think about, if Frau von Mitterer had let him) with the moving in of this unusual man. With him everything went smoothly and without wasted motions, just as it did in his official work. There was no messing about with the luggage, no overlapping or duplication among the servants. All things found their proper places, as if by themselves, everything was simple, purposeful, clear cut, numbered, and named. The servants understood one another simply by a glance, without words, shouting, or noisy instructions. There was no equivocation over anything, or the least shadow of ill-temper, uncertainty, or disorder.

Always, in everything, a clean account with no balances.

When it came to taking over the inventory and reviewing the work in progress and the staff of the Consulate-General, von Paulich used much the same approach.

Speaking of Rotta, the chief assistant, von Mitterer dropped his eyes unwittingly and his voice sounded uncertain. Hemming and hawing, he said about the chief interpreter that he was somewhat—in a way—peculiar and was not exactly— well—the choicest flower in the garden, but he was loyal and very useful. Throughout the conversation von Paulich looked sideways, all but away: his big eyes narrowed and a cool gleam of irritation appeared in the corners. He listened to von Mitterer's briefing in stony silence, without any sign of either approval or disapproval, evidently having made up his mind to handle the inventory and other matters under discussion in his own way and by his own method of accounting, in which there would be no errors or outstanding balances.

Considering the kind of man he was, his sudden arrival in Travnik and his confrontation with the fluttery Anna Maria were bound to arouse her attention and give fresh point to her old unquenchable urge for passionate admiration and her vague hankering for a "concord of souls." She at once nicknamed him "Antinoüs in uniform," which the Lieutenant-Colonel took without a word or a flicker of an eyelash, as something that neither had, nor could possibly ever have, the slightest connection with him or the world around him. Von Paulich was quite unmusical and did not hide the fact; indeed, he could not have made a secret of it if he had wanted to, since he was quite unable to sham that genial air with which unmusical people participate in musical discussions, as if by doing so they hope to atone for their shortcoming. Their talks about mythology and Roman poets were more successful, although here Anna Maria was the weaker, for the remarkable Lieutenant-Colonel countered each one of her distichs with a whole string of verses. On most occasions he was able to recite from memory the entire poem of which she knew only a line, and would also, in passing, correct the mistake she usually made in that line. But his quoting had a dispassionate, factual ring, as if the thing had nothing whatever to do with him or with the surroundings or with live mankind in general, and all her lyrical allusions bounced off him like an unintelligible sound.

Anna Maria was taken aback. All her encounters so far— and there had been a good many of them—had ended in disappointment and in running away, yet in all her "strayings" she had always managed to force the man to take a step forward or a step back, or both; never yet had it happened that he stayed exactly where he was, like this robot Antinoüs for whose benefit she now put on her fluttery, preening game in vain. He was to her a new and particularly acute form of self-torture. This promptly made itself felt in her home life. (Right on the first day, Rotta was heard saying in the office, in that caustic jargon in which petty bureaucrats discuss their superiors, that "Frau Konsul was putting on quite a performance.") While von Mitterer was familiarizing the new Consul with his duties, Anna Maria blustered through the house, changed her husband's instructions, sat on the packed cases and cried. One moment she would try to delay the departure, and in the next she would excitedly try to speed it up. At night she shook her husband awake just as he had fallen asleep, to berate him and tell him all the reproachful things she had thought up while he slept.

Hardly was the packing finished when it turned out that nothing was in its proper place, that no one knew where anything was or how it had been put away. When the luggage was ready to be moved, the pack horses which the Chief of Police had promised to the Consul failed to arrive in time. Anna Maria alternated between outbursts of fury and moody resignation. Rotta scurried around, shouted, and threatened. When finally, on the third day, enough horses were rounded up, it was found that some crates were too bulky and would have to be repacked. Even this might have been accomplished somehow if Anna Maria had not insisted on issuing her own orders and lending a helping hand. As a result, packing cases broke and things were damaged even before they got under way, and the Consulate was surrounded by a whole camping caravan of animals and drivers.

At length everything was loaded and sent on its way, and the family von Mitterer followed a day later. With compressed lips and dry unfriendly eyes Anna Maria bade an insultingly icy farewell to von Paulich in front of the devastated Consulate, in a courtyard littered with straw, broken boards, and horse droppings. She and her daughter drove off first, followed by von Mitterer and von Paulich on horseback.

Daville, accompanied by D'Avenat and a groom, saw them off as far as the first crossroad. Here Daville and von Mitterer said good-bye and parted, in a manner not so much cold and insincere as rigid and awkward—in fact, in the same way in which they had first greeted each other on that autumn day more than three years before and in which they had lived and associated ever since.

On the crossroad too Daville could see the Catholic women and children approaching von Mitterer from both sides, to kiss his hands and clutch his stirrup shyly, and he could see that the Colonel was greatly moved by it; there was a whole crowd of them waiting their turn at the edge of the road.

With this image of von Mitterer's last triumph before his eyes, Daville turned to go home and discovered that he too was moved quite considerably, not because von Mitterer was gone, but because his departure touched off memories of their common past and fresh speculations about his own future. His actual going seemed almost to be a relief; it was not so much

that he was getting rid of a tricky rival, since judging from all
he'd heard the new Consul was even cleverer and more formidable than von Mitterer, but because this sallow-faced Colonel, with his weary eyes and woebegone look, had with time
become a kind of embodiment of their common, unconfessed
misery in this wilderness. No matter what came after him,
Daville was more content to part from and bid farewell to
this difficult man than to have to meet him and welcome him.

Around noon, at the first resting place by the river Lashva,
von Paulich also took leave of his predecessor. Anna Maria
exacted her punishment by giving him no opportunity to greet
her once more. Letting the carriage trudge empty up the slope,
she went on foot along the green edge of the road and refused to turn and look down into the valley where the two
consuls were saying good-bye on the riverbank. That tearful
sadness which overcomes even steadier women on leaving a
place where they have spent a part of their life, whether that
life was good or bad, now choked Anna Maria too. Her lips
pouted, her throat tightened, as she fought to keep back her
tears. But more than this, she was tormented by thoughts of
the handsome, cold Lieutenant-Colonel, whom she no longer
called Antinoüs but "the glacier," since she had found him to be
even colder than the marble statue of the beautiful youth of
antiquity. (She had named him that the night before and so
gratified her need to invent a special name for everyone she
met, appropriate to her feelings of the moment toward the
person in question.) With an air of rigid solemnity, Anna
Maria walked up the mountain road as though it were a stair-
way to some poignant, mystical height.

Parallel to her, on the other side of the road, her daughter
Agatha walked along the other shoulder, timid and silent.
Unlike her passionate mother, the little girl did not feel that
she was making a grandiose ascent, but rather that she was
going downhill under a cloud of sadness. She too was struggling to keep back her tears, but for quite different reasons. She
was the only one in the family who genuinely grieved to leave
Travnik and the silence and freedom of its gardens and ve-
randas, who was sorry to be going back to huge and unfriendly
Vienna where there was no quiet, no view to the open sky,
where the moldy breath of houses chilled one's heart right in
the doorway, where this mother of hers, who made her feel

uncomfortable even in her dreams, would be ever-present and inescapable.

The tears in Agatha's eyes went unnoticed by her mother, who seemed to have forgotten that she was there. Angry, disjointed words came from Anna Maria's lips, and she was furious with her husband for tarrying so long and "making up to that glacier, that nonhuman," instead of turning his back on him as she had done. And as she muttered to herself, she felt the wind inflating the long, light green veil tied to the back of her traveling hat, fluttering it and tugging at it. She found the sensation lovely and somehow moving and her mood suddenly lifted and changed, exalting her in her own eyes, so that all the trivia of her present existence faded away and she saw herself as a noble victim treading the lonely path of renunciation before the awed gaze of the world.

That was all she would deign to give that cold unfeeling man: a blurred glimpse of herself on the horizon and the last proud, imperious flutter of her veil as it faded and receded without appeal.

Lost in these dreams, she went up along the edge of the hill with a firm deliberate step, as though the landscape around her and the sky above were some great deep stage.

But down below, in the valley, her husband was the only one who noticed the mountain; he glanced up anxiously, while "the glacier," not noticing a blessed thing, went through the amenities of parting with the utmost politeness and finesse.

The touchy and emotional Anna Maria was not the only one whom the personality of the new Consul had fascinated and then disappointed.

Even during the first visit von Paulich had paid him, in the company of von Mitterer, Daville had seen that he would be dealing with a totally different kind of man from the latter. In matters of consular business, von Paulich was more forthright and much clearer. One could also talk to him on virtually any other subject, especially on the subject of classical literature.

In their subsequent exchange of visits, Daville had got an even better impression of his ample and thorough knowledge of classic texts and commentaries. Von Paulich had looked through Delille's French-language translation of Virgil, which Daville had sent him, and had described his reaction lucidly and earnestly; he had maintained that a true translation must follow the meter of the original, and had criticized Delille's use, and misuse, of rhyme. Daville had defended his idol Delille, happy to have someone to discuss it with.

But the first flush of Daville's pleasure at having this cultivated and well-read man available paled rather quickly. It didn't take him long to realize that chatting with this learned man produced very little of that glow of satisfaction which is the usual aftermath of an exchange of ideas on a favorite subject with a cultivated partner. A conversation with the Colonel was, in fact, an exchange of data—which were invariably accurate, interesting, and copious, on any and all subjects—but hardly an exchange of thoughts and impressions. Everything about these talks was impersonal, dispassionate, and general. Having said all he wanted to, the Colonel would leave with his rich and precious bag of facts, as fresh, neat, cool, and upright as he had come, and Daville would be left just as lonely as he had been before, his craving for a good talk unappeased. A discussion with the Colonel left nothing for the senses or the soul; one could not even recall the timbre of his voice. His conversation gave the partner no clue to his inner personality, and invited no confidence from the latter. In general, everything that was personal, close, and intimate recoiled from the Colonel as from a rock. So Daville had to forego all hope of discussing his own poetic work with this cold-blooded lover of literature.

At the time of the happy event in the French ruling family, Daville had written a special poem commemorating the baptism of the King of Rome and had sent it to his Ministry with the request that they pass it on to the august parents. The poem opened with the words: *"Salut, fils de printemps et du dieu de la Guerre!"* (Son of spring and god of War, we salute you!) Further along, the poem voiced a hope for peace and well-being among the nations of Europe and made a passing mention of those who, "scattered in wild and desolate regions," did their humble bit toward that goal.

Daville read the poem to von Paulich during one of his visits, but there was no reaction. The Colonel not only failed to understand the allusion to their joint work in Bosnia but did not comment with a single word either on the verses or their subject. What was worse, he kept his usual polite and affable manner

throughout. And while Daville felt disappointed and even annoyed, he could not very well show that he was offended.

20

The period after the Peace of Vienna, the years 1810 and 1811
—which we have called the quiet years—were in reality a
time of strenuous work for Daville.

There were no wars, no visible crises or open clashes, but
now the whole Consulate was deep in work on problems of
commerce, the gathering of information, writing of reports,
issuing of certificates of origin and recommendations to the
French authorities in Split or to the Customs House in Kostaynitsa. There was a saying among the people that "trade
moved across Bosnia," and Napoleon himself was alleged to
have said somewhere, "The time for diplomats is over, these
are the Times of the Consuls."

Three years before, Daville had drawn up a plan for the development of trade between Turkey and France and the countries under French occupation. He had strongly recommended
that France organize her own postal service through the Turkish lands and not be at the mercy of the Austrian service or
the whims and confusion of the Turks. All those proposals had
got stuck somewhere in the bursting files in Paris. Now, however, after the Peace of Vienna, it became evident that Napoleon himself stood to gain enormously if they were put into
effect with all possible speed, on a scale much greater and more
significant than the Consul at Travnik would ever have dared
to suggest.

Napoleon's Continental System called for sweeping changes
in the network of communications and trade routes on the European continent. The creation of Illyrian Provinces, with their
center in Ljubljana, was to serve this purpose exclusively, according to Napoleon's ideas. Due to the English blockade, the
old routes through the Mediterranean, by which France obtained her raw materials, especially cotton from the Levant,
had become risky and dangerous. Now trade had to be shifted

to an overland route and the new Province of Illyria was to serve as a link between France and the Turkish lands. These routes had always existed—from Istanbul along the Danube to Vienna, and from Salonica through Bosnia to Trieste—and commerce between the Austrian lands and the Levant had always made use of them. Now it was necessary to expand them and suit them to the needs of Napoleonic France.

As soon as the first proclamations and newspaper articles revealed Napoleon's thinking on this, French authorities and institutions began to vie with each other in carrying out the Emperor's wishes with the greatest zeal and to the best possible effect. All of a sudden there was prolific correspondence and lively collaboration between Paris, the Governor-General and Intendant-General in Ljubljana, the Embassy at Istanbul, Marshal Marmont in Dalmatia, and the French consulates in the Levant. Daville worked with enthusiasm, referring with pride to his three-year-old proposals which showed how close, even at that time, his viewpoint and line of thought had been to the ideas of the Emperor.

Now, in the summer of 1811, this work was in full swing. During the past year Daville had tried very hard to find reliable men and to organize a supply of horses in all the places through which French goods passed, and to establish some kind of supervision over the pack drivers and freight. It had been a slow, uphill, and unsatisfactory task, like every other thing in this country; but now, with "Napoleon breathing on the sails" as it were, it was all beginning to perk up and look more promising, and the work went more easily and cheerfully.

The day came at last when one of the leading trading houses at Marseilles, Freycinet Brothers, which so far had used the sea route to transport goods from the Levant, opened an agency at Sarajevo. The French government had approved the agency, directing it to work with the Consul. One of the Freycinet brothers, a young man, had arrived in Sarajevo a month earlier to supervise the work personally; and now he came to Travnik for a couple of days to visit the Consul-General and discuss further developments.

The lovely but short Travnik summer was at its zenith. A dazzling clear day, all sunshine and blue skies, glittered over the Travnik valley. On the big terrace in the shade of the Consulate Building a table was laid out with several white wicker chairs.

The air in the shade was fresh, though touched now and then by the waftings of the torrid heat that rose from the huddled streets of the bazaar down below. The steep green sides of the narrow valley gave off a dry heat and seemed to pulse and throb like the underbelly of a lizard stretched out in the sun. Madame Daville's hyacinths on the terrace were long past their bloom, both the white ones and the colored varieties, the single- as well as the double-petaled ones; the borders now sparkled with red geraniums and delicate violet Alpine flowers.

Daville and the young Freycinet sat at the table in the shade. Spread out before them were copies of their reports, back issues of *Le Moniteur* containing the government announcements and decrees, and paper, ink, and quills.

Jacques Freycinet was a hefty young man, with fresh pink and white cheeks and that calm, self-possessed voice and bearing common to children of well-to-do families. Business was obviously in his blood. No member of the clan had ever done or wanted to do anything else, or had ambitions to belong to another class, and he was in no way different from the rest of them. Like all the others in his family he was neat, polite, alert, tactful, ready to stand up for his rights, conscious of his interests, though not in a blinkered, unimaginative way.

Freycinet had traveled the route from Sarajevo to Kostaynitsa both ways; he had rented an entire inn at Sarajevo for his depot and was now negotiating with merchants, pack drivers, and local authorities. He had come to exchange information with Daville, to tell him of his observations and to make certain proposals. The Consul was pleased to have this lively and polite southerner as a co-worker on problems that had often seemed to him insurmountable.

"*Alors*, let me repeat once more," said Freycinet with that stolidity which creeps into a businessman's voice when he is marshaling facts to serve his interest, "we must allow seven days for the trip from Sarajevo to Kostaynitsa, including these overnight stops: Kiselyak, Busovacha, Karaula, Yaytse, Zmiyanye, Novi Han, Priedor, and, of course, Kostaynitsa. In the winter we must reckon with twice as many, that is to say fourteen stages. We'll need at least two more caravanseries along the road, if we're to keep the freight out of the weather and prevent stealing. Transport costs have gone up and are still rising. The reason for that is Austrian competition and, I'm inclined to think, certain Sarajevo merchants, Serbs and Jews, who seem to be working hand in hand with the English. Currently we had better count with these prices: from Salonica to Sarajevo at the rate of 155 piasters per load, from Sarajevo to Kostaynitsa 55 piasters. Two years ago the costs were exactly one half of that. And we should do all we can to prevent further increase, because that might put the route out of business altogether. And we'd better make an allowance for the whims and greed of Turkish officials, for the inclination of the natives to pilfer and steal, the danger that the Serbian uprisings may spread and result in banditry along the Albanian frontier, and, finally, the risk of epidemics along the way."

Daville, ever ready to see the fingers of the English Intelligence in everything, wanted to know the reasoning behind Freycinet's suspicion that the Sarajevo merchants were working for English interests, but the young man would not be flustered or diverted. Holding his notes in front of him, he went on: "Well, to recapitulate and conclude. Dangers to traffic are the following: unrest in Serbia, Albanian bandits, pilfering in Bosnia itself, rising costs of transport, arbitrary duties and tax, competition, and, lastly, plague and other epidemics. The measures that ought to be taken are: first, two new caravansaries between Sarajevo and Kostaynitsa; second, stabilizing the wild fluctuations of the Turkish exchange by a special firman at the rate of 5.50 piasters to a thaler of 6 francs or one Maria-Theresa thaler, 11.50 piasters to a Venetian zecchino, and so forth; third, enlarging the quarantine station at Kostaynitsa, building a bridge to replace the ferry, enlarging the warehouse to accommodate at least eight thousand bales of cotton, establishing resthouses for travelers, et cetera; fourth, special gifts to the Vizier Suleiman Pasha and to certain other key Turks at the time these demands are put to them. The whole plan would cost approximately ten to thirteen thousand francs. It would solve the main difficulties and make the route safe and practical."

Daville made a note of these things, to include them in his official report. At the same time he decided, with a certain pleasurable anticipation, to read the young man his own report, written in 1807, in which he had so accurately foreseen Napoleon's intentions and all the measures they were now putting into effect.

"Ah, *mon cher monsieur*, I could tell you a good deal about what happens in this country when you come up with a sensible scheme or a useful enterprise. I could tell you some tales, but you can see for yourself the kind of country this is, the kind of people, the kind of government, and the enormous trouble one has to go through for every blessed little thing." The young man, however, had nothing more to say; having pithily stated the problems and outlined the means for solving them, he had no appreciation of generalized complaints and "psychological" subtleties. He consented politely to listen to Daville's report of 1807, which the Consul began to read.

The shadow in which they sat grew longer and longer. The lemonade that was set before them in tall crystal glasses grew more tepid by the minute, for they had both forgotten it.

In that same summer stillness, two blocks above the Consulate where Daville and Freycinet conducted their business, only slightly to the left and nearer the stream which, shrunken and out of sight, cascaded down into the valley, Musa Krdzaliya and his companions sat in the former's garden.

The steep and neglected slope of the garden was choking in vegetation. On a small outcropping, the top of which offered a narrow strip of near-level ground, under a tall pear tree, a rug had been spread and on it were remains of food, coffee cups, and a bottle of chilled plum brandy. Here the sun was already gone, though it still lay on the other side of the Lashva. Musa the Singer and Hamza the Crier lay in the grass. The third man Murad Hodzich, known as the Swaying Hodja, half sat and half lay on the slope, his feet braced against the pear tree. Also propped against the tree was his *tambura,* a stringed instrument resembling a mandolin, the tip of which was covered with an inverted brandy glass.

He was a swarthy little man, as compact and mottled as a cockerel. A pair of big dark eyes, with a fanatical gleam in them, stared, unblinking, from his small sallow face. He came from one of the better Travnik families and had once gone to school, but brandy had not allowed him to finish or to become an imam at Travnik, as so many in his family had done. It was said that when he came up for his final examination and faced the head of the school and the board of examiners he was so drunk he could barely stand on his feet; he swayed and reeled, and the Head dismissed him and called him "the Swaying Hodja." And the name had stuck. Deeply offended, the sensitive and temperamental young man then became a chronic drunkard. And the more he drank the greater became his resentment and wounded vanity. Dropped from the ranks of his contemporaries so early in his life, he dreamed of surpassing them all one day with a spectacular feat of some kind and so revenging himself for everything. Like so many failures who have a mousy physique but a passionate temperament, he was consumed with a burning secret ambition not to spend the rest of his days as an unknown, unrespected nobody, but to make the world sit up and take notice by some forceful and astounding deed—how where, or with what, he himself did not know. As time went on this obsession, fanned by heavy drinking to the pitch of insanity, took hold of him completely. The lower he fell, the more he deceived himself with big words and lies, with vain daydreams and flamboyant tales. This often made him a butt of jokes and mockery among his companions, who were drunkards like himself.

As always in those fine summer days, the three of them began to drink in Musa's garden and later, in the gathering dark, went down to town to continue drinking there. Waiting for the night to fall and light up the big stars along the narrow blue strip of the Travnik sky, and already floating in a haze of brandy, they hummed or talked in undertones, with sluggish tongues, disconnectedly, without particular reference to one another's words. It was the talk and singing of men sodden with drink, a substitute for the work and movement they had long become unused to. In these conversations they traveled and lived adventurously and saw the fulfillment of ambitions which they would never be able to realize in any other way; they looked at one another with unseeing eyes, they listened without hearing, they puffed themselves up, swelled, basked in their own greatness, took wing and soared, they became all the things they never were and never would be, and possessed things that were nonexistent and which only brandy can bestow, for a fleeting moment, on those who give themselves up to it body and soul.

Musa was the least talkative of the three. He lay, completely sunk in the thick, dark green grass, with arms folded under his head, his left knee bent and his right leg flung over it, as though he were sitting in a chair. His gaze was lost in the bright sky. Through the skein of grass his fingers felt the touch of the tepid earth which, it seemed to him, rose and fell in long measured breaths; and he was conscious, at the same time, of the soft stream of warm air entering his sleeves and the loosened leggings of his baggy pants. It was a hardly perceptible wafting, a special Travnik breeze that gets up in the early summer evenings, creeping languidly and staying close to the ground as it moves along, gently ruffling the grass and the undergrowth. Musa, who was somewhere halfway between the morning's hangover and a new haze that was fast thickening, reveled in the warmth of the earth and in this gentle, steady flow of air, which made him feel as though he were being lifted up, floating and soaring, not so much because the breeze was strong and insistent but because he himself was no more than a breath and a bubble of restless heat, so light and feathery that he became airborne of his own account and just soared away with them.

And as he took off and flew and lay unmoving, he heard the voices of his two companions as in a dream. Hamza's voice was hoarse and hard to understand, but the Swaying Hodja's was deep and clear; he was speaking slowly and solemnly, his eyes fixed on one spot, as though he were reading from a book.

A few days before, the three of them had come to the conclusion that they had ran out of money and must try to get hold of some at all costs. It had long been the turn of the Swaying Hodja to see to it, but he had trouble raising it and preferred to drink on other people's money.

They talked now about the loan which he was supposed to get from his uncle in Podlugovo. The uncle had become quite rich lately.

"Where does his money come from?" asked Hamza, suspiciously and irritably, for he knew this uncle and rather doubted that the money could be got out of him.

"He made it on cotton this summer."

"Pack driving for the French?"

"No, buying and selling the cotton that 'drops off' in the villages."

"And the cotton is still coming?" drawled Hamza.

"They say it is. Makes you wonder. The English closed up the sea road, you know, and Bonaparte's left without cotton. But he's got to dress that big army of his, so now they're sending it through Bosnia. All the way from Novi Pazar to Kostaynitsa it's just one horse after another, one bale after another. The roads crowded, the inns bursting at the seams. You can't get a pack driver anywhere, the French have hired them all, and they pay with real solid ducats. Anybody that's got a horse these days, it's worth its weight in gold. Anybody that deals in cotton is a rich man inside a month."

"All right, but how do they get the cotton?"

"How? Well, they get it. The French wouldn't sell it for anything. You could offer them a house for an armful of cotton and they wouldn't. So the people learned to steal. They steal in the inns, where the drivers unload the horses for the night. When they take down the freight all the bales are there, but next morning, when they load again, a bale of cotton is missing. So there's a hue and cry. Where is it, who was it? But you can't hold up the whole caravan for a bale of cotton, so they start without it. And in the villages it's the same thing. The children go out, hide in the bushes by the road, and slit the bale sacks with their little knives. The road is narrow between the bushes, the cotton starts falling out and getting caught on the branches on both sides. The caravan goes by, the kids come out and gather the wisps in their little hampers, then hide again and wait for the next caravan. The French blame the drivers and take the damage out of their wages. In some places they send guards and catch the kids, but you can't round up a whole countryside of children. So they keep plucking Bonaparte's cotton off the bush and the trees, like it was Egypt, and people come from the market towns and buy it. Plenty of them got dressed that way and made a little pile besides."

"And it all goes through Bosnia?" Hamza asked drowsily.

"No, not just Bosnia. Happens all over Turkey. Bonaparte's got himself concessions from Istanbul and has sent consuls and merchants with wads of money all through the land, and there you are. Do you know, for Bonaparte's cotton my uncle . . ."

"Well, get the money then," Musa interrupted with quiet contempt, "and we won't ask whether it comes from your maternal or paternal uncle, or where it grows, or how it collects. What we need is money."

Musa did not care for these tales of the Swaying Hodja, which, as a rule, were overlong and exaggerated and served to show, more often than not, that he'd had a little schooling and knew his way about and was at home in the affairs of the world. Hamza, on the other hand, was more patient and listened to them quietly and with good humor, which never left him even during the periods when he hadn't a penny to his name.

"God knows we need money," said Hamza in a kind of croaky echo. "We need it badly."

"And I'll get it, Allah help me, or perish in the attempt," the Swaying Hodja promised earnestly.

His promise and oaths brought no reaction from the other two. Silence fell. Three bodies, weakened by idleness, steadily burning with alcohol or burning for it, breathed quietly and pretended to relax, sprawling on the grass in the warm shade.

"Quite a man, this Bonaparte." The Swaying Hodja spoke thickly, as if talking to himself. "Quite a man. He can beat and conquer anyone living. And they say he's small and puny, nothing much to look at."

"Small, about your size, but with a big heart," Hamza said with another yawn.

"Never carries a sword or a pistol, they say," the Swaying Hodja went on. "Just turns up his collar and pulls his hat over his eyes and runs off at the head of his army. Anything that lives, he just walks over it. Fire spurts out of his eyes. No sword can cut him down, no bullet can touch him."

The Swaying Hodja plucked the empty brandy glass from the tip of his *tambura,* filled it and drank, all with his left hand, while the right one remained inside his open shirt front; with his chin on his chest, he kept his vacuous gaze riveted on the grainy bark of the pear tree. The brandy promptly sang out of him. Hardly opening his lips, not shifting his gaze or changing his position, he sang in his deep baritone:

"Lovely Naza was taken ill
Her mother's only child . . ."

Again he reached for the glass, filled it, tossed it back and took up his *tambura.* "Ah, if I could meet him just once . . ."

"Meet whom?" asked Hamza, even though he'd heard these and similar fantasies a hundred times.

"Whom did you think? Bonaparte. If I could get my hands on him, just the two of us, damn his infidel soul, and then whoever wins good luck to him."

The crazy words petered out in complete silence. Once more the Swaying Hodja plucked his glass from the instrument, shook noisily after drinking it, and continued in a much deeper voice: "If he wins, he can have my head. I wouldn't care this much. But if I win and tie him up, I wouldn't kill him. I'd simply march him through the Turkish army, tied up like that, and make him pay taxes to the Sultan, same as the lowest infidel shepherd from below Karaula."

"He's a long way off, Murad. A long way off, this Bonaparte,"
Hamza said good-humoredly, "And that's a great big army he's
got. And, brother, what about all those other infidel empires you'd
have to go through first?"

"Oh, there'd be no trouble with those." The Swaying Hodja
gave a deprecating wave. "True, he's far away when he's home
in his own land, but he wanders around all the time and won't
sit still. Last year he came to Vienna to get married to the
Austrian Emperor's daughter . . ."

"Well, yes, here around Vienna it might've worked out," said
Hamza with a grin, "if you'd only thought about it in time."

"That's what I'm trying to tell you. We've got to pull ourselves
together and get out into the world, instead of moping and rot-
ting away in this Travnik mildew. Let's get a little glory before
we die. I've been saying it over and over, but all I hear from you
two is, 'No, don't. Wait. We'll do it today. Let's do it tomorrow.'
So what do you expect . . . ?"

Saying this, the Swaying Hodja resolutely snatched the
brandy glass off his *tambura*, filled it to the brim, and tossed it
back sharply.

Neither Hamza nor Musa commented any more on his loud
musings. With deft, practiced movements, they too reached for
their glasses and helped themselves to the flask in the grass. Left
to himself, the little Swaying Hodja sank into that proud and
disdainful silence which is the aftermath of hard-fought bouts
and great feats of valor, the kind that never receive their just
recognition and due reward. Sullen, his chin on his chest, his
right hand on his unbuttoned shirt, he gazed absently in front of
him. "Three long years she ailed . . ." His doleful baritone
burst forth once again, as if another person were singing from
inside.

Hamza coughed and perked up. "Good luck to you, Murad,
you old war horse! You'll be going yet, by the will of Allah. Wait
and see, you'll be on your way. The world will find out who
Murad is and the stuff he's made of, where he comes from and
who his people are."

"Your health, my friend," the Swaying Hodja said, deeply
moved, raising his glass wearily like a man whose arms were
heavy with the weight of glory.

Time passed again. Musa lay quietly, unmoving, and he
floated up and soared on the breeze and on the warm exhalation

of the earth under him, freed, at least for a while, from the laws
of gravity and the shackles of time.

Over the Travnik valley, daylight seemed to grow more limpid
and incandescent, glittering with the pure light of the sun under
the ultramarine dome of the sky.

21

When at the beginning of the year 1812 signs began to multiply,
and rumors began to spread, about a likely new war, Daville
recoiled from those voices with the pained shudder of a man
who knows what labors and anguish lie ahead.

"Dear God! Dear God!" he muttered to himself, with a deep,
drawn-out sigh, slumping in his chair and pressing the palm of
his right hand over his eyes.

It was the old story all over again, like two years before about
this time, like those earlier years 1805 and 1806. And everything
would repeat itself: the unrest and the worries, the pervading
doubts and the sense of shame and loathing; and with it all, an
abject hope that this time, too, everything might somehow end
up well—this one more time!—and that life (this incongruous,
sad, sweet, one and only life!), the life of empires, of human
society, his own life and the life of his family, might somehow
remain stable and enduring; that this trial might be the last;
that there would be an end to this kind of existence in which a
man was hurled up high and then plummeted earthward as in a
swing run amuck, with just enough breath left in him to prove
that he was alive. Doubtless it would all end up again with bulletins of victory, with advantageous peace treaties, but who
could stand a life like this, a life that slowly and inexorably
crushed one's spirit and ate away at one's conscience, who
could find it in himself to go on paying the price such an existence demanded? What could a man give who had already given
his all, whose strength had been wrung out of him? And still
they were asked to keep on giving all they had and to accomplish
the impossible, so that these eternal wars might finally be won
and a man might take a breath and snatch a moment of peace
and stability.

"Peace, a little peace! Peace, peace," he thought aloud, and the word was enough to lull him into a half-sleep.

But before his closed eyelids, under the cool palm of his hand, there suddenly rose up the forgotten visage of the forgotten von Mitterer, sallow and woebegone, his deep wrinkles filled with greenish shadows, the ends of his pomaded mustache standing up stiffly, an unhealthy light burning in his dark eyes. It was with the same face, in this same room, this time last year, that von Mitterer had told him, in a voice of amiable equivocation, that next spring there was "sure to be quite a bit of noise." (Yes, that was the exact barrack phrase he used!) And now he came back, implacably punctual, like some soulless, pedantic apparition, to remind him of that prophecy and tell him again that peace was an illusion and they were not to have it. Bitterly and with a kind of malice, as it had done the year before, when they were parting, the head of von Mitterer spoke the words: "*Il y aura beaucoup de tapage.*"

Ugly words, spoken in an ugly voice, with a distinct edge of perfidy.

"*Beaucoup de tapage . . . de tapage . . . de tapage . . .*"

As if echoing the words, von Mitterer's face began to nod in rhythm, growing more and more bloodless and deathlike. And then it was no longer von Mitterer; it was the pale and bloody severed head on the tip of the sans-culotte pike which he had glimpsed one morning from his Paris window more than twenty years before.

Daville started, dropped the hand from his eyes and shattered his dream; with this he exorcised the apparition that had come to frighten him in his exhaustion and helplessness. The big wooden clock ticked steadily in the uncomfortably warm room.

The spring began badly for Daville.

The circular instructions, the growing frequency of couriers, and the shrilling tone of the press all seemed to indicate that big things and new campaigns were in the offing, that the whole war apparatus of the Empire was once again in motion. But Daville had no one he could discuss it with, no other opinions to compare with his own; there was no one to help him examine the general outlook and verify his doubts and fears, so that, in the light of a rational give and take, he might decide which part of his fear was real and which was only a figment of his imagination, apprehension, and weariness. Like all isolated people who are weak and worn out, whose self-confidence may be shaken from one moment to the next, Daville sought to find in the words and looks of others some confirmation and support for his opinions and actions, instead of searching for them in himself. But the misery was that while talk and advice were always plentiful, he could not have them when he most needed them; there was no one he could talk to clearly and openly about the things that truly worried him.

Von Paulich tended to his own business, polite and cool, handsomely unapproachable, the imperial Austrian robot who did not waver or make mistakes. When they saw each other, they talked about Virgil or discussed the intentions of the European courts, but in none of these talks could Daville get around to testing the accuracy of his fears and forebodings, because von Paulich confined himself to decorous phrases like "alliance and family ties that exist between the Austrian and French courts," or "the farsighted wisdom of those who nowadays jointly guide the destinies of European states," and obstinately avoided saying anything clear or outright about the future. And Daville himself lacked the courage to ask those direct questions, for fear of giving himself away; instead he peered feverishly into the man's strange dark blue eyes and was met again and again by the same unrelenting forbidding reserve.

Talking to D'Avenat was no help either. He only recognized tangible things and practical questions. Anything that fell short of that stage of development did not exist for him.

There remained his visits to the Vizier Ibrahim Pasha, and his talks with the people at the Residency. What he heard from the Vizier was a rehash of things repeated down the years, always the same, by now quite ossified, like the man himself.

It was the first week of April, a time of the year when the Vizier grew restless and irritable at the prospect of having to fit out an army against Serbia, when he was swamped by demands and instructions from Istanbul that far exceeded his strength and patience.

"They don't know what they're doing over there," he complained to Daville, who had been hoping to ease his own mind through this conversation. "They don't know what they want, that's all I can say. They want me to move together with the Pasha of Nish, and at the same time, so that we should attack the rebels on two sides. But they don't know, and don't want to know, what my real resources are. How can my oxen keep pace with their horses? Where will I find ten thousand men and feed them and fit them out? You can't put three Bosnians together without a squabble about who's to be first—none of them would dream of being the last, of course. And even supposing I could manage all this, what good are these Bosnian heroes when they refuse to fight on the other side of the Drina and Sava? Their bravery and proverbial heroism go as far as the Bosnian frontier and no farther."

It was obvious that the Vizier was unable to think or speak of anything else at that moment. He became almost animated, if one could use that word in describing him; he waved his hand as if trying to chase away a persistent fly.

"Furthermore, one shouldn't waste words on Serbia, it's not worth talking about. Ah, if Sultan Selim were alive, it would all be quite different."

And once the subject of the unfortunate Selim III was broached, then, for that day at least, it was useless to expect conversation on any other topic. And that was exactly what happened.

About this time Daville sent a special gift to Tahir Beg, the Vizier's Secretary, just to be able to visit him and hear what he had to say.

After having vegetated through the winter, more in bed than on his feet, Tahir Beg was now beginning to revive; he was more agile and talkative, almost unnaturally lively. His face was already lightly touched with the April sun and his eyes shone as though he were a little drunk.

The Secretary talked breathlessly and feverishly about Travnik, about the winters they had spent there together (it was his fourth and Daville's fifth), about the feelings of friendship and the bond of common suffering which their long stay in the town had forged between the Vizier and his staff and Daville and his family; about Daville's children; about the spring; about a great many other things that may have sounded irrelevant on the surface but were in fact close to Tahir Beg's heart in his present mood. Quietly, with a small but lively smile, as though he were saying something that had only just occurred to him and which he hoped would convince Daville no less than himself, he said like a man reciting: "Spring makes up for everything, straightens everything out. As long as the fields keep flowering, over and over again, as long as there are people who look at them and enjoy them, everything is in the best possible order."

With a brown, sunburned hand, the nails of which were strangely ribbed and bluish in color, he made a movement indicating how all things evened out.

"And there will always be people to do that, because those who cannot or don't know how to see the sun and the flowers pass on constantly, and new ones arrive in their places. As the poet says, 'Children replenish and purify the river of mankind.' "

Daville nodded approvingly and had to smile, looking at the man's beaming face, but privately he thought: "He's saying these things because, for a reason God only knows, they mean something to him at this moment." And he began at once to maneuver the conversation from spring and children to empires and wars. Tahir Beg took up every subject and discussed it with the same mild and smiling eagerness, as if he were opening a new, fascinating book.

"Yes, we too hear that new wars are imminent. Who shall join whom and who shall fight whom, we'll soon see. But that there will be war this summer, that's certain."

"You really think so?" Daville asked, dismayed.

"According to what one reads in your newspapers, it would seem certain," the Secretary replied with a smile. "And I have no reason to disbelieve them." Tahir Beg tilted his head a little and gave Daville a very bright, almost piercing look, a look reminiscent of that of a wild marten or weasel, nimble little beasts that kill and gorge on blood but will not touch the flesh of the slain animal. "I say certain," the Secretary went on, "because, to the best of my knowledge, the Christian powers have not stopped fighting one another in all these centuries."

"The Eastern, non-Christian states haven't either," replied Daville.

"No, that's true. But the difference is that the Moslem countries wage war in an open manner, without hypocrisy or prevarication. War has always been an important part of their mission in the world. Islam came to Europe under a warrior's banner and has managed to stay here up to the present day either by making its own wars or by taking advantage of the wars among the Christian powers. And, as far as I know, the Christian states condemn wars so strongly they're always blaming one another for starting them. But while they're condemning them, they never cease to wage them."

"There's much truth in what you say," Daville encouraged the Secretary, hoping at last to make him talk about the Russo-

French conflict and hear his opinion, "but do you really believe that the Tsar of Russia will risk incurring the wrath of the greatest Christian ruler and the most irresistible army in all Christianity?"

The eyes of the Secretary lit up more strongly and became more piercing still. "I have not the vaguest idea about the Tsar's intentions, my respected friend, but allow me to draw your attention to something I observed a long time ago, namely, that war is constantly raging over the face of Christian Europe, only it keeps shifting from here to there, just as a man carrying an ember of coal in the palm of his hand would shift it from one side to another to avoid burning himself. At this particular moment the ember happens to be somewhere on the European frontiers of Russia."

Daville began to realize that he was not, after all, going to learn anything here that was either interesting to him or had some bearing on his uncertainty, for this man, like the Vizier, was only saying things which his inner need of the moment compelled him to say. Nevertheless, he decided to make one more attempt, a blunt and direct one. "It is no secret," he said, "that the principal aim of Russian policy is to liberate subject peoples of the same faith, which, of course, would include these territories here, under the Ottoman rule. Therefore, many consider it a foregone conclusion that Russia's real war plans are directed against Turkey, rather than against countries of western Europe."

The Secretary refused to be sidetracked. "What are you to do? Foregone conclusions don't always turn out to be right. But if the thing that 'many consider' should really come about, then it is not difficult to foresee what the course of events would be. Everyone knows that these territories have been at the point of the sword, that they shall be defended by the sword, and, if it must be, lost by the sword. None of which changes what I have said by one iota."

With that Tahir Beg stubbornly went back to his original subject. "If you will think back with an open mind you will see that wherever Christian Europe extends her authority and brings in her customs and her kind of order, war usually follows —war between Christian and Christian. You can see it in Africa, in America, in the European territories of the Ottoman Empire that have gone to some Christian state. And if it ever happens, through the will of Fate, that we should lose these territories to some Christian country, as you mentioned just now, it will be the same story here. It might easily happen, in fact, that in another hundred or two hundred years, on this very spot where you and I at this moment are discussing the possibility of a Moslem-Christian war, Christians will mark their liberation from Ottoman rule by mutual bloodletting and slaughter."

Tahir Beg laughed aloud at his vision. Daville smiled too out of politeness, for he was anxious to keep things amiable and artless, even though he felt displeased and fretful over the drift of the conversation.

What remained of their talk was garnished and scented by Tahir Beg with fresh reflections on the wonders of spring, on youth—which was eternal, even though the young ones were not—on friendship and good-neighborly feelings that made even harsh countries tolerable and pleasant to live in.

Daville listened to them with a smile, which he hoped would mask his dissatisfaction.

On the way back from the Residency, as often happened, he exchanged impressions with D'Avenat. "How does Tahir Beg seem to you?" he asked, by way of opening the conversation.

"He's a sick man," D'Avenat said flatly and promptly fell silent.

Their horses came together again.

"He seems to have recovered quite well this time."

"That's just what's wrong with him, he's recovering all the time. If he keeps recovering at this rate, one day he'll . . ."

"You mean . . . ?" Daville left his question unfinished.

"Yes, exactly. Did you see his hands and eyes? The man is just barely this side of death, by the grace of drugs," D'Avenat said in a low voice, but firmly and gravely.

Daville did not reply. Now that his attention was drawn to it and he remembered part of the Secretary's talk without the benefit of his peculiar smile and manner, he did find it disconnected, exaggerated, and not quite normal.

Yet all that D'Avenat had said, and especially the crude and brusque manner in which he had said it, grated on Daville in a way he could not explain to himself, like some painful discord or a personal affront. He spurred his horse a length ahead of D'Avenat's. It was a sign that the conversation was over. "Strange," thought Daville, his eyes resting on the broad shoulders of the Vizier's sergeant who rode ahead and made way for them, "strange how no one here shows any pity or natural com-

passion which among us is a common and spontaneous reaction
to another person's suffering. Here one had to be a beggar or a
cripple or have his home burned down from under him to
arouse any pity at all. There is no pity here between men of
the same rank and station. One might live here a hundred years
and never get used to their heartless way of talking, to their
bleak morality and uncouth directness. One might never
become thick-skinned enough not to be pained and offended by
it."

Like a sudden loud explosion, the voice of the muezzin from
the Speckled Mosque rang out above them. The voice rose and
vibrated with a forceful, aggressive, shrilling kind of piety that
seemed to burst from the fullness of the muezzin's chest. It was
the hour of noon. A second muezzin, on a minaret somewhere
out of sight, joined him; his deep ringing voice trailed after the
voice of the bazaar muezzin like a devout and eager shadow.
The voices accompanied Daville and his escort all the way back
to the Consulate—mingling, catching up, and fading in the air
above them.

About that time, on the Feast of the Annunciation, there came
the anniversary of the christening of Daville's little daughter.
Daville took advantage of it to invite to lunch von Paulich and
the parish priest of Dolats, Fra Ivo Yankovich, with his young
curate. The friars accepted the invitation, but it was obvious
right away that their attitude had not changed. They were both
overpolite, avoided Daville's eyes and looked past his shoulder,
in a furtive, oblique fashion. Daville knew this look of the Bosnians (long years and many dealings with the Bosnians had
seen to it), and he knew well too that whatever was hidden behind it was quite outside his powers of persuasion. He was no
stranger to the crabbed and mysterious inwardness of these
Bosnians, who were as touchy about themselves as they were
harsh and callow when the boot was on the other foot. And he
braced himself for this luncheon as though it were a tricky
game which he knew in advance he could not win but which
had to be played all the same.

The conversation before the meal and at the table was confined to general topics; the note was one of genteel but harmless
insincerity. Fra Ivo ate and drank with such gusto that his normally flushed face turned a faint shade of purple and his tongue

loosened up. The copious meal had quite the opposite effect on his young curate, who grew paler and more taciturn.

As they were having their first smoke, Fra Ivo deposited the large fist of his right hand on the table—a fist tufted with red hair at the joints—and, without any preamble, waded into a lecture on the relations between the Holy See and Napoleon.

To Daville's surprise, the friar seemed to be quite at home with the many different aspects of the struggle between the Pope and the Emperor. He knew in detail about the National Council which Napoleon had called in Paris the year before and about the resistance of the French bishops, just as he knew all the places the Pope had been banished to and all the various pressures to which he had been subjected.

Daville set out to defend and explain the French conduct (his voice sounded lame and unconvincing even to himself). With it he tried to guide the conversation to the current international situation, hoping to hear what the canon, and his brothers and the whole congregation with him, thought and expected of the immediate future. But the canon had no interest in generalities. He could only talk about things that were congenial to his passionate nature and his fanatical beliefs; as for the rest, he merely glanced down the table toward von Paulich, who was talking to Mme Daville, as if deferring to him. It was obvious that the canon had little use for either the French or the Russians. In that tart voice of his, which was strangely thin and strident for so hefty a man, he kept painting a dark picture of a nation that treated the Church and its anointed Head so poorly.

"I can't say, *monsieur le Consul,* whether your army will march against Russia or against some other enemy," Fra Ivo said to Daville, "but I do know for certain, and tell you so openly, that it will find no blessing anywhere, no matter where it marches, because treating the Church like that . . ."

Here followed a fresh series of accusations with quotations from the last Papal Bull against Napoleon about the "new and ever deeper wounds inflicted daily upon the Apostolic authority, the rights of the Church, the sanctity of the Faith, and upon Us personally."

Seeing him so humorless, monolithic, and unshakable, Daville was struck by a thought that had crossed his mind off and on for many years and was as pertinent that day as it had ever been: that this man, for some reason, was filled up to his gills with chagrin and defiance, which spilled over with every word he uttered and gave an acid edge to his shrillness, and that everything he thought and spoke of, even the Pope himself, was only a handy, welcome excuse to get the gall and the spite out of his system and give it expression.

At the canon's elbow sat the motionless young curate, a silent miniature of the parish priest and his exact duplicate in manner and attitude. He too kept the clenched fist of his right hand on the table, save that the fist was white and delicate and the red hair on it no more than a down.

At the other end of the table Mme Daville and von Paulich were in a lively tête-à-tête. Ever since she had first met him, she had been surprised and charmed by his genuine interest in everything that had to do with home and household and by his remarkable knowledge of domestic affairs and needs (just as Daville had been astonished and charmed with his fluency in Virgil and Ovid, and von Mitterer, in his time, had been amazed and intimidated by his versatility in military matters). Whenever they met, they talked long and pleasantly on these subjects. At the moment they were discussing furnishings and how to preserve and keep things in the peculiar climate of their present domicile.

The Colonel's knowledge was indeed wide and inexhaustible. He approached each one of these topics as though it were the only one that interested him for the time being, and on each he spoke with the same cool and poised detachment untainted by anything personal or ambiguous. Now he was discussing the effects of humidity on different kinds of wood in furniture and on the sea grass and horsehair in the upholstery, and did so with the assured knowledge drawn from experience and also with a certain scientific objectivity, as though the subject were furniture in general and not just his own possessions or his likes and dislikes.

The Colonel spoke in a slow and bookish but choice French that was a refreshing change from the bastardized vocabulary and rapid-fire Levantine delivery which had been so jarring and discomforting in von Mitterer. Here and there Mme Daville helped him by furnishing a word he could not find right away. She was delighted to be able to talk with this courteous, precise man about the things that were foremost in her mind and around which her life revolved. In her conversation, as in her work and prayer, she was gentle and forthright, unwavering and free from prejudice, staunch and confident in her acceptance of heaven and earth and anything that time might bring or men might accomplish.

Watching and listening to all these people around him, Daville thought: they are at ease and content, they all seem to know exactly what they want, at this moment anyway, and I am the only one who's confused and afraid of tomorrow, and tired and fretful, condemned to hide the fact and carry it inside me like a secret, anxious not to give myself away even by a sign.

His musing was interrupted by Fra Ivo who got up abruptly, as always, with a sharp reminder to his curate, as though it was his fault that they had sat around so long, and shouted that it was late and they had a long way to go and there was work waiting for them back home. This increased the chilly atmosphere of the gathering.

That same spring Travnik saw the arrival of the Metropolitan Kallinik and the suffragan bishop Joannike, who came on the business of the Orthodox Church. Wishing to find out what they thought about the events in prospect, Daville invited them to lunch.

The Metropolitan was a stout, lymphatic, sickly man, wearing thick-lensed spectacles that gave his eyes a fearfully distorted and shapeless look as if they were about to spill and trickle away at any moment. He expressed himself in the unctuous and suave manner of expatriate Greeks, and his comments on the great powers were tactful and conciliatory; he was careful to give each one his due. All told, he operated with a limited set of phrases which he applied to things and concepts alike, all of them favorable and affirmative without exception, and he used them apropos of anything that was said to him, by a sort of rule of thumb, not choosing them particularly, indeed sometimes quite out of context. The cynical overpoliteness, so often found in elderly clergymen, thinly veiled his utter indifference to everything that other people might be saying or to things that could usefully be said on a subject.

Bishop Joannike, on the other hand, was a different type altogether. He was a large heavy monk, with an overgrown black beard, a cross expression always on his face, and something brusque and military in his whole bearing, as if beneath his black cassock he wore a breastplate and heavy equipment. The Turks had long suspected this bishop of being implicated in the Serbian rebellion but had never been able to prove it.

His replies to Daville's queries were short, but firm and candid. "You would like to know whether I'm for the Russians, and I tell you that we are for those who help us to stay alive and work in freedom. And you, at least, who live here, can see how things are and what we have to put up with. And so it's no wonder . . ."

The Metropolitan turned to the bishop and gave him an admonishing look out of his expressionless eyes, watering hugely behind their thick lenses, but the bishop would not be stopped.

"The Christian states are at one another's throats instead of settling their differences and working together to put an end to this misfortune once and for all. This has been going on for hundreds of years, and now you would like to know whose side we're on . . ."

The Metropolitan stirred again and, seeing that a glance was not enough, spoke up quickly in a prayerful tone of voice: "May the Lord bless and uphold all Christian powers, which are God-sent and God-nurtured. We never cease to pray . . ."

Now it was the bishop's turn to interrupt the Metropolitan, and that rather sharply: "We are for Russia, monsieur, and for the liberation of Orthodox Christians from the antichrist. That's what we're for, and don't believe anyone who tells you otherwise."

Here the Metropolitan broke in again and made some affable observation that consisted almost entirely of honeyed adjectives, doing so in bits and pieces, and not very accurately.

Daville watched the dour-faced bishop. His breath came in quick asthmatic puffs and his wheezing voice was unsteady and ragged, with a distinct rasp in it, like the bursts of an obscure, long-suppressed fury that seemed to fill him up to his Adam's apple and escaped from him with every word and every gesture.

Daville did his best to explain to the Metropolitan and the bishop the aims of his government and to place them in as good a light as possible, but his diffidence increased as he went on, for the look of angered slight did not leave the bishop's face for a moment and the Metropolitan did not seem to care particularly one way or another; indeed he seemed to listen to all human speech as though it were a jumble of nonsensical sounds and gave all of it the same affable and vacuous inattention, the same honeyed insincere assent.

The prelates had come to the Consulate in the company of

Pakhomi, the pale and haggard monk who looked after the Orthodox church in Travnik. This ailing bent man, with the pinched and sour face of a person who is never free from dyspepsia, seldom visited the Consulate and regularly declined all invitations, pleading ill-health or fear of the Turks. Whenever Daville met him and tried, after a friendly greeting, to engage him in conversation, he would double up even lower and twist his face, his eyes would sidle furtively (those Bosnian eyes Daville knew so well!), and he would shy away from his gaze and look up from under, obliquely, past one or the other of his shoulders. D'Avenat was the only person to whom he sometimes talked more freely.

Forced that day to accompany his superiors, he sat cramped and still, a burdensome guest, on the edge of his chair, as if planning to flee at any moment, and stared in front of him the whole time, not saying a word. But two or three days after the Metropolitan had left Travnik, when D'Avenat met him on the road and began to talk to him "in his own way," the sallow and frail monk suddenly came alive and found his tongue. His eyes sparkled up and didn't flinch away. One word led to another, the conversation grew livelier. D'Avenat tried to draw him out by saying that any people, regardless of religion, who expected something of the future, had better look to the all-powerful French Emperor and not to Russia, whom the French were sure to vanquish that summer, thus removing the last opposition to their "unified Europe."

At that the monk's large and normally tight mouth opened wide, displaying a row of white, regular, and wolflike teeth whose healthy ferocity one would not have expected in so small and delicate a face; the corners of his mouth dimpled away in a couple of surprising lines, new to D'Avenat, expressing a roguish, mocking sort of mirth; the monk threw his head back and roared a hearty, scornful laugh that flabbergasted even D'Avenat. It lasted only a moment. Immediately afterwards the monk's face shriveled back to its old rumpled size and grew peaked, diminutive, and frail. Turning away a little, he glanced around quickly to make sure that they were alone, then brought his face close to D'Avenat's right ear and said in a rich, fruity voice that would have gone much better with the earlier laughing expression than it did with the one he now wore: "Listen to what I'm telling you, neighbor. Knock that idea out of your head!"

Leaning over confidentially, the monk said this in a friendly indulgent tone of voice, as though he were making a gift of some value. Then, with a breezy greeting, he was on his way, steering clear of the bazaar and the main streets, as he always did, and taking the side alleys instead.

22

Things were fast coming to a head for these foreigners who had drifted in and become stranded in the narrow, damp valley and were condemned to live there for indeterminable stretches of time, under extraordinary stipulations. The unfamiliar conditions in which they found themselves had the effect of quickening the inner tendencies they had brought with them when they came, and drove each of them more decisively and mercilessly in the direction marked out for him by his own instincts. In the local alchemy of things, these drives took on a form and momentum which, under different circumstances, might never have come about.

Already in the first few months after von Paulich's arrival it became fairly clear that relations between the new Consul-General and the interpreter Nicholas Rotta were strained and were bound to lead to a clash and, sooner or later, to a break; for it would have been hard to find two people more unlike each other and more predestined to misunderstand and foil each other.

The cool, laconic, and sober Colonel, who cast around him an atmosphere of sharp, crystalline frost and clarity, bewildered and irritated the vain and touchy interpreter by his very presence and stirred in him the old convulsive tangle of uncertainties which had lain dormant and quiescent up to that moment. It would have been inaccurate to say that the aversion of the two men was reciprocal, because, in fact, it was Rotta who quailed away from the Colonel as from a bleak and monolithic iceberg; even worse, by some inescapable quirk of fate, he kept coming back and lunging at it again and again.

It is hard to imagine that two such clever, self-possessed, and cold people would have a devastating effect on each other, but that was the case here. Rotta had worked himself into a state of inner despair and laceration in which this superior of his was bound to mean his utter ruin. The calm and all but inhuman impartiality of the Colonel could not fail to act as poison on the already poisoned interpreter. If Rotta's chief had been someone soft and permissive like von Mitterer, or someone blustering, unpredictable, and given to human passions, even of the worst kind, he might still have held out somehow. With the former type he would have thrived on the softness; with the latter, his own dark and conflicting urges might have found a point of contact and reassurance in combat with the other man's passions, and in this steady attrition and clashing he might have kept his balance. But against a superior like the Colonel, Rotta could only hurl himself like a frenzied creature against a wall of ice or an imaginary shaft of light.

In his very ideas, his methods and procedures, von Paulich represented a marked and grave change for the worse, as far as the interpreter was concerned. To begin with, Rotta was far less essential to him than he had been to von Mitterer, to whom he had long become indispensable. To von Mitterer he had been a kind of shelter from the roughest and most wearying chores of the service, a kind of glove for the dirtiest work. Then too in many ways, and increasingly so in the last few years, the interpreter had become a sort of Gray Eminence. Whenever, at times of family crisis or official troubles, von Mitterer fell prey to a momentary paralysis of the will, made acute by his exhaustion or liver ailment, Rotta had been there to hold him up, to take "things" in his own hands, and in doing so had given the flagging man a sense of relief and grateful dependence. As for "things" themselves, he had never had any difficulty in settling them, since, as a rule, they were not complicated; they had only seemed hopeless and unsolvable to von Mitterer, in his condition at that particular moment.

All this, of course, was quite unthinkable with the new chief. With von Paulich, all work was as plain and regular as a chessboard, on which he moved like a calm and deliberate player who ponders long and feels no anxiety before a move and no doubt after it, who needs no advice, support, or guidance from anyone.

Moreover, von Paulich's conduct of business took away the last gratification left to the interpreter in his barren and unsuccessful life. His arid browbeating manner toward his juniors and office visitors, toward all those who either depended on him or could not retaliate, was for Rotta a pleasure, a wretched one it was true, but the last and only pleasure amidst the chaos and debris of his existence, a wan illusion of strength and a visible mark of that superiority for which he had vainly sacrificed his energy, his youth, and his soul.

After a dressing-down of this kind, in which, puffed up, red in the face, his legs astraddle, he had harangued and shouted down some wretch who dared not or did not know how to answer him, the interpreter would feel—for a moment it was true, but a thrilling moment—a delicious and heady satisfaction at having crushed something, having shattered and routed someone. He would stand over the silenced and humbled opponent and his own thrill of happiness would seem to lift him high above the earthly creatures, yet not too high either, just high enough for them to see him, to measure and feel his greatness. And now the Colonel took away from him even this mirage of spurious happiness.

His very presence now discouraged such behavior. Under the gaze of his cold, dark blue eyes no illusion could hold out for long and every self-deception would crumble and vanish in the void from which it had sprung.

Right at the outset, von Paulich had warned Rotta that there was a way of talking to people quietly and of getting their cooperation in a decent and civil manner. In any case, he did not want any member of the Consulate to use that tone with anyone, either in the building or in the town. The interpreter tried, for the first and last time, to influence the Consul and impose his own views. Rotta, with whom arrogance and bullying had become second nature, felt all but paralyzed in this man's presence. His lips twitched at the corners, his eyelids drooped even more heavily on his tilted head, he clicked his heels together and said brittlely, "Just as you wish, Herr Oberstleutnant," and with that he left.

Whether he forgot this or whether he wanted to test the stamina and quality of the new chief, Rotta went twice more against his explicit orders and gave his juniors a noisy and offensive tongue-lashing. The second time this happened, the Colonel summoned the interpreter and told him that if it occurred once more, even in the mildest form, he would immediately apply the clause in the regulations covering repeated grave breaches of discipline. As he was saying this, Rotta could see his blue eyes narrow and taper to a hard murderous light at the

corners, a light that completely changed his look and the expression on his face from one moment to the next. From that
time on the interpreter, thoroughly cowed, withdrew into himself and nursed his hatred of the Colonel out of sight and in
secret, but with all the intensity and fury he had earlier
wreaked on his victims.

Von Paulich, who treated Rotta's case with the same cool
equanimity he showed toward everything else in the world, tried,
in turn, to use him as little as possible. He sent him as a courier
to Brod and Kostaynitsa; he even hoped to see von Mitterer
assigned to another job in which he might be able to use Rotta
and ask for him. He himself made no move to get him out of
Travnik. Ironically enough, it never crossed Rotta's mind to
leave this position which, as he realized himself, was not doing
him any good; instead, like one bedeviled, he continued to circle
and fluster around his cold and brilliant superior and clashed
with him at regular intervals, each time more sharply, though
all of it loomed bigger in his mind than it was in reality.

D'Avenat, who knew, or at least guessed, everything that
was going on in Travnik, soon got wind of Rotta's predicament
in the Consulate and promptly began to speculate how and
where, in the ripeness of time, the French interests might benefit by it. Once, during one of those typical conversations which
the two interpreters sometimes struck up after meeting accidentally in the bazaar or on the way to the Residency, D'Avenat
jokingly told Rotta that if anything happened he could always
count on finding asylum in the French Consulate. Rotta parried
his joke with a joke of his own.

After the first clashes, there was an ominous calm between
von Paulich and his interpreter that lasted a whole year. Had
the Colonel loaded the interpreter with too much work or harassed him with unfair demands, or had he thrown tantrums and
displayed ill will, Rotta might have learned to live with it and
might perhaps have found the patience to bear up with his new
chief and last out to the end. But von Paulich's Olympian attitude and the way in which he simply ignored Rotta's personality
were bound, sooner or later, to lead to a break.

The actual rupture took place in the spring of 1812. The
diminutive, hunchbacked interpreter could not live unnoticed
in this way, reduced to his basic duties, frustrated in all his
deepest instincts and ingrained habits. Losing his self-restraint,
he abused the servants and junior office clerks and in quarreling

with them addressed certain unmistakable threats and messages to his chief, in his desperate need for some relief. In the end, he clashed with von Paulich himself. When the Colonel coldly informed him that he was throwing the book at him and sending him away to Brod, Rotta found strength, for the first time, to challenge him openly and impertinently, asserting at the top of his voice that the Consul had no such authority and that he, Rotta, would perhaps send him packing, and much farther from Travnik at that. Von Paulich ordered Rotta's effects to be thrown out of the house and forbade him to enter the Consulate. At the same time he informed the town Mayor that Nicholas Rotta was no longer in the service of the Austrian Consulate-General, that he no longer enjoyed imperial protection, and that his presence in Travnik was undesirable.

Dismissed, Rotta at once went to D'Avenat and through him applied for the protection of the French Consulate.

Not since the advent of the consuls and the establishment of the consulates had there been such a scandal and uproar in Travnik. Not even the strange conversion and mysterious death of Mario Cologna had made such a stir or set so many tongues wagging, so many people scurrying. Cologna's death had happened at a time of general unrest and had, indeed, been a part of it, whereas now the times were quiet. Moreover, the "Illyrian doctor" was dead and silent forever, whereas Rotta was more alive and noisier than ever.

Rotta's defection from his Consul and his country was generally regarded as a great success for D'Avenat. D'Avenat shrugged it off and bore himself like a modest and reasonable winner. In reality, he was scheming to make the best possible use of Rotta's quandary, but he was going about it carefully, without unseemly haste.

The event, like so many others, left Daville with a feeling of unease, divided in himself. He could not, dared not, ignore all the advantages that Rotta's defection offered to the French cause, the more so as the hunchback interpreter, driven by circumstances and swept along by his own passions, was edging closer and closer to open treason and was revealing, bit by bit, all he knew about the activities and intentions of his superiors. On the other hand, he felt pained and humiliated at the thought of having to use his official reputation as a cloak for the plotting of two interpreters, low and unscrupulous Levantines, against a gentleman like von Paulich, a man of honor and intelligence.

In his heart of hearts he hoped that the whole thing—once D'Avenat had made all the use of it he could—might simmer down and be hushed up. But that was not what the two interpreters had at heart, and Rotta especially. In his fight against von Paulich he had at last found a worthy object for his denied and repressed passions and appetites. He sent long letters not only to the Consul but also to the commanding officer at Brod and to the Ministry in Vienna, presenting his case but suppressing, of course, the fact that he was in touch with the French Consulate. Accompanied by a kavass from the French Consulate, he rode out to the Austrian Consulate and demanded some of his things that were still there, he quarreled loudly and made public scenes, he invented new demands, ran about town in a huff, went up to the Residency and to the town Mayor. In short, he basked in his own scandal like a demented woman who has lost all shame.

Von Paulich kept his composure. Nevertheless, he made the mistake of formally asking the town Mayor to arrest Rotta as a common thief of official documents, which forced Daville to write to the Mayor informing him that Rotta had placed himself under French protection and could therefore not be arrested and prosecuted. He sent a copy of the letter to von Paulich, adding that he regretted the whole thing but could not act otherwise, as Rotta, who was perhaps a man of unstable and volatile temperament but otherwise an upright person, had placed himself under the French protection, which could not be denied to him.

Von Paulich replied bluntly, protesting the action of the French Consulate in giving asylum to paid spies, embezzlers, and traitors. He requested Daville to mark all his future letters to him as "not containing a reference to Rotta," for otherwise he would return them unopened, so long as this sordid dispute over the interpreter continued.

This further offended and saddened Daville, to whom this affair of Rotta's was becoming increasingly distasteful and troublesome.

The morose old town Mayor, finding himself in the middle of two contending consulates, one of them firmly pressing for Rotta's arrest and the other firmly opposing it, fell into a dither and was equally annoyed with both, and especially with Rotta. Several times a day he snorted and muttered aloud to himself: "The dogs are fighting, and in my own back yard!"

He notified the two consuls through one of his men that he would sooner hand in his resignation than permit the pair of them to squabble around Travnik while their emperors were at peace, and that across his already overburdened back. He would not wish to give umbrage to either of the consuls over anything, and particularly not over the question of this rabid little fellow who was, after all, no more than a lackey and an errand boy and as such hardly deserved to be the subject of conversation between imperial officers and people of rank. And, with much less ceremony, he advised Rotta to pipe down and keep what little head he had on his shoulders, since for many weeks now he had been a cause of upset to the leading people of the town, which up till now had been as peaceful as a temple of God; he would not be worth all this trouble even if he had a head of gold and the brain of a vizier. If he wanted to live on quietly and decently in Travnik, well and good; but if he chose to throw the town on its ear by dashing between the two consulates, stirring up trouble, and dragging in both the Turks and the Christians, he'd better take one of the two roads that led out of Travnik, the sooner and quicker the better.

And in fact Rotta had filled the town with his vendetta and dragged into it everyone he could. He had rented the upper floor in the house of one Pero Kalydzich, a single man who lived alone and had a bad reputation. He brought in gypsy blacksmiths and had them put up iron bars on his windows and fit all doors with special locks. Besides two good English pistols, which he kept under his pillow, he also bought a long musket with powder and shot. Afraid of being poisoned, he made his own food; he cleaned the place himself, for fear of thieves and tricks. His rooms were pervaded with that chilly bleakness that invests the living quarters of eccentrics and solitaries. Rags and refuse began to pile up, dust and soot settled on everything. The house, which had been quite humble to begin with, grew more neglected by the week, even from the outside.

Rotta himself began to change rapidly, to waste and disintegrate. He became careless of his dress and stopped caring about cleanliness. His shirts were soft and crumpled and he wore them over and over again; his black cravat was spattered with food, his shoes trampled and dirty. His hair, which had turned completely gray, now developed greenish and yellow streaks. His nails were black, he stopped shaving regularly, he began to reek of the kitchen and drink. In his bearing he was not the old Rotta any more. He no longer walked about with his head thrown back, swaggering and looking down his nose, but scurried around the town with a mincing, preoccupied step, whispering conspiratorially to those who were still willing to talk to him, or ranting against the Austrian Consul in some low-down pothouse, defiantly and at the top of his lungs, buying his listeners with drams of the brandy which he himself was beginning to consume in greater and greater quantities. Day by day the gilded veneer of his erstwhile dignity, his spurious power and gentility grew thinner and more threadbare.

So Nicholas Rotta lingered on in Travnik, convinced that he was waging a great fight against his mighty and various enemies. Blinded by his morbid hate, he never even noticed his own backsliding and transformation, or realized that on the way down he was retracing the whole long and tortuous road of his former climb. He never even felt how countless petty circumstances were fusing together to create an imperceptible but powerful stream that would carry him back into that life which he had left as a child in the slums of San Giusto in Trieste, right back into the world of ugly squalor and besetting vice from which he had run with all his strength for thirty years and which, for a long time now, he had believed was behind him.

23

Daville had no patience with petty superstitions, yet often caught himself entertaining them. One of these was to the effect that the summer months in Travnik were unlucky and usually brought along some unpleasant surprise or other. He told himself that this was entirely natural. All wars and rebellions usually began with the summer; the summer days were longer and people had more time, *ergo* more opportunity, for getting up all those follies and mischiefs which are a deep inner necessity to them. And after he had reasoned it all out very neatly, he would catch himself a few minutes later in the same thought: that summer brings trouble and that the summer months ("those without the letter r") are in every respect more dangerous than the others.

That summer, indeed, got off to a bad start.

One morning in May, which had begun rather well with a couple of hours of work on his Alexandrines, Daville was sitting with young Freycinet, who had come to report personally on the difficult situation at the French depot at Sarajevo and the various problems in the French transit commerce in Bosnia.

The young man sat on the veranda, among the potted flowers, and talked in his lively and quick southern manner.

It was his second year at Sarajevo. In all this time he had visited Travnik only once, but he had been in constant correspondence with the Consul-General. In his letters of late more and more space had been taken up with complaints about people and conditions at Sarajevo. The young man was completely disillusioned and discouraged. He had lost weight, the hair above his forehead was beginning to thin, his face had an unhealthy color. Daville noticed that his hands shook and that his voice was full of bitterness. Of that cool clarity, with which he had outlined his plans and intentions during his first visit the summer before, on this same terrace, there was not a vestige left. ("It's the East," thought Daville, with that unconsciously malevolent thrill one feels when discovering and observing the symptoms of one's own disease in other people. "The East has got into this young man's blood; it has sapped, unnerved, and embittered him!")

Young Freycinet was indeed bitter and fed up. That rankling dissatisfaction with everyone and everything which eats into and overcomes Westerners who come to work in these countries, had obviously got the better of him and he had not the strength to fight it or contain it.

His proposals were sweeping. The whole enterprise should be liquidated, the sooner the better, and they should look for an alternative route through some other territory where conditions of life and work were more human.

It was clear to Daville that the young man was infected with the "oriental toxin" and that he was in that phase of sickness in which, as in a fever, a man is incapable of seeing reality or forming a sober judgment and can only battle and flail, with every nerve and thought, against everything that surrounds him. This state of mind was by now so familiar to him that he could afford to play the part of the healthy, balanced elder who consoles and reassures. But the young man shrank from all consolation as though it were a personal slur and offense.

"No," he said bitterly, "they haven't the faintest idea in Paris about what goes on here. No one could possibly know. Only when you've lived and worked among these people can you get an inkling of how undependable, stuck-up, primitive, and treacherous these Bosnians can be. Only we can know it."

Daville thought he was hearing his own words, the same ones he'd spoken and put in letters so many times. But he listened to them attentively, not taking his eyes off the young man who fairly trembled with barely contained emotion and deep disgust. "So that's how I must have sounded to Desfosses and to all those others to whom I have so often said the same thing, in the same tone of voice, with the same show of nerves," Daville thought. Aloud, however, he tried to calm and soothe the excited young man. "Yes, conditions are hard, we know that from experience. But we have to be patient. In the long run French reason and pride are bound to overcome their conceit and quick tempers. Only we had better . . ."

"We'd better get out of here, *monsieur le Consul,* and as quickly as possible. Because we're going to lose our reason and pride, not to speak of the effort we've put in, and all for nothing. That much is certain, at least as far as my own work is concerned."

"The same sickness, the same symptoms," thought Daville, as he continued to calm him and reassure him that it was all a matter of patience and waiting, that the work cannot be simply abandoned, that in the great imperial plan for a Continental System and in the European economic organization as a whole Sarajevo was a vital point, thankless but vital, and that a slackening of effort at any point now might jeopardize the whole concept and damage the plans of the Emperor.

"This is our share of toil and bitterness and we have to accept it, no matter how hard it is. Even if we can't see the sense and direction of the plan on which we are collaborating, results are bound to show eventually, so long as each of us sticks to his post and doesn't give way. And we should bear in mind at all times that Providence has given us the greatest ruler in all the centuries, that he guides the destinies of all, including our own, and that we can blindly trust his leadership. It is not an accident that the fate of the world is in his hands.

His genius and lucky star guide every enterprise to a positive end. Believing in that, we can do our work quietly and confidently, in the face of the greatest difficulties."

Speaking slowly and calmly, Daville listened to himself in growing wonder: he was using words and arguments he had never been able to muster in his own daily waverings and doubts. He grew more and more eloquent and persuasive. He was experiencing the sensation of an old nurse who lulls a child to sleep with a long fairy tale and in the end gets drowsy herself and nods off beside the wide-awake child. By the time he finished talking he was relaxed and convinced of his own words, while the young man, whose life was being poisoned by the Sarajevo merchants and pack drivers, shook his head slowly and watched him bitterly, nibbling at his lips, with a twitching face that showed signs of bad digestion and overflowing spleen.

At that moment D'Avenat came in. After apologizing for the intrusion, he informed the Consul in an undertone that a courier had arrived from Istanbul the night before, bringing news of an epidemic in Ibrahim Pasha's harem. The plague that had been ravaging Istanbul for some weeks had spread to the Vizier's house on the Bosporus. In a short space of time fifteen people had died, mostly servants, but the Vizier's oldest daughter and a son of twelve years were also among them. The remaining inmates had fled to the mountains in the interior.

As he listened to D'Avenat's bad news, Daville could almost see the tall figure of the Vizier in front of him, dressed up in his gaudy clothes and leaning slightly to the left or right, as he always did, and now rocking under new blows.

On D'Avenat's advice and in accordance with wise oriental custom, they decided not to seek an immediate audience with the Vizier, but to let a few days go by, in which time the first shock of the tragedy would have passed.

When he resumed his conversation with Freycinet, Daville felt himself even more patient and understanding, steeled as it were by another person's misfortune. Boldly and without hesitation, he promised the young man that he would personally visit Sarajevo the following month in order to see, on the spot, what he could do with the authorities to improve the conditions for French transit commerce.

Three days later the Vizier received Daville in his summer divan on the upper floor.

From a blazing summer day Daville passed without any transition into the dusky, cool ground floor of the Residency, and shivered as if he had entered a catacomb. There was more light on the upper floor, yet there too the shade was heavy and cool in comparison with the heat and glitter of outdoors. One of the windows had been raised and a thick-leaved vine spilled lushly over the sill and into the room.

The Vizier sat in his usual place, unchanged, in his full ceremonial dress, but leaning to one side like an ancient tombstone. Seeing him like that, Daville tried to appear casual and unchanged himself, while concentrating hard on what he had to say about the misfortune that had occurred; he wanted to express it warmly and with circumspection, without specifically mentioning those who had died, and particularly not the women, while nevertheless showing his understanding and sympathy.

The Vizier made Daville's task easier by his usual unbending style, which perfectly matched his grim physical stiffness. Having listened to Daville's words, in D'Avenat's translation, almost without a movement or change in his expression, he wasted no words on the dead but passed on, forthwith, to the destinies and actions of the living.

"So the plague came to Istanbul and struck some districts where it has never struck before," the Vizier said in his grave cold voice, as if he were speaking through a mouth of stone. "We were not to be spared even that, it seems. The plague had to come, because we sinned. And I must be a sinner too, for it came into my house."

The Vizier fell silent, and Daville instructed the interpreter D'Avenat to say, in his capacity as doctor, that the nature of pestilence was such that even saintly, innocent people and homes were sometimes accidentally infected through a chance carrier of the dangerous germ.

The Vizier turned his head slowly and looked at D'Avenat for the first time, as if only just noticing him, with that blind look in his black eyes which, though open, seemed not to see, like eyes of marble; then he turned back to the Consul.

"No, it's because of sin, all because of sin. The people in the capital have lost their reason and honor. They have all gone mad with their scramble after luxury and vice. And they have no guidance from those on top. This would never have happened if Sultan Selim were alive. So long as he was alive and in power, sin was banished from the capital; drunkenness, mischief, and dissipation were driven back. But now . . ."

Once again the Vizier ran out of words, suddenly, like a mechanism that has run down; and again Daville tried to say something comforting and soothing, to explain how in the end sin and punishment must inevitably balance each other out and how, presumably, one day, there will also be an end to atonement.

The Vizier refused to be comforted. "God is one. He knows the measure," the Vizier said.

Through the open window came the twitter of unseen birds, whose hopping sent a tremor through the vine leaves that overflowed into the room. On the steep slope opposite that cut off the view, they could see fields of ripe wheat divided by green boundaries of grass and hawthorn thickets. Suddenly, in the silence that had fallen after the Vizier's words, they heard the shrill loud neighing of a colt somewhere on the slope.

The audience came to an end with another brief allusion to Sultan Selim, who had laid down his life as a martyr and saint. The Vizier was moved, although neither his voice nor his face showed it. "May God give you every joy with your children," he said as Daville began to take his leave.

Daville replied by expressing the hope that the Vizier's sorrow might soon give way to radiant joy.

"As for myself," said the Vizier, "I have lost so much in my life that I would be very happy indeed if I could now put on some plain clothes and hoe my garden far from the world and events. There is only one God!"

The Vizier uttered this as though it were a set and long rehearsed phrase, or as if it were a vision that was uppermost in his mind, possessing a special and deep significance for himself which others could not understand.

That summer of 1812, which had begun so badly, continued in the same vein.

During the last war, against the Fifth Coalition, in the autumn of 1810, Daville had had it much easier in many respects. In the first place, although his struggle with von Mitterer and his collaboration with General Marmont and the fortress commanders on the Austrian frontier had been difficult and tiring, they had at least filled his time and occupied his mind with concrete problems and tangible goals. Secondly, Napoleon's military campaign had gone well, from victory to victory, and, more important still, it had gone swiftly. Already the early autumn had brought the Peace of Vienna and at least a temporary quietus. This time, however, everything was distant and quite beyond grasping. The obscurity and the sheer gigantic size of it were frightening.

Having to center one's life and thoughts on the progress of an army somewhere on the steppes of Russia and having no clear idea about this army, its lines of advance, its resources and prospects, but having to guess and await developments, even the worst, while ambling up and down the steep garden paths around the Consulate—such was Daville's life in those summer and autumn months. And there was nothing to make his waiting easier, there was no one to help him!

Couriers came and went more often now but they brought scant news of the war. There was no comfort or reassurance to be had from official bulletins, in which strange names of unknown cities were mentioned, cities one never heard of before —Kovno, Vilna, Vitebsk, Smolensk. And the couriers themselves, usually full of tales and all kinds of news, were overworked, short-tempered, and silent. One missed even the untruths and wild speculation that normally filled the air at such times, which at least might rouse one and provide a welcome respite from brooding and uncertainty.

The work of transporting French cotton through Bosnia had finally settled down and was progressing quite well, or so at least it seemed in comparison with the worries and fears that hung over the larger enterprise going on in the far north. True, the pack drivers kept raising their prices, the peasants continued to steal cotton en route, the Turkish customs officials changed their minds all the time and their venality was bottomless. Freycinet wrote despairing letters, couched in the fevered tone of foreigners who have had to contend too long with unsuitable food, with intractable people and inimical conditions. Daville followed the all too familiar symptoms of the disease and sent back wise, moderate, and statesmanlike replies, counseling patience in the service of the Empire.

Yet even as he did this, he too was casting about desperately for some hopeful sign that would encourage him and quiet his own uncertainties and his hidden but nagging fear of it all. But there was nothing a man could hold on to or depend on. As always in such cases, as once it had happened with the young

captain from Novi, Daville felt himself surrounded by a living
wall of faces and eyes that were cold and dumb, as in a
wordless conspiracy, or else enigmatic, empty, and lying. Who
was there to turn to, who was there to ask, who might know the
truth and be willing to say it?

As often as he saw the Vizier, the question asked was always
the same terse one: "Where is your Emperor now?"

Daville would mention the town cited in the last bulletin, and
the Vizier would wave his hand lightly and say in a quiet voice:
"May he soon enter St. Petersburg, God grant it." Saying this,
he would give Daville a look that chilled his insides and made
his heart still heavier.

And the attitude of the Austrian Consul was no less disheartening. It only exacerbated Daville's apprehensions.

Immediately after the French army had moved against Russia
and the news had come that Austria was this time marching
alongside Napoleon as an ally, with a force of over thirty thousand under Prince Schwarzenberg, Daville had called on von
Paulich in the hope of discussing the prospects of the great
campaign in which both their courts were now happily on the
same side. He was met with a quiet and frosty politeness. The
Colonel was more strange and distant than ever before; he
behaved as if he had never heard of the war or the alliance, and
he left Daville to brood about it alone, to rejoice in the successes
and tremble at the thought of failure all by himself. When
Daville pressed him for at least one word of agreement or disapproval, the Colonel lowered his fine blue eyes to the ground,
and those blank eyes of his suddenly seemed wicked and dangerous.

After every visit to von Paulich, Daville came home even more
puzzled and despondent. In other ways too the Austrian Consul
was plainly fostering the impression, with the Vizier and among
the people at large, that he was not in the least sanguine about
this war and preferred to stay aloof, and that the whole undertaking was exclusively a French affair. D'Avenat's observations
in the bazaar seemed to bear this out.

Coming home preoccupied with such thoughts and impressions, Daville would find his wife busily organizing their winter
stores. Taught by the experience of the past years, she now
knew exactly which vegetables kept longer and better, which of
the local fruit varieties were the most suitable for preserving,
and what to do against humidity, cold, and seasonal changes.

Her bottled fruits and jar preserves had improved in quality from year to year; her meals had become richer and more varied, the waste and spoilage more and more negligible. She trained and personally supervised the women helpers and worked with them whenever she could.

Daville knew well (he too from long experience!) that it was idle and useless to interrupt her in the midst of work, the more so as she had no head for abstract discussions and would not know what to say about the fears and anxieties that preyed on his mind. The least concern over the children or the house or even himself, was to her a far more important and more suitable topic of conversation than the most complex "states of mind" and preoccupations which obsessed him so constantly, and which he would have dearly loved to confide to someone. He knew only too well that his wife (a peerless and dependable companion otherwise) was now, and always had been, totally engrossed in the work of the moment, as if nothing else in the world existed and the whole human race, from Napoleon down to the Consul's wife in Travnik, was equally up to its ears, each in his own way, in their preparations for the winter. As far as she was concerned, God's will was done every moment of the day and night, everywhere, in all things. And what else was there to talk about?

So Daville sat in his big chair, pressed his eyeballs, and, after a faint sigh ("Dear God. Oh dear God!"), reached for his Delille and opened a volume at random, in the middle of a poem. He was, in fact, looking for something that neither life nor books could give: a compassionate fellow spirit who would be willing to listen and would have an endless capacity for understanding, to whom he might talk openly and receive lucid and honest answers to all questions. In this dialogue he might then, as in a mirror, see himself for the first time as he really was and learn the true value of his work and determine, without ambiguity, his own position in the world. Here at last he might be able to separate all that was real and well founded in his scruples, premonitions, and fears from all that was imagined and not based on fact. In this sad valley which now contained the sixth year of his loneliness, that might have been a true release.

But such a friend did not come. He never would come. Instead of him, there appeared only strange and undesirable guests.

.   .   .

Even in the years past a traveling Frenchman would sometimes arrive, or a foreigner carrying a French passport, and he would stay on in Travnik, seeking Daville's help or offering his services. Lately, however, they had become more frequent.

Travelers arrived, suspicious-looking merchants, adventurers, impostors, who had lost their way and had departed from their itinerary for a side trip to this impassable, poor country. They were all in transit or fleeing from somewhere, en route to Istanbul, Malta, Palermo, and looked upon their stay in Travnik as a punishment and a piece of bad luck. To Daville each of these unexpected and undesirable guests meant a series of troubles and excitements. He had grown unused to dealing with his compatriots and people from the West altogether. And like all easily disturbed people who are not sure of themselves, he found it hard to tell a lie from the truth and was apt to waver between unfounded suspicion and unwarranted trustfulness. Intimidated by the ministry circulars which kept up a barrage of warnings to the consulates to be on the lookout for English agents, who were alleged to be very cunning and cleverly disguised, Daville saw an English spy in each of these travelers and went to a great deal of trouble either to unmask him or defend himself against him. In reality, these men for the most part were lost souls, strays and unfortunates, dislocated people, refugees, the flotsam and jetsam of a stormy Europe which Napoleon's campaigns and policies had furrowed and whipped every which way. From them too, Daville was often able to get some idea of what "the General" had done to the world in the last four or five years.

Daville disliked them for another reason. Their almost panicky eagerness to get out of Travnik as soon as possible, their exasperation with the slovenly, crude, equivocating local folk, the despairing helplessness of their struggle against the land, the inhabitants, and the conditions, were a poignant reminder to Daville that he himself was marooned and wasting the best years of his life in a backwater.

Every one of these uninvited guests meant trouble and pain for Daville; they seemed to come expressly to be a stone around his neck, to make him a laughingstock in the eyes of all Travnik. And so he used every means he could—money, indulgence, persuasion—to get them out of Bosnia as soon as possible, so as not to have to look at these embodiments of his fate, these witnesses of his bad luck.

A number of these chance travelers had passed through before, but never as many as this year, when the campaign against Russia began, and never had they been such a weird, suspicious-looking, and disreputable lot. It was fortunate that D'Avenat was a type of man who never, not even in circumstances like these, lost his sense of reality, his coolly arrogant presence of mind, and his consummate indifference to most people and things, which came in handy in settling even the toughest cases.

One afternoon on a rainy day in May a group of travelers arrived in front of the main town inn. A crowd of children and bazaar loafers collected right away. Out of wraps and shawls there appeared three people in European dress. A small dapper man; a tall sturdy woman with a rouged and powdered face and dyed hair, like an actress's; and a plump little girl of twelve years. All three were tired and sore from long riding over rough roads, hungry, cross with one another and with everyone around them. They wrangled no end with the caravan drivers and the innkeeper. The little man, who was dark-haired and sallow, hopped around in the lively fashion of a southerner; he shouted, gave orders, bawled out the woman and the child. At length their trunks were unloaded and stacked at the inn entrance. The agile little man took the girl under both armpits, lifted her and sat her on the topmost case, ordering her not to budge from there on any account. Then he went to look for the French Consulate.

He came back with D'Avenat, who could barely conceal his disdain. The man gave his name as Lorenzo Gambini, born at Palermo; he explained that he had been a merchant in Rumania until quite lately and was now returning to Italy, as he could no longer bear living in the Levant. They had cheated him, plundered him, and ruined his health there. To go back to Milan, he needed a visa. He had been told to get it here at Travnik. He had an old passport issued by the Cisalpine Republic. He was anxious to move on right away—without a moment's delay—because, he said, every extra day he spent among these people drove him crazier and he would not be responsible for himself and his actions if he stayed here any longer.

D'Avenat arranged with the innkeeper to find them quarters and food, without listening to the traveler's breathless outpouring.

The woman broke into the conversation, in the weary tearful voice of an actress who knows she is getting older and can neither forget it nor learn to live with it. From the top of her trunk the little girl cried that she was hungry. They all spoke simultaneously. They wanted to get to their room, to eat, rest, get the visa, leave Travnik as soon as possible, and clear out of Bosnia. But what they needed most urgently, it seemed, was to talk and quarrel, for they neither listened to nor cared to understand each other.

Oblivious of the innkeeper and turning his back to D'Avenat, the little Italian shouted at the woman who was twice his size: "Keep out of it! Don't say anything! If you hadn't talked and I hadn't been a fool to listen to you we wouldn't be here now, damn you!"

"You blame me? Me? Oh!" screamed the woman, rolling her eyes to heaven and glancing around the circle of bystanders as if calling on them to be her witness. "Oh, my youth, my talent, everything, everything have I given him! And now I'm to blame!"

"So you are, my beauty! Yes, my sunshine! If I suffer and sink, it's all your fault. And if I finish it all right here and now, that'll be on your head too . . . !" With a practiced movement, the little man whipped a big pistol from his voluminous traveling cloak and pressed the muzzle to his temple.

The woman gave a shriek and rushed toward the fellow, who had no intention of carrying out his threat; she threw her arms around him and began to babble.

Perching on top of the pile of trunks, the plump little girl quietly ate a piece of Albanian yellow cake that someone had given her. D'Avenat scratched himself behind the ear. The Italian had already forgotten the woman and his suicide gesture, and was passionately explaining to D'Avenat that he must have the visa the next morning; he brandished a crumpled and dog-eared passport, scolding the girl in the same breath for getting up there instead of helping her mother.

D'Avenat promised to let him know in the morning. After a last instruction to the innkeeper, and without another glance at the curious family or a word of reply to the stream of explanations and appeals from the Italian, he set off for the Consulate.

A large and inquisitive crowd remained at the gates of the inn. Puzzled and wondering, they stared at the foreigners and their dress and unusual behavior, as if the scene were a stage or a circus. The Moslems on their shop platforms and the working people who were passing by looked on darkly from under their eyebrows and at once averted their heads.

No sooner had D'Avenat returned and managed to tell the

Consul about the peculiar visitors they had acquired, and had shown him Gambini's passport, a fantastic affair of loose pages and stitched extension flaps, full of visas and endorsements, than there was a hue and cry at the gate of the Consulate. Lorenzo Gambini had come in person and was demanding a private interview with the Consul. The gate kavass barred the entrance. A group of bazaar urchins was watching him from a distance, evidently having sensed that wherever this foreigner went there was bound to be trouble, noise, and excitement. D'Avenat came out and sharply warned the sputtering man to pipe down; however, he babbled on about how well he'd served the French cause and how he would have a few words to say in Milan and in Paris as well. But he obeyed in the end and went back to the inn, threatening to shoot himself on the Consulate's doorstep if he did not get his passport back by the next morning.

Daville was shaken, disgusted, and indignant. He told D'Avenat to settle the thing with all possible speed, to prevent further bazaar spectacles of the same or possibly a worse kind. D'Avenat, to whom these qualms were a matter of utter indifference, and who had long accepted squabbling as an integral feature of doing business in the East, assured the Consul in his dry and matter-of-fact manner: "That fellow is not a suicidal type. When he sees that he will get nothing out of us, he'll clear out as fast as he came."

And that was exactly what happened. Two days later the whole family left Travnik, after a stormy quarrel between D'Avenat and Lorenzo, in which the latter threatened at one moment to shoot himself on the spot and in the next swore that he would protest to Napoleon in person about his treatment at the hands of the Travnik Consulate, while his sizable wife flashed her eyes at D'Avenat in the highly dramatic style of a former beauty.

Daville, who was always concerned with the prestige of his country and the Consulate, sighed with relief. But three weeks later another uninvited guest made his appearance at Travnik.

This time it was a Turk, conspicuously well dressed, who took up quarters at the inn. He came from Istanbul and sought out D'Avenat right away. He called himself Ismail Raiff but was in fact a converted Alsatian Jew by the name of Mendelsheim. He too asked for a private interview with the Consul and claimed to have important information for the French government; he boasted of wide connections in Turkey, France, and

Germany and of membership in the leading Freemason Lodge in France and claimed to know many of the plans of Napoleon's opponets. He was strong, of an athletic build, a redhead with pink cheeks, talkative and overweening. There was a bright, almost drunken glaze in his eyes. D'Avenat tried to get rid of him with a stratagem he often used: he advised him in all earnestness to continue his journey without a minute's delay and to convey all he knew to the military commander at Split, who had the sole authority to receive such information. The Jew demurred, complaining that French consular officials showed no understanding whatever of these matters, which an English or an Austrian consul would welcome with open arms and pay for with fourteen-carat gold. Still, after a few days he too left.

The day after he departed D'Avenat learned that before he left the man had visited von Paulich and offered his services against Napoleon. D'Avenat immediately reported this to the commanding officer at Split.

Hardly two weeks later Daville got a long letter from Bugoyno, signed by the same Ismail Raiff, informing him that he was stopping at Bugoyno and had entered the service of Mustapha Pasha Suleimanpashich. He was writing on Mustapha's orders and requested in his name that they send him two or three bottles of cognac or Calvados, or any other French drink, "as long as it is strong."

Mustapha Pasha was the oldest son of Suleiman Pasha Skoplyak, a spoiled and debauched young nobleman, given to many vices and especially to drink, and quite unlike his father, who was shrewd and dissembling but also a brave, upright, and hard-working man. The young Pasha led an empty and dissolute life, molesting his women tenants, drinking with idlers, and tearing about the countryside on his horse. Suleiman Pasha the Elder, who was otherwise stern and a skillful handler of men, was weak and indulgent with this son of his and always found excuses for his laziness and bad habits.

D'Avenat at once understood what drew those two men together. With the Consul's approval, he promptly wrote to the young Pasha himself that he was sending some bottles of spirits by a separate messenger, but that he would advise him not to put too much trust in this Ismail as he was an adventurer and quite possibly an Austrian spy.

Ismail Raiff sent back a long letter, defending and justifying himself, in which he tried to prove that, far from being any-body's spy, he was a good Frenchman and world citizen, an unhappy man whose only sin was that he had lost his bearings. The letter, which reeked of plum brandy, ended with some mawkish verses in which he bemoaned his fate:

"*O ma vie! O vain songe! O rapide existence!*
Qu'amusent les désirs, qu'abuse l'espérance.
Tel est donc des humains l'inévitable sort—
Des projets, des erreurs, la douleur, et la mort!"

(Oh life of mine, oh idle dream, oh swiftly passing span!
Teased by fond desire, mocked by hope.
Such, then, is the inescapable lot of men—
Plans, mistakes, pain, and death.)

He wrote a few more times in this vein, remonstrating and justifying himself in alcoholic prose garnished with verses, signing the letters with his original name and an assumed masonic title, "Cerf Mendelsheim, Chev . . . d'or . . ." until drink, wanderlust, and events swept him out of Bosnia.

As if they had arranged to succeed each other, the moment Ismail stopped writing another French traveler arrived in Trav-nik, one Pepin, a tiny, nattily dressed man, powdered and per-fumed, with a shrill voice and a mincing gait. He told D'Avenat that he had come from Warsaw, where he had kept an acting school, and was stopping here because he had been robbed on the way; that he was returning to Istanbul, where he used to live at one time and where some people owed him money. (How he got to Travnik, which could not, by any stretch of the imagina-tion, be said to lie on the Warsaw-Istanbul route, he did not explain.)

This little man was as forward as a tart. He stopped Daville as he was riding through the bazaar, placed himself in front of the horse, and requested him in ceremonious language to receive and hear him. Afraid of another public scene, Daville consented. Once he got home, however, trembling with anger and excite-ment, he called D'Avenat right away and implored him to get rid of the pest.

The Consul, who saw English agents even in his dreams, was sure that the man had an English accent. D'Avenat, unshakably calm as usual, lacking imagination and incapable of seeing anything that was not there, or of embellishing anything he did see, formed an accurate idea of the traveler right away.

"Watch out for this man," the Consul had warned D'Avenat in some excitement. "Get rid of him, please. He's obviously an agent, sent here to compromise the Consulate or for some such purpose. He is an *agent provocateur*. . . ."

"He is not," D'Avenat said flatly.

"How not? What do you mean?"

"He's a pederast."

"He's what?"

"A pederast, *monsieur le Consul*."

Daville clutched at his head. "O-o-o-h! That's all we need in this Consulate. You say he is . . . oh, *mon Dieu!*"

D'Avenat calmed his chief and the very next day he rid Travnik of M. Pepin. Not saying anything to anyone, he cornered the man in his room, got a firm grip on the immaculate lace ruffle of his shirt, and told him that unless he moved on right away the Turks would give him a public lashing in the middle of the bazaar and then throw him into the fortress dungeon.

Daville was relieved when this last vagabond had gone, but he remained apprehensive and kept wondering what trash and human flotsam and debris blind and senseless chance would bring next into this valley where life was quite hard enough without them.

Daville's sixth autumn in Travnik had nearly run its course and was fast moving to a dramatic climax.

Toward the end of September the news came of the fall of Moscow and of the great fire. No one came to congratulate him. Von Paulich continued to maintain, with barefaced calm, that he had no news whatever of the campaign, and avoided all talk of it. And D'Avenat reported that von Paulich's staff took the same line in their conversation with the local people and behaved in all respects as if they were unaware of the fact that the Austrian Empire was at war with Russia.

Daville made a point of visiting the Residency more often and meeting the people of the town, but all of them, one after another, as if by mutual agreement, shied away from any discussion of the Russian campaign and retired behind meaningless generalities and noncommittal pleasantries. At times it seemed to Daville that they were all looking at him in awed

wonder, as though he were a sleepwalker teetering on the edge
of some perilous abyss and they were anxious not to startle him
awake with a careless word.

Nevertheless, little by little, the truth came to light. One
rainy day when the Vizier, as was his custom, asked Daville
what news he had from Russia and Daville told him the latest
bulletin about the capture of Moscow, the Vizier expressed his
pleasure, despite the fact that he already knew this; he con-
gratulated Daville and hoped that Napoleon would continue to
march forward, like Cyrus of antiquity, a just and true conqueror. "But why is your Emperor marching north at this time
of the year, just before the winter? That is dangerous, dangerous.
I would prefer to see him going south," said Ibrahim Pasha,
gazing anxiously through the window, into the distance, as if he
were looking at Russia itself and trying to fathom her dangers.

The Vizier said this last in the same tone of voice in which he
had recited his good wishes and made his analogy with Cyrus,
and D'Avenat translated it in the same flat and uninspired fashion in which he did all his interpreting. Yet Daville felt a stirring
of queasiness in his innards. "Here, then, is this thing I am
afraid of, and they all seem to know it already, only nobody
wants to say it openly," thought Daville, waiting tensely for the
Vizier to go on. But Ibrahim Pasha was silent. ("He will not say
it either," Daville thought, distressed). After a long pause,
however, the Vizier spoke up again, but on another subject. He
recalled how many years before Ghisari Tchelebi Khan had
marched against Russia and, in a series of battles, had routed
the enemy army, which kept retreating north, deeper and deeper
into the country. Then, winter suddenly overtook the victorious
Khan. His great army, irresistible till then, became demoralized
and afraid, while the infidel barbarians, inured to cold on
account of their hairiness, began to ambush it from all sides.
Ghisari Khan then spoke the unforgettable words:

"When a man leaves his country's sun behind him
Who shall light the way on his return?"

(Daville had never had much patience with this Turkish
custom of sprinkling conversation with weighty aphoristic lines,
whose pertinence and aptness more often than not were lost on
him, and at the same time he could not help feeling that the
importance and meaning they attached to those verses was

something special in itself which he ought to make it his business to divine and understand.)

Young Ghisari Khan flew into a rage at his astronomers, whom he had purposely brought with him and who had forecast a much later onset of winter. So he gave orders that these wise men, who had turned out to be less than wise, be tied up and made to march barefoot and lightly clad at the head of the army, so that they might rue their colossal fumble with their own bodies. And then it turned out that these emaciated scholars, with less flesh on them than bedbugs, withstood the cold much better than the army. They remained alive, while the hearts of the young warriors cracked in their chests like green beechwood in the first frost. You could not touch steel, they said, because it stung you like white-hot iron and the skin of your palms remained stuck to it. And that was the sad end of Ghisari Khan's expedition. He lost his magnificent army and barely escaped with his head.

The Vizier terminated the audience with blessings and good wishes for the success of Napoleon's undertaking and the defeat of the Muscovites who, as was well known, were bad neighbors and warmongers and never kept their word.

The tales of Ghisari Tchelebi Khan and Cyrus had not, as it happened, come out of the Vizier's head but out of Tahir Beg's. He had produced them in conversation with the Residency inmates when they were discussing the fall of Moscow and Napoleon's further adventures in his march across Russia. The ever-alert D'Avenat found that out in the course of his pulse-taking at the Residency; and the stories left no doubt about what the Turks really thought of the French army's chances in Russia.

Tahir Beg had apparently told the Vizier and the others that the French had already gone too far and could no longer pull back without considerable losses. "And if Napoleon's men spend another week where they are," the Secretary had said, "I can see them turning into grave mounds covered with Russian snow."

D'Avenat's informant had repeated the statement word for word, and D'Avenat in turn reported it to Daville exactly as he heard it.

"In the end, all fears become reality," Daville told himself, calmly and aloud, as he woke up one winter day.

It was an unusually cold December morning. He had woken

up with a start, imagining that the hair of his own forehead was somebody's cold hand. He had opened his eyes and spoken these words as if they were a message from someone.

He spoke them again, a few days later, when D'Avenat came in to tell him that the Residency was agog with rumors of Napoleon's defeat in Russia and the French army's complete disintegration. The newest Russian war bulletin, with full details of the French debacle, was circulating around town. One could safely assume that the Austrian Consulate had procured and secretly distributed these bulletins through its agents. In any case, Tahir Beg had the bulletin in his possession and had shown it to the Vizier.

"It's all coming true," Daville told himself over and over again as he listened to D'Avenat's account. Then he pulled himself together and quietly ordered the interpreter to go visit Tahir Beg on some pretext and, in the course of the conversation, ask for the Russian bulletin. At the same time he called in the junior interpreter Rafo Atias and told them both to try to scotch these unfavorable rumors around the town and assure everyone that Napoleon's army was invincible, in spite of temporary setbacks which were the result of the distances and the winter weather and not of any Russian victories.

D'Avenat managed to see Tahir Beg and ask him for the Russian bulletin, but the Secretary would not give it to him. "If I gave it to you, it would be proper for you to pass it on to M. Daville, and I don't want that. What they write here is too disagreeable for him and his country, and I esteem him too highly to have him receive this news from me. Tell him that my good wishes are with him constantly."

D'Avenat repeated this to Daville in his flat, faithful, and exasperating way and left the room at once. Alone with his thoughts, Daville mulled over Tahir Beg's oriental compliment —the kind of compliment that made a man's flesh creep. When the Osmanlis began to pussyfoot like that with a man, he was as good as dead, or the unluckiest man alive! Such were Daville's thoughts as he leaned on the window sill, gazing into the winter dusk.

In the narrow band of dark blue sky above Vilenitsa the new moon came on stealthily, cold and sharp, like a graven metallic letter.

No, this time things would not end as they had before, with triumphal bulletins and victorious peace treaties.

What until then had lurked like a premonition at the back of Daville's mind now rose up before him as a full and clear realization, in the cold night of a foreign land under a sinister young moon, forcing him to consider what a complete breakup and ultimate defeat might mean for him and his family. He made a concerted effort to think about it but felt that the problem required more strength and courage than he was capable of that evening.

No, this time the end would come not, as it had earlier, with a victorious bulletin and a peace treaty bestowing new territories on France and fresh laurels on the Imperial Army, but, on the contrary, with a rout and dissolution. A hush was falling over the entire world: the dull, bated-breath kind of pause before the dreadful crash that was certain to come. Or so, at any rate, it seemed to Daville.

During these months Daville remained without any news, almost without any contact with the outside world on which all his thoughts and fears were centered, and to which his personal destiny was bound.

Travnik and the whole countryside were in the grip of a long, cruel, and unusually severe winter, the worst of all winters Daville had spent here. The townspeople recalled a similar winter twenty-one years before, but, they said, this one was colder and fiercer. As early as the month of November the winter bore down hard on all life and changed the face of the earth and the appearance of people. It filled and flattened the valley, hardening and settling like a fatal desolation and leaving no hope of change. It emptied the granaries and shut off the roads. Birds fell dead from the air, like phantom fruit from invisible branches. Wild animals came down from the high mountains and wandered into the town, their fear of winter stronger than their fear of men. In the eyes of the poor and homeless one could see terror of a defenseless death. People froze on the roads, in their quest of bread and warm quarters. The sick were dying, for there was no medicine against winter. In the arctic night one could hear the shingles on the Consulate roof crack open with the force of pistol shots, and the wolves howling above Vilenitsa.

Fires in the earthen stoves were kept going all through the night, as Mme Daville feared for the children and could not help remembering the boy she had lost four years before.

During these nights Daville and his wife sat after dinner,

she fighting sleep and exhaustion from the day's work, he with sleeplessness and endless worries. She would be aching for sleep, while he would want to talk. To her all talk and brooding about the winter and poverty sounded gloomy and unwelcome, for she had spent the whole day struggling against them, frail as she was, muffled to her chin in shawls, yet nimble and always on the move. He, on the contrary, found at least momentary comfort in such talk. Still, she listened to him, although dying to go to sleep, and so gave him his due, just as all day long she had done her duty by all the others.

Daville kept on talking, saying everything that came to his mind, apropos of the disastrous winter, the general misery, and his secret fears.

He had, he told her, seen and lived through many bad things that overtake a man in his tussle with the elements, both those around him and the ones that dwell inside him and are generated by human conflicts. He had known hunger and every kind of want during the Terror in Paris twenty years before. At the time it had seemed that violence and chaos were the nation's only prospect and future. Greasy, tattered *assignats* of thousands and thousands of francs were not worth the paper they were printed on, and for a scrap of pork fat or a fistful of flour one had to traipse at night into the remote suburbs and haggle and bicker with shady characters in dark cellars. Day and night you had to scramble and worry about keeping alive, though life itself was worth very little and you might lose it at any moment through someone's denunciation or a police error or simply by a quirk of chance.

And he recalled his years of war in Spain, when for weeks and months on end he had worn one single shirt that molded on him with sweat and dust, and dared not take it off and wash it for fear that, at the least touch, it would split and tear into strips and rags, like something rotted through and through. Besides his musket, bayonet, a little powder and shot, his only other possession had been a waist belt of untanned hide, which he'd taken off of a dead Aragon peasant, who, for the glory of God, had taken up arms against the French vermin and Jacobins. The belt had seldom contained anything except, on a particularly lucky day, a piece of stone-hard barley bread which too had been snatched from someone or stolen from an abandoned house. And it was the time of stinging blizzards when neither warm clothing nor solid boots afforded any protection, when men forgot everything in their single-minded quest for cover and shelter.

All these things he had known in his life, but never yet had he seen or felt the horror and force of winter in quite the same numbing, devastating degree as now. He had never dreamed that such a thing as this oriental poverty and want could exist, or this utter paralyzed helplessness which went with a long withering winter and lay heavy over the entire mountainous, spare, and luckless countryside like the wrath of God. This he had got to know only in Travnik, and only this winter.

Madame Daville was not, in general, too fond of recollections of this kind and like all active, genuinely religious people she shrank from the kind of "loud musing" that led nowhere and was only a form of self-coddling that weakened one's resistance to the environment and often led one's thoughts astray. Up to that point she had listened dutifully, with a distinct effort, but now she rose, overcome by fatigue, and announced that it was time to sleep.

Daville remained alone in the big room which was getting colder by the minute. He sat on alone for a long time yet, without anyone to talk to, and "listened" to the cold creeping into all things, shattering the core of everything it touched. As far as his mind could stretch, whether he thought about the East and the Turks and their disordered and unstable life, a life without value or purpose, or whether he tried to guess what was happening in France and what had become of Napoleon and his army, returning in defeat from Russia, everywhere his mind came up against misery, suffering, and dark uncertainty.

So passed the days and nights of that winter, a winter which seemed endless and unrelieved.

Sometimes when the cold let up for a day or two, there would be a heavy new snowfall that piled up high on top of the old layer, which was crusted over with a hard shell of ice that gave the earth, as it were, a new visage. Immediately afterwards there would be another wave of cold, bitterer than the first. One's breath froze, the water turned to ice, the sun darkened. One's brain grew numb, deadening all but one thought: how to survive the cold. It was only by a great effort that a man could rouse himself to remember that somewhere down below was the earth, the warm and living nurse-mother, capable of blossom and fruit-giving; for between him and the fruit there was now a white, frosty, and impassable no man's land.

The price of everything had soared right in the early months of the winter, but especially the price of grain; now there was no grain to be had at all. There was famine in the villages, and the town suffered from an acute shortage. One came across starved peasants in the streets, with empty sacks over their arms, desperately looking for corn. Street corners swarmed with beggars, wrapped in rags and blue from cold. Neighbors enviously counted each other's meals.

Both consulates tried to help the people and alleviate the miseries of hunger and cold. Madame Daville and von Paulich vied with each other in helping with food and money. Crowds of hungry people, mostly children, collected outside the Consulate gates. At first they were only gypsies, with here and there a Christian child, but as the winter grew longer and privation increased, one began to see Moslem orphans and poor who had come down from the outskirts. During the early days, Moslem children from the town houses waited for them in the bazaar and mocked them for begging and eating infidel food. They threw snowballs at them and shouted: "Starvelings! Infidels! Did you gorge yourself with pork? Starvelings!"

But later the cold became so intense that these town youngsters would not set foot out of doors. In front of the consulates the throng of frozen children and beggars hopped and chattered with cold, so bundled in rags and tatters of every kind that it was hard to tell to what faith they belonged or where they came from.

The consuls gave away so much grain that they remained without it. However, as soon as the winter let up enough to allow the pack drivers to come from Brod, von Paulich, with his usual skill and resolution, arranged for a steady supply of flour and food for his Consulate as well as for Daville.

The French consignments of cotton via Bosnia had been halted at the start of the winter, though Freycinet continued to write despairing letters and made plans to discontinue the whole enterprise. Moreover, there was common agreement among the people that the French, by paying excessive wages to the pack drivers, had not only pushed up the cost of living but had created the food shortage by tempting the peasant away from agriculture. All in all, "Bonaparte's War" was responsible for everything. As so often in history, the people made of their *bête noire* a victim who must carry on his shoulders the sins and transgressions of everyone; and there were more and more of those who, without even knowing why, began to look for relief and deliverance in the rout and disappearance of this Bonaparte, of whom they knew nothing except that he had become "a burden on earth," for he spread war, unrest, rising prices, sickness, and want wherever he went.

Over in the Austrian countries, on the other side, where the people groaned under a load of taxes, fiscal crises, compulsory military service, and bloody casualties, Bonaparte had already become a subject of story and song, and was looked upon as the main cause of all misery and an obstacle to personal happiness for everyone. In Slavonia, lone girls of marriageable age sang:

> "Oh Frenchman, thou mighty Emperor!
> Let the lads go, the girls were left behind;
> The quinces and apples are rotting away
> And the gold-spun bodices as well."

This ditty crossed the river Sava, was taken up all through Bosnia, and reached Travnik.

Daville was familiar with the way these generalizations sprung up, took root, and spread in these regions, and how difficult and futile it was to try to combat them. And besides, now as earlier, he could only struggle against them halfheartedly and with insufficient strength. He went on writing the same reports and giving the same instructions to his staff and his agents, and he kept up with the Vizier and everyone else in the Residency. All of these things were the same as before, only he, Daville, was no longer the same.

He walked upright and conducted himself quietly and with assurance. Outwardly everything was the same. And still there were some things that had changed forever, both around him and within him.

Had it been possible for someone to measure his will-power, the trend of his thoughts, and the force of his inner urges and outward movements, he would have found that the rhythm of all Daville's actions was by now much closer to the rhythm in which this Bosnian town breathed, lived, and worked, than to the rhythm which had animated his movements six or seven years before, when he first arrived here. The transformation had taken place slowly and imperceptibly, but it had been steady and relentless. Daville now shrank from putting things in writing, from instant and clear decisions, he was afraid of novelty and of guests, and shuddered at every change or the thought of change. He preferred a fleeting moment of assured peace and respite to the years that were yet to come, bringing no one knew what.

The external changes too were difficult to hide. People who live together in huddled proximity and are thrown upon one another day after day are slower to notice that they are ageing and changing. All the same, the Consul had visibly grown feebler and older, especially in the last few months. The vigorous shock of hair above his forehead had wilted and become flatter and was turning a grayish hue, like the color of blond people whose hair begins to go gray all of a sudden. His cheeks were still rosy, but the skin was drier and beginning to sag under the chin and lose its freshness. In the aftermath of the painful toothaches that had plagued him that winter he was beginning to lose some teeth.

These were the tangible ravages which, in the course of years, had been imprinted on Daville by the Travnik frosts, rains, and humid winds, by family worries, small and great, and by the never-ending consular duties, but especially by his inner conflicts and unrest over the recent events in the world and in France.

Such was Daville's situation at the end of the sixth year of his unbroken residence in Travnik, as he faced the new developments after Napoleon's return from Russia.

24

When, in the middle of March, the cold wave broke at last and the ice, which had seemed everlasting, began to thaw, the town was left cowed and limp as after an epidemic, its streets washed out, the houses scarred, the trees bare, the people worn out and troubled, as if having survived the cold was only a prelude to the still greater extremity of having to find food and spring seed and a way out of the tight, remorseless squeeze of debts and loans.

One such day in March, once again in the morning, and once again in that deep and dire voice in which D'Avenat had for years, monotonously and implacably, conveyed pleasant and unpleasant news, important as well as irrelevant, the interpreter informed Daville that Ibrahim Pasha was being transferred, though he had not yet received a new assignment. According to the firman, he was to leave Travnik and await further orders at Gallipoli.

When, five years before, he had been told in the same fashion of Mehmed Pasha's transfer, Daville had been excited and had felt a strong compulsion to talk about it, to busy himself and plot ways and means of countering that decision. This time, however, although the news hit him badly and meant a great loss in the present circumstances, he no longer found the strength to protest and oppose it. Ever since this last winter and the catastrophe at Moscow, he had come to feel more and more that everything was tottering and crumbling; and each new loss, no matter what side it came from, seemed only to corroborate and justify that feeling.

All was coming down—emperors, armies, institutions, fortunes, ambitions that were sky-high—so why shouldn't this unfortunate half-dead Vizier also come down one day, he who had sat all these years leaning now to one side, now to the other? Everyone knew the meaning of the phrase "await further orders at Gallipoli." It was banishment, pining away in isolation, and virtual penury, without a chance of appeal, explanation, or redress.

As he thought about it longer, Daville realized that he was losing an old friend and a dependable protector, and at a moment when he perhaps needed him most. Yet try as he might he could not summon up any of that excitement and zeal and eagerness to write, warn, criticize, and ask for help which he had felt at the time of Mehmed Pasha's departure. Everything must come down, even one's friends and supporters. And the man who got up in arms and tried to save himself or the others, achieved nothing in the end. And so the Vizier, with his perpetual list, must also collapse and go away like all the rest, and all one could do was nurse one's sorrow.

While he was still pondering this, unable to come to a decision, a message arrived from the Residency that the Vizier wanted to talk to him.

At the Residency there was an atmosphere of confusion and

scurrying, but the Vizier seemed unchanged. He talked of his transfer as though it were merely the latest and perfectly natural link in the long chain of misfortunes that had been dogging him for years. As though he were himself anxious to complete the chain process, he had decided not to tarry here but get under way in the next ten days—that is, at the beginning of April. He had been informed that his successor was already proceeding to Travnik, and he would on no account wait for him here.

Like Mehmed Pasha once, the Vizier claimed to be a victim of his pro-French sentiments. (Daville was well aware that this was one of those oriental lies or half-truths which circulate and intermingle with genuine bonds and true kindnesses, just as bad money circulates together with the good.)

"Yes, yes. So long as France was advancing and conquering, they kept me here and didn't dare to touch me. Now that she's down on her luck, they're replacing me, so that I should not have any contact or opportunity to work with the French."

(At that the counterfeit money suddenly turned into legal tender, and Daville, forgetting the Vizier's inaccurate premise, woke up to the reality of French defeat. That chilling cramp of queasiness, now tightening, now lessening, which had so often gripped his stomach here at this Residency, seized him now again as he quietly heard the Vizier's recital, from its false cordiality to its bitter truth.)

"Lies and truth are mixed up," thought Daville as he waited for the interpreter to translate words which he himself had understood perfectly well—"everything is so mixed up that no one can tell what is what, but one thing is certain: everything is tumbling down."

The Vizier had already passed from the subject of France to that of his own relations with the Bosnians and with Daville personally. "Believe me, these people need stricter and tougher viziers. True, they say the poor of the country call me a blessing —which is all I ask for. The rich and the strong hate me. They misinformed me about you too, in the beginning, but then I got to know you and soon realized that you were my only friend. Praise be to Allah, the One and Only! And, believe me, I myself have asked the Sultan several times to recall me. My needs are infinitesimal. I would best of all like to work my garden like a common hired hand and spend my last days in peace."

Daville expressed his good wishes and spoke reassuringly of the future, but the Vizier spurned all comfort.

"No, no! I know exactly what to expect. They will find something to blame me for, to get me out of the way and seize my lands—I know, because they've tried it before. I can almost hear them plotting against me in the high places, digging the ground from under me, but what can I do? Allah is One! Ever since I lost my favorite children and so many of my family, I have been ready for further bad news. If Sultan Selim were alive, things might have been different. . . ."

Daville knew the mechanics of what was to come. And D'Avenat translated almost from memory, as though it were the text of a familiar ritual.

As he was coming out of the Residency, Daville could not help observing how the bustle and tension were mounting by the minute. The extensive and motley household of the Vizier, which in the last five years had multiplied, taken root, and blended itself into the dwelling and the surroundings, was now suddenly beginning to totter as if about to fall.

Behind every partition and door there were voices, hurried footsteps, the banging of hammers, the thudding of chests and trunks. They were all trying to save themselves. The large, intriguing, yet closely knit family was turning back toward the great obscurity of Turkey and was seething, creaking, and toiling in every fiber. The only one who remained aloof and immovable in this hustle and commotion was the Vizier; he sat in his usual place, Turkish fashion, leaning slightly to one side, like a caparisoned stone idol borne aloft by a swaying, bewildered throng.

Next day servants brought to the French Consulate a whole flock of domestic and tame animals, Angora cats, greyhounds, foxes, and white bunnies, which Daville solemnly awaited and received in the courtyard. The page who had accompanied the menagerie stood in the middle of the yard and announced in his best courtly manner that these creatures had been pets in the Vizier's household and the Vizier was now leaving them in the care of a friend. "He loved them, and must now leave them to the one he loves."

The page and the servants were given presents and the animals were taken to a shelter in the courtyard at the back of the house.

Madame Daville was appalled, but the children were jubilant.

Several days later, the Vizier called Daville once more, to say good-bye privately, unofficially, and as a friend. This time he was genuinely moved. He shunned all blandishments and half-truths and would-be compliments. "Man must part with everything, and now our time has come. We have met like two exiles, cast out and thrown among these wild people. We have long been friends here and will always remain thus, if we should meet once again in some better place."

Then a great new thing happened, unknown in the five years of ceremonial at the Residency. The pages rushed up to the Vizier and helped him get up. He rose with that sudden clipped movement of his, and it was only now that Daville saw how tall and powerful he was; then he crossed the room slowly and heavily, without a wasted motion, gliding on invisible feet like a hulking upright cannon shell on wheels. All of them descended into the courtyard. There stood the polished and spanking black carriage, an old gift of von Mitterer's, and a little beyond it a fine thoroughbred bay horse with dappled white and red nostrils, in full harness.

The Vizier stopped beside the coach and muttered something that sounded like a prayer, then turned to Daville. "On the eve of my departure from this sad country, I leave you this, so that you too may depart as soon as possible . . ."

Then they brought the steed and the Vizier again addressed Daville: ". . . and this noble animal as well, to carry you on to every kind of good fortune."

Touched, Daville was on the point of saying something, but the Vizier went on, gravely and scrupulously, to conclude the prearranged ceremonial. "The carriage is a symbol of peace and the horse of good luck. These are my wishes for you and your family."

Only then did Daville manage to express his gratitude and convey his good wishes for the Vizier's journey and for his future.

And while they were still on the premises, D'Avenat learned from one of the minor functionaries that the Vizier had given no presents to von Paulich and had taken his leave of him coolly and rather curtly.

At the foot of the Residency, a whole caravan of pack horses and drivers had struck camp, and they were loading and weighing the packs, calling one another and standing around. The empty house was echoing to footfalls, loud orders, and dickering, and above it all Baki's shrill voice could be heard.

Baki felt wretched and ill at the very thought of having to

travel in such cold weather (there was still snow in the mountains) and over such appalling roads, while the expense of it
and the damage and the sheer impossibility of taking every last
thing along drove him to distraction. He kept dashing from room
to room for fear that something might be left behind, warning
the men not to toss things around and break them, imploring
and threatening in turn. He was angry with Bekhdjet, who
never stopped grinning throughout the upheaval. ("With that
bird brain of his, naturally, I'd be grinning myself!") The reckless and carefree ways of Tahir Beg offended him. ("He's ruined
himself, so why shouldn't he ruin all the rest!") The gifts the
Vizier had earmarked for Daville had upset him so much that
he forgot the baskets and the pack drivers. He had expostulated
with everyone and finally gone to the Vizier, begging and demanding that at least the horse be withheld. When that didn't
help him, he had flopped down on a coverless sofa, choking
with tears, and told everyone how Rotta had once confided to
him, on the very best authority, that at the time of his transfer
from Travnik von Mitterer took with him fifty thousand thalers
which he had saved in just under four years.

"Fifty thousand thalers! Fi-f-t-y thou-sand! That Austrian
swine! And in four years!" shouted Baki and asked himself
aloud how much more the Frenchman was likely to save in
that case. He beat the palm of his hand against his silken jacket,
where the pocket was.

At the end of the week, in a cold rain that turned to snow in
the mountains, Ibrahim Pasha and his retinue set out on their
journey. He was escorted out of town by the two consuls and
their kavasses. They were joined by a fair number of mounted
Travnik begs and town worthies on foot who went part of the
way, for Ibrahim Pasha's departure was not a clandestine affair
and he left no hatred behind him, as had been the case with
Mehmed Pasha.

In the first two years he too, like the majority of his predecessors, had had to contend with intrigue and rebellion among the
local notables, but these had calmed down with time. The Vizier's unbending rigidity, his honesty in money matters, and
then Tahir Beg's skill, moderation, and generous, forward-
looking administration of the land had in time produced a
climate of tolerance and cool but peaceable relations between
the Residency and the landowning begs. They had held it
against the Vizier that he did nothing for the country and had

no master strategy against Serbia, but this was a kind of fault-finding that the begs had felt they must keep up more for the sake of their conscience and the public image of their zeal than from any real desire to ruffle the barren but pleasant "silence" that had become a feature of Ibrahim Pasha's long vizierate. (While, in his turn, the Vizier had complained, and with good reason, that the only thing which prevented his mounting an armed expedition agains the Serbs was the sluggish, disorderly, and quarreling Bosnians themselves.) And as the years had gone by and the Vizier had begun to resemble a dead man more and more, the public judgment of him had softened and the opinion of his rule grown more and more favorable.

Now, little by little, the cavalcade that was seeing the Vizier off dwindled and scattered. The first to fall away were those on foot, then the horsemen, one by one. Finally only the Moslem religious leaders were left, a few town notables, and the two consuls with their escorts. The consuls took their leave at the same little coffeehouse where Daville had once said good-bye to Mehmed Pasha. The tumble-down arbor was still there, black from the rain, lying in a puddle of water. Here the Vizier halted the train and bade farewell to the consuls in a few mumbled words which no one translated. D'Avenat loudly repeated his Consul's greetings and good wishes, while von Paulich replied in Turkish for himself.

A cold drizzle was coming down steadily. The Vizier sat on his big, placid, broad-rumped horse, which had been nicknamed "Cow" back at the Residency. He wore a cloak of dark red cloth and heavy fur and its bright color contrasted strangely with the glum and sodden surroundings. Behind the Vizier one could see the sallow face of Tahir Beg, with its burning eyes, the long hunter's figure of Eshref Effendi, the doctor, and a stuffed, almost round bundle of clothing out of which peered Baki's blue eyes, wrathful and ready to burst into tears.

They were all in a hurry to get out of the rain-soaked hollow, almost as if they were at an official funeral.

Daville rode back with von Paulich. It was past noon. The rain stopped and a diffused sunlight filled the air intermittently, wan and lacking any warmth. Their casual small talk was pregnant with unspoken memories and thoughts. The closer they came to the town, the narrower and tighter became the gorge. On the steep slopes young grass was pushing up, crisscrossed by wet, dark blue shadows. At one spot along the way Daville noticed several half-opened flowers of yellow primrose and all at once the gloom of his seventh Bosnian spring broke over him with such force that he could just barely manage to make a few suitable, monosyllabic noises in reply to some quiet remark from von Paulich.

Daville was surprised when, ten days after the Vizier's departure, he received the first news of him. At Novi Pazar, Ibrahim Pasha had met Silikhtar Ali Pasha, his successor to the Bosnian vizierate, and they had spent a few days together. As the French courier from Istanbul happened to pass through at the same time, Ibrahim Pasha had used the opportunity to send his friend the first greetings from the journey. The letter was full of friendly memories and good wishes. By way of a postscript, Ibrahim Pasha had added a few lines about the new Vizier: "I should like, my esteemed friend, to describe my successor to you, but that is quite out of the question. I can only say: May God have mercy on the poor and on those who have no protection. Now the Bosnians will see!"

What Daville learned from the courier, and later from Freycinet's letters, fully bore out Ibrahim Pasha's impressions.

The new Vizier arrived without any official staff, without pages or a harem, "lone and naked as a bandit in the woods," but with one thousand and two hundred well-armed Albanians of "sinister appearance" and two large pieces of field artillery— preceded by his reputation as the most unpredictable butcher and the meanest Vizier in all the Empire.

Somewhere on the open road between Plevlye and Priboy one of the Vizier's field guns had got mired down, as the roads were barely passable at the best of times, let alone at this time of the year. As soon as he got to Priboy, the Vizier cut off the heads of all the government officials there, without exception (fortunately there were only three), and those of another couple of leading citizens.

Then he sent a herald ahead with strict orders that the roads be mended and surfaced. But the order was superfluous: the example of Priboy had produced its terrible effect. Along the entire road from Priboy to Sarajevo there were swarms of workmen and overseers, the deep ruts and potholes were filled up, the wooden bridges were repaired. Terror had paved the way for the Vizier, literally.

Ali Pasha traveled slowly, spent considerable time in each

town, and promptly introduced his kind of rule. He collected taxes, executed insubordinate Turks, threw local notables into jail, and all Jews without exception.

At Sarajevo, according to the lengthy and graphic report from Freycinet, the terror was so great that the most powerful begs and bazaar elders went all the way up to the Goats' Bridge to greet the Vizier and offer the first gifts. Knowing the reputation of the Sarajevo begs for being cool and haughty to the viziers who passed that way from Istanbul to Travnik, Ali Pasha gruffly refused to see the delegation, shouting loudly from his tent that they were to get out of his sight immediately. As for those he might need, he said, he would find them in their homes.

The following day, in Sarajevo, all wealthier Jews and some of the most respected begs were taken into custody. If one of them as much as dared to ask why he was being held, he was at once tied up and lashed in the Vizier's presence.

All of this was carried to Travnik and bruited about town in advance, and popular rumor was already building the new Vizier into a monster. But his actual arrival in Travnik, the way he received the town notables and gave them the first audience, surpassed even the reputation that had preceded him.

On that spring day, the first to enter Travnik was a detachment of three hundred of the Vizier's Albanians. Marching in wide regular ranks, they were all as like as beads on a thread and as easy on the eye as girls. They carried short muskets and advanced in a short parade step, looking straight ahead. Then came the Vizier with a small escort and a detachment of cavalry. They too rode at a short funeral pace, with no sound or talking. In front of the Vizier, at the head of the escort, marched a great big giant of a man carrying a long naked sword before him in both hands. Not even the most wanton mercenaries, not a horde of wild Circassians, yelling and firing their guns, could have terrified the people as much as this slow and voiceless procession.

That same evening Ali Pasha carried out his usual arrests of the Jews and leading citizens, on the principle that "a man talks differently after spending a night in jail." If any relative or friend of the arrested man cried or wailed or wanted to give him something or help him in any way, he was whipped on the spot. All the heads of Jewish households were taken in, as Ali Pasha had an exact list and operated on the premise that no one paid as much ransom as the Jews and that they spread the bad news through the town much faster than anyone else. And the people of Travnik, who had long memories, witnessed, among other portents and ill-omens, the spectacle of the Atias family being led away on a single chain.

The same night the parish priest of Dolats, Fra Ivo Yankovich, Brother Guardian of the Gucha Gora monastery, and the monk Pakhomi were also taken in custody, fettered, and thrown into the citadel.

Early the following morning, all those who had previously been jailed for murder and major thefts and had been awaiting sentence under Ibrahim Pasha's court of justice, which had been slow and considerate, were led out from the fortress and tried. By sunrise they had already been hanged on the town's crossroads. And at noon the arrested notables purchased their freedom at the first divan held in the Residency.

The Hall of Audience could remember many stormy and fateful assemblies, it had heard many grave words, important decisions and sentences of death, but it could not remember this kind of silence—a silence that caught a man's breath and turned his innards to jelly.

Ali Pasha's art of government rested on his skill of creating, maintaining, and spreading such an atmosphere of terror that even men who were not afraid of anything, even death, were crushed and broken.

The first thing the Vizier told the assembled notables after he had read the Sultan's firman of appointment, was that the Mayor of Travnik, Ressim Beg, had been sentenced to death. Ali Pasha's surprises were the more frightful for being unexpected and incredible.

When Ibrahim Pasha had left Travnik three weeks before, Suleiman Pasha Skoplyak was somewhere on the Drina with his army and he declined, on some pretext or other, to come back and deputize until the arrival of the new Vizier. So the old Mayor, Ressim Beg, had been left in supreme command at Travnik.

The man had already been arrested, the Vizier said, and would be executed on Friday, because during the time he had acted for the Vizier he ran the affairs of the government in such a feeble and slipshod manner that he deserved to die, not once but twice over. And that was only the beginning. After him it would be the turn of all those others who'd agreed to work for the Empire and look after the business of state but had done their duty inadequately or had publicly and secretly shirked it. After the pronouncement, coffee, pipes, and sherbet were served.

Following the coffee, Hamdi Beg Teskeredjich, the senior beg among the assembled, spoke a few words in defense of the hapless Mayor. While he was still speaking, one of the servants attending the Vizier backed away toward the door on the right and there collided with one of the pipe bearers, knocking over a lighted clay chibouk. As if this were the last straw, the Vizier's eyes blazed up, he jerked himself up to his full height and, drawing a knife, threw himself on the stunned boy. There was a frantic scuffle among the servants as they carried out the poor bloodied wretch, and a wave of shock passed over the begs and dignitaries, who forgot the smoking pipes in front of them and dropped their eyes, each staring into his own coffee cup.

Only Hamdi Beg kept his calm and presence of mind and wound up his defense of the old Mayor, requesting the Vizier to consider his age and previous services rather than his recent mistakes and failings.

To this the Vizier replied in a clear, lashing voice that was like a sharp thunderclap. Under his government every man would get what he deserved: rewards and recognition for those who were obedient and worked for it, death and whipping for the shirkers and insubordinates. "I was not sent here to have wool pulled over my eyes, or to smoke chibouks with you, or lounge around on these cushions," concluded the Vizier, "but to make order in this country which is famed all the way to Istanbul for taking pride in its disorder. There's an axe for every head, even the hardest. Now you still have your heads, I have the axe in my hand, and the Sultan's firman is under my cushion here. Let each man who wants to eat his bread and see the sun, behave and act accordingly. Make a note of this and then tell your people, so that together we can begin to do things which the Sultan wants us to do."

The begs and the dignitaries got up and took their leave with silent greetings, happy to be alive and as dazed as if they had watched a magician's performance.

The very next day the new Vizier received Daville in a solemn audience.

Daville was given an escort of his Albanians, in full dress and well mounted. They rode through deserted streets and a bazaar that was almost dead. Not a door opened, not a window shutter was raised, there was not a head to be seen. The reception went according to protocol. The Vizier presented Daville and his interpreter with furs. The rooms and corridors of the Residency were conspicuously empty, devoid of furniture and decoration. And the number of courtiers and servants was unusually small. After the throb and bustle of Ibrahim Pasha's tenure at the Residency, the place now looked naked and desolate.

Curious and excited as he was, Daville was quite taken aback at his first sight of the new Vizier. He was a strong and high-set man, but small-boned, and he moved with a springy brisk step, with none of that ponderous dignity which so many high Turkish personages affected. His face was swarthy, the color of his skin dull, his eyes were large and green, while his beard and mustaches where completely white and trimmed very short.

He was relaxed and talked freely and laughed often, though perhaps too loudly for a Turkish dignitary. Daville asked himself if this was the same man of whom he had heard all those dreadful things, who only yesterday, in the course of a single audience, had condemned the old Mayor to die and had stabbed one of the servants.

The Vizier laughed and told Daville of his plans to set the country to rights and lead a serious and energetic military expedition against Serbia; then enjoined the Consul to keep up his good work as heretofore, assuring him of his good will, his attention and protection.

On his part Daville too was unstinting with compliments and assurances, but he could see right away that the Vizier's stock of fine phrases and amiable grimaces was rather limited, because the moment he stopped talking and the smile died on his lips, his face darkened and hardened and his eyes grew restive, as if looking for a spot to strike. The cold flame of these eyes was hard to bear and it was in strange contrast to his loud laughter.

"These Bosnian begs have probably told you about me and my methods of government. Don't let that bother you. I can well believe they are not enamored of me. But I didn't come here to be liked. They are fools who want to live on empty gentility and talk big and loud. But that cannot be. The time has come for them to use their brains. Only you can't make them see that by appealing to their heads, but by appealing to the other end, the soles of their feet. I've never yet seen a man who forgot a good bastinado, but I've seen a hundred times how men forget the best advice and lesson." The Vizier laughed out loud and there was a youthful, devilish expression around his mouth and the trim mustaches and beard. "They can say what they like," he continued, "but I intend to strike discipline and order into these people's marrow. Don't pay any attention to it, but if ever you need anything, come straight to me. It is my wish that you should be content and quiet in your heart."

It was the first time Daville was confronted with one of those unlearned, coarse, and bloody Turkish governors about whom he had so far known only from books and popular tales.

There followed then one of those intervals of time during which everyone tried to make himself small and inconspicuous, when everyone sought cover and shelter, and the saying went around the bazaar that "even a mouse hole was worth a thousand ducats." Fear spread over Travnik like a bank of fog, pressing down on everything that breathed and thought.

It was the kind of great fear, unseen, imponderable, but all-pervading, that comes over human communities from time to time, coiling itself around some heads and breaking others. At times like these many people, blinded and bedeviled, lose sight of reason and courage and of the fact that everything in life is fleeting, and that although human life, like every other thing, has its value, that value is not unlimited. And so, cowed by the passing specter of fear, they pay a price for their bare life that is far in excess of its value, they do low and mean things, they humble and shame themselves, and when the moment of fear has passed, they realize that they have ransomed their life too dearly, that they have not even been in real jeopardy but have simply knuckled under to the irresistible wraith of fear.

The garden of Lutva's coffeehouse was left deserted, although spring had set in and the lime tree above the garden was turning green. All that the Travnik begs dared to do was entreat the Vizier humbly to forgive the Mayor his mistakes (although no one knew what these were) and to spare his life out of consideration for his old age and previous services.

All the other prisoners in the fortress, the dice players, horse thieves, and arsonists, were tried in short order and led to the chopping block and their heads were stuck on poles and displayed in public places.

The Austrian Consul promptly interceded for the arrested friars. Daville did not wish to be outdone—save that, in his own petition, he mentioned the Jews as well as the friars. The Brothers were released first; they were followed by the Jews who came out one by one and were immediately assessed and fined. They left so much money at the Residency that all the Jewish cashboxes were emptied down to the last penny—that is to say, the last penny of the funds set aside for bribery. The one who remained longest in the fortress was the monk Pakhomi, whose case no one took up. At length he too was ransomed by his small and poor congregation for a round sum of three thousand groschen, of which more than two thirds were contributed by two brothers, Peter and Jovan Fufich. As for the begs of Travnik and other towns, some were let go while others were being arrested, so that there were always ten or fifteen of them in the fortress.

That was how Ali Pasha began his rule in Travnik and hastened to get up an army against Serbia.

25

The sense of extremity that gripped Travnik with the coming of the new Vizier, preying on the whole town but especially crushing to those individuals who happened to be the immediate victims of it, was of course localized in this mountain range which rings and hems in the city, and was echoed only dimly in the reports of the two Travnik consuls, reports which in those days hardly anyone in Paris or Vienna had the time to read with any attention. For the great outside world was then filled with rumors of the momentous drama of Napoleon's collapse.

Daville spent the holiday period of Christmas and New Year's in terrified waiting, obsessesed by the thought that all was lost. When it was learned that Napoleon was back in Paris, things took a turn for the better. Reassuring comments began to arrive from Paris, instructions and circulars as well as news that the Grande Armée was being reorganized and that the government was taking firm measures in all departments.

Once again Daville was ashamed of his faintheartedness. Yet this same timidity drove him now to seek refuge in nebulous hopes, so great is weak man's need to deceive himself and so boundless his capacity for being deceived.

At the end of May came the bulletins of Napoleon's victories in Germany, at Lutzen and Bautzen. The old game was resumed once more. But in Travnik, at this time, there was so much woe and dejection and fear of the new Vizier and his Albanians that no one was in the mood to listen to victory bulletins.

At about that time Ali Pasha marched against Serbia—having first "struck order and discipline" into everyone without exception. Even here his methods were unlike those of his predecessors. In the old days these "departures for Serbia" used to have the aspect of a public festival. Day by day, week by week, the drilling field at Travnik was the scene of a gradual mustering of fortress captains from the interior of Bosnia. They came in their own sweet time, arbitrarily, bringing whatever type of force suited them, in any size they thought fit. And having reached Travnik, they would settle there and start haggling with the Vizier and the local authorities, making demands and laying down conditions, asking for provisions, equipment, and money, while for the public benefit they put on a show of martial enthusiasm and sword-rattling pomp.

While this was going on, armed, uniformed, and sinister strangers could be seen loafing in the streets of Travnik. The noisy and flamboyant circus on the drilling field would go on for weeks. Tents were hitched and campfires burned. In a clearing in the center, a lance with three horsetails was stuck into the ground, spattered with the blood of rams which had been killed as a sacrifice for the good luck of the expedition. Drums throbbed, bugles sounded, prayers were read. In short, everything that could possibly delay departures was done. And often the principal and climactic attraction of the whole thing lay in this mustering and in the attendant festivities, so that the majority of warriors never saw the battlefield at all.

But on this occasion, under the beady eye of Ali Pasha, the affair went off in grim silence and under a cloud of fear, with no special celebration but also without any wrangling and tarrying. As food was scarce, the men lived on scant rations from the Vizier's store. No one felt like singing or making music.

When the Vizier came down to the field for a personal inspection, he ordered the beheading of the commander from Cazin, for having brought ten soldiers fewer than he had promised; immediately afterwards he chose a man from the commander's mortified contingent and made him the new captain.

This was how the present expedition set off for the Serbian frontier, where Suleiman Pasha was already waiting with his force.

Once again Travnik was left in the supreme command of the old Mayor, Ressim Beg, whom Ali Pasha had sentenced to death upon his arrival and whose life the begs had only just managed to save. The ordeal to which the old Mayor had been subjected was, in the Vizier's opinion, the best guarantee that this time he would carry out his office satisfactorily, in accordance with the Vizier's wishes and plans.

What earthly purpose would it serve, mused Daville, to burden the pathetic old man with bulletins of Napoleon's new victories? What point was there in telling anyone about them?

The Vizier had gone off with his army and his Albanians, but the terror had remained behind him, as cold and hard and lasting as the hardest wall; behind him too lingered the ghost of his return, more potent than any threat and crueler than any punishment.

The town remained as if deaf and dumb; empty, drained, and hungering as never before in the last twenty years. As the days grew longer and sunnier, there was less time for sleeping and more for the pangs of hunger than during the short days of winter. Groups of wasted scabby children ambled through the streets, looking for what was not to be found: wholesome food. People journeyed as far as Posavina beyond the river Sava, looking for grain, or even for seed.

The market days began to resemble ordinary days. Some shops did not bother to open. The merchants squatting on their wooden platforms were sullen and glum. There had been no coffee or imports from overseas since the previous autumn; staple foods were nonexistent. The only customers were those shopping for things which were not there. The new Vizier had levied such high taxes on the bazaar that a good many store owners had had to borrow in order to meet them. And the fear was so pervasive that no person dared to utter a complaint, not even within the four walls of his home.

In the shops and houses there was talk of how six Christian

emperors were banding together to strike at Bonaparte, how they had all conscripted every last male into their armies and how there would be no plowing, no digging, no sowing or harvesting until Bonaparte was brought to his knees and destroyed.

Now even the Jews took care not to be seen around the French Consulate. Freycinet, who had set about liquidating the French agency at Sarajevo, wrote that the local Jews had suddenly presented all their demand notes and bills and that he was quite unable to meet all his obligations. And Paris had stopped answering letters altogether. As for the Consulate, the payroll and expense funds had not been received for three whole months.

While viziers were being changed at Travnik and Europe was preoccupied with great events, in the little world of the Consulate things continued their natural course: new lives were born and old ones came to the end of their span.

Madame Daville was again pregnant and in her last months. She bore the pregnancy as easily and unobtrusively as the one of two years before. She spent the whole day with her helpers in the garden. Thanks to von Paulich, she had managed once again to obtain the necessary seeds from Austria and was looking forward to great things from her seedling flats, even though the confinement came at an awkward time for her, just when her presence in the garden would be most needed.

At the end of May a fifth child was born to the Davilles, this time a boy. The child was weak and was therefore christened right away. He was registered under the name of Auguste-François-Gérard in the parish of Dolats.

Madame Daville's delivery brought forth the same lively reaction as her previous one: gossip and the sympathies of the whole distaff side of Travnik, visits, inquiries, and good wishes from all sides, even birthday presents, despite the shortages and the general want. The only thing missing was a gift from the Residency, but that was because the Vizier had gone to the Drina with his army.

Although so many things had changed in the last two years—particularly relations between people and conditions in the country—the general idea of family life had remained unchanged. Everything that had to do with it exacted a strong and unchanging fascination for these people, like a hallowed relic whose value was universal, lasting, and unbounded by changes and events in the world at large. For in communities like these the life of every person was firmly centered in the family, as in a perfectly wrought closed circle. Yet these circles, though strictly separate, had an invisible common center somewhere, so that a part of each impinged on and overlapped the others. Therefore nothing that happened in one family could fail to leave the others indifferent, and every person took a sympathetic interest in all family events, births, weddings, and deaths, and did so heartily, eagerly, with the spontaneity of a natural reflex.

About the same time, the former interpreter of the Austrian Consulate, Nicholas Rotta, fought his last, pathetic, and desperate fight with his destiny.

The von Mitterer family had for years employed an old Hungarian woman who was so obese and rheumatic that she could hardly move. She was an excellent cook, genuinely devoted to the family, and at the same time an unbearable tyrant to all the staff. Anna Maria had quarreled and made peace with her for fifteen long years. However, as the Hungarian was getting heavier and slower, they had taken a young woman from Dolats to help her. Her name was Lucia, and she was strong, useful, and energetic. She took the moody old cook in stride so well that she learned cooking and scullery work from her. When the von Mitterer family left Travnik, taking, naturally, their "house dragon" with them, as Anna Maria called the old Hungarian, Lucia stayed behind as von Paulich's cook.

This Lucia had a sister, Andja, who was the black sheep of the family and a disgrace to the whole Dolats community. When still a girl, she had gone on the primrose path and had been cursed from the pulpit and thrown out of Dolats. Now she owned a roadside coffeehouse at Kalibunar. Lucia, like the rest of her family, suffered a great deal on account of this sister, whom she loved very much and with whom, despite everything, she never could break completely. From time to time she would go to see her in secret, although these visits caused her more pain than even her longing for her sister, for Andja obstinately stuck to her ways, while Lucia, after pleading with her in vain, would cry over her every time as if she were already dead. And still they could never entirely give up seeing each other.

Wandering aimlessly around Travnik and the countryside, with nothing to do, yet trying to appear busy and important, Rotta often came as far as Andja's coffeehouse at Kalibunar. Little by little he struck up a friendship with the loose woman, who, like himself, was an outcast and was beginning to age and take to drink.

Some time around Easter, Andja came to the Consulate to see her sister Lucia. After they had talked for a while, she came out with the blunt and startling suggestion that they poison the Austrian Consul. She had brought the poison with her.

It was just the sort of plan that might be hatched in a disreputable coffeehouse in the dead of night, between two sick and unfortunate creatures whose brains were in a fog of alcohol, ignorance, hatred, and warped infatuation. Rotta had apparently quite turned Andja's head, for she swore to her sister that the poison was a very special one designed to make the Consul waste away and die by slow imperceptible degrees, as from a natural disease. She promised Lucia a huge reward and a life of luxury with Rotta, whom she, Andja, planned to marry and who was certain to get another high post after the Consul's death. And she produced a sum of cash in solid ducats. In short, all three of them would be happy and without a care in the world for the rest of their lives.

Listening to her sister's proposition, Lucia almost died of fright and shame. She quickly took the two white phials and hid them in the pockets of her skirt, then grabbed her sister by the shoulders and began to shake her, as if to bring her out of a morbid trance, imploring her, on their mother's grave and in the name of all that was holy, to push these thoughts and designs from her head and come to her senses. In order to convince and shame her, she told her of the Consul's kindness and what a mortal sin it would be even to think of repaying his goodness in this ghastly way. She urged her to break off with Rotta immediately and have no more truck with him.

Taken aback by this resistance and censure, Andja pretended to give up her plan and asked her sister to give her back the two phials, but Lucia would not hear of it. And so they parted— Lucia dazed and in tears, and Andja in silence, with a peeved and enigmatic expression on her red face. Unable to close her eyes that night, Lucia tossed in her bed and went through agonies. And when the morning came, she set out for Dolats, without telling anyone, and confided the whole thing to the parish priest, Fra Ivo Yankovich. She gave him the poison phials and asked him to do what he thought best to avert a sin and a catastrophe.

The same morning, without losing a moment, Fra Ivo called

on von Paulich, told him everything, and handed over the poison. The Consul at once wrote a letter to Daville, in which he informed him that his protégé Rotta had tried to poison him, and that there were witnesses and evidence to prove it. The wretch had made a mess of it, as was to be expected, but he, von Paulich, left it to Daville's good judgment to decide whether he wanted to extend the further protection of the French Consulate to a man of that caliber. In a similar letter, he also reported the whole business to the town Mayor. Having done that, the Consul quietly resumed his work and his old life; he went on eating the same food, kept the same servants and the same cook. However, everyone else was greatly distressed: the Mayor, the friars, and especially Daville. D'Avenat was ordered to give an ultimatum to Rotta: either he was to leave Travnik forthwith or lose the protection of the French Consulate and be arrested by the Turkish authorities for a proven attempt of poisoning.

Rotta vanished from Travnik that same night, together with the woman Andja from the Kalibunar coffeehouse. D'Avenat notified the French authorities in Split about Rotta's recent exploits and his treacherous, untrustworthy character. He advised them not to give him a service job of any kind and recommended that they pack him off back to the Levant and let him fend for himself.

26

This time the summer months brought some relief and a semblance of quietude. The season of fruit came, wheat and barley ripened, the people ate better and felt a little easier. But the talk of war, of the great account settling and Napoleon's inevitable collapse before the end of summer, did not cease. The friars, especially, encouraged a whispering campaign to that effect among the people. They did it so stealthily and efficiently that Daville could neither catch them red-handed nor combat them as he should have.

One day in early September von Paulich, with a bigger escort than usual, paid a visit to his French colleague.

All through the summer, while fantastic rumors and highly improbable items of news had been circulating against the

French, von Paulich had remained composed and impartial in his relations with everyone. Every week he had sent Mme Daville samples of his flowers and vegetables, raised from seed they had bought together. In his rare meetings with Daville he had given as his opinion that a general war was unlikely and that there was no indication whatever that Austria might abandon her neutral position. He had quoted Ovid and Virgil. He had discussed the causes of famine and shortages in Travnik and sketched out a method by which such trouble might be circumvented. And, as always, he had talked of these things as if the point of discussion were a war on some other planet and the famine in another part of the world.

And now, exactly at noon of that quiet September day, in Daville's study on the ground floor, von Paulich sat across from Daville, more solemn than usual, but calm and cool as always.

He had come, he said, because of the persistent rumors that were circulating among the local populace about an imminent war between Austria and France. As far as he knew, these reports were unfounded, and he wanted to reassure Daville on that point. Nevertheless, he also wanted to take this opportunity to tell him how he envisaged their relations in the event that war really did come. Gazing at his folded white hands, the Colonel calmly outlined his views.

"In all matters of politics or war our relations should, in my opinion, remain the same as heretofore. In any case, as two Europeans and men of honor who have been tossed into this country in the line of duty and forced to live in exceptional circumstances, I do not think we should harass and malign each other before these barbarians, as once may have been the case perhaps. I thought it my duty to tell you so, in view of the gossip-mongering, which I believe is quite unfounded, and to ask your opinion about it."

Daville felt his throat tighten.

From the uneasiness of the French authorities in Dalmatia in recent days he had gathered that something was afoot, but he had no other information and did not want von Paulich to see this.

Collecting himself a little, he thanked von Paulich in a voice hoarse with emotion and added at once that he was in full accord with his ideas, that this had always been his own attitude, and that it was no fault of his if things had sometimes been different with von Paulich's predecessor. He even wished to go a step further. "I hope, my dear Colonel, that war can be avoided, but if it cannot be, then I hope it will be waged without hatred and will not last long. In that case, I hope very much that the tender and exalted family ties which link our two courts will be a mitigating element and will hasten the conclusion of peace."

At this point von Paulich, who until then had looked him straight in the eye, glanced away and his averted face grew stern and distant.

And that was how they parted.

A week later special couriers arrived, the Austrian one from Brod and after him the French courier from Split, and the two consuls learned almost simultaneously that war had been declared.

Next day Daville had a letter from von Paulich, informing him that their two countries were at war and recalling all they had verbally agreed to concerning their mutual conduct so long as the war lasted. He wound up the letter by assuring Mme Daville of his undying respect and repeating that he was at her disposal for any service of a nonofficial nature.

Daville answered promptly, averring that he and his staff would observe their agreement to the letter, as "here in the Orient, all nationals of Western countries, without exception, must regard themselves as members of a single family, no matter what their differences in Europe itself." He added that Mme Daville thanked him for his remembrance and was sorry to lose the Colonel's company for a while.

And so, in the autumn of 1813, entering another period of war, the two consuls also commenced the last year of the "Consular Era."

The steep paths in the great garden around the French Consulate were strewn with fallen leaves that trickled in dry rustling rivulets down toward the terrace, already seeded for the next season. On these tumbling footpaths, under the leaning, harvested fruit trees, it was warm and quiet, as always during the days when the whole of nature relaxes in momentary peace, in that bewitching, lulling pause between summer and autumn.

It was here that Daville, hidden away, with only a fragmentary view of the neighboring hill in front of him, searched his heart very earnestly and saw his past exaltations, plans, and conviction for what they were.

It was here, in the last days of October, that he learned from

D'Avenat the outcome of the Battle of Leipzig, and heard of the French defeats in Spain from a passing courier. For it was here in the garden that he spent his entire days, until the weather grew quite cold and the early autumn rains turned the yellow, rustly leaves into a clammy mass of shapeless mud.

One Sunday before noon—it was November 1, 1813—the cannon was fired from the Travnik fortress, shattering the dead humid silence between the steep and bare hillsides. The people down in the bazaar lifted their heads and counted the shots, while glancing at each other with mute questioning eyes. Twenty-one shots were fired. The white gun smoke above the fortress thinned and faded and silence descended once again, only to be broken again a little later.

The voice of the town crier rose up in the middle of the bazaar. It was the goitered and asthmatic Hamza, whose voice was growing noticeably feebler, just like his laughter and sense of humor. Still, he gave it all he had and tried to make up with gestures for the voice he no longer had.

Laboring for breath in the damp winter air, he announced that Allah had blessed the arms of the Crescent Moon with a glorious and just victory over the rebellious infidels, that Belgrade had fallen into Turkish hands, and that the last traces of the infidel insurgents in Serbia had been wiped out forever.

The news spread like a flash from one end of the town to the other.

On the afternoon of that same day D'Avenat went down into the city to find out how the populace was taking the news.

The top crust of Travnik, the begs and the bazaar folk, would not have been true to character if they had shown their joy openly and aloud, even at such great news as a victory of their arms. They condescended to mumble a few monosyllabic banalities, not even bothering to pronounce them distinctly; anything else would not have been in keeping with their ideas of dignity and restraint. They seemed, in fact, to look upon the news as a mixed blessing; for good as it was to know that Serbia had been pacified, it was not especially pleasant to think of Ali Pasha returning as a victor, since now, presumably, he would be even harder and tougher to deal with than he had been thus far. And besides, they had been hearing a good many criers and victorious announcements down the years, but none of them could remember a time when one New Year was an improve-

ment over the old. That was how D'Avenat "read" them, although not one of them deigned to give him as much as a
glance in answer to his unseemly questioning.

He also went to Dolats, to find out what the Brothers were
saying. However, Fra Ivo pretended he was busy in the church;
he dragged out the service as never before and refused to leave
the altar until D'Avenat tired of waiting and went back to Travnik.

He looked in on the monk Pakhomi at his house and found
him lying in bed like a hermit, in a chilly room bare of furniture, wearing all his clothes, green in the face. Instead of questioning him as he had intended, he offered him his services
as a doctor, but the monk declined all medicines and claimed
that he was well and lacked nothing.

Next day, both Daville and von Paulich paid an official visit
to the Deputy Vizier and offered their congratulations on the
victory, but they timed their calls so as not to meet either at the
Residency or on their way in and out.

When the first heavy snow fell, Ali Pasha returned to Travnik.
He entered the town to a roaring gun salute and a blare of
trumpets, while children scampered alongside. The Travnik
begs suddenly found their tongues. Most of them praised the
victory and the victor with moderate and dignified phrases, but
took care to do so aloud and in public.

On the very first day Daville sent D'Avenat to the Residency
to convey his felicitations and deliver a present to the victorious
Vizier.

Some ten years before, when Daville was Chargé d'Affaires in
a mission to the Knights of Malta at Naples, he had bought a
heavy, beautifully wrought gold ring that had no stone but an
exquisite carved laurel wreath in the place where the stone
would normally have been. Daville had bought it from the estate
of an heirless and indebted Knight of Malta. According to the
family tradition the ring had once been used as a victor's trophy
in the tournaments of the Knights of the Maltese Order.

Lately, as things had taken an irrevocable turn toward defeat
and he had lost his own sense of direction and suffered agonies of
uncertainty about his homeland, his future, and that of his family, Daville gave things away more often and more easily, and
found a strange new satisfaction in presenting other people with
the objects he had loved and jealously guarded till now. In giving away these dear and precious things, which so far he had

looked upon as part and parcel of his personal life, he felt as though he were bribing Fate, who now seemed to have forsaken him and his family. At the same time the act filled him with a deep and genuine joy, quite like the joy he had once felt when he was buying these things for himself.

D'Avenat was not allowed to see the Vizier, but delivered the present to the Secretary, with the explanation that for hundreds of years this treasure had been awarded to the man who won in combat and that the Consul was now sending it to a happy victor with his compliments and good wishes.

Ali Pasha's Secretary was one Assim Effendi, called "the Stammerer." He was pale and haggard, a shadow of a man, with an impediment in his speech and a pair of squinting eyes of dissimilar color. He had a look of being perpetually frightened to death and so infected every visitor in advance with a terror of the Vizier.

Two days later the consuls had their audiences, first the Austrian and then the Frenchman. The days of the French preeminence were over.

Ali Pasha was worn out but content. In the reflected glare of the snowy winter day, Daville noticed for the first time that the Vizier's pupils flickered every now and then restlessly; the moment his eyes steadied and his gaze became even, the strange flickering would begin. The Vizier was apparently conscious of it and felt awkward about it, for he kept turning his eyes and shifting his glance, which once again gave an unpleasant and wary expression to his whole face.

Ali Pasha, who for this occasion had placed the ring on the middle finger of his right hand, thanked Daville for his gift and good wishes. He hardly mentioned the Serbian campaign and his successes; the little he said about them had the ring of false modesty typical of vain and touchy people, who prefer to keep silent because they consider all words inadequate and insufficient, and because their silence cows the man in front of them and takes their success out of the realm of description and so places it beyond the reach of average people. By this stratagem, successful people of this type manage to shut up anyone who talks to them about their victory, even years after the event.

The conversation began to drag and sound insincere. Silences kept occurring in which Daville searched for fresh and stronger words of praise for the Vizier's triumph; and the Vizier let him search, while his own eyes cruised around the room and his face bore an air of restive boredom, as though he were privately convinced that the right and proper words could never be found.

And as usually happens in such cases, in his eagerness to show as much sympathy and sincere joy as possible, Daville unwittingly hurt the feelings of the Vizier.

"Does anyone know the whereabouts of the rebel leader Karageorge?" asked Daville, perhaps because he had heard that Karageorge had fled to Austria.

"Who knows or cares where he is," the Vizier said contemptuously.

"But isn't there a risk that some country might give him asylum and help, and that he might afterwards return to Serbia?"

The corners of the Vizier's mouth twitched in anger, then curled in a smile. "He will never come back. Besides, there's nothing for him to get back to. Serbia is so thoroughly ravaged that it'll be many years before he or anyone else can think of another uprising."

Daville had even less luck in steering the conversation to France and the war plans of the Allies, who at this time were preparing to cross the Rhine.

On his way back to Travnik the Vizier had been met at Busovacha by a special courier sent by von Paulich, who had handed him, together with von Paulich's congratulations, a comprehensive written report on the state of the European battlefront. Von Paulich had written the Vizier that "God had finally struck down the unbearable pride of France and the united efforts of the European nations had borne fruit." He had described in detail the Battle of Leipzig, Napoleon's defeat and withdrawal behind the Rhine, the relentless advance of the Allies, and the preparations for the crossing of the Rhine and final victory. He gave exact figures for the French losses in killed, wounded, and equipment, as well as the armed strength of the subject states which had broken away from Napoleon. And on his arrival in Travnik, Ali Pasha had found other reports that fully confirmed what von Paulich had written.

That was why he now adopted this tone with Daville, and was careful not to mention either his ruler or his country by a single word, as if he were talking to the representative of a nameless and obscure never-never land which had no concrete shape and no fixed position in space; or, as if he were superstitious and reluctant to rub elbows, even mentally, with those whom Kismet had snubbed and who had long passed to the side of the vanquished.

Daville glanced once more at his ring on the Vizier's finger, then took his leave in a studiedly cheerful manner, which seemed to come more easily the more difficult and equivocal his position grew.

When they left the Residency, the covered courtyard was already in darkness, but as they rode out through the gates Daville was dazzled by the whiteness of the soft wet snow that lay heaped in the streets and thick on the house roofs. It was around four o'clock in the afternoon. Blue shadows stretched over the snow. As always on those very short days, dusk came early and sadly in this mountain valley, and beneath the heavy snow the purl of water could still be heard. Everything exuded dampness. The wooden bridge echoed with a hollow sound under the horses' hoofs.

As always when he left the Residency, Daville felt a momentary relief. For a while he forgot who was the victor and who the vanquished, and thought only of how to ride, this one more time, quietly and with dignity through the town. A shudder ran through him, partly from excitement, partly from the overheated air at the Residency and the damp air of the evening. He tried not to shiver. It reminded him of that February day when he had ridden for the first time through this same bazaar, to the abuse, the spitting, or the contemptuous silence of these fanatical people, as he was on his way to his first audience with Husref Mehmed Pasha. And all of a sudden he had the feeling that all his life, since he had reached the age of sensibility, he had done nothing else but ride along this same road, with the same escort, deep in the same thoughts.

Slowly and through necessity, he had inured himself in these seven years to a great many distasteful and painful things, but he still went to the Residency with the same feeling of unpleasant apprehension. Even in the happiest of times and in the most favorable circumstances, he had always, as far as he could, avoided going to the Residency and tried to accomplish his errands through D'Avenat. And when an item of business seemed to require a visit to the Vizier and could really not be settled without it, he girded himself for it as though it were a major expedition, and slept badly and ate little for days ahead. He rehearsed what he would say and how he would say it, he tried to anticipate their answers and wiles and so wore himself out in advance. And to give himself at least some rest, peace, and comfort, he would tell himself in bed at night: "Ah, tomorrow at this time, I shall be lying here again, and those two bitter hours of torture will be far behind me."

The enervating game would start right in the morning. Grooms would scamper and horses would clatter in the courtyard and in front of the Consulate. Then, in due course, D'Avenat would appear with his dark suffused face which would have taken the heart out of a heavenly angel let alone an ordinary worried mortal. This was the sign for the agony to begin.

From the gathering children and loafers the town usually knew that one of the consuls was due to pass through to the Residency. Then, from the bend at the top of the main market street, Daville's procession would appear, always the same. In the van, the Vizier's mounted guard, whose job it was to escort the Consul both ways. Behind him, the Consul on his black horse, dignified and expressionless; two paces farther back, D'Avenat on his frisky bay mare, which the Travnik Turks hated almost as much as D'Avenat himself. Bringing up the rear were two consular kavasses on good Bosnian horses, armed with pistols and daggers.

That was how they expected him to ride through every time, mounted straight as a ramrod, looking neither to the left nor to the right, neither too high nor between the horse's ears, neither tense nor woolgathering, neither smiling nor glum, but calm, grave, and yet alert, with something of that improbable air of generals in their portraits as they look out over the battle into the distance, at a point somewhere between the road and the line of horizon, where, at a decisive moment, certain well-deployed reinforcements are supposed to appear.

He himself hardly knew how many hundreds of times, over the years, he had passed like this over the same road, but he knew that, always and under all viziers, it had been an experience very akin to inquisition. He used even to dream about the road and suffer all kinds of agonies in his dream, riding with a ghostly escort between a double row of menace and ambush, on his way to a Residency that was utterly beyond his reach.

And now, as he was remembering all this, he was riding once more, in exactly the same fashion, through the twilit bazaar, full of snow.

Most of the shops were already closed and shuttered. Passers-by were few and they walked slowly, bent forward as if dragging chains behind them, through the deep and lumpy snow, with their hands stuck in their waistbands and their ears muffled in handkerchiefs.

When they got to the Consulate, D'Avenat asked Daville to see him for a few minutes, so that he could tell him what he had heard from the Vizier's retinue.

A traveler from Istanbul had brought word of Ibrahim Halimi Pasha. After a two-month stay at Gallipoli, the former Vizier had been banished to a small town in Asia Minor, after all his estates in Istanbul and on the Bosporus had been confiscated. His entourage had gradually dispersed, every man looking to his own bread and interests. Left almost alone, Ibrahim Pasha had set out for his exile; and as he journeyed to the distant little Anatolian hamlet, where the land was barren, craggy, and scorched, a stony desert without grass or a drop of running water, he passed the days rehashing his old daydream—the dream of how, cut off from the world and dressed in the simple clothes of a gardener, he would till his parcel of soil in silence and solitude.

A few days before his departure into exile, his former Secretary, Tahir Beg, had suddenly died—of heart failure, it was said. His death had been a heavy blow to Ibrahim Pasha, who had only one remedy against it, an old man's failing memory, as he spent his last days in the rocky and waterless region.

Daville dismissed D'Avenat and remained alone in the snow-bound dusk. A swelling cloud of humidity rose up from the valley below. All sound was muffled in the high soft snow. Down at the bottom, the snow-capped mausoleum of Abdullah Pasha was barely visible. The tower window above the grave shone with the feeble light of the taper that was burning inside.

The Consul shivered. He felt weak and feverish. A bright welter of recent impressions and news swirled through his weary, passive mind. Then, as often happens to people who are exhausted and worried to distraction, everything he had heard and gone through that day, all the difficulties and embarrassments that might still be in store for him tomorrow and in the future, suddenly drained out of his consciousness and he thought only of what he saw before him—of the octagonal stone mausoleum by which he had walked so often, of the flickering taper flame inside that now barely pierced the evening mist and which he and Desfosses had once called "eternal light," and of the origin of the tomb and the story of Abdullah Pasha who was resting in it.

He thought of the low stone sarcophagus covered with a green pall, on which was written "May the All-Highest light his tomb!"; of the thick wax candle on its high wooden candelabrum which burned day and night over the dark grave in a feeble effort to persuade God to grant the prayer in the pall inscription, and which God was unwilling to grant, it seemed. He thought of the Pasha, who had risen high when still a young man, and had died accidentally on a visit to his native country. Yes, he remembered it all, as if the fate of other people and his own were one and the same thing. He remembered how Desfosses, before he left, had finally managed to see and read Abdullah Pasha's testament.

Knowing how little light there was in this valley, the Pasha had made over his houses and tenant holdings to an endowment fund, to which a cash legacy was later added, all for the purpose of having at least one great taper burn over his tomb to the end of time and the world. And he had arranged and legalized it all while he was still alive, in writing, before the magistrate and witnesses—specifying the kind of wax that was to be used, the weight of the candle, the wages of the man who would light it and change it—so that no successor of his or an outsider would ever be able to deny or betray his will. Yes, the Pasha knew well about the dark evenings and foggy days in this narrow valley, where he would have to lie till Judgment Day, and he knew too how quickly men forgot the living and the dead alike, how they betrayed trust and broke their promises.

And while he lay ill in one of these townhouses, without a hope of recovery, without a hope that his eyes, which had seen so much of the world, would ever again behold a more generous view than that from his bedside, the only thing that could soften his boundless grief over a misspent life and a premature death was the thought of the pure beeswax that would burn over his tomb with an even, soundless flame, with no smoke or molten gobs. And so, all that he had won by great effort, courage, and acumen in his short life, he gave for this little flame now trembling delicately over his helpless remains. In his stormy life, having seen many countries and kinds of people, he had learned that fire was at the root of all creation; it was the breath of life and also its destroyer, visible or invisible, in one degree or another, in forms without number. And so he devoted his last thoughts to fire. True, this little orange tongue of flame was not very secure or significant, nor was it likely to be there till the very end, but it was the best one could do—shed a small, permanent light on a puny fragment of a gloomy and cold land.

Yes, it was a strange bequest—but they were a strange people! Yet any man who had lived here for some years and passed his nights like this by the window could understand it easily and well.

He could hardly take his eyes off the faint glow that sank deeper and deeper into the humid miasma of darkness. Then, all at once, the memories of the day flooded back into his mind again, the strained conversation with the Vizier, the memory of Ibrahim Halimi Pasha, and Tahir Beg, the former Secretary, of whose death he had learned that evening. More real than he had been when he lived at Travnik, the Secretary rose up before Daville; bent at the waist, with shiny eyes that pierced a little with their unnatural glitter, the Secretary was saying, as he once had said on a cold evening like this: "Yes, monsieur, everyone sees the victor in a golden cloud. Or as the Persian poet says, 'A victor's face is like a rose.' "

"So it is!" Daville thought. "The victor's face is like a rose, but the face of a defeated man is like a graveyard that makes people turn their heads and run."

Daville spoke this aloud—it was the answer he should have made to the Secretary when he was still alive. And then he recalled the rest of his talk with the late Secretary. He felt another cold shudder and a trembling in his whole body, and he rang for the servant to bring in the candles.

And even after that Daville kept going to the window, watching the taper glow in Abdullah Pasha's tomb and the tiny, dull lights in the houses of Travnik; and he pondered further on the meaning of fire in the world, the lot of victors and vanquished, remembering the living and the dead, until all the windows guttered one by one, even those of the Austrian Consulate. (Victors go to bed early and sleep well!) The only light left was the sad taper of the mausoleum and at the opposite end of the town one other light, bigger and different. There, in a still-house, they were making plum brandy, as they did every year at this time.

At the other end of the Travnik gorge, where the wet snow was high, they had set up the first still in the coopery of Peter Fufich and begun to distill brandy. The shop was outside the city, on

the bank of the Lashva itself, below the road that went to Kalibunar.

The hollow was packed with soggy snow and full of cold
drafts. In the coopery by the water's edge the "witches' cauldron" sang and hissed all night long and smoke coiled through a
vent under the roof.

Logs of green wood squealed under the cauldron, around
which there was a constant coming and going of muffled, grimy,
and frozen men, who fought the smoke and flying sparks, the
wind and the drafts, and, on top of it all, the sharp tobacco
smoke which kept burning their lips and stinging their eyes.

One of them was Tanasiye, the well-known expert on stills
and brandy. During the summer he worked off and on for short
periods, but as soon as the first plums fell he would go from
house to house, in every town in the Travnik district, and sometimes even farther afield, for no one knew better how to ferment
the plums, how to judge when the mash was ripe, or how to
"cook" and draw the finished brandy. He was a dour man who
had spent a lifetime in drafty and smoke-filled still-houses, always pale and unshaven, sleepy and in bad humor. Like all masters of their trade, he was perpetually dissatisfied with his own
work and with his helpers. Angry mumblings and sharp words
of disapproval constituted his entire conversation.

"Not like this! Don't let it burn over! No more! Don't touch it!
Stop, that's enough! Take your hands off! Get away!"

After these bad-tempered and slurred growlings, which both
he and his helpers understood very well, there would finally
emerge from Tanasiye's cracked and sooty hands, from the
smoke, the mashy ooze, and the seeming disorder, a perfect
and thoroughly professional end product—a fine clear brandy,
decanted according to type into "single still," "sharp," "mild,"
and "double still"—a shining fiery liquid, clear and "medicinal,"
free of sediment and burnt taste, showing no trace of the labor
and filth that had gone into its making, no tang of smoke or rot,
but smelling of plums and orchards and flowing nobly into the
casks like a pure and precious essence.

Up to that moment Tanasiye had fussed over it as though it
were a delicate newborn babe. Now, when it was done, he forgot to grumble and harp and only twitched his lips, as if whispering a wordless spell; with a practiced eye he watched the
slow trickle of the spirit and, without ever testing it on his
tongue, he determined its quality, proof, and class.

Around the fire that burned under the still there would always be a few visitors, people from the town; and among them, more often than not, there would be an idler or a gate crasher, a fiddler or a storyteller, for it was pleasant to eat and drink and tell stories by the cauldron fire, even though one's eyes watered from the smoke and one's back was always icy from the draft. As far as Tanasiye was concerned, these people were as good as nonexistent. He muttered and went about his work, forever ordering and telling his helpers what not to do, and in doing so he simply walked through or over the men by the fire as if they were made of air. He seemed to accept these loafers as an integral part of the still-house. At all events he neither addressed them by name nor made a move to drive them away nor seemed to notice them.

That was how Tanasiye had made brandy for over forty years in town after town, hamlet after hamlet, monastery after monastery; and he was still the same, except that he had visibly aged and shriveled. His growling was not as fierce as it had been, and often ended up in a coughing fit or in an old man's rasp and wheeze. His thick bushy eyebrows had turned gray, and were smeared, like the rest of his face, with the soot and clay used in the coating of the still-pot. And under those matted brows one could barely make out a pair of eyes that were like glass chips, flashing out one moment and guttering the next.

Tonight the party around the fire was bigger than usual. There was Peter Fufich himself, the owner of the coopery, and two other Travnik Serbs, merchants, one ballad singer, and Marko of Djimriye, a fortuneteller and a saintly man who traveled around Bosnia all the time and sometimes dropped in at Travnik, though he never ventured beyond the coopery or went into town or the bazaar.

This Marko was a grizzled, neatly turned-out peasant from eastern Bosnia, small but wiry, with an air of deftness and authority about him. He was known as a soothsayer and diviner. In his home village he had grown-up sons and married daughters, a house and lands. After the death of his wife, he had begun to lead a life of prayer, to admonish people and divine the future. He was not greedy for money, and refused to tell fortunes indiscriminately. He was brusque and unsparing with sinners. The Moslems knew him and winked at his soothsaying.

When Marko came to a town, he did not look for well-to-do houses but sat down in a coopery or a humble hut, beside the

fire. He talked with the men and women gathered there. Sometimes, in the course of the evening, he would go out into the
night and remain there for an hour or two; on his return, damp
with dew or rain-soaked, he would squat by the fire where his
audience was still waiting for him, and, gazing at a thin board
of larchwood, would start to talk; often, however, before he did
that, he would turn to one of the group, scold him sharply for
his sins, and ask him to leave the company. He did that with
women especially. He would stare long and fixedly at some
woman and then tell her quietly but firmly: "Daughter, your
arms are on fire right up to the elbows. Go and put out the fire
and stop sinning. You know the sin I'm talking about."

Blushing crimson, the woman would slink out of the room
and Marko would then begin his soothsaying on matters of general interest to all the assembled.

Tonight too Marko had gone outside, despite a cutting wind
and sleet. Now he looked at his little board, tapping it with the
index finger of his left hand, then gazed at it some more and
slowly began. "There is a fire smoldering in this town, smoldering in many places. It cannot be seen, because people carry
it inside them, but one day it will blaze out into the open and
strike the guilty and innocent alike. On that day the upright
ones will not be in the town, but outside it. Far outside. Let
every man pray that he shall be among them."

Then, all of a sudden, he turned slowly and intently to
Peter Fufich. "There's a sound of weeping in your home too,
Master Peter. It is a loud one and will get louder still, but there
will be a change for the better. The change is about to begin.
But you must go to church and remember the poor. Keep the
candle burning under the icon of St. Dimitri."

As the old man spoke this, Peter Fufich, who was ordinarily
a proud and arrogant man, bowed his head and stared at his
silken waistband. There was an awkward silence, until Marko
resumed gazing at his little board and tapping it with his nail,
deep in thought. Out of that scratchy sound there came, imperceptibly, his gentle but firm voice, first in a thick mumble
of slurred words, then clearer and more distinct: "Oh, wretched
Christians, wretched Christians!"

It was one of those dire oracular pronouncements that Marko
made from time to time, which were afterwards spread from
mouth to mouth among the Serbs.

"Lo, they walk forth in blood. The blood is up to their ankles, and rising still. Today, for a hundred years more, and then one half of the next hundred, nothing but blood. That much I can see. Six generations adding their blood one to another in bucketfuls. All of it Christian blood. And a time will come when every child will read and write and people will talk to each other from one end of the world to the other. They will hear every word, but will not understand one another. Some men will gather up power and wealth such as the world has never seen, but their riches will vanish in blood and all their skill and cunning will not help them. Others will grow poor and hungry, they will eat their own tongues from hunger and pray for death to finish them off, but death will be slow and deaf. And whatever the soil shall bear, all food will have the bitter taste of blood. The Cross will tarnish over by itself. Then a man will come, naked and barefoot, with no staff or satchel, and he will blind everyone with his wisdom, his strength and beauty, and cast out the tribe of blood and violence, and he will comfort every soul. And the era of the Third One of the Trinity shall begin."

Toward the end of the speech, the old man's words had grown less audible and distinct, grading finally into a soft murmur that was indistinguishable from the faint rhythmical tapping of his nail on the thin dry board of larchwood.

They all gazed into the fire, deeply affected by the words.

They had not understood the message, but its veiled content held them spellbound and filled them with the vague excitement which prophecies usually kindle in simple folk.

Tanasiye got up to look at the still. Then one of the merchants asked Marko whether Russia would be sending a consul to Travnik. There was a silence, in which everyone felt that the question was out of place at that moment. The old man was irritated and answered sharply: "There will be neither a Russian Consul nor any other. The ones who are here will soon be gone. And soon the years will come when the main road will bypass this town. You will long to see a traveler or merchant, but they will not come near the town. You will buy and sell amongst yourselves. The same money will pass from hand to hand, but will not stay long enough in any hand to get warm or make a profit."

The merchants looked at one another. There was an uneasy silence, though a very short one, for it was broken almost immediately by an argument between Tanasiye and his helpers. Then the merchants too started talking, and the old man once

more assumed his usual modest and smiling expression. He
opened his ancient leather bag and began to take out cornmeal
bread and several dark red onions. The young helpers laid some
cuts of beef on the coals and the meat began to sizzle with a
zesty, pervading aroma. They did not offer any to the old man,
for it was well known that he never ate anyone's meals but
lived only on the dry food from his little leather bag. He ate
slowly and with relish, then went to a corner of the still-room
where the smoke and the smell of roast meat would not reach
him, and there, curling up quietly like a schoolboy, his right
cheek in the hollow of his palm, he went to sleep.

As brandy was passed around, the conversation among the
merchants grew more lively; but still they kept glancing toward
the corner where the old man slept, lowering their voices as they
did so. His presence filled them with a sense of unease and a
certain solemn gravity which they rather liked.

Tanasiye went on stoking the fire with beech logs, drowsy
and churlish as always, undaunted and patient like Nature herself, unaware that at the other end of Travnik a French Consul
was watching the red glow of his fire, not even aware, in his
simplicity, that there were consuls and living people in the
world who could not sleep.

27

Daville spent the opening months of 1814, his last months in
Travnik, in utter isolation, "ready for anything," without any
instructions and without news of any kind either from Paris or
Istanbul. He paid the kavasses and servants out of his own
pocket. Among the French authorities in Dalmatia there was
near anarchy. French couriers and travelers had stopped coming.
News from Austrian sources, which reached Travnik slowly and
irregularly, grew less and less favorable. He stopped going to the
Residency, for the Vizier showed him less and less attention
and treated him with a certain vacuous and offensive kindliness,
which hurt him worse than any rudeness of insult. Moreover,
his harshness and intolerance were becoming an unbearable
strain on the whole country. His Albanian detachment treated

Bosnia as though it were a conquered land, and took from the Turk and Christian alike. Discontent rose and swelled among the Moslem population—not the loud kind that spent itself in roistering and headless frenzy in the streets, but the stifled, rankling kind that goes on smoldering a long time and, when it breaks out, leads to blood and slaughter.

The Vizier's Serbian victory had gone to his head. True, according to the stories of eyewitnesses and people in the know, the victory subsequently turned out to have been somewhat dubious, and Ali Pasha's role in it less than notable, but to himself, apparently, it was a great and significant victory; in his own eyes, at any rate, his stature as victor seemed to increase with every day that passed. His reckless outbursts against the begs and prominent Moslems, too, gained momentum by the day. And it was precisely this that weakened his position. For although violence can spread terror and achieve some useful ends, it is not enough for a lasting rule. Terror soon blunts as an instrument of government. And every one seems to know this except those who, impelled by circumstances or their own instincts, perpetrate terror.

The Vizier knew no other way of governing. He never even noticed that the begs and the notables had stopped fearing him and that his policy of ruthlessness, which had spread panic to begin with, no longer terrified anyone and was therefore, from his own point of view, no longer effective. Earlier they had trembled from fear, but now they were "numb and indifferent"; whereas he, on the other hand, shook with fury at the least sign of obstinacy or insubordination, even at their pregnant silence. There was a flurry of correspondence between the fortress commanders, the begs were whispering among themselves, and an ominous hush settled on the bazaars throughout the country. With the approach of warmer weather, there might well be an open movement against Ali Pasha's regime. D'Avenat, for one, felt certain that this would happen.

The friars avoided the French Consulate, although they continued to show Mme Daville every courtesy when she came to Mass at the Dolats church on Sundays and holidays.

The kavasses wanted to know from D'Avenat how long they could count on remaining in the French service. Rafo Atias began to look around for another job as interpreter or agent, as he could not bear the idea of going to his uncle's warehouse. By tireless underground work, the Austrian Consulate fed the local populace a steady diet of news about the Allied victories and Bonaparte's eclipse, now supposedly only a matter of days. The idea gained ground among the people that the era of the French had passed and the days of the French Consulate at Travnik were numbered.

Von Paulich himself did not go anywhere or speak to anyone. Daville had not seen him for almost six months, ever since Austria had come into the war, but he felt his existence at all times; he thought of him with a special emotion which was neither envy nor fear but had a little of both in it. He thought he could see him in the large building on the other bank of the Lashva, quietly going over his business, completely cool and self-possessed, knowing exactly what he wanted, never doubting or hesitant, correct and yet shrewd, incorruptible but somehow inhuman. The exact opposite of the sick demented victor at the Residency, he was, in fact, the only winner in the game that had been going on for years in the Travnik valley. He seemed only to be waiting, with a quietly merciless air, until the quarry they had driven into a corner should fall and, in falling, signify his victory.

And that moment inevitably came. When it did, von Paulich behaved like someone taking part in an ancient and solemn game, the rules of which were painful and inflexible, but logical, just, and honorable alike to winners and losers.

One day in April, an Austrian kavass came to the French Consulate, for the first time in seven months, and brought a letter for the Consul.

Daville recognized the handwriting—an orderly pattern of perfectly straight lines that were like a salvo of metal arrows all streaming in the same direction, all with the same barbed point. He recognized it and guessed the meaning of the letter, but was nevertheless startled by the contents.

Von Paulich wrote that he had just received news that the war between the Allies and France had been happily concluded. Napoleon had abdicated. The lawful heir to the French throne had been reinstated. The Senate had voted a new constitution and a new government had been formed, headed by Talleyrand, Duke of Benevento. Since he assumed that this news relating to the fate of his homeland would be of interest to Daville, he was sending it on, delighted that the end of hostilities would once again enable them to see each other. He tendered his warm respects to Mme Daville, and so forth and so forth.

The Consul's dismay was so great that the full import and true significance of what he had read did not at once penetrate his mind. His first reaction was to drop the letter on his desk and get up, as though he had just received some message he had long expected from von Paulich.

For some time past, and especially since the defeat in Russia in December of the year before, Daville had been trying to visualize the possibility of such an ending. He had turned it over in his mind and tried to define his attitude toward it. In this way, slowly and imperceptibly, he had come to live with the idea that the Empire might fall, even with the fall itself. Day by day, with each new event, that old and distant threat had come a little closer, gradually shading into reality, finally becoming reality itself. And now beyond the Emperor and the Empire, life beckoned once again, everlasting, all-powerful, unfathomable, life with all its infinite possibilities.

He himself had no idea just when he had begun to accept the thought of a world of affairs and events without Napoleon as its *sine qua non*. The process had been hard and painful at first, a kind of inner swooning; he had tottered and reeled inwardly like a man who feels the earth shifting and moving under his feet. Later all he had felt was a sense of great desolation, a loss of foothold and absence of any enthusiasm, and only life itself remained, the bare dreary life, stripped of vision and of those marvelous shimmering forms in the distance which might not be real but which give one strength and a little dignity in the passage through life. And by then he had thought about it so much and grown so accustomed to the sensation that he fell into the habit of judging the world and France, his own and his family's destiny, from that imagined point of view.

Throughout that time, even as now, Daville had conscientiously gone about his duties, had read circulars and articles in *Le Moniteur*, listened to the couriers' and travelers' stories of Napoleon's plans to defend metropolitan France and the chances of his reaching a settlement with the Allies. Then, once more, he had resumed his brooding—wondering what it would be like when there was no more Emperor or Empire—and the spells of brooding had steadily grown longer and more insistent.

But, in fact, his agonizing was one of a piece with the great drama that was being played out at the time in the hearts of thousands of Frenchmen, worn out in the service of a regime that had long been doomed by having to ask more of the people than they had to give. And when a man grows used to a thought and reconciled to things, he begins sooner or later to seek confirmation in reality, all the more so when that reality hews close to his thoughts and often even overtakes them.

In recent months Daville had been astonished to discover what a tremendous distance he had already gone in that direction. Forgetting the many long conflicts he had fought with himself in these last twelve months, he had the sensation of having reached his present viewpoint all at once and with perfect ease. In any case, he had long felt like a man who was "ready for anything," which was another way of saying that he had already detached himself from the regime now in its last throes in France and was willing to make his peace with anything that came after it, whatever that may be.

And yet now, at the moment when all of it loomed before him as reality, Daville could not help staggering, as if from an unexpected and crushing blow. He paced around the room and the import of what he had read in von Paulich's letter welled up inside him in wave after wave of confused emotion: wonder, horror, sorrow, even a kind of abject gratitude that he and his family were spared and alive amidst so much ruin and change; and then again fear and uncertainty. He was suddenly reminded of the line from the Old Testament, "God is great in His Works"; and the sentence kept haunting him like a persistent tune that he could not get out of his mind, although he was unable to say what kinds of "works" they were or what their greatness was or what any of it had to do with the Lord of the Bible.

For a long time he paced like that around the room but was unable to come to grips with any one thought, and still less to grasp and sort out what he had heard. He felt that for this he would need much more time.

He told himself that no pondering, foresight, or shallow mental comfort was worth very much, nor were they any help at the moment when the blow fell. For it was one thing to project one's fears in imagination, to anticipate the worst, to determine one's attitude and the mode of one's defense, while at the same time feeling smug in the knowledge that everything was still in order and in its proper place, and quite another thing to find oneself facing an actual collapse which required one to make instant decisions and take concrete action. It was one thing to listen to a tipsy and wrought-up colleague from the Ministry of the Navy saying with round eyes, "The Emperor is mad! He and all of us together are rushing headlong to ruin, which is waiting for us just beyond the last victory," and quite another to grasp and accept the fact that the Empire was defeated and in pieces, that there was no longer any Napoleon but only a throneless usurper, whose worth was less than if he had perished in one of his own victories. It was one thing to doubt the value of conquests and the permanence of armed successes, as he had so often done in recent years, and to speculate what would happen to him and his family "in the event that . . ."; it was something else again to learn suddenly that not only the Revolution and all it had brought but also "the General" and the irresistible magic of his conquering genius and the whole scheme of things founded on it had vanished overnight as if they had never been; and that now the clock would have to be turned back to the time when as a boy, in the main square of his home town, moved by the "King's goodness," he had cheered Louis XVI.

Even in a dream that would have been too much to ask.

Unable to concentrate or think clearly, to divine the essence of what was happening and to pierce the future, Daville clutched at the fact that his old protector Talleyrand was now at the head of the new government. This struck him as his only hope of salvation, an extraordinary gesture of grace on the part of Fate toward him personally, in the midst of general ruin and chaos.

As with "the General," Daville had spoken with Talleyrand only once in his life, more than eighteen years before, when the latter was not yet famous or had the title Duke of Benevento. In the old Ministry of Foreign Affairs, which was then in an appalling muddle of transition, reflected not only in the quality of work and personnel but in its furnishings and system as well, he had been received for a few minutes in an improvised salon. Talleyrand had noticed his articles in Le Moniteur and had wanted to see him. The chaotic mood of the Ministry also played over their short interview.

The well-set man who received him standing and remained like that throughout the conversation, gave him a quiet, barefaced, once-over kind of look, as if the object of his attention were not young Daville but something behind him. His talk too was superficial and absent-minded, as though he regretted having shown an interest in the articles and in meeting the young man. He told Daville that he "must go on," that he would always back him up in his work and in the service. And that, in reality, was all Daville ever saw or heard of his patron. Nevertheless, throughout these eighteen years most of the Ministry officials and Daville himself had taken it quite for granted that he was Talleyrand's protégé and that his official career was hitched to Talleyrand's star. And in fact, whenever Talleyrand had been in power and in office, he had supported Daville. Cases of this sort were not uncommon: in which powerful individuals obstinately trailed behind them a horde of protégés, not for the sake of the protégés themselves, whom they neither knew nor sometimes esteemed very highly, but for their own sake, because the shelter and backing they afforded these people were a visible proof of their own power and nobility.

"I must get in touch with the Duke," Daville told himself, unclear as yet as to how and on what grounds this might be done. "I shall appeal to him," he kept saying to himself all through the night, unable to think of any other scheme and oppressed by regret that he had no one with whom to talk it over. And the next day found him exhausted, but still as bewildered and undecided as the day before.

Watching his wife, as she bustled around the house without any idea of what had happened, planning the work of the garden as though she intended to spend the rest of her life in Travnik, he felt like a damned creature who knew what the other mortals did not know, and was therefore both superior to them and unhappier than they were.

The arrival of a courier from Istanbul shook him out of his lethargy. The courier bore the congratulations of the Ambassador and his staff to the new government and messages of loyalty to the new ruler Louis XVIII and the House of Bourbon. He also brought orders to Daville to inform the Vizier and the local authorities of the changes in France and to notify the Vizier that henceforward he would be in Travnik as the representative of Louis XVIII, King of France and Navarre.

As if carrying out a long-laid plan or listening to some unspoken directive, Daville wrote all that was necessary to Paris that same day, without any further hesitation or delay.

"I learn from the Austrian Consul here of the happy change that has returned a descendant of Henry the Great to the French throne and peace and a firm promise of a better future to France herself. So long as I live, I shall regret not having been in Paris on this occasion, to add my own voice to the manifest enthusiasm of the people." So began Daville's letter, in which he placed his service at the disposal of the new government, with the request that his "expressions of devotion and loyalty be laid at the feet of the Throne," and adding modestly that he was a "plain citizen, one of the Twenty Thousand Parisians who had signed the well-known petition in the defense of the Martyr King, Louis XVI, and the Royal House." He concluded his letter with the hope that the "Age of Steel may be followed by a Golden Age."

At the same time he sent a congratulatory poem to Talleyrand, as he had often done before when Talleyrand was in office. The poem opened with the verses:

"*Des peuples et des rois heureux moderateur,*
Talleyrand, tu deviens notre libérateur."

(Blessed guide of peoples and kings,
Talleyrand, you now become our liberator.)

And because the courier could not wait, Daville had no time to complete the poem and designated the two-dozen-odd verses as a "fragment."

In the same letter he proposed that the Travnik Consulate be closed, as the changed circumstances had removed the need for its further existence. He requested permission to leave Travnik with his family in the course of that month, and to appoint D'Avenat, whose loyalty was proven and had been demonstrated so many times, to supervise the office and carry out the liquidation. In view of these exceptional developments, unless he received contrary instructions by the end of the month, he would proceed with his family to Paris.

Daville spent the night writing these congratulations, requests, and letters. He slept no more than a couple of hours, but got up feeling fresh and invigorated, and accompanied the courier to the gate.

From the terrace, where the still unopened tulips were bent under the great weight of dew, Daville watched the courier and his companion descend the steep hill toward the road down in the valley. Their horses waded through a dense ground mist that reached above their knees and was suffused with faint morning sunlight; and then, sinking deeper and deeper into it, they disappeared from view.

He went back to his study on the ground floor. All over the room there were visible traces of the night just past, a night spent in work and writing: candles askew, burnt down to their base, strewn sheets of paper, crumbs of sealing wax. Daville sat down among the litter of copies and torn paper, not touching a thing. A wave of deep weariness broke over him again, though lightened by the knowledge that everything had been written and forwarded to the proper quarter, finally and beyond recant, that there could be no more doubts and agonizing over it. He bent over the desk and put his drowsy head on his folded arms.

And still it was hard not to think, not to remember, not to see. He had spent twenty-five years of his life questing for a "middle road" that would lead to serenity and the kind of dignity without which an individual could not endure. Twenty-five years he had blundered, groping and finding, losing and regaining, swinging from one enthusiasm to another; and now, tired, spent, inwardly wrung dry, he had arrived at the point from which he had started when he was eighteen. There was plainly no such thing as a road leading onward; in reality all roads led one around in a circle, like those tricky mazes in Eastern tales; and so now they had brought him, weary and despondent, back to this spot among the shreds of paper and the jumble of drafts, to the point where another circle began, as it would from every other point on its circumference. It meant that there was no such thing as a middle road, the true road leading onward to peace, dignity, and stability; that all men simply groped around and around, always along the same paths that led them up the garden path eventually. The only things that changed were the men and the generation who traveled the path, forever deluded. It meant—the tired, stumbling mind of this tired man concluded—that no roads of any kind existed and that this new direction, in which his game-legged protector, the great Duke of Benevento, was supposed to lead him, hobbling, was only a part of that circle which was utter roadlessness. One simply went on. The long trek had no point or value, save those we might learn to discover within ourselves along the way. There were no roads, no destinations. One just traveled on. One traveled on, spent oneself, and grew weary.

And so he, too, was now moving along without a pause or rest. His head was nodding, his eyelids drooped, and behind them a sun-kindled pile of mist rose higher and higher, lapping at a couple of shadowy horses, mincing along daintily, until, finally, it enveloped and swallowed them up, together with their riders. But fresh horses and riders kept appearing, an endless host, looming up without surcease and quietly vanishing in the mother fog, where one dropped from exhaustion and longed for sleep.

Letting his head fall on his crossed arms, overcome with exhaustion and the strain of thinking, Daville fell asleep at his writing table, among sheets of paper and guttered candles from the night before.

If only they would let him sleep. If only he could keep his eyes shut and his head down, even in this dank reddish mist, among the swarming and lurching horde of riders! But they would not leave him alone. One of the riders, behind him, kept placing a cold implacable hand on the nape of his neck and talking to him indistinctly. He bowed his head lower and lower, but it stubbornly tugged him awake.

When he lifted his head and opened his eyes, he saw the smiling, reproachful face of his wife. She scolded him for over-tiring himself, and told him to undress, lie down, and rest. But now that he was already wide awake, even the thought of lying alone in bed with his ghosts appalled him. He began to make order among the papers on the table, while talking to her. Up until now he had been reluctant to tell his wife, clearly and in so many words, just what had happened in the world and in France and what it all meant for them. Now, all of a sudden, the act came easily, it was simplicity itself.

On being told so clearly and unequivocally that the entire scheme of things had radically changed, and their own situation right with it, and that their stay in Travnik had indeed come to an end, Mme Daville was at first shattered and thrown off balance. But only for a moment—until her mind cleared and she could see what this meant for her family and what practical problems it entailed for her personally. As soon as she understood that, she calmed down. And, forthwith, they began to discuss the journey, the moving of household things and their future arrangements in France.

28

Madame Daville set to work. Just as once she had furnished and made this same house livable for them, she now made everything ready for the move—quietly, with concentration, energetically, without complaining or seeking anyone's advice. The household, which she had put together in these seven years, was dismantled slowly and methodically. Everything was marked, well wrapped, and got ready for the trip. The part of it that most distressed Mme Daville was the flower terrace and the big garden with its vegetable beds.

The white hyacinths, which Frau von Mitterer had once christened "Wedding Joy," or "Imperial Bridegroom," were as sturdy and full-flowered as ever, but the center of the terrace was now given over to Dutch tulips which Mme Daville had managed to obtain in recent years in great quantity and a variety of colors. The previous season they had been spotty and uneven, but this year they had done well and had just come into bloom, in a uniform, showy display that was like rows of schoolchildren in procession.

In the garden, the German sweet peas were already out. She had got the seed from von Paulich the year before, a few weeks before the war was declared. Now the deaf-mute Mundjar was hoeing them.

Mundjar was still at work, as he had been every spring. He knew nothing about the events in the world or the change in these people's fortunes. To him this year was like any other. Forever bent double, he crumbled the soil with his hands, clod by clod, he spread manure, watered, transplanted, smiled at Jean-Paul, or at little Eugénie when the nanny brought her out on the terrace. With a quick and expressive flip of his soiled fingers, grimacing and making the emphatic, worldless sounds of a mute, he tried to tell Mme Daville that in von Paulich's garden this same sweet pea was pushing up higher and flowering much better, though in itself that meant nothing, as it was no yardstick of the final results. These they would be able to judge when the pods came out.

Madame Daville looked at him. She let him know by signs that she had understood him, then went back into the house to resume her packing. Only there did she remember that in a few days she would have to abandon everything, the garden as well as the house, and that neither she nor any of her family would see the ripe pods of that pea. And at that tears came to her eyes.

And so at the French Consulate they quietly made preparations to leave. There was, however, one thing that worried Daville— the question of money. Some time before, he had sent to France all the savings they had. For months now he had received no pay. The Sarajevo Jews who had worked with Freycinet and often loaned money to the Consulate were now distrustful. D'Avenat had some savings, but he was staying on at Travnik in an ill-defined capacity and in a state of complete uncertainty, and it would not be fair to deprive him of what he had and ask him to lend money to the state, and without security at that.

Both the interpreters, D'Avenat and Rafo Atias, were well aware of Daville's predicament. And while he was fretting and wondering which way to turn, old Solomon Atias, Rafo's uncle, came in one day, unannounced. He was the most respected of the Atias brothers and the head of the whole numerous clan of Travnik Atiases.

Short, running to fat, and bowlegged, in a greasy kaftan, with a short-necked head that sat almost flat on his narrow shoulders, he had the large bulbous eyes of those who suffer from a heart defect. He was out of breath and sweating profusely from the heat of the May day and the unaccustomed walk up the steep hill. Timidly he shut the door behind him and slumped panting into a chair. A scent of garlic and uncured hides enveloped him like a cloud. His hairy, dark-skinned fists lay clenched on his knees and a tiny bead of sweat glistened on every hair.

They exchanged greetings several times and floundered for a while in meaningless civilities. Daville would not come out and admit that he and his family were leaving Travnik, and the fat, panting Solomon was quite unable to say why he had come. At length, however, in that hoarse, throaty voice which always reminded Daville of Spain, Solomon began to discourse about unexpected changes and the great needs of states and state officials, which to him were perfectly understandable, and how times were hard for everyone, even an ordinary merchant who was only concerned with his own little bailiwick, and finally— well, finally—if *Monsieur le Consul* did not receive official funds in time, and, after all, a trip was a trip and one couldn't very well put off an official schedule, he, Solomon Atias, was here, always at the service of the French Imperial—or rather, French Royal—Consulate, and what little he possessed or was able to do was entirely at the disposal of *Monsieur le Consul*.

Daville, whose first thought had been that Atias had come to request or demand something of him, was surprised and touched. His voice shook with emotion: the muscles of his face, between the mouth and the chin, where his ruddy skin was beginning to wither and wrinkle and sag, twitched visibly.

Daville thanked him and, in the embarrassed pause that followed, pressed some refreshments on him. At length they agreed that Atias would lend the Consulate twenty-five imperial ducats on a bill of exchange.

Solomon's large bulging eyes grew moist, which made them glitter more than usual, so that their yellowish, blood-veined whites became less conspicuous. Daville's eyes, too, filled with tears of emotion—indeed, emotion seemed to be a permanent state with him these days. But now they could talk more easily and freely.

Daville sought to give his gratitude a wider, more encompassing expression. He spoke of his sympathy and understanding toward the Jews, of compassion and the need for people to know and help each other, without distinction. He confined himself to vague and general sentiments, for he could no longer speak of Napoleon, whose name had a special meaning for the Jews and still exerted a powerful attraction; nor could he speak openly and definitely about his new government or mention his new sovereign by name. Solomon perspired and breathed heavily, his big eyes resting on Daville, as if all that were clear to him and pained him also, as much as it pained Daville, if not more, as if he knew and thoroughly appreciated what trouble and what danger all those emperors, kings, viziers, and ministers really were, whose coming and going was not of our making, yet had the power of lifting us up and grinding us into dust, us and our families and all that we represented or possessed; as if, in fact, he were distressed at having had to leave his dark warehouse with its stacks of hides and climb up to this high and sunny place, to sit with gentry on unaccustomed *fauteuils* in luxurious rooms.

Relieved that the problem of traveling money had been solved in this unexpectedly simple fashion, and wishing to give the conversation a more cheerful tone, Daville said half-jokingly: "I am really most grateful and shall always remember that with all your worries you found time to think about my predicament. And to tell you honestly, I am astonished to see that, after all that's happened here, after all those fines you've had to pay, you are still in a position to lend anybody anything. The Vizier was boasting that he'd emptied your cashboxes to the last thaler."

At the mention of the persecution and ransom which the Jews had suffered at the hands of Ali Pasha, Solomon's eyes took on a fixed, woebegone look of inexpressible sadness. "It has cost us a great deal and deprived us of very much. Truly our cashboxes are empty to this day. But I can tell you . . . you ought to know . . ."

Here Solomon looked down in confusion at the sweating hands in his lap and, after a short silence, went on in a different, subdued voice, quite changed, as though he had suddenly decided to approach it from another viewpoint: "Yes, it scared us and cost us quite a bit. Yes indeed. The Vizier is a hard man, truly hard and difficult. But he has had to do with us once, whereas we've had to do with dozens of them. Viziers come and go . . . and each of them takes something with him, that's true. They go away and forget what they have done and how they have treated us; and then a new one arrives and it's the same thing all over again. But we remain, we remember, we keep a tally of all we've been through, of how we have defended and preserved ourselves, and we pass on these dearly bought experiences from father to son. And so our cashboxes have two bottoms. One is just deep enough for the Vizier to reach down and scoop clean, but underneath a little something always remains for us and our children, for the salvation of our soul, for helping ourselves and our friends when they're in need."

Now Solomon looked straight across at Daville, no longer with those comically baleful and frightened eyes, but with a new expression that was direct and bold.

Daville laughed heartily. "Ah, that's good. I like that. And the Vizier thought he was so clever."

Solomon interrupted him at once in a lowered voice, as if to let him know that he too should speak lower. "No, I am not saying that he is not. They are wise and shrewd people, that they are. But you know how it is, our masters are fine and mighty gentlemen, they're like dragons, our masters are, but they have to have their wars and fights and expenses. You know, we have a saying: big lords are like a big wind; they blow, they break things, they blow themselves out. And we lie low and keep on working and put something away for a rainy day. That's why we last longer and always have something."

"Ah, that's good. Very good," Daville said with a nod, smiling as before and encouraging Solomon to continue.

But now the smile caused Solomon to falter suddenly; he

searched the Consul's face more closely, again with that earlier woebegone and timid look, as if afraid that he had gone too far or said something he should not have; as though he realized that what he had said was not what he had wanted to say, although what that should have been he hadn't the least idea. But still, something drove him to speak out, to complain, to praise and explain himself, like a man who, for a few precious minutes, had been given a unique opportunity to pass on an urgent and important message. From the moment he had left his warehouse and climbed up the steep hill where ordinarily he never went, and had sat down in this sun-filled room, surrounded by a beauty and cleanliness he was not accustomed to, it had seemed to him a rare and important thing to be able to talk to this foreigner who planned to leave town in a few days, to discuss things which, perhaps, he would never again dare or be able to discuss with anybody.

As his sense of wonder and acute discomfort began to wear off, he felt more and more impelled to tell this stranger a few other things, about himself and his family, and other secret and pressing things, from this weasel hole that was Travnik, from the musty warehouse where life was hard and devoid of justice and honor, without beauty and order, without judge or witnesses; and he felt it ought to be some kind of message addressed to some vague but telling entity, perhaps to that better, more orderly, more enlightened world to which the Consul would presently return. Just once, he felt, he ought to say something that was not shrewd or cautious, not connected with gain or money, with haggling and workaday accounts, but rather with giving and spending freely, with the pride of generosity, with sincerity and secret pain.

But the very desire that filled him so intensely all of a sudden, to convey and impart something more, some important and sweeping truth about his own life and situation and the indignities which the Travnik Atiases had had to endure all these years, prevented him from finding the right manner and the words needed to express, briefly and adequately, what now choked him and started the blood pounding in his ears. And so he began to stammer out, not the things he was so full of and which he longed to express—how they struggled and managed to preserve an invisible strength and dignity—but only the disjointed phrases that came to his tongue. "So you see . . . that's how we keep going and how things are, and we don't regret . . .

for our friends, for the justice and good will shown to us . . . because we . . . we too . . ."

Now abruptly his voice broke off and his eyes began to swim. He got up in confusion. Daville rose too, moved by an inexplicable feeling of warmth and friendship, and gave him his hand. Solomon grasped the hand quickly with a jerky and unaccustomed movement, and stammered another few sentences, begging the Consul not to forget them and to put in a good word for them wherever and whenever he could over there, about their life here and how they paid for it with trouble and suffering. But the words were disconnected and unintelligible, and they mingled with Daville's expressions of gratitude.

No one would ever know what it was that was choking Solomon Atias at that moment, that brought tears to his eyes and sent a shiver down through his whole body. Had he known how, had he been a man used to speaking his thoughts, he might have said something like this: "Monsieur, you have lived here among us for seven long years and have shown us Jews the kind of consideration we have never received either from the Turks or from foreigners. You have treated us like human beings, without discrimination. You may not even be aware how much decency this has brought into our lives. And now you are leaving. Your Emperor has had to fall back before overwhelming enemies. Your homeland is now the scene of wrenching upheavals and great change. But yours is also a noble and powerful country which in the end will turn everything to good account. And you shall certainly find your way there. The ones who are to be pitied are we who remain here, we the handful of Sephardic Jews here in Travnik, of whom two thirds are Atiases, since to us you have been a small and hopeful ray of light. You have seen the life we lead and have been as good to us as it is possible for a man to be. And when a man does good, everyone expects him to go on doing it. And that is why we take the liberty of asking one more thing of you: that you be our witness in the West, which once was our cradle too, and which ought to be told what has become of us. For it seems to me, if we could but know that there are some who realize and acknowledge that we are not what we appear to be, not the kind of people our lives suggest, everything we have to bear would be more tolerable.

"More than three hundred years ago we were torn from our homeland, the unforgettable Andalusia, by a dreadful, insane, fratricidal storm which even today we cannot understand and which to this day has not understood itself. It has scattered us around the world and reduced us to a beggary that even gold cannot help. A few of us here were swept eastward, and life in the East is neither easy nor blessed for us; the farther a man travels and the nearer he gets to the Rising Sun, the worse it gets, for the land grows coarser and more barren, and men are creatures of the soil. It is our misfortune that we have not been able to give our whole heart to this land to which we are indebted for having welcomed us and given us haven, and have been incapable of hating the land which has unjustly driven us out and banished us like some unworthy progeny. We don't know which is the greater grief to us: being here or not being there. No matter what part of this earth beyond Spain we might be in, we would always suffer, for we would always have two homelands. This much I know. But here in this place, life has been particularly harsh and degrading for us. I know that for a long time now we have not been the same, yet we no longer remember what kind of people we once were, we only know that we were different. Ages have passed since we first set out on our journey, and the journey itself lasted an age, and we strayed to this ill-starred place and settled, and that is why we're no longer even a shadow of what we once were. Like the blushing fuzz on a fruit that is passed from hand to hand, a man too first sheds what is finest in him. That's why we are the way you see us now. But you know us better than that—us and the kind of life we lead, if it can be called a life.

"We are wedged between the Turks and the Christian peasants, the poor downtrodden peasants and the terrible Turks. Utterly cut off from our own kind, we try to preserve everything that reminds us of Spain, the songs and the food and the customs, but the change within us goes on relentlessly, we can feel the erosion, the fading of memory. We still remember the tongue of our country, the very same one we took with us more than three centuries ago, which is no longer spoken even there, and we mangle the language of these poor peasants who are victimized as we are, and of the Turks who lord it over us. And the day is perhaps not far off when the only pure and decent speech left to us will be the language of prayer, which needs no words anyway. Isolated and few that we are, we marry among ourselves and watch our blood grow thinner and paler. We bow and scrape to everyone, we writhe this way and that only to survive—as they say, we make fire on ice. We toil, make a living, and save, and not only for ourselves and our children but, alas, for those too who are stronger and more arrogant than we, who threaten our lives, our self-respect, and our material security. That is how we have managed to keep our religion, the same one for which we had to abandon our lovely homeland, though we lost almost everything else in the process.

"Fortunately, and to our sorrow too, we have never lost from memory the vision of this dear homeland of ours as it once was before, like a stepmother, it cast us out; and by the same token, we shall never stop longing for a better world, a humane and well-ordered world in which a man can walk upright and speak openly, without a shadow of fear in his eyes. This longing we shall never be able to suppress, nor the feeling that, in spite of everything, we belong to such a world, even though, banished and unhappy, we now live in another.

"This, then, is the story we would like you to tell *over there*, so that our name will be kept alive in that brighter and more civilized world which is forever crashing and dimming, forever shifting and changing, but which will never perish and will always exist somewhere for some men. Tell that world that we carry it in our hearts, that even here we serve it in our own fashion, that we feel ourselves part of it, although we are hopelessly and eternally separated from it. And this is not vanity or an idle wish, but a genuine need and a plea from the bottom of our hearts."

That, more or less, would have been what Solomon Atias might have told the French Consul on the eve of his leaving Travnik forever, at the moment when Solomon gave him his hard-earned ducats to enable him to travel. That, or something like it, is what he might have said. But none of it was very clear or explicit in his own mind, still less was it ripe for saying; it all lay inside him, a living, kicking fetal weight as it were, dumb and inexpressible. And was there a man alive who could express his subtlest feelings and his noblest yearnings? No one, or almost no one. So how could a hide merchant of Travnik give tongue to them, a Spanish Jew who was no longer at home in any language? And even had he spoken all the languages of this world, what use would they have been, since even in his crib they had not let him cry out loud, let alone speak freely and clearly during his lifetime? But that was the reason and the import, hard though it was to decode it, of his stammer and trembling during his last visit to the French Consul.

If the making and furnishing of a house is as hard and slow a job as going up a hill, the dismantling of an institution or a household is as quick and easy as going downhill.

Sooner than he could have hoped, Daville received an answer from Paris. They granted him a three-months leave of absence, but he was to take his family with him right away and leave D'Avenat to deputize at the Consulate. The question of liquidating the French Consulate at Travnik would be settled when he got to Paris.

Daville requested an audience with the Vizier, to advise him of his departure.

Ali Pasha now wore the look of a sick man. He was unusually friendly toward Daville. It was plain that he had been informed of the imminent shutdown of the Consulate. Daville made him a present of a hunting rifle, and the Vizier gave him a fur-lined cloak, which meant that he considered Daville to be leaving for good. They parted as two people who did not have a great deal to say to each other, since both were preoccupied with themselves and burdened with their own worries.

The same day Daville sent von Paulich the gift of a gun, a valuable carbine of German workmanship, and several bottles of Liqueur Martinique. He enclosed a long letter in which he let him know that he and his family would be leaving Travnik in a few days, on "an extended leave of absence which, God willing, may become permanent." Daville requested the necessary visas and letters of recommendation to the Austrian frontier authorities and to the quarantine commander at Kostaynitsa.

"I hope," wrote Daville further, "that the treaties now being negotiated in Paris will give the world peace, as just and durable as the Peace of Westphalia, and so vouchsafe the present generation a long, deserved respite. I hope and wish that our great European family, united and at peace, will henceforth desist from giving the world a sorry example of discord and strife. These, as you know, were my tenets of belief before the last war, during the war, and they are that today, more than ever before."

"Wherever I may be," wrote Daville, "wherever destiny chooses to send me, I shall never forget that in the barbarous

land where I was condemned to live, I found the most enlightened and most amiable man in Europe."

As he was finishing the letter on this note, Daville decided to
leave without a personal good-bye to von Paulich. He felt that of
all the difficulties he had to bear, the hardest would be the self-
possessed and victorious visage of the Colonel.

Reporting to his own Court Chancellery about the imminent
closure of the French Consulate-General at Travnik, von Paulich
added the recommendation that the Austrian Consulate-General
be closed down as well. The Consulate was no longer warranted,
he wrote, not only because the French would cease to be active
in these parts, but also because, judging by the straws in the
wind, Bosnia might be convulsed at any moment by internecine
violence and an open struggle for power between the Vizier and
the begs. The struggle would consume all their attention and
energies, and therefore no armed forays against the Austrian
frontier might be expected in the foreseeable future. Intelligence
concerning these internal Bosnian affairs might easily be obtained by Vienna through the friars or special agents at all
times.

To this proposal of his von Paulich attached a copy of
Daville's letter. In the margin, against the passage where Daville had written of him flatteringly, von Paulich added in his
own hand: "I have often had occasion in the past to draw attention to M. Daville's luxuriant imagination and his tendency
to exaggerate."

Daville spent a whole summer afternoon with D'Avenat,
putting the papers in order and giving him instructions.

D'Avenat was his usual lugubrious self, the muscles on his
cheeks knotted and tense. According to Paris, his son had been
detailed to the Embassy office in Istanbul, but the actual appointment had been delayed in the great flurry of take-over in
France, and Daville now promised to use his influence at the
Ministry to see it through. Thinking only of his son, a bright
and goodlooking youth of twenty-two, D'Avenat assured the
Consul that he would carry out the liquidation in good order and
pack everything away, down to the last pen and the smallest
scrap of paper, even if they hacked him to pieces.

As they were still not finished by dinnertime, they continued
to work after dinner. About ten D'Avenat went home.

Remaining alone, Daville looked around the half-empty room
in which a solitary burning candle flickered in vain against the

gathering gloom. The windows were bare, curtainless. The white walls were checkered in pale rectangles, where pictures had hung till yesterday. A watery purl flowed into the room through an open window. Two of the clock towers chimed some kind of Moslem hour, first the one in the neighborhood, then a distant one in the lower bazaar, as if mocking the first.

The Consul was worn out, but his excitement, a tingling sort of energy in its own right, kept him awake and alert, and he went on making order among his personal papers.

In a hard binding tied with green ribbons, there was the manuscript of his epic poem about Alexander the Great. Out of the twenty-four cantos he had originally planned, seventeen were already written, although even those were not in final form. In the past, writing of Alexander's military campaigns, he had always had "the General" before his eyes, but for over a year now, ever since he had begun to identify the downfall of the living conqueror with his own personal destiny, he had felt incapable of saying anything about the rise and fall of the long-dead conqueror of his epic. And so here before him now was this half-finished work in all its absurdity of logic and time sequence: Napoleon had completed the great arc of his rise and fall and had once more landed on earth, while Alexander was still somewhere in mid-flight, storming the "Syrian passes" at Issus, with never a thought of falling. Daville had often struggled to get the thing going again, but was defeated each time by the realization that his poetry invariably lost tongue in the presence of real-life events.

Here too was the beginning of a tragedy about Selim III, which he had started writing the year before, after the departure of Ibrahim Pasha, prompted by his long talks with the Vizier about the enlightened but hapless Sultan.

Here also was a sheaf of those encomiums and verse letters penned on various gala occasions and celebrating various men and regimes. Poor orphaned verses, dedicated to lost causes and personalities who today meant less than the dead.

Finally, there were stacks of bills and personal letters, tied up with a string, yellow and dogeared. As soon as he tore the string, the papers fell apart in tatters. Daville recognized single letters at a glance. He saw the regular, firm handwriting of one of his best friends, Jean Villeneuve, who had died on a ship the year before within sight of Naples. The letter was written in the

year 1808, in reply to some agitated communication from Daville himself.

"... Believe me, *mon cher*, your dark broodings and fears
have no basis in fact, and less today than ever before. The great
and extraordinary man who now guides the destiny of the
world is laying the cornerstones of a better and lasting order
for generations to come. That is why we must rely on him un-
questioningly. He himself is the best guarantee of a happy future,
not only for each of us but our children as well, and the children
of our children. So be quiet in your mind, my dear friend, as I
am, whose peace of mind rests firmly on the acceptance of the
foregoing. . . ."

Daville lifted his eyes from the letter and gazed at the open
window where the night moths, attracted by the light, were
darting into the room. And then from the nearby Moslem
quarter a song arose, faintly at first, then growing stronger. It
was Musa the Singer, coming home. His voice was short-winded
and hoarse, and his song fitful, but drink had not yet finished
him; he was still alive, and alive inside him too was what von
Mitterer once had called *"Urjammer."* Now Musa had turned the
corner of his alley, because his voice sounded fainter and
fainter, spaced out more and more, like the throttled cries of a
drowning man. It rose again to the surface, to cry out once
more, then sank again deeper then before.

Now the singer must have staggered into his courtyard, for
his voice was heard no more. Once more silence was complete,
unruffled by the gurgle of water, which only made it fuller and
more even.

And so too everything else was drowned out. It was the way
"the General" had drowned and, before him, so many other
powerful men and great movements!

Left once more in the steady silence of the night, Daville sat
on a few moments, with his arms crossed and his eyes vacuous,
as if transfixed. He was wrought up and thoughtful, but no
longer frightened or lonely. In spite of the uncertainty and
difficulties that still lay in wait, it seemed to him as if, for the
first time since he had come to Travnik, the air around him was
growing lighter and a fragment of a road was looming dimly
ahead.

Since that February day, more than seven years before, when,
after his first audience with Husref Mehmed Pasha, he had

returned upset and humiliated to the room of Baruch's ground floor and sunk down on the hard sofa, all his work and struggles with Bosnia and the Turks had conspired to drag him earthward, to shackle and weaken him. Year by year, the coursing of the "oriental poison" had mounted in his veins and sapped him— that poison which dims a man's vision and eats at his will, with which the country had plied him from the very first day. Neither the proximity of the French army in Dalmatia nor all the dazzle of great victories could reverse the process. And yet now, when, after defeat and collapse, he was getting ready to leave everything and face an uncertain future, he felt a stirring of will and purpose such as he had not known in these seven years. His worries and needs were greater than ever, but strangely enough they no longer drove him out of his mind as once they used to, but rather they honed his thoughts to a keener edge and broadened his outlook; they no longer pounced on him unsuspected, like a curse and a calamity, but were part of the mainstream of his life.

At that moment a sound of rustle and scratching could be heard from the next room, like a mouse in the wainscoting. It was his wife, tireless and methodical as always, wrapping and putting away the remaining things. In this same house were his children, now asleep. They too would grow up one day (he was determined to do all he could to see them grow up good and happy), and they would set off in quest of the road which he himself had never succeeded in finding; and even if they never found it, they would at least go after it with more strength and dignity than he had been able to marshal. Asleep now, they were growing. Yes, there was life and movement in this house, no less than in the world outside, where prospects were opening up and new possibilities were ripening in the sun.

As if Travnik were already far behind him, he no longer thought of Bosnia, of what it had given him or how much it had taken away. All he felt was an undercurrent of new strength and patience surging back into him, and a resolve to save himself and his family. He went on making order among the faded papers, tearing up all that was outdated and superfluous, saving and filing away anything that might be of some use in the changed circumstances of life in France.

And playing over this humble, mechanical chore was a vague but obstinate thought, like a recurring tune: that somewhere out there the "right road," the one he had sought all his life in vain, must nevertheless exist. And not only did it exist, but sooner or later someone was bound to stumble on it and throw it open to all men. He himself had no idea how, when, or where, but it was sure to be found some time, perhaps in his children's time, or by his children's children, or by a generation still to come.

Like a soundless inward melody, that thought lightened his work.

Epilogue

For three weeks now the weather had held fairly steady. The begs had already started going out for coffee and a chat on the Sofa at Lutva's coffeehouse, as they did every year. But their talk was restrained and cheerless. Throughout the land the silent consensus was growing that the time was ripe for rebellion and resistance against the mad and intolerable government of Ali Pasha. In the minds of people the idea was already as good as settled, and now it was coming to a head by itself. Ali Pasha, too, was speeding up the process by his own actions.

On this day, the last Friday in the month of May 1814, all the begs were present in force and the conversation was lively and earnest. They had all heard the news of the defeat of Napoleon's armies and of his abdication; now they were merely comparing, swapping, and checking their information. One of the begs, who had talked to the Residency staff that morning, said that all arrangements had been made for the departure of the French Consul and his family; moreover, according to a dependable source, he would soon be followed by the Austrian Consul, who had been sitting it out in Travnik on account of the Frenchman anyway. So it was quite safe to assume that before the summer was out Travnik would be rid of the consuls and the consulates, and of everything they had brought with them and started here.

They all received the news as though it were the tidings of some victory. Although in the course of years they had in many ways grown accustomed to the presence of foreign consuls, they were all pleased, nevertheless, at the thought of their going. The foreigners' way of life was alien and outlandish, and they had been arrogant enough to meddle in Bosnian affairs.

They speculated who would take over the "Dubrovnik Depot," which now housed the French Consulate, and what would become of the big Hafizadich house when the Austrian Consul too left Travnik. They all raised their voices a little so that Hamdi Beg Teskeredjich, who was sitting on the fringe of the gathering, might also hear what was going on. He had grown very old and wizened, fallen in like a disused, ancient house. He was getting hard of hearing. He had trouble lifting his eyelids, which had grown heavier of late, and had to throw back his head when he wanted to take a better look at someone. His lips were bluish and tended to stick together when he talked. The old man raised his head and asked the last speaker: "When was it they came, these . . . consuls?"

The company exchanged glances and there was some loud guessing. Some replied that it was six years ago, others that it was longer than that. After a brief argument and some counting, they agreed and established that the first Consul had arrived more than seven years before, three days before the Bairam of Ramadan.

"Seven years, eh?" Hamdi Beg said thoughtfully, drawling a little. "Seven years! And do you remember what a hue and cry there was over these consuls and over that . . . that Bonaparte! Bonaparte here, Bonaparte there. He was going to do this, he was going to do that. The world was too small for him. His strength was boundless, no one could match him. So this infidel rabble of ours lifted up their heads like some cobless corn. Some hung on to the coat tails of the French Consul, others to the Austrian, and the third lot waited for a Russian. The rayah went plain off their heads and ran amuck. Well, that was that and it's over. The emperors got together and smashed Bonaparte. Travnik is sweeping out the consuls. The people will talk about them another year or two. The children will play at consuls and kavasses down by the river, riding on wooden sticks, and afterwards they too will forget them as if they'd never existed. And everything will be the same again, just as, by the will of Allah, it has always been."

Hamdi Beg stopped, as his breath gave out, and the others remained silent in case he had anything more to say. And as they drew on their pipes, they enjoyed their relaxed, victory-scented silence.

A NOTE ABOUT THE AUTHOR

Ivo ANDRIĆ was born in 1892 in Travnik in northern Bosnia. At the outset of the First World War, while he was still a student, Andrić was arrested for his participation in a revolutionary movement which opposed the Habsburg regime and sought unity and independence for the South Slavic peoples. He was in prison for three years. After his release, he completed his studies, and received a doctorate in history from the University of Graz in Austria. He then entered his country's diplomatic corps and served in a number of European capitals, including Berlin, where he was stationed at the outbreak of hostilities between Yugoslavia and Germany in 1941. During the Nazi occupation of Yugoslavia, Andrić remained under vitual house arrest in his Belgrade apartment, and devoted himself to writing. The publication of his Bosnian Trilogy—of which this volume serves as the centerpiece—in 1945 firmly established his reputation in his native land. In 1961 he was awarded the Nobel Prize for literature. He died in 1975.

A NOTE ON THE TYPE

THE TEXT of this book was set on the Linotype in a face called PRIMER, designed by *Rudolph Ruzicka,* earlier responsible for the design of Fairfield and Fairfield Medium, Linotype faces whose virtues have for some time now been accorded wide recognition. The complete range of sizes of Primer was first made available in 1954, although the pilot size of 12 point was ready as early as 1951. The design of the face makes general reference to Linotype Century (long a serviceable type, totally lacking in manner or frills of any kind) but brilliantly corrects the characterless quality of that face.

Typography and binding design by
VINCENT TORRE